CW01626781

SINNER'S VOWS

SOPHIA KARLSON

Cover Art: Qamber Designs

Editing: Zee Monodee

Copyright © 2025 by Sophia Karlson

All rights reserved.

No part of this book may be reproduced in any form or by any electronic or mechanical means, including information storage and retrieval systems, without written permission from the author, except for the use of brief quotations in a book review.

To my lovely ARC Team.
Thank you for your love and enthusiasm for my writing! It means the world to me.

FOREWORD AND TRIGGER WARNINGS

This is the third book of the MAFIA VOWS Series. (Originally *Il Consiglio - A Mafia Dynasty* - Series).

These books **can't** be read as standalones (well, they can, but I don't want you to get lost here, and trust me, by book 3 you are going to get lost). Please read HATED VOWS (book 1) and BROKEN VOWS (book 2) first.

This is a dark Mafia romance and has elements of suspense. Other trigger warnings include: on-page violence, gun violence, gore, references to domestic violence, abuse of all kinds, scarification, rape (not detailed on the page) and torture. Please read with care.

1

DOMINIC

I open the door, step inside, and let my eyes adjust to the darkened room. Center stage is a four-poster bed, covered in black satin. On top lies a woman, spread-eagled and strapped to the four wooden bed posts.

She's been waiting. Good. Just lying here, open to nothing but meditation, is the best place for her to be before we start. I bet she's been visualizing everything I'm going to do to her, already ramping up her need. As always, they've set the scene exactly as I instructed. Only the best satin sheets and the softest hemp Shibari rope from Japan to tie her down with—I want her to be as comfortable as possible.

As the door closes quietly behind me, she'll be aware of my arrival, what with her other senses heightened seeing how she's also blindfolded. For a moment, I stand and just breathe. Even this she'll hear in detail, tuning in with anticipation to every sound I make.

When I don't move, she strains against the inch of space she has, her limbs shifting the black satin sheet covering her naked body.

Good. Nice and tight. They followed my instructions to the letter.

I take in a few deep breaths, on a knife's edge. This is what she wanted, what she needs, and now I tilt towards the slow and sensual, focusing on her needs all the way, serving. Because this isn't about me. It's for me, too, but my needs are met by meeting hers. For a moment, I close my eyes and shut the doors in my mind. Doors leading to places I don't want to go when I'm with her.

My steps sound quietly over the hardwood floor as I make my way to the console table where my items are laid out. The consent form. I pick it up and scan through it, making mental notes along. Once done, I reach for the matches, take one out, and strike it into a hot flame.

A match can burn twice. First in flame and then on flesh, during those last seconds before it turns to ash. I push the thought away as the mixed scent of sulphur and phosphorus drifts up when I light the row of candles standing sentinel along the wall. They are slightly scented, nothing overpowering but more like a warmth of clean linen with a hint of pine.

I take two and carry them over to the nightstands flanking the bed. As I put down the first one, she shifts, aware of my every move, her nostrils flaring as the new scent fills the space. I round the bed and place the other candle down. I'm right there by her hand, and when I do nothing more, she grapples for the rope and pulls it taut against the bedpost.

It's her first real sign of distress, that her trust in me might be wavering. If only she knew what I am capable of.

I reach for her inner arm in a tender touch.

"Easy, baby," I murmur to reassure her, leaving my hand there so my warmth can sink into her skin and calm her. Her fist clutches the rope and battles the restraint. "Deep breaths." I wait until she inhales long, slow breaths, exhales them just as shirt to the floor, I however keep myself contained, belt buckled, willpower harnessed. Then I reach for the edge of the sheet and slowly drag it off her, exposing her beauty inch by inch, her body lifting into the erotic glide of satin flowing over skin.

She's a beautiful canvas on which I'm going to draw with my tongue, my lips, my fingertips, then maybe with more, depending on how I feel.

As I drop the sheet to the floor, I kneel onto the bed and move on my hands and knees until I'm hovering over her body. We're not touching, but she's pushed her hips up to mine, seeking connection. I dip my head, my mouth at her temple, my lips soft as I inch them over her delicate skin to her ear, where I run them along the shell and down to the lobe.

She's exquisite, so soft, with the faint scent of lilies clinging to her skin, but it's the helpless moan escaping from her that only hardens me more.

"I'm slow, baby, so bear with me," I murmur, my warm breath popping a rush of goosebumps down her neck and beyond.

She moans again, and now, I'm completely into it, sinking into the moment, my blood thrumming with the beat. My lips press to her skin, tasting her, licking and nibbling and placing open-mouthed kisses on every inch of her, sucking and teasing her nipples, then going down until I've reached her lower belly, where I pause.

I'm still perched over her, touching her with nothing but my lips and tongue, but now, I shift my weight so I can press my palm to her pelvic bone. She quivers, and when I massage her there with just the right amount of pressure, her breathing becomes strained.

"No. Not yet," I instruct, lifting my hand, leaving only my fingertips connected to her skin. She'd cry out in protest if she could, but it's too soon to remove the gag.

For a minute I wait, allowing her pending orgasm to retreat.

slowly, and her chest rises and falls in a steady, regular rhythm. It would help if I removed the gag, but it's too early in the evening for that. "Good girl. Just like that."

It's a waiting game, and once she's settled, I glide my fingers over her arm to her hand and for a moment caress her fingers. She's let go of the rope, her grip relaxed, and as I stroke her gently, lacing our digits, sliding them together, seducing her with the smallest of touches, she traps my hand with her own. It isn't a desperate hold, more like a lover's touch, and a smile toys on my lips as I rub a slow circle with my thumb in the heart of her palm.

A small foundation of trust is here. Now to build on it. I study her face in the flickering candlelight. I don't know this woman. We haven't had each other before, but Luca sure knows how to deliver. She's beautiful—darker skin with smooth, soft cheeks and plump lips circling the gag, black hair that tumbles loose over the satin pillow, its length seeming to melt into the fabric.

My gaze glides lower, to the elegant column of her neck, exposed and so delicate. It won't take much—

Fuck. This isn't why I'm here. I close my eyes as my mind slips and I know I've left it too long. I need this more than she does—she isn't the only one trying to reconnect with a part of herself that's buried under debris.

Shut the door, Dominic. Just fucking shut it.

With a measured exhale, tension seeps from my body, cleansing my mind.

As I open my eyes, my gaze dips to her chest. With the slightest move, the satin slips and teases her nipples into hard peaks, and they are etched out against the sheet.

I bet she's ready for me. Wet and willing. It would be as much her pleasure as mine to rip the sheet off her body and fuck her right now, but I've hardly started. I need this. The slow seduction. The tenderness and care. Having echoes of touch reverberating into her darkest parts, letting every sensory input turn as tight as the spring in her can go. When she finally orgasms, it would feel like a meteorite burning through the ozone layer to Earth. Shattering with such intensity that for weeks, she'd think of nothing else.

And for a few hours tonight, I will think of nothing else but getting her there. Fuck knows, I need my thoughts channeled into something positive, use my hands to gently weave every nerve ending in her body into bliss and not pain. Give her pleasure, and in the process, drain out the bottled-up poison in me.

I let go of her hand and stretch my fingers, releasing tension in all of them except my left-hand pinkie, which stays crooked. The woman arches her back at the missing connection, so I graze her cheek with a knuckle.

"Soon."

But it's a lie.

This is a test of her willpower just as much as mine. She can come at any time, whatever her mind dictates. Some women can orgasm through thought alone, and if she's one of those, my purpose here would be to arrest her mind so she only comes on my command.

If she isn't one of those women, I'm here to guide her there.

I take my time to set up the rest of the room, putting the remaining candles in place and then turning on the sound system. It's a slow, heavy baseline, blended with other beats which only lure you into the most primal of rhythms.

Once everything is in place, my mind is in the right space, too, and I turn to her. In the flickering glow of all the candles, her breathing syncs with the music. It's a sight I relish like a delectable treat. The beats vibrate through my body as I palm my erection. Soon.

I toe off my shoes and strip my socks, then start to unbutton my shirt as I pad over to the foot end of the bed. Dropping my

I get off the bed and pad over to the console, my gaze roaming over the selection on display. Nothing here will inflict pain, because I don't do that shit outside of office hours, but sexual torture is real. The only difference is that sublime pleasure is the ultimate outcome, and women will endure everything I do to them, knowing I'm getting them there with a helluva bang.

I pick up a peacock feather and make my way back to the bed.

By the time I deem her ready for me, I've worked through several props, and she's soaked the sheets, but still she hasn't come. Her scent overpowers every candle in the room, and my cock is begging me to make it end. I strip my belt and pants, and when I fist my cock, need ripples through my body. I want that tight pussy now, and with trembling hands, I rip open the condom and roll it on. She's gone quiet, maybe sensing freedom and release are seconds away.

I unhook her legs, one after the other, and she pulls her knees up, opening as wide for me as she possibly can. I'm on her in seconds and force myself to ease into her with slow thrusts. She comes on the third one, and her whole body trembles, her thighs shaking as I drive in and out, maxing her orgasm to the deep beats of the music which set this rhythm in the first place.

And still she comes. I don't stop pounding into her, my own release stalling. I haven't earned this.

Her cheeks are wet, and I curse softly. I reach for the gag and unclip it, and it falls to the side.

"Shh, baby girl," I try to soothe her, but she's full-on sobbing now.

"Harder," she pleads as if she knows exactly what I need. "Fuck me harder. Please."

And it's the only way I'm going to get there. I slam into her, thankful that nothing about her is fragile, that her body can take mine, that she is ready for my need. By the time my release rockets out of me, I feel another orgasm hugging my own. She cries out, her feet hooking over my thighs, pressing me as deep into her as I can go as we peak together.

It's intense. Powerful. Our bodies one. All tension seeps out of me as I press into her, acknowledging again that I've waited too long for this, for my antidote. For my own sanity, I need to do this more often.

When her legs go slack, I adjust my weight, lifting off her inch by inch. She slides her feet down my calves, trapping me.

"Baby—"

"Let me touch you," she whispers. "Let's me see you."

I lower my head to kiss her, finally connecting our lips and forcing her to be quiet. It's a slow, deep, and erotic kiss, aimed to distract her, because none of that's happening. With us kissing, my cock stirs afresh where it's still lodged in her body. Fuck. I can just start again. I bet she'd be there for it all. We can probably go the whole night.

With a last soft sweep of my tongue, I close off the kiss and slip from her body. "I've got to go."

"Why? Please stay."

I know she needs aftercare, somebody to hold her and talk to if she wants this. It isn't going to be me. It's never me. "I've a funeral in the morning."

She stills. "What? I'm sorry...whose funeral?"

"My dad." And the only way I'd be able to get through tomorrow is by fucking a stranger tonight.

I deal with the condom as she says nothing, probably digesting my words and fucked-up attitude. Her arms are still tied and she's still blindfolded, but she's relaxed now, sinking into the mattress with a sated afterglow. I stop the background music, find my clothes, and get dressed. My head is shifting away from the space of release, back to reality.

"Who are you?" she asks.

Somebody you don't want to know in real life.

"Someone will be here as soon as I leave to take care of you." In every way I can't. *Hold you, talk to you, make you laugh. Love you.*

I walk out, never answering her question.

2

DOMINIC

Trust the sun to fucking shine on the day we bury Don Giuliano Scalera. It doesn't help with my mood which has been pretty sour for the past few months. That's not exactly new, but it's become worse ever since the fucking Don came up with his last requests and dragged us back into a world we've been trying to break away from.

Dad, the psycho, has been dead a week, and none of us would have cared a flying fuck to give him a proper burial if it weren't for keeping up pretenses and appearances. Now's not the time to appear weak or weird.

Good news travels fast. There're at least two hundred people here, most of them men. Beyond the swath of somber suits and bowed heads, I spot the two black SUVs crawling past. I know the cops when I see them, even disguised in unmarked vehicles. Always keeping an eye on us; even more so when there's a shift in leadership.

My clenched fists unfurl, and I stretch my fingers to release some tension. As always, my left-hand pinky battles the movement as if the Don still restrains my whole body through this one digit alone, and I push down hard on every emotion I've bottled up for years. This finger serves as a reminder. *Know your place.*

Matteo glances at me, then at my hand. I shrug, and with a sigh, he tracks how I'm taking in the solemn crowd of mourners. People will meet his bold, confident stare, but as soon as my eyes land on them, they all look down.

"Don't scare the children now, Nicky," he mutters under his breath.

A smile hides in his voice, making me suppress a smirk. Seeing me here is unsettling because most people think I've left *Il Consiglio*. Good. That's a rumor we like to keep circulating. There's another one keeping people on their toes around me: *Don Scalera trained his son Dominic to be his interrogator.*

Yep, everybody here is right to shit their pants if I so much as glance at them. And no, I haven't left *Il Consiglio*. As if I'll ever leave my family. I've only been running the back office. My legit security company and thriving business is the perfect front to make people think I've left the Mafia...except I'll always have a role to play.

The pallbearers lower the coffin into the grave, and eventually, the soft thuds of soil hitting the wood sound through the eerie quiet of the gathered crowd. The priest has done his thing, but we all know Don Guiliano Scalera is going straight to Hell, where he'll be keeping seats for us. You don't become the most feared and hated Don on the East Coast without paving the way there with sin. As for us Scalera boys, I'd like to think we've toned things down, though Heaven is very far from rolling out the red carpet for us when our time comes.

"Come on. Let's go." I nudge Matteo with my elbow. "Enough of this shit. By the time they line up, you have to be in the right headspace."

Moving on—that's what we need to be thinking about.

"You really want to do this today?" he grunts under his breath.

"As the new Don—"

"I can make my own rules."

"Maybe, but fuck it, Matty, you can't afford to put this off a single hour." If someone comes for Matteo, especially now he's had the idiocy of getting a wife, I'll protect him with my life. But fuck knows, I'm not in the mood for a blood bath. "You now have Tasha to think of, too, and appearing weak could cost her."

Matteo draws in a sharp, if controlled, breath. "Fuck it."

"Yep, you have no choice."

And neither do I. I'm now his lieutenant, and the second in command. I never willingly assumed this position but was shoved into it the night our brother Alex got killed.

Matteo takes the lead as he turns away from the grave first. I fall in beside him. We're headed for Don Scalera's compound, where the capos at the funeral will swear allegiance to my brother. I'll take roll call, and those members of *Il Consiglio* who fail to show up today... Well, I'll have some questions to ask. By the surreptitious glances these men shoot me, most here know better than to let me interrogate them.

As we walk abreast and part the crowd, we're signaling the new hierarchy to everybody here.

Matteo Scalera, the new Don of *Il Consiglio*.

Me, his second.

And then, the mystery of the other Scalera brothers. Luca, Stephano, and Benedict aren't at the funeral. Lucky fuckers. *Keep them guessing* was the Don's slogan. It won't pay for us all to be seen together, never mind being photographed so people can identify us as the core of *Il Consiglio.*

Our bodyguards flank us, and soon we're in our bulletproof SUV and heading out to the exclusive and wildly expensive

Matteo meets my gaze, and a silent promise travels between us. We have each other's backs, no matter what.

With Don Scalera and Don Randazzo dead, a new era is unfolding. From what we've seen on the dark net, shit's still flying round and hitting the fan. When I went over there more than a month ago to secure Matteo's security detail while in Sicily and Cannes, I didn't foresee anything spinning out of control like this. There's more to his resistance to doing this initiation than merely stepping into Don Scalera's shoes. Matteo was the last person to see the Don alive, and well, beyond Tasha and the need to fuck his wife, my brother has been weirdly distracted lately.

Cars are coming up the driveway, and I signal to our bodyguards to do crowd control.

"Party's starting, Matty. Best get ready for a line-up. The capos are right behind us, and they can't wait to kiss your ass."

"Fuck's sake," he grunts as he pulls off his wedding band and makes it disappear into his jacket's pocket again. With resignation, he turns towards the wide corridor and makes his way to the Don's office.

I don't blame him. I'll never be the idiot to get hitched because that's just courting trouble, but if I did, I wouldn't soil my wedding band with the capos' blood, either, even if it were just a droplet. We might all be sinners, but crime doesn't belong within the confines of sacred wedding vows.

It's almost midnight by the time we're done.

I hold out a printout of the five members of *Il Consiglio* who haven't bothered to show face and swear the oath of *omertà* to my brother yet. This isn't something you do over a Zoom call, and if you know what's good for you, you prioritize this in-person meeting.

"I'll give these fuckers two weeks." I toss the paper to his desk. "We'll make examples of those who don't show up."

You never know what slackers do in their spare time. I'd love to find out.

Matteo leans back in his seat and rubs down his face. "Fine. Deal with them as you see fit and do it here."

"Here? In the basement? Your place is easier."

Not only does Matteo have his own special room for interrogations, but he also has an elevator directly to the promession site to deal with bodies.

"Let the butcher deal with it," he says as he stifles a yawn and picks up his phone.

"Fine." I don't relish the prospect of any of this, but I'm loyal if nothing else. I lean back in my chair, nursing a whiskey as I scroll on my phone. "I see they've identified Randazzo's body. His death has finally hit mainstream news in Europe."

"Took them long enough."

I glance up. "You're worried about it?"

This could be bugging him. He might have eliminated Randazzo, but that doesn't mean the police aren't going to hunt down the assassin.

"Should I be? The mole assured me that all video footage of that day or any other evidence got destroyed. We've covered our tracks. Nobody involved in that operation will talk, not even the Trapanis."

The Trapanis aren't my biggest worry. Don Trapani wanted Randazzo dead. But we've put an enormous amount of trust in one man. The mole better live up to the promises he made. If he doesn't, we'll move to the defense. I'm not worried. Not for now, at least. There's a reason why I started a security company: my brothers will always be protected by every layer of modern security out there.

I've been on the giving side of interrogations. There was only one time where I got caught on the receiving end, and it was a lesson I only needed to learn once. By instinct, I reach for my left-hand pinkie and rub the scar ringing the digit. All the physiotherapy in the world and the little fucker is still as stiff as a corpse.

I made a vow that day: no kin of mine will ever end up in such a situation. None of them would be subjected to what I've been subjected to. Over my dead body we'll get into a situation that can break us.

In our brotherhood, there is no weakest link.

3

ARIANA

Where the hell is Lorenzo? I've been in this hole of a room for more than five hours, and there's been no sign of him. With no windows, there's only one exit, and two bulky bodyguards have been blocking the narrow door—in itself hard to navigate—ever since we got shoved in here to prepare for the night.

I know my strengths and limitations. Without a weapon, there's no way I can take out two men, not without backup lined up or having a plan to get out of this fucking deathtrap warren.

There was an unexpected guard change a minute ago. I haven't been on the job long enough to establish their routines, and now, I could kick myself. It was the perfect moment for me to get the hell out of here because this wasn't the plan. *Fuck, Lorenzo.*

For all I know, it was the only opportunity to get the hell out of here.

I've lost all contact with my team. I keep raking my mind to understand how it happened, but it was so subtle. First, my makeup case and my clothes—both replaced with their standard-edition fare. There went all my tracking devices. I've never had a phone or a gun with me as I had to be in character. That was Lorenzo's job. My partner was supposed to have my ass covered while I'm undercover in this God-forsaken ring.

Fuck.

"Ten days," one of the new bodyguards says. "Ten fucking days since his compound got burned to the ground. That's how long it took them to identify his body."

I glance surreptitiously at them. Useful gossip is coming my way.

"Randazzo? They really found his body? You've got to be kidding me. Don Emilio Randazzo dead?" The other bodyguard is stunned. "How can they be so sure?"

What the actual fuck? Randazzo dead? He's the most notorious Capo Crimini and head of this ring we've been trying to crack for years.

I swallow and blink, homing in on the two bodyguards' muttered discussion to catch more words. I steady myself by leaning with my hip against the desk, needing to be so freaking careful not to show how this news affects me. But already, tremors run through me. Premonition tightens my already cramping gut. Is this why they moved us two extra times in the past twelve hours?

"They found his body, eighty percent charred," the bodyguard says. "No eyes, no ears, and missing a finger. And his ring, apparently. That fucking insignia on which every capo has sworn alliance to for decades."

"Where have you had all this intel?" the other bodyguard asks.

"My friend in the *sbirri*. The one that likes to talk."

Both bodyguards chuckle, and I close my eyes with an inward scream. The Italian police talking to Mafia bodyguards. This corruption is why we've been so careful, so slow to go undercover, and why it's almost impossible to get ahead. My plans for Franco Fiore—Randazzo's henchman and my little steppingstone to the man himself—would be much further along if it weren't for the police holding hands where they choose to with organized crime.

Fury engulfs me, and with a steel grip, I suppress my rage and frustration at being so stymied, keeping my facial expression blank and focused on the girl in front of me.

Someone got to Randazzo first.

Fuck.

Randazzo is an enigma. Long ago, he went underground and ran his operations through a three-dimensional maze of henchmen so thickly layered, with so many twists and turns, getting to the man proved impossible.

But Randazzo took everything from me, and I'd vowed I'll get my revenge. I've committed the past seven years of my life to this task, preparing to take him down...only for him to go bask in Hell without ever having to look me in the eye. Because someone got to him first. How the fuck did he do it?

"Get on with it, Ana," one bodyguard says as he steps up to me. "Shop opens in half an hour."

This wasn't the plan. Sweat breaks out between my breasts and down my back. The plan was to stop this sex-slave auction from happening, but nobody has raided this place yet. Where the fuck is my team? I clamp down on the anxiety eating my gut and telling me this operation has been compromised. How? We were fool-proof, unbreachable. This can't happen. It can't be real.

"Yes," I say, playing my part even if my sixth sense tells me to run as self-preservation makes me fall back into character. *Observe, adapt, and react only when the time is right.*

Shit.

"Blink, *cara,*" I instruct softly so I can blend the fake eyelashes with the girl's real ones, trying to bring life to the hollow look in her eyes.

The girl blinks, but it's like one of those old dolls whose

eyes close as you tip their heads. She's so young. On paper, it says she's eighteen, but she could be fifteen for all I know. Apparently, she signed up for this herself, but guns held to your parents' heads could make a lot of people do things they don't want to, especially if you're not from Italy and in a moment of misunderstanding handed over your passport.

We're all in serious trouble here. Hyperventilating won't get me anywhere, so best I think rationally. Or attempt to, at least. My team is missing in action, and my type don't get out of here alive. Not with what I've observed three days into this operation. With my luck, I'll end up on that auction stage, too.

At least one thing stands true: comparing me with the women for sale would be like putting a donkey next to a unicorn and asking a stallion which one he'd like to fuck. All the bidders tapping into this sex-slave market think they're Italian stallions, and for their money, they only want pretty unicorns. The prosthetics I apply protect me up to a point, but now I can't risk even being here, never mind hiding behind fake burnt skin covering half my face.

As I apply a second mascara coat, feet shuffle, and an unnatural quiet descends over the room. A chill prickles down my spine, as if Death itself has swept in, suffocating even the soft breathing of the drugged women lined up in chairs along the wall.

Without moving, I glance up into the mirror to see who has walked in.

He meets my gaze, and shock zaps through me like an electric current. The mascara wand drops from my hand as fear cuts through me like an Arctic wind, making goosebumps pop on my arms and freezing the blood in my veins.

Franco Fiore.

God. How is it possible? This demon from hell was supposed to have been apprehended by now. I was never meant to come face to face with him during this operation—I made sure of it.

Something went wrong. Very wrong.

I swallow hard as I blink, making sure I'm not seeing a ghost.

But he's real. So fucking real in his black suit and black shirt and black tie and black scowl, even his stained teeth seem grey against his tanned skin and the black ink of the tattoo reaching up to his chin.

He stares at me as if he came for me. How did he know—

I cower back as he steps closer, the very Devil in disguise, shoving his hands in his trouser pockets, inspecting me with those little shark eyes that see everything. The bodyguards have closed the only escape with the bulk of their bodies, blocking the narrow door.

I should have run. As soon as my sixth sense had told me to get the hell out of there, I should have bolted.

Now, it's too late. I can't break eye contact with Franco, hypnotized as if he's a snake. *That* night flashes back in my mind, as it still does, often and without invitation. Those memories have helped me get this far, fueled my vendetta against this man, but now he's *here*?

This wasn't the plan. It hits me that my team doesn't know where I am anymore. I'm on my own.

"Ariana Morelli," Franco says in greeting, his voice deep and grainy. "I preferred Emilia. It's been a long time."

Twelve years. Twelve long and harrowing years of looking behind my back, treading water, and diving deep to stay hidden between the reeds of this life I've been running from. From a world I have vowed to bring down if it's the last thing I do. A mission I'm willing to die for.

Oh, I'm staring death in the eyes.

If he knew where to find me, what else does he know?

Everything.

"You're a clever little one, Ariana, but not clever enough." He finds the edge of the prosthetic, works it loose for a stretch, and rips it off in one go.

"Fuck!" I yelp as pain sears my skin.

"Open wide," he says as he squeezes my jaw. My skin burns, and even if I could bite those fingers, he's too fast. He shoves the prosthetic into my mouth as a gag. "Tasty shit, isn't it?"

It's all chemical and oily with a weird placating scent that comes with cosmetics. I'd take it any day over the number of other things he could shove into my mouth. Soon, I'm dropped into a car's trunk, and we're on the dirt road, my body bouncing along with each bump and pothole.

When we slip onto smoother tar and the car speeds up, I lose all sense of space and time. Eventually, the car stops, and the engine switches off. Right on cue, my pulse races and pounds in my temple. This could be it.

Franco will have his fun with me first. He'll push to see how much I can take before he kills me. I steel myself, praying my mind will hold its ground. Mind over matter. Mind over body. *Whatever happens next, don't lose your mind.*

When the trunk opens, a henchman pulls a bag over my face. He grunts as he cradles me in his arms and huffs as he carries me through a garage, the smell of motor oil and lubricant heavy in the air beyond the man's stale stink of old cigarettes. Metal bangs on metal, and then we're descending some stairs. Endless stairs. The air becomes moldy, like wet cement and stone.

I'm dropped onto something that bounces with creaky springs. It reeks of piss.

Someone rips the bag off my head, and a torchlight blinds me.

"You know, Ariana, at some point, you were my only hope." Franco stands in front of me where I'm sitting on a dirty mattress, raised off the floor by an old steel bed frame. The torchlight haloes his body, making him look like the Angel of Death. "Now, Randazzo is dead, and I've stepped into his position as *Capo Crimini* as if it were held for me by the gods."

The gods. As if.

But if Randazzo is really dead, and Franco just took over his operations, then we're fucked. He's not even the man's legitimate successor. Not that it matters to him. Franco is unhinged. Always has been.

I glance around frantically. Nobody is going to find me here.

"You've gone from being my only hope to being as useful as shit in a bucket." He sighs. "So, while I sort everything out and establish myself as Don, you're going to stay here where you can't come and fuck things up for me. We're going to count the days, *cara*, and maybe if you're lucky, I'll find a use for you in the bigger scheme of things."

In the bigger scheme of things means only one thing—sex trafficking. Where he'd wanted me in the first place and what he told me he was preparing me for.

He snaps his fingers, and his henchmen come forward, grip me by the arms and legs, and force me on my back.

"She's a frigid little thing, but she won't lie still. Tie her to the bed frame. Both sides."

Raped, by this man. Again. I can't. He might have had me once, but I vowed no man will ever have me like that again.

But this is worse. This is going to be a gang rape, and then what? Franco's meticulous precision and his love for ritualistic barbarism make me want to beg already.

Quiet tears slide down my temples and into my hair as I'm spread-eagled on the bed. It hits me that none of the prep work or training they do could prepare you for this.

Franco puts a medical carrying case on the mattress. He starts to dig. I close my eyes as fingers fiddle with my jeans, unbuttoning them and pulling at the zip. Soon, someone tugs them down, but not far enough to violate me.

I open my eyes only to spot the glint of metal in the light.

Franco runs his fingertip along my panties, and I know the exact moment he sees Randazzo's tattooed seal, because he laughs.

"You lot are fucking idiots. Even from here—" he stands tall as he shakes his hand holding the scalpel, "—I can see this isn't Mara's work. Dumb fucks, all of you."

He puts the scalpel on my stomach, and I shudder at the metal's cold tip and warm handle burning my skin. Now he's lighting a cigarette, staring at me, deep in thought.

"Cut or burn?" he asks after a few deep drags.

His meaning sinks in, and I cower.

"Meh, I'm working on my brand. The scalpel it is." He tosses the half-smoked cigarette to the floor and grinds it with his heel then picks up the scalpel again. "Now hold still, *cara*. A line a day until I figure out what to do with you."

4

ARIANA

I've disappeared off the face of the Earth. My team will never find me in this dungeon where Franco has left me to die. They will have given up by now.

I don't know whether it's night or day anymore. The only way to guess is by the noises infiltrating the layers between me and the outside world. They're not much to go on.

A chair scraping in anger. Something crashing to the floor with such force, even I hear it. And then, there's the men who come to clean up my prison cell and leave me some food, but there's no set time for that. Sometimes, I'm so hungry by the time they come, for all I know, a whole day could've passed.

One is always holding a machine gun trained on me. The other does his thing while I'm too stunned to do more than blink, as my eyes need to adjust. There's no way out. I've felt my way around the space, looking for cracks in the cold stone walls, searching for a weakness in the bolted wooden door. There's nothing.

I'm rotting away like some medieval peasant who stole bread. Only one difference here: I know exactly how long I've been in here. Franco Fiore makes sure to keep count so I can be grateful for spending my last days like this, at his mercy.

He's been here four times, but each visit has been such a painful ordeal, I have nightmares. I dread his return, the mere thought making my heartbeat spike, fear paralyzing my limbs. Even now, I'm unable to unfurl from where I'm curled up in a ball. I know how this ends. How else? There's going to be that moment when his scalpel digs too deep and when he finally slaughters me by skinning me alive.

I've tried to detach from this situation and meditate myself into a state of calm, but I lapse. More and more often. I've always imagined if I get caught by the Mafia, they'd kill me kindly with a bullet to the head. Or anything else that would do the trick in minutes. Not this slow, starving uncertainty, death row in the dark, with no set execution date.

My ears home in on the noises that vibrate through the building. From far above, someone is descending to this dungeon. I still, overly conscious of every little sound. Metal against metal, scraping, slamming. Keys forced into locks, twisting as if it's a chicken's neck, breaking. Steps. I've counted them. Twenty-five down to this cellar.

Voices. I start to quiver uncontrollably. *Franco*. Not again? Not so soon? He was here yesterday, and I'm still raw.

By the time he has banged open the wooden door, I've all but pissed myself in fear. Light blazes into the space, and I cower away. I'm slowly going blind in this dark existence.

"*Piccola ragazza*."

His little girl. If only I were never born.

I should defy him and show no fear, but it's become hard. I should fight, but it's been nineteen days since I've been locked up here, and without enough food, I'm losing muscle mass. I'm weak. In the beginning, they tied me up, leaving me on this mattress for days, until I withered and all the fight drained out of me.

"Ariana," Franco says again as he comes closer. "Come now, look at me."

I squint in his direction, taking in the two looming male figures etched out in the torchlight Franco points to my chest. By the door, a henchman with a machine gun is on standby.

"And you call that a prize?" the other man says. It's a new voice. *He* hasn't been here before. "Fuck, just look at her. And the stench—"

"Nothing a good scrub can't fix, Vincenzo." Franco comes up to me, harshly takes my jaw in his hand, and forces me to look up at him. "To think I planned to marry her at some point."

"Trust me, Gigi will be a much better fuck than this hag."

Both men smirk as Franco shoots this Vincenzo a glance. Gloating. He's gloating, showing Vincenzo his *prize*.

"Why are we wasting time here, Franco? You took over from Randazzo. It's been a month, and nobody has contested your rule. Once you're married to Gigi, you'll have access to all the money you'll ever need."

I can't hear my own thoughts over the rush of adrenaline through my veins, over my heartbeats that hammer in my temples. My eyes hurt, but at least Franco isn't shining the torch in my face.

I peer up at him, trying to make sense of the words. *Vincenzo*. Franco is marrying *Gigi*. My thoughts tick over, one by one. I've studied every last known Mafia family in Italy. Vincenzo is such a common name, but there's only one Gigi I know of. Gigi Trapani. Vincenzo Trapani. And there's the youngest one, Carla Trapani, still a girl. Maybe not. She must be finishing school this year.

Franco lets go of my jaw, and I don't make a sound. He retaliates too quickly with his fists.

"You say you guarantee me access to your family's millions,

Vincenzo, but until I've seen the physical stacks of gold, the diamonds—"

Vincenzo pulls a packet of cigarettes from his jacket's inner pocket and holds one out for Franco.

"Don Trapani will bend to your rule, Franco," Vincenzo says as he searches for a lighter. "You'll see tomorrow night. We just need to be there early enough to make sure he understands his new position. He won't stand in the way of you marrying Gigi. I'll make sure of it."

God help Don Trapani. And Gigi. As a woman, I already weep for her. From here, I can't do anything to help her. I've done nothing to help anybody or stop that auction from happening the night Franco came for me. Where are all those women now? Mere girls drugged into slavery?

Franco tosses the torch to the mattress, and it rolls, comes to a standstill, and beams onto the stone wall, leaving half my body lit up but my face in the dark. I bite down on my jaw, fear already choking me because I know what men like these do with cigarettes.

Franco pulls a lighter from his pocket and toys with it. Each time he flicks it into flame, a tremor zaps up my spine.

Vincenzo nods to him, and as Franco holds the flame to his cigarette, he mutters between drags, "Does she even talk, or have you cut out her tongue?"

"I dunno. When I first met her, she used to be a real chatterbox. As a kid, you know," Franco says as he lights his own cigarette.

I was a kid once. A girl, innocent and pure, with an easy laugh.

A thin ribbon of smoke finally reaches my nose. At least that part of me is still working a hundred percent.

"They always seem to become really quiet around me after our first introductions," Franco says after another deep puff.

Both men smirk, and I bite down on my lip, sealing my mouth as tight as I can. Nothing is beyond Franco Fiore.

I watch the men's quiet movements as they smoke in silence, the two cigarette tips glowing in the dark, almost hypnotic. They're waiting...for what? To hear me plead for my life? Probably. They'd like that. Assholes.

"Nineteen days, Ariana," Franco says eventually. "And now, we're at a crossroads."

"Fuck," Vincenzo says with a laugh. "So long? You're such a fucking psycho."

"That I am," Franco says, his eyes blazing into mine.

"Just kill her already. There'll be *nobody* to contest you. No surprises out of the middle of nowhere."

Franco just grunts then passes Vincenzo his cigarette, which has almost burned to the end. "Hold this."

He pulls his own packet from his pocket and lights another two cigarettes and then leans into me.

"This is what's going to happen, Ariana. Tomorrow is Friday, and we'll be in Lake Como. This weekend, I'm marrying Gigi Trapani. Once I have the Trapani fortune in hand, you'll really be obsolete. For old time's sake, you get to live a couple more days until I've sealed the deal."

I swallow down the nausea that comes with his cigarette breath in my face, at his creepy closeness and the very threat he poses.

Money. Franco's quiet obsession. Money and power at all costs. Ambition is one thing. Ambition is planned, calculated, acted on with precision. Ambition, anybody can respect. Greed, on the other hand, is another beast altogether. Greed makes people do stupid things.

Marrying Gigi Trapani for her money sounds like a sudden, greedy move, unless he disposes of her, too, which is probably his long-term plan. Here's the problem, though—you don't kill the daughter of one of the oldest Mafia families in Italy without retaliation. Unless he wipes out the whole Trapani family including Vincenzo in one go. But these two appear to be more than Mafioso messing around—they look like they're best friends. Friends who share everything. Ambition, money, women.... I can't wait for all of this to go sour.

Greed is going to be Franco Fiore's downfall, and I already feel cheated. First, someone kills Randazzo and denies me the pleasure of doing so myself. Now, I'm going to be dead before Franco Fiore meets his match. It will serve him right to find a knife in his neck one morning, compliments of Don Trapani. No chance in hell Don Trapani would allow his son to match his daughter with this psycho.

Franco's next action is so swift, I hardly have time to breathe. He fists me by the hair, and I yelp in pain as he twists the dirty strands tight. I reach up for his hands, but it only exposes a sliver of skin between my panties and T-shirt.

"Until then—" he whispers, his sickly breath ghosting my skin as he traps my legs with one of his, "—and to save myself some time, let's count together. This is for today. And Friday."

I gasp as he kills the glowing tips of the two fresh cigarettes on my body, the sound strangling somewhere between my throat and my lips, the burn too intense for me to keep completely quiet. I want to push him away, but Vincenzo holds me in place, his hand circling my wrists where I'm yanking at Franco's grip on my hair.

Franco holds out his hand for his other cigarette which Vincenzo passes to him. "Saturday."

I hiss at the sudden and intense burn, right next to the other ones which still glow with pain.

"And Sunday."

The fourth and final cigarette burn. Tears seep from my eyes as my chest heaves with sobs I contain in a death grip in my throat. I will not cry openly. I will not let go in front of these men.

"Seems she's lost her voice. No nagging," Vincenzo says as he lets go of my hands. He picks up the torch, shining the light on my side. "Good job, Franco."

They smirk at each other, and I could vomit except the only thing that will come up is bile.

"Not my best work, but she's been a good canvas to play on."

Franco lets go of my hair and steps away, and before I can even orientate myself, the men are gone. I'm hulled in darkness again, slowly trying to calm down with each sound that bangs farther and farther away.

Time slips past as I let the pain, the radiating, pulsing burning take over, and I just exist there in the dark, forcing myself to breathe slow and deeply. I reach for the latest addition of the *art* Franco has created on my skin. I'm hurting everywhere he's been. It will be over soon.

By Monday, I'll be dead.

5

DOMINIC

Ever since Gigi and Carla Trapani flew in from Italy without warning, I've been on high alert. I'm always tense and overcautious, but something in their arrival triggered a new layer of worry in me.

Two Italian Mafia princesses running away all the way to the States isn't normal, but *this. This* isn't normal. Here's Matteo married to Tasha Armstrong of all women, and now Stephano is falling like a brick for Gigi Trapani. This marriage they've entered into is a farce, but I can read my younger brother like a book. He's trying his best not to develop feelings for her, but soon I'm going to have two brothers telling me all they want to do is *fuck their wives.*

Women. They are nothing but distractions.

Distractions I can't afford.

In our line of work, this means nothing but our downfall. Failure, at best. Death, at worst. Weakness throughout.

As for Gigi, something happened to her before she fled Lake Como and Franco Fiore. She probably ran because of what Franco did to her. Even if Stephano would never say a thing, I can read between the lines. I can see it in the way he is protective over her. She's been a rabbit caught in a snare, ready to chew off her own leg to ensure she got away from Fiore. It makes my blood boil.

The newlyweds leave Matteo's apartment, and once Tasha and Carla have taken the stairs to their bedrooms, it's just me, Matteo, Luca, and Benedict left at the dining table.

"Franco Fiore." Now isn't the best time, but I've spent the past week upgrading Stephano's apartment's security system and getting things in place to protect Gigi from that devil's inevitable arrival in Boston.

"Really, Dominic? Now?" Matteo says with a groan as he picks up his wineglass. "You're like a fucking dog with a bone sometimes."

Yep. I'm extra because I know what happens when things go wrong. Out of habit, I reach for my left-hand pinkie and start to massage the stiff little fucker. *Things don't go wrong* under my watch.

"Keeping my finger on the pulse, Matteo. Do you have anything new, Benedict?" We can't afford to let any details slide just because we had our first family wedding today.

"The mole says that Franco is losing his shit. His 'fiancée' is on the run, and he doesn't like it. He's hunting Gigi down in every corner of Europe where his network extends to. For now, the only thing we can do is wait."

So much for Franco's fiancée. She just married another man. And it's going to be our problem.

I hate being a sitting duck. Plus it stalls other projects I have going. Ever since the Don's funeral where *Il Consiglio's* capos lined up to swear their *omertà* to Matteo, I've been uneasy. Too many eyes stole to corners of the Don's office to figure out the setup and how to gain access to serious confidential paperwork in said office. For all I care, we can put a match to the whole lot, but Mom's things might be in the mix.

"We're ready," I say and shoot a glance to Luca. "Best you lie low for now."

"Sure," Luca says with a shrug. "I'll hang out with Benedict."

The twins were split apart early on to the outside world. People might know the Don had six sons, including one set of twins, but images of Luca and Stephano together are nonexistent, and the fact that they are identical has been a closely guarded secret.

We were homeschooled, because 'the system' didn't teach us the shit we needed to know to survive in our world. Stephano is the only one who went to a private school due to his behavioral issues, and then got expelled from said school for beating a kid to a pulp. It was a bad move on the Don's part, as it put us on the radar of social services and everybody else wanting a sneak peek into our lives. Stephano paid by spending two years in a juvenile facility just to keep the rats out of our business.

The Don roped in some of the best tutors in Boston who knew how to keep their mouths shut, reinforcing the mystery around the Scalera brothers. Benedict scrapes the internet for images of us daily. The twins are never together in public, and ever since that fatal night, when six became five, we've been even more careful. Benedict is probably the biggest enigma of us all. Going from homeschooled to hacker, if it wasn't for a birth certificate, he might not exist at all.

As for Luca and Stephano, it's always handy to have two of the 'same person' when you deal with fuckers like Franco Fiore. There's no chance Franco will know what any of us looks like if he tries to hunt us down. We know what we're up against. He doesn't. I know one when I see one, and images of him are just as impossible to find. The question really is whether he is a psycho by nature or by training.

Time will tell.

"I'm heading out," I say, standing up.

"You're still at the Don's house?" Luca asks.

"Yep."

"Have you found anything interesting?" Matteo asks.

I might be like a dog with a bone, but Matteo is like a hawk, scouting for prey. I can't shed this feeling he's waiting for me to discover something only so he can swoop in and snatch it away. This feeling has been lurking around for weeks now, ever since he came back from Sicily.

"Nothing noteworthy. A lot of dated documents I doubt have any value."

The only thing with value for me would be Mom's journals. What I really want is to extract everything of hers from that house and put it in a shrine, but her journals, in her handwriting, is even more personal. I used to love watching her write and the calmness that seemed to descend on her when she did.

I don't know if her journals are even still around, or if I'd have the stomach to read any of them, but she had to deal with her circumstances somehow, and a lot of shrinks would tell you to *try journaling*.

Fuck me. Maybe I should take up the pen.

"Keep me posted if you find anything—" Matteo breaks off with a shrug. "Just keep me posted."

"Will do." There are too many cabinets with paperwork to sort, so I moved back into the old family house to save myself the drive and make a dent in the paperwork.

Whatever I'm looking for, I bet Matteo is banking on me finding it before anybody else does. He's looking for something, but he won't say what. Maybe he doesn't even know what he's looking for.

I head to the parking garage in the building's basement where my driver, Stan, and my bodyguard, Gus, have been killing time.

We hit the road to the Don's house, and forty minutes later,

I take in the beautiful grounds in the twilight. At this time of year, it's truly an oasis with rolling lawns and big trees that will soon show hints of the coming fall. With the estate still under guard and being maintained by the same trustworthy staff the Don employed, it's immaculate.

As the house comes into view, I already spot Bruno where he's waiting at the front door. My heart clenches.

Dang that dog. Nobody has ever waited for me like this.

I'm a loner. Always have been. Mostly because of the Don, but also because I can't let anybody close to me. All Scalera boys have done illegal things that come with being in the Mafia, but there are layers here. Where Matteo and Stephano have only killed in self-defense, to protect someone else, I've killed on command.

I've tortured and maimed; I've dragged information out of people like I would their nails, all with a cold-hearted brutality that's been fine-tuned over years in the Don's service. I know what I'm protecting my brothers from—I'm protecting them from someone like me.

The only way to survive in this world is to be the strongest, and now Matteo and Stephano have both gone and weakened our foundation by bringing women into the picture. *Fucking madness...*

There are unwritten rules about being in the Mafia and getting married, such as wives and children are off-limits when it comes to retaliations, discipline, or hostile takeovers. None of those rules will ever apply to me. I've done things nobody ever talks about—because they're dead—but rumors are rife. There will be no mercy if I, or any woman associated with me, get caught by our enemies.

With a sigh, I clamber out of the car. Bruno wags his tail and hastens towards me.

"Hey, bud. Good day, hmm?" I say softly, a warm spot glowing in my heart.

Fuck it. To think this mutt is growing even more on me in his old age. Every day he does this: waits for me and then trails behind me as if I'm his last connection to the man he evidently loved. Then he whines so much when I leave, testing me like no human ever has.

For Bruno's sake, we can't sell the house in a rush. He shatters my resolve with those eyes that seem to search for a face, only to lean into me with his head against my thigh when he realizes it's me and not the Don. Then nuzzling my hand as if it doesn't matter, as if he's happy to have his world revolve around *me*.

I sink down on the stairs to sit next to him and drive my hands into his thick fur to give him a good rub. He pants happily, and for a long time, we're just sitting there, in companionable silence as twilight turns darker and darker.

Just like my soul.

It's pitch black by the time I make the call. The fucker in the basement won't see the next day. He's the only capo still standing who hasn't sworn his *omertà* to Matteo. He won't talk, and I bet it's because he's involved in another crime ring, one that might be coming for us or stealing our business. In moments of delirium, he's spewed out some Russian at me, basically sealing his fate. No kid puts the Bratva and *Il Consiglio* in the same sandbox and gets to play along.

With this Franco Fiore situation coming to a head sooner or later, there's going to be blood and bodies. Matteo's promession site has a limited capacity, and we wouldn't want this fucker to cause a bottleneck.

Time to go do the thing I've been trained for.

6

ARIANA

I blink at the oval-shaped window that only opens to darkness. The low hum of engines drone in my ears. Far off, a single light blinks.

I don't move, waiting for the fog in my head to lift. The past few days have blurred into a mess of distorted memories. Wearing sunglasses indoors to have my eyes adjust to the light after weeks underground. Food. I could eat for days. A shower. Washing my hair...brushing my teeth. Luxuries I'll never take for granted again.

Franco never lived up to his promise. Monday—execution day—came and went. I recall his henchman dragging me up the stairs out of the dungeon, just before I went completely mad.

Of all the inhumane things to do to someone, isolation in the dark is probably the worst. Franco could have asked anything of me, and I'd have given it to him. A list of my colleagues' names who are out to get him? Done. Where do they live? Give me a map, and I'll show you. Wives and kids he can eliminate en route? Here's the exact headcount.

Staring at the far-off blinking light, it sinks in. How the hell...? I'm on an airplane, and I don't recall getting on it at all.

As I shift in my seat, my head sways. God. I've been drugged. With a deep drag of air, I come up again only to see Franco Fiore sitting across from me. The sight is so sudden and creepy, a shudder runs through my body, and I gasp.

"Welcome back, Ariana. You've been so well-behaved, I almost want to give my little girl a golden star."

I start to tremble. It's in fear, but for all I know, it's the first hint of withdrawal.

The last time I saw him was when he came to my hole of a jail cell with Vincenzo Trapani. I glance around slowly. I have no idea how long I've been on this flight. We're on a private jet heading straight to...hell? "Where're we going?"

"The end of the road."

And the worst is, even if I want to fight him with everything in me, this drugged, my body won't have the strength for it.

He stands, and I turn my face into my seat to ignore him, but then he leans over me.

"Come on." He takes hold of my chin and forces me to look at him. He studies my eyes, checking how out of it I am. Then he lets go of me to casually slap me on the cheek a few times. "Snap out of it now. You have work to do." He straightens and calls to the back. "Food and water for our *piccola ragazza*."

Two of his henchmen are on the plane, and one comes over with a sandwich and a bottle of water. He uncaps the water, and I take it with a hand that seems to dumb for the task.

"What work?" Probably prostitution, and for that I don't want to sober up at all. But I'm not dead yet, and my mouth is parched. Base needs first.

Franco nods to the henchman, and he brings a case over, perches it on my seat's armrest, and opens the lid. Makeup. My gaze jumps over the array of brushes, containers filled with cottonwool and cotton buds and other essentials—it's filled with everything I need to transform someone—then snags on the beard prosthetic.

"Drink up, *piccola ragazza*, so you can sober up. Otherwise I'll have to funnel it into your stomach." Franco pulls out his phone and checks the time. "You have four hours."

"And then?"

"And then you're going to behave like my darling wife while we collect my fucking AWOL fiancée. Or else..."

Or else what? Death is hardly a threat anymore. Keeping me alive and doing what he'd done to me over the weeks in that dungeon is a far worse fate.

"Imagine arriving with *a wife* on your arm to fetch your fiancée," I joke, defiant. Something's gone wrong with his plans for the Trapanis, and Franco has lost his cool and is on the warpath. There might be hope, after all. "Awkward, much?"

Franco grinds his jaw. "I've packed my kit. There's a lot of you left, Ariana."

My stomach turns, and I push down the bile by drinking all the water in one go. There's no hope. Just this monster still on a mission to take me down.

I have so many questions, but respect for Gigi Trapani blooms in me—she's given the maniac the slip and an up-yours in the process. Good for her. If only I can help her keep it that way. A pang of guilt blooms in me. I shouldn't be helping the Italian Mafia and their offspring in any way, but a woman with Franco on her scent? Anytime.

Franco starts to strip. First his jacket then his shirt. I want to look away, but I'm mesmerized by those hands with the snake tattoos. Hands, unmarred at the time, that once touched me in places no fifteen-year-old is ready for. Franco had said it was in preparation for the work Randazzo had lined up for me. After that night, I'd known my only option was to run. No man has ever touched me again.

My gaze drops to his chest. Franco's tastes have evolved, and so has the man. He was already into tattoos back then, but nothing like this. He's covered, and my job is probably to hide it all. I stare into the case and reach for the full-coverage concealer and the biggest brush there is. I'll have to mix and blend it, and that's going to take time. At least that's doable with my head seeming to float separate from my body as it's doing right now. Anything more complicated, I'd mess up.

Three hours later, I have a blistering headache, and I can't drink enough water, thirst constantly scratching my throat. But I'm done, and through the ritual of applying makeup, I've claimed back my inner calm. The bearded man in front of me looks so different from Franco, even I buy into it. He looks like some American country star, cowboy boots and all.

"Dress the part, darling," he says as the henchman tosses a plastic bag filled with clothes by my feet. "And do it here."

I'm used to this. Since being taken out of the dungeon, I've been afforded zero privacy. Even when I showered or used the washroom, someone was always right there, watching me. I don't question anything. I still have no idea where we're going, but this flight has been long, and once the morning dawned, the small oval window gave glimpses over the ocean. America? That's all I can think of...and that I'm screwed. Dead in a country where I don't belong. I'd be a body they'd never be able to identify, *if* they find me. No chance in hell my team will be looking for me anywhere but in Italy.

Apparently, we're landing in forty minutes. I strip, overly aware of every pair of eyes on me, how pale and sickly my skin must look, and how fragile I've become in just weeks. My hands skim my ribcage which is mere skin on bones now. Parts of me seem to have died, every want and need and desire, everything except this desperation to stay alive at all costs. Screw human nature and the need to survive.

I'm going through the motions because I have no choice. The denim miniskirt and tank top sit loose even though I've been eating everything that came my way. A white denim jacket and cowboy boots round off my outfit. The henchman hands me a brush, and I drag it through my hair.

"Good enough?" I venture, no longer daring to poke at Franco's mood. He seems to hang over the precipice of something here, probably his sanity.

"Color in your face," he snarls. "Do you think I'll walk around with someone who looks like this?"

I haven't looked at myself in the mirror. Not if I can help it. Obediently, I dig through the makeup box and take twenty minutes to hide the dark circles under my eyes and do the best I can to look like some dolled-up version of someone on death row. It's sickening.

"Just so you understand what's happening next, *cara*," Franco says as we're strapping in to land. "I know who you work for. I have names, addresses, family connections, everything. One wrong move on your side, and triggers start pulling all over Europe."

Of course he does. Why am I not surprised? He found me with such ease, I bet he has a list of agents all over Europe. They might not be connected to me, or even to Randazzo's case, but for Franco, we're just no-name bodies in a much bigger war.

"Do you understand, Ariana?"

I could claw his eyes out, but then he just reaches for my hand and wraps his fingers around mine.

"I'd hate for anything to happen to Pietro Garlini's twin girls, don't you agree?"

The casual way in which he throws my team lead's name out there sends chills down my spine. How much intel does he really have? How did he manage to dig so deep into our operations to know *this*?

"You know what they say, *piccolo ragazza*. Keep your friends close but keep your enemies closer. You know better than to underestimate me."

I close my eyes, not doubting him for a second. He could do whatever he wants to me now. I'd rather die than have something happen to my boss's ten-year-old twins. Without a doubt, Franco won't hesitate to let men do to them what he'd done to me.

We land, and by the time we've gone through passport control and got into a taxi, I'm rattled with shock at how easy it was to get into the States. I'm done for, though. What else could Franco possibly use me for now?

Observe, adapt, act only when the time is right. My little go-to mantra pops back in my mind. I'm not dead yet.

We're pulling up into a truck rental company, one of those dodgy places outside of the city where line upon line of vans and trucks bake in the sun.

"This is us, darling," Franco says as he pays the taxi driver. We all clamber out, his hand steel around my arm, squeezing in warning.

This might be in the middle of nowhere, but I should run while I can. Even just try my luck...but I choke the notion. Whatever I do today will have repercussions on the most innocent people out there, and even though I'm already dead, I won't be able to live with myself if Franco retaliates.

The henchmen also get out of their taxi, and we wait for the vehicles to drive away. Then one of the men walks off and returns minutes later with car keys and nods, so we follow him. Franco never lets go of the death grip on my arm, but he doesn't need to force me along like this. His warning about Pietro's daughters sucked out the little energy I had left.

We stop at a white van standing at the end of a row. The henchman opens up its double back doors.

Only one thing is certain here: once I'm inside, I'm done for. I gather my strength and strain against Franco's hold for one last futile second. We're far off in a corner of the yard, and even if there were security cameras, the men and the doors block everything that's happening from view. Nobody is going to come to my aid.

"Bad timing, Ariana," Franco hisses as he punches me in the gut. I fold into the back of the van with such force, I stumble and hit the side of my head on the hard metal floor. My head spins, but I'm not out for the count—not yet. Feet step over me, and arms drag me deeper into the van by my hands.

The doors close, swamping the space in darkness.

7

DOMINIC

It's been weeks of planning, and now Franco Fiore has finally hit our turf. The rush is real. Ever since he landed at one of the smaller commercial airports outside of Boston, and we've realized he's given us the slip, adrenaline has been crashing through my veins.

Now, he has Gigi and Carla Trapani in his hold, and fuck knows, Stephano is losing his mind.

Good. I need my brother at his peak when he deals with Franco. Over the weeks, I've watched Steph. Everything to this point had been eating him. His past, the Don, the fuckup that was every single one of our youths, and then the love he has for Gigi Trapani. A deep, immovable love that makes me want to step away from it, because it hurts so fucking much. A type of love that shakes the world and makes men do stupid fucking shit.

Yep, protecting his wife is my brother's only goal, and Steph's final day of retribution has come. This is what he needs, and I will hand it to him on a platter.

But first, we need to ensure the safety of the women, and somehow the numbers have grown from two to three.

We didn't expect for Franco's entourage to contain an unknown female he strong-armed out of the private jet airport and shoved into the back seat of a taxi as if she were a piece of meat. That security footage spoke volumes. Fuck knows, it riled me up. All I want is for her to be safe. I don't care who she is, but to be manhandled like that gave me flashbacks of Mom and the Don. That airport staff didn't pull them aside for intimate partner abuse just goes to show how little people care, and how negligent Franco has become. The man is mental, but this we knew.

Mental or not, I give anybody who treats a woman like this a bullet in the head.

I'm in a truck with Benedict, our sniper rifles loaded. My phone pings with the latest location share, and I quirk a brow.

"Dumb fuck." I can't help but smirk. "I thought this was going to be a challenge, but it's going to be a walk in the park."

I turn my screen towards Benedict, and his eyes widen before he meets my gaze. "Gotta be kidding me?"

"Nope."

Every scheme we hoped would catch Franco failed, but he has gone and picked his own deathtrap. His van is heading straight for our abandoned warehouses on the Boston harbor's periphery, and we couldn't have asked for a better outcome.

For the next minute, we're on a video call with Matteo and Stephano, strategizing. Once our plans are in place, I instruct the driver to speed up. He finally slows down to a quiet crawl as we enter the dead-end road with the row of warehouses the Don used for his import and export business.

"We keep the woman for last if we kill her at all." The plan is to eliminate Franco's team with a few neat shots and leave Stephano to end Franco. It looks like he only brought the woman along as a human shield, and I don't want to take out an innocent thrown into this mess. "She might come in handy."

Benedict nods as his leg jolts up and down. He isn't

nervous; he's pumped. My youngest brother doesn't get enough action, and I can't deny him the thrill of the chase.

"Turn and stop here on the side," I say as Franco's white van pulls into a warehouse, at least two hundred yards from us.

The driver parks, and we wait twenty seconds, scouting the surroundings for unwanted traffic. Behind us, farther down the road, one of our vehicles has pulled up to block anybody from coming this way.

As soon as we're sure the coast is clear, we pull down our masks and clamber out of the truck. We head for the fire escape connecting a set of offices attached to the warehouse bordering the street. From the top of the staircase, it is easy to clamber to the roof and make our way to the structure in the middle.

None of us has been here for ages, but nothing much has changed. The flat roof only has the slightest incline to guide rain to the gutters, but it's rusted and pock-marked with holes. It's basically a deathtrap of its own, but it will hold. It must hold, one last time.

We crouch down and soft-foot it along one of the bolted metal beams that offers sturdy support, and when we reach the edge of the middle warehouse, lower down to a leopard crawl until we spot holes big enough to look down into the empty space. What a dump. Farther along the roof, it gets even worse as much wider gaps have peeled open where the bolts have rusted away.

I signal to Benedict to stay behind me as I make my way forward until we both have opportunity to look down at the same time. My breathing stalls. Inside the warehouse, Gigi Trapani—Steph's *wife*—is on her knees, mouth taped and hands tied, legs bound. Her sister, Carla, is lying on the floor, motionless. *Fuck*.

A good twenty feet away, Franco has jerked the other woman to his side. Her hands are tied, and she has duct tape covering her mouth, but now, he's doing something with the contents of an open case... *Is that cotton wool? What the fuck, dude?*

Franco clearly has no idea we're here.

I shift my focus from the crazy to the two other men in the warehouse. One is picking Carla up and carrying her across to where some barrels are stacked in a corner. Well, that isn't going to happen now, is it?

The other man leans against their van. Probably the driver. I signal to Benedict. We don't need words. We take half a minute to position ourselves and our weapons, and in seconds, take out the two men.

Chaos doesn't erupt. It's even quieter now than it was before. Franco glances up, but he is slow in his disbelief as this new reality sinks in. He reaches for his gun, unsure where to shoot. The garage door starts to rattle open, and he homes in on it. We need one last distraction.

I pull my handgun from its holster and nod to Benedict. I aim, knowing the distance between everybody down there is far enough if I shoot with precision. As I fire several shots in a row, Benedict runs across the roof. We repeat the action, but this time, he shoots, and I run.

I kneel down, peering through a hole. Franco is frazzled, unsure which side the bullets came from, and those three seconds cost him. Benedict is back in position already, his sniper rifle pointing to our target as Stephano, Matteo, and Luca walk in, coordinated, with bodyguards flanking them. So many guns are pointed at Franco, he stands no chance.

I don't look at the others, though. I watch on in horror as the unknown woman slowly crumbles to the floor.

8

ARIANA

Everything flashes by me. The moment in the dark underground parking garage where Franco and his men ambushed Carla Trapani and her bodyguard, one of the henchmen coming from behind and killing the guard with a perfect stab in the back.

How Franco lured Gigi Trapani in with the simple threat of a mass shooting. I had to sit by, gagged and tied up, unable to do anything to stop her from getting into the van.

I've slumped to the cold cement floor and curl into myself as heat seeps out of my body. I knew from the start this is how it ends, but I underestimated Gigi Trapani. A whole gang of men has come for her, shooting to kill.

A sharp stab penetrated my body seconds ago, and now a throbbing pain has settled in my lower abdomen. I can hardly breathe with the duct tape covering my mouth, and a cold sweat sparks over my skin. I close my eyes, trying to zone out the shouts echoing in the warehouse so I can focus on my breathing.

A warm hand rests on my shoulder, and I startle. A man is crouching by my side. When he pulls a knife out, I flinch.

"Easy," he murmurs, his voice calm and soft, measured. "I'm going to cut your ties and roll you onto your back so I can see how bad it is."

He works quickly, gently shifts me, and my arms flay out to the sides, no energy left in my muscles. His fingers are on my stomach, lifting the thicker denim and slicing right through it to fold the fabric away.

Footsteps rush in our direction, and another man places something next to me.

"You'll manage?" the newcomer asks.

"Yes," my caretaker says as his hands still on my stomach, and it's the most peace I've felt in years. Maybe this is the finally the end and I'll gently slip away, his soft touch my final memory of a life not really lived.

"Get Gigi the hell out of here. Steph won't want her to see him go at Franco."

Tears seep from my eyes. *Franco.* He isn't dead yet.

The other man walks off, and I open my eyes to look at the stranger. He's staring back at me. God, he's gorgeous. A high forehead and a regal nose, with the beginnings of a beard lining his jaw, but it's his soft gaze that draws me in. Warm brown eyes that tell me everything. He'll make the pain go away. He'll never hurt me. His arms are strong. He is indeed the angel coming to carry me home to Heaven. I've sinned, but not so much that the only doors standing open for me are those leading to Hell.

"I'm taking off the tape," he says, interrupting my hazed thoughts. "It's going to hurt, but you'll breathe easier."

I don't respond, and his fingers are at the edge of the duct tape, working it loose, and then with care, inching it off. I gasp at the stings, but it's more in relief than pain. In comparison to everything I've lived lately, this is nothing, and with Franco, I've learned long ago to be quiet.

His fingers brush along my temple to gather my hair from

my face, and his thumb wipes at my wet cheek. I can't stop the tears—they're flowing of their own volition.

"It's going to be okay. Bullet went in on the lower left side. No vitals there."

And then, his hand stills. Right there where his fingertips could feel my pulse if they press down a bit harder on my neck, his thumb hovering over my lips. He's no longer looking at me, but to the others.

The air in this vast warehouse seems to have twisted tight, and I prick my ears, trying to listen.

"Franco Fiore. You hit my wife," a man snarls. "You bruised her beautiful face. You hurt her sister. You've cut into her flesh, leaving a mark I'll still erase. Let me show you how *Il Consiglio* deals with men like you."

His wife? *'Leaving a mark I'll still erase.'*

I'm not alone. Shudders course through me, and the man starts to stroke the hair by my temple again. It's the smallest, most gentle gesture, but it does everything it intends to do. It calms me enough to make me breathe slower.

The wife could be Carla. Or Gigi Trapani. But I've never heard of *Il Consiglio*. Or have I?

The man by my side is looking on, not stopping the gentle caress of his thumb over my skin.

"Fight to the death?" Franco's voice cuts through the leaden silence.

Just die already.

"And that after I brought you someone in exchange for Gigi Trapani," Franco continues. "Someone you can all share."

I shudder. The fucker still plans to sell me out as a whore to these men. I turn my head to see, but the man's hand cups my cheek and forces me to look at him.

"No. We don't do that type of shit," he murmurs to me as he shakes his head. "Whatever you do, don't look. I'll take care of you and get you out of here as soon as I can, but I don't want to distract my brother."

His brother? I want to look at all the men here, but his hand holds my face so gently, his gaze locked with mine.

"You are a sick fuck, aren't you?" another voice says.

"That depends." In Franco's voice, I can hear the sadistic grin he has before he cuts into you. "If you're into incest or not."

The man's hand stills on my cheek, and I reach for it, trapping it in a weak grip and dragging it to my chest where I press it to my heart. He doesn't tear his eyes from mine. Instead, they start to search my gaze, then jump all around as he maps the contours of my face.

"What the fuck are you talking about?" someone asks...and here's the moment where it all goes downhill.

I can already sense it. Franco knows how to play everybody —even these strangers. I can't watch on as he comes for them and close my eyes.

"I'm talking about a baby sister you all took for dead," Franco says.

'A baby sister you all took for dead.'

It's so quiet, his words echo like a bomb's aftershocks.

"Sick way to buy yourself some time, don't you think?" another man says.

I can no longer distinguish the voices. So much rage pulses through the air, but the man by my side doesn't show any of it as he just lets me squeeze his hand. I'm clutching it as if it's my last lifeline, right there where my heart beats like a horse's hooves on a racetrack. As long as he's here, I'll be okay. I can die in peace, whatever happens to Franco next.

"If you kill me, you'll never know."

Franco sounds pained now, and I loll my head to the side to look at him.

The man doesn't stop me this time. He lets me look on. Someone has Franco in a choke hold. My gaze jumps to the others surrounding him. Franco hasn't got a chance. One against many, and they look menacing. I can already see the matching traits. Brothers. All of them.

They're not *my* brothers. It's impossible.

"If you know, others will know, and we will hunt them down," one man says, and it slowly sinks in that he has a look-alike; they are so similar, they must be twins.

"If she survives your bullets," Franco croaks out.

"Oh, she'll survive," my guardian angel says to me as he starts to dig with his free hand in an emergency medical kit.

Franco is going to die in the next few moments, I just know it, and for the first time in weeks, a spark of hope flares up in me.

My will to survive kicks in, and I let go of his hand. As long as he's here, I'll be okay.

He puts on surgical gloves, and I know what he's going to do next. Contain the bleeding, cover the wound, and get me to hospital as soon as possible.

Except I'm an illegal here on a fake passport with a madman who isn't going to live through the next hour.

Then, the sounds of a fight break out. Feet scuffle, fists hit, bones crack. It's blood sport.

"Don't look, sweetheart," my guardian angel murmurs as he tears something open that smells like disinfectant. "It's the thing of nightmares."

As if my rapist's and tormentor's murder could give me anything but sweet dreams.

His hands are on me, gentle, warm, prepping the wound, folding my skirt's fabric even lower and exposing my under-wear so he can apply the bandage. He stills, and then his fingers dip underneath the band of my panties and peels them away.

"Fuck," he mutters under his breath.

I fall to pieces. He said earlier it was going to be okay? No vital organs… I can feel it's bad, the end of the road as Franco called it, but for a good five minutes, I had hope.

"Franco did this to you?"

His question sinks in slowly. This man isn't looking at my bullet wound—he is looking at everything else. Franco's cigarette burns and how he kept tally on my skin.

He turns my face with the back of his hand so I'm forced to look at him.

"Did he do this to you?" he asks again, and the only answer I can give are tears streaming down my temples.

"*Fuckfuckfuck.*" He picks up the urgency. "Watch all you want, sweetheart. It's the last time anybody hurts you like this. Watch that fucking maniac die."

9

DOMINIC

This woman has been tortured. At the hands of Franco Fiore.

"Hang in there, sweetheart," I whisper now, only wanting to get her away from the hands that did this to her. "You're doing well, so well."

I've zoned out the grunts, cracks, and thuds coming from the death spar going on ten yards from us. I told her not to watch—fuck, *I* don't want to watch—but with what he's done to her, I don't blame her for wanting to see Franco Fiore meet his end.

My fingers are trembling. The notion this woman could be my little sister, our baby Gabriella, is so far-fetched, but it's affecting me. I don't buy into anything, least of all manipulative shit like this, but I'm rattled.

Gabriella was stillborn. Mom died in childbirth. It's impossible.

You weren't there. You never saw a body. Without a body, anything is possible.

I grind my jaw to keep my focus on the task at hand: getting this woman out of here without letting Stephano lose his concentration. Whether she is Gabriella or not, she needs to get to the clinic as soon as possible. I've already alerted our emergency response team, and the surgeon will be waiting, operation table ready. Ever since that night with Alex's death, we've put systems in place to guarantee us the best possible outcome in situations like these. We would never be taken unawares again or suffer such an immense loss—not if I could help it.

I glance down at where I need to close the wound for transportation. When I first cut away her skirt to assess the bullet wound, I was too focused on where and how many bullets to look for anything else. It's only when I inched down her underwear to stick on the bandage that I noticed the rest.

Cigarette burns. Cheap torture, and unrefined.

But then my gaze homed in on the lines cut into her flesh—four down, one straight across. Old-school tally marks, counting sets of five. *What the actual fuck?*

She also has a tattoo I've seen before. Randazzo's seal. She's one of *his* girls.

For the hundredth time, I curse Don Guiliano Scalera for this final post-mortem fuck-you farewell. First Gigi Trapani, and now this unknown woman, both landing into our laps just because Emilio Randazzo is dead.

Matteo has slowly been extracting us from Mafia business over the past ten years, trying to be above board wherever possible. By killing Randazzo, we've been dragged back into the dregs. Human fucking trafficking.

I won't have it.

To prove whether she's our sister or not is the easy part. A quick swab and a few days' wait. It's the aftermath that's already trying to take shape in the back of my head. If she is our sister, then how the fuck didn't we know about her existence?

My hand stills where it's way too close to her sex as I stick the dressing over the oval-shaped bullet wound. It looks shallow, and I already know it's not deep enough for a direct hit.

One of our bullets struck metal, deformed in the process, and ricocheted to hit her.

I retract my hand and pull her skirt back up for what it's worth. I might be into all kinds of deviant shit, but incest—never. To my knowledge, none of the Scalera boys likes to share. As for me, I find it so fucking demeaning, as if a woman's body is only there to serve.

As soon as I've covered her, I aim to pull away, but she reaches for my hand again. A soft touch sliding across my knuckles, but then a desperate squeeze follows as she reels from fatigue or blood loss or just plain desperation. I hold on gently, but she's quivering and gripping my fingers as if she could tap life out of me to keep going. She's still staring at the fight, eyes barely open. From afar, she'll look zoned out, but she's fully aware in this moment.

When Franco finally sinks to the ground, a shattered breath escapes her lips, and she rolls her head away.

She's crying, but without a sound. In fact, she hasn't spoken a single word. Here I've been going on in English, not even considering she might not understand me. Franco is—was—fluent.

"*Cara, parli inglese?*" I whisper.

She looks into my eyes, and I can almost see her mind working. "Yes."

"The axe!" Stephano shouts out, and I look up to where he has straddled Franco. "Bring me the fucking axe."

I shudder. He's actually going to do it. I've done worse, but it's never reassuring to see the Don's hold on you mirrored in your brothers, even if I know this is what Steph needs to sever his past and carry on with his life.

Stephano has the upper hand, and it's time to get this woman out of here.

I brush my fingertips over her face, instructing her silently to close her eyes. This is the last thing she should see. Her breath is warm against my palm, and I caress her cheek. I shouldn't, but I only want to reassure her she's safe. That ever-present need always hums in me when it comes to women, and now it grows louder. I want to wrap her in safety and keep all the world's darkness away from her. This need is born out of everything I've lived and seen, and now it's just what I do, who I am. One half of me, anyway, the one I'd choose every day if I could.

Matteo walks up to Stephano, the axe we always have in the emergency kit in our SUV's trunks hanging from his hand. The sight tears me from my thoughts. He pauses for a moment next to Stephano and Franco, in silent conversation with our brother.

"Do it," Matteo says. "It's like shedding old fucking skin."

"Jesus Christ," I huff as I guide her arm around my neck, gather her to me, and stand. This is going too far.

"Where's Gigi?" Stephano asks.

"Benedict took her and Carla to the clinic," Luca says. "Carla was coming to. Dominic is still with the other woman. She's unconscious."

But she isn't. She wasn't. She's witnessed everything that's happened here.

She's watched us shoot down two men, and now Steph is going to hack Franco Fiore to death.

Sister or stranger, she's witnessed these crimes.

Which means she's trapped.

She's just been passed from Randazzo, to Franco, to the Scaleras, as if she's a fucking parcel and not a human at all. Yet, her body is warm in my arms, if too light. Not only has Franco been torturing her, but he's also been starving her, too.

Now isn't the time to ask questions, but she will answer them. Everything she knows, I'll get it out of her.

I hasten towards the exit with her in my arms. Franco might be dead already, and there will be no scope for revenge, but whoever she is, she isn't going back to Italy and whatever she was doing before in Randazzo's network. Not under my watch.

"If I do this—" Stephano says, "—there'll be no more information from him."

"I don't care," Matteo replies. "If there's any truth to his words, the woman will talk."

And that's going to be my problem.

"If she lives," Stephano says.

"I have her," I say in passing. "She'll live."

I lengthen my strides even more, eager to get out of the warehouse before Stephano finishes Franco off. I may be a death dealer, yet it doesn't mean I enjoy watching the shit show happening, and it's the last thing the woman in my arms should see. We're at the closed garage door, waiting for one of the bodyguards to open it, when the crush of metal through bone cracks through the space.

At the sound, she stiffens in my arms, pulling up with her hand around my neck, pressing deeper into me. By instinct, I hold her tighter, hugging her close. Warm tears wet my skin where she's hidden her face in my neck, and now a suppressed sob racks through her body.

"Shhh," I murmur, wanting to soothe her, not quiet her. She's hardly made a sound since I found her, and it would probably be good for her to finally cry her heart out. "It's done."

Outside, one of our SUVs is on standby, and a bodyguard opens the back door. When I try to get her into a seat, she only clams up closer in my arms, unwilling to let go. She's overwrought, I get it. And in this storm, I'm the only safe harbor she knows. I contain the huff that wants to escape. I'm more the death-inducing sharp reefs all around the lighthouse than the beam of salvation.

"Sweetheart," I mutter under my breath. It will be safer if she's strapped in. I don't know her name, and I don't want anybody to realize she's fully conscious. It will be safer if nobody knows she's witnessed everything that happened in the warehouse.

I close my eyes at the feel of her warm breath against my skin. She's seeking comfort, safety, an anchor. Everything women usually seek from me. Everything I can never give her.

"I'll hold her," I say to Gus, my bodyguard, and he just nods but goes to the front passenger seat and pulls the seat as far to the front as possible.

I manage to settle in the back with her on my lap. It's only when we slip into traffic fifteen minutes later that she finally relaxes in my arms and her hand inches down to my chest.

"You're safe, sweetheart. You're really safe now," I vow, and like a real dumbass, I seal my promise with a brush of my lips along her hairline. "You're going to be fine, sweetheart. I've got you."

10

ARIANA

His arms are gone. Without the warmth of his body and his rhythmic breathing which soothed me, I'm cold. Metal cold. Voices. So reassuring...but I sink back into indifference. Without his soft voice and tender touch, I don't care to be here.

When I open my eyes, I wake up for the first time in weeks without pain, then take in the drip standing close, the soft, clean linen covering my body.

"Hey," a familiar voice says.

A man stands and steps up to my bed. I blink. My guardian angel. Protecting me. Probably with me in that dungeon all this time, keeping me going. Protecting me from Franco.

Franco.

Shards of memory pierce my mind, and I gasp.

"Easy, sweetheart," the man says, his hand on my arm, with just the right amount of pressure to reassure me. "It's all done. They extracted the whole bullet and closed the wound. You lucked out. No damage. You can even eat. You're going to be fine."

I exhale a slow breath, trying to wrap my head around the

memories infiltrating my mind. Bullet? Wound? Nothing makes sense right now.

A nurse walks into the room, and he steps aside. They don't talk, but I watch him watch her as she checks my vitals.

"Are you in any pain?" the nurse asks.

"No." My lips are dry, but I don't feel thirsty. I eye the drip, the brain fog slowly lifting.

This isn't Franco's dungeon. There was a plane, and then...a warehouse. A lance of fire burning my gut. Falling. Then this man with his soft touch and even gentler voice.

"Doctor will be here soon to check in on you." She smiles at me, nods at the man, and walks out.

For a few seconds, it's quiet, then I shift my hand in his direction. As if he reads my mind, he takes my hand in his, his thumb brushing my knuckles.

"Where am I?"

Clearly, this isn't Hell. It doesn't strike me as Heaven, either, even if my guardian angel is standing there, tall and handsome, wingless but just as protective as I remember him in that warehouse.

It feels like ages ago now, a warped reality, what with his touch that's languid and gentle, each brush of his thumb over my delicate skin in sync with my breathing.

"You're in a private clinic in Boston. You're safe here. I'm Dominic Scalera. What's your name?"

Emilia Korhonen.

No. I swallow. Too many things have moved too fast, and now my head is stuck in my earliest memories.

I want to buy into this promise that I'm safe, but I'm no fool. When was the last time I was really safe? Lying might be the best option here, but I can't—not to him. "Ariana Morelli."

"Nice meeting you, Ariana." He smiles, and it softens the angular lines of his face.

More like...*nice saving you, Ariana.* I'm in this man's debt, and not in a way I want to be. Already, I'm adding up all the crimes I've witnessed. His promise of safety is a very thin net that can snap at any second under the weight of it all.

"Not Gabriella, then?" he asks as he squeezes my hand.

"No?"

"Never been called that?" Another squeeze to my fingers.

"I'm not your sister," I whisper.

I was my mother's only child. This man is looks like he's about ten years older than me, and it would've meant my mom started to have babies when she was like...ten? In the realm I grew up in, shit like that isn't that far-fetched, but I don't want to even go there.

"Okay. How do you know Franco Fiore?"

At his question, I pull my hand away and turn on my side, giving him my back. I probably shouldn't. Not with the bullet wound, but I'm not ready for this. I regret telling him I'm not his sister, giving away how I was fully conscious in that warehouse. I can't randomly answer more questions as if all my training's deserted me. I've no idea where this is going to lead me.

"Ariana—"

I feel him behind me, his eyes on my back. A shutter is drawn down the room's window, but a thin slit into the outside world is open at the bottom. It's night already. "Where are the other women?"

Dominic's footsteps sound around the bed, and he comes to stand in front of me. "Carla is here in another room. She's got a concussion, but she's going to be fine."

When I don't look up to meet his gaze, he goes on his haunches to be at my eye level. Now I have no choice but to look into his eyes, his gaze warm on me.

"Gigi's home. She didn't get hurt. Not like you or Carla."

"And Carla's baby?"

"They don't know yet."

I nod. At least it's not worse news.

He rests his hand on the edge of the bed and straightens again. It's a beautiful hand. Long, strong fingers, neat nails, veins branching out to a muscular forearm. He is still in the same clothes from the warehouse, his shirtsleeves rolled up. As I slide my gaze along his arm back to his hand, it snags on his little finger. It has a black ring tattoo, right in the middle knuckle.

It must be a marking of sorts, identifying him as belonging to some gang.

I close my eyes, blocking out the visual of him, of his hand as it hovers, indecisive, on the edge of the bed. I sense he wants to touch me, stroke my hair as he did in that warehouse.

"I'll be back to see you in the morning," he says. "And then we'll talk."

I don't respond, but in me, the coil that gave a bit tightens again. I can't talk, not to him, not to anybody but the police. If I'm lucky, I can make my way to the Italian Embassy, but that might not even be in Boston. I have no clue. I'm in a foreign country, cornered, in the hands of some new crime ring. This is my life coming full circle. Born into it, dying the only way out.

He sighs, and then a featherlight touch brushes my hair. "Sleep tight, Ariana."

I don't want Dominic to go. After all the time in that dungeon, I don't want to be alone with my thoughts that can't channel to anything else but impeding death. Or how I failed the mission I set myself in my life: honoring my mother's death, saving those girls from that sex-slave auction, from men like Franco Fiore. Killing Franco first, and eventually getting so close, I kill Randazzo, too, dismantling his sex-trafficking ring in Europe.

I don't want him to go, because I want him to hold my hand, to remind me that I'm alive and managed to swerve away from Franco's final destination for me at the last second.

His footsteps fall softly, and I keep listening, counting, until all is quiet around me. For a long while, I lie still, my mind grappling with the fact I'm alive. *Observe, adapt, act only when the timing is right.*

Eventually, I roll onto my back and run my palms down my body. I'm dressed in a hospital gown which gives easy front access to the bandage covering my wound. I glance to where my personal items could be, but there's nothing in this room except the usual hospital paraphernalia and an occasional chair.

One night. I give myself one night of peace and quiet to recover, and then I'll deal with this new situation and find a way back to my team.

When a stranger's face peeks into the room and our gazes clash, I sag. Everything about him screams *bodyguard.*

Dominic Scalera plans for me to stay put.

I've jumped from the pan into the fire.

11

DOMINIC

It's almost eleven p.m. when I walk into the service road at the back of our private clinic. Gus is waiting for me, and we both get into my SUV. With a nod, I give Stan the go-ahead to drive home.

I lean back in the seat and close my eyes. What a fuckup. We have an unknown woman in our custody—for lack of a better word—thanks to Franco Fiore. By the look of her, she isn't just any woman, either. She might have Randazzo's mark tattooed on her skin, but my gut tells me she's too beautiful to be a run-of-the-mill prostitute. Not with those blue eyes, blond hair, and creamy skin that screams Scandinavian heritage like nothing else. I'm guessing she's in her mid to late twenties, and the women who have worked the circuit for some time have a certain look about them, a hollowness in their eyes that nothing takes away.

It's a look Ariana Morelli doesn't have.

The way Franco treated her has something to do with this gut feel, too, but there's more to it. It's the way she clung to me earlier and how she fell asleep in my arms on the way to the clinic that speaks to me. As if she felt safe with me.

Fuck it. I'm not a better man at all. I'm probably worse.

With a sigh, I reach for my phone in my pocket and glance over the latest messages. Luca and Benedict were in charge of the warehouse's clean up, and Matteo stayed with Stephano. When I last checked in on Steph, he was still with Dr. Wong, having his hands and other wounds looked after.

Everybody has gone home already. I stayed at the clinic to be with Ariana when she woke up to reassure her. It's late, but I need to talk to Matteo.

Me: *Are you still up?*

I bet after a day like today, he isn't going to look at his phone again once he's with Tasha.

Matteo: *Yep. We got home over two hours ago.*

Enough time to fuck his wife, then. Why isn't he sleeping?

Me: *Gigi's ok? And Tasha?*

Matteo: *All good. Steph is with Gigi now. She's going to be fine.*

He keeps on typing, probably asking the question I'm already answering.

Me: *She came out of anesthesia just fine. Ariana Morelli. Does the name ring a bell?*

There's a pause, and it takes him a minute to respond.

Matteo: *No. What's the damage?*

It's our fault she got shot in the first place. I don't want to do a ballistics report to figure our whose rogue bullet hit her. Whether it was Benedict's bullet or mine, it's irrelevant because it wasn't intentional.

Me: *Ricocheted bullet. No serious damage. She'll be up and about in no time.*

Provided she rests. And eats. All the signs are there: this woman has been tortured, and I bet she's going to suffer from PTSD. Whatever Franco subjected her to, she'll need time to heal. That's one side of the coin. The other side is *why*.

I have so many questions. If she is our little sister, how did Franco know about her whereas we've been oblivious for decades? How did he know about us to such an extent that he brought her to Boston...and why did he burn her with cigarette ends and cut into her skin?

My thoughts zap to Gigi and how she was when she came to Boston. I bet she carries the same scars, but neither she nor Steph has ever mentioned it. Not until today in the warehouse, when Steph accused Franco of cutting into Gigi's flesh. I shudder.

Matteo: *That's good news at least.*

Yep. At least we don't need to get rid of another body.

Me: *I've asked someone on my team to arrange some DNA tests for us. They should deliver them in the morning. Results take two days.*

Matteo: *That's a start. I'll come with you to see what she says.*

I get it. Ariana Morelli will have to talk. She parachuted into an *Il Consiglio* war zone what with Stephano beating Franco to death and us taking down two of his henchmen. Now, we need to manage the situation. With Randazzo's seal tattooed on her lower belly, Matteo will have questions.

Another message pops up before I can respond.

Matteo: *By the way, two men were apprehended this morning at Steph's gym. They were asking after him, or his lookalike for that matter. They weren't playing nice.*

What the fuck?

Me: *Who?*

Matteo: *Sounds like more of the Ukrainians Franco hired. Bait and switch works every time, but this was too close a call.*

Shit. Some new crime ring was poking around in our salad while we took out Franco Fiore. This is more than smoke—this is a full-on wildfire shaping to blaze out of control.

Me: *Where are they now?*

Matteo: *They're at your place, Nicky. A gift from me to you.*

I drop my head back with a grunt. Fuck it. This day can be done already. I don't want to deal with this right now. Vincenzo

Trapani is still hanging by a thin thread in that special room next to Matteo's apartment, so I get why he sent these new ones my way. There will be five bodies to deal with once we're done on that side: Vincenzo plus the four Ukrainians we picked up en route with this Gigi Trapani fuckup. Now, there're two more at the old Don's house.

It all started when Matteo went and took out Randazzo.

Fuck my life. There I thought we were cooling things down. Taking a calmer approach to this whole Mafia business.

I drag in a slow breath and type back a closing message: *It's not my fucking place, Matty. I'll see you in the morning.*

When we arrive at the Don's compound half an hour later, I spot Bruno waiting for me as usual. All I want to do is sink my fingers into his thick fur and find some equilibrium in my mind and body. Instead, I give him a quick rub and make my way down to the basement of the house with Gus in tow. I acknowledge the other guards as we head deeper into the dungeon. Gus doesn't speak much, and that suits me just fine.

The place is a maze, mostly because the house's square footage is so massive and the Don liked his prisoners confused with the several twists and turns. Before the cells come into view, I open a linen cupboard and pull out medical masks and sterile gloves from a container and hand Gus some, too.

They weren't playing nice.

I know what that means. Our side wasn't playing nice either. No wonder Matteo is still up. He's had a rough start to his career as Don, and now, we have wannabe Bratva trespassing on our territory. The least I can do is prove to my brother that I'm his right hand and he can rely on me.

Masked and gloved, we walk into the dimly lit space where cages separate and hold our subjects. Two men are tied to shackles hanging from the beams overhead. They're still clothed, but they're pretty banged up. Swollen eyes, dried blood trails down their chins, heads bobbing as they realize someone's arrived. Gagged.

Good. By the look of them, they'll last another day or two. I don't need to take care of this now. I'm not in the fucking mood.

"I'll deal with this tomorrow. Keep them alive, will you?" I tell Gus.

"Yes, boss," he says with a nod.

My command will find its way down the chain.

As I retrace my steps and ascend the stairs to the main house, I roll my shoulders and stretch my fingers and curl them into fists, an age-old method I use to release tension. All my fingers obey the movement, except my left hand pinkie.

Let's get one thing straight: I've *never* been in the fucking mood for any of this shit.

12

DOMINIC

First thing the next morning, I arrive at the clinic with the DNA tests and my head in a better place—for now.

It is a late summer's day, the crisp promise of fall a soft whisper in the cold dew sparkling on the shrubs lining the street. On a day like this, it's hard to imagine yesterday was such a clusterfuck and I need to deal with that shit later.

I don't spot Matteo's car. He's five minutes away when I check in, so I don't wait for him and head into the clinic alone. When the nurse tells me Carla is having a shower, I hand her one bunch of flowers and continue to Ariana's room. Our stationed bodyguard, Marco, acknowledges me as I lean into the door, not wanting to barge in.

Ariana is sitting up in bed, still on a drip, and looking better than yesterday. Not that it would take much. Without the layers of makeup and mascara she quietly cried away and rubbed over my clothes on the way here, the dark circles under her eyes are too prominent. So is the rest of her, mere skin and bones. My heart seems to stall before it hits the right gear again.

Our gazes meet, and it strikes me we can't be related at all.

Never mind my unnatural reaction to a woman who could be my sister—nobody in our family has those sky-blue eyes, or such blond hair. We'd have seen some of that pop up somewhere. The DNA tests in my pocket seem superfluous now, but we're here to investigate and deal with the consequences. We might have a little sister somewhere in the world who is alive, and she can't be well. Not if she's stuck in Franco Fiore's or Randazzo's world, the world this woman hails from. We'll need to fix that as soon as possible.

I walk into the room, flowers in hand and suddenly feeling like an idiot.

"These are for you." I hold the yellow roses out to her.

Ariana bites her lip in an attempt to hide a smile, but her eyes light up just enough to reassure me. She hasn't checked out yet, not in that way. She might be a lot of things, but she's also just a woman, with a bullet wound in her stomach and cuts on her skin. I'll do anything to make the pain go away, hers and any woman's, so I relax despite the anger at everything she must have gone through. I hardly know anything.

She takes the bouquet in both hands and drops her nose into the rose petals' fragile folds. Quiet tears run down her cheeks and disappear into the buds.

Fuck. Those tears undo me.

"Ariana—" I start but break off, not knowing what to say.

"Thank you." She wipes at her face. "You're so— *These* are so...unexpected."

Well, that goes both ways.

"My brother's going to be here soon."

The nurse walks in with a glass flower vase she sourced from who knows where. Probably from Portia, who lives next door and used to be the Don's housekeeper. The nurse is probably related to her because that's how we roll. Portia's retired now, but at the current rate, I might have to call her back into service, what with Ariana and the bomb Franco dropped yesterday. Someone must know something about Gabriella.

Ariana hands the flowers to the nurse with a soft *thank you* and clamps her hands together in her lap.

I wait for the nurse to leave then close the door behind her. *Il Consiglio* works on a need-to-know basis, and even though our hiring policies are incestuous, and the clinic's staff has been put through their paces when it comes to security, this matter is more personal than our usual fare.

"How're you feeling today?" I've already gone over the doctor's report from his visit early this morning. Physically, she's going to be fine. Mentally is another story.

"I'm better," she says softly, her gaze shy to meet mine.

Must she be so fucking submissive? It does nothing for this building need in me to take care of her.

"You know we have questions." I walk around the bed to place the DNA tests on the nightstand. I've sourced five tests, one for each brother to compare a DNA sample with Ariana's, and now that I look at them, they're extra, but I wasn't thinking clearly yesterday.

She doesn't say anything, and when I look at her again, there's a pull to her beautiful mouth that spells out everything to me. This one is going to give me a hard fucking time.

There's a knock on the door, and when Matteo swings it open, I shove my hands into my pockets, watching him as he walks inside.

Jesus Christ. Yesterday was rough, but by the look of it, he hasn't slept at all. The dark circles under his eyes match Ariana's, but there's a haunted look in his gaze which hints to more than exhaustion.

Despite the evidence of a sleepless night, he is dressed impeccably and makes quick work of the few steps to the bed.

"Matteo Scalera," he says in greeting, his eyes drinking in

her face and without a doubt coming to the same conclusion as me. "Welcome to Boston."

There's a hesitant moment when he looks as if he'd shake her hand, but she wrings her hands in her lap and then folds her arms over her chest, protective.

"Thank you." Her gaze volleys between the two of us before dropping back to her lap.

I hold back a huff. This is the last thing she needs—men like us hovering over her hospital bed. None of us have tattoos up to the jaw and down to the wazoo and wherever else, but like this, flanking her bed, we'd be intimidating. We are. She already looks like a fawn curled up in hiding between the sheets, us wolves on the prowl.

Matteo rolls on his heels, and when he meets my gaze across the bed, my heart sinks. If she isn't going to talk, he's going to make me make her, because that isn't his game—it's mine.

I pull the chair closer and sit down, my hand resting on the edge of the bed, wanting to reach for hers and indicate it's okay. It's all going to be okay because I'll protect her.

"Ariana," I start. "I've DNA tests here. We'll begin with those, and then—"

"Who are you? How do you fit in with Franco Fiore?" Matteo cuts in, in that tone only Tasha has ever defied. "Why would he want to kill you?"

"Give Ariana a break, Matteo. Once we have the results, there'll be time for questions."

"We have a sister at large, and we don't have time to waste." He drags his hands through his hair and then cups them to his face, breathing into them as if he is warding off a panic attack.

Our gazes clash over the short stretch of the bed, and cold dread spears through me like a thousand needles as it hits me: Matteo knew. He fucking knew about Gabriella.

I fist my hands, my fucking pinkie scraping the linen as if it would dig a hole in its obstinance to not bend like the others.

Until this moment, I'd thought it was all a lie, because *how*?

I want to grab him by his fucking collar and shove his face into mine and give him a piece of my fucking mind, but I can't. Not with her here, watching our truth crumble out of him like an earth-quaked tower. The tension is so thick with all the unanswered questions, I can hardly breathe.

Instead, I reach for a DNA test packet with a trembling hand and throw one to Matteo. It's not a nice throw. He catches it, though, and I pick one up for myself.

"Do the fucking swab," I say, my tone clear that I'm not taking no for an answer from anybody. "And then, we're going to have a little chat."

I don't care that he's the new Don of *Il Consiglio* and can have me whipped if he wants to for insolence, but I *will* drag the truth out of him today. And fuck knows, I'm not having this talk with Matteo in front of a stranger, whether she's related to us or not.

"Surely, one test would do," he says as he stares me down.

"I got five fucking tests, non-refundable. The others will take them, too, Matteo, so why don't you start and lead by example."

Not waiting for his reaction, I tear open the box and take out the various foil-wrapped pieces and instructions. My hands are shaking so much, I lean onto the bed with the instruction leaflet to stop it from quivering. It's quick and simple, but I need a moment to work through the emotions raging through me.

A soft touch to my hand makes me take a deep breath.

"Let me."

Ariana's fingertips brush over mine to take the tip of the paper. When I let go and she picks it up, I notice she's trembling, too.

This woman is scared, and it's fucking killing me because she has no reason to be. We might be the brutal fucking Mafia —and yesterday, she's seen us at our worst—but of all the lines I've crossed, this is one line I never have and never will: I will never hurt a woman.

I let go of the instructions and fall back in the chair. As I meet Matteo's gaze where he stands rigid and unyielding, it strikes me that my brother has kept more than one secret.

But so have I. It started the night Alex died, and the most recent one concerns this woman between us.

Everybody else thinks she saw nothing yesterday. Only I know this woman witnessed everything in that warehouse and could have us all hanged for it. And that secret is only the latest joining the list.

13

ARIANA

I stare blindly at the paper in my hand.

I just want to shrink away, drown into the bed, and disappear. I'm not well, whatever the doctor might say. I hardly slept, and when I did, nightmares flooded my mind, jerking me out of my restless sleep. Nobody knows because I'm quiet. I don't call out, I don't stir and kick in my bed, but I wake up with a soft gasp as if I'm finally allowed a breath after being waterboarded.

Worst of all is how the nightmares weren't about yesterday, or about Franco and the time I spent in that dungeon. They were all about that night twelve years ago when he came for me.

I compartmentalized that night and packed it away so deep in me, the memories are only embers, glowing with the occasional trigger I've never allowed to catch flame. But the job I was on before Franco came for me was like a ball of oxygen waiting to explode. I've trained to separate my body from my mind, but now, after all these weeks and everything that's happened, my systems are failing, and I'm broken.

If my team knew my history with Franco, they would never have let me on the job in the first place. There was always the risk of running into him, exactly as I have. But I'm a closed book. I've learned long ago to keep my mouth shut. You can tell your team everything...except how personal a job—a vendetta—really is.

Worst of all is yesterday, I was in Dominic's arms, and he felt so unexpectedly safe. Nobody has ever held me like this, least of all a man. I've never allowed one close, not after what Franco did to me.

And now, he's brought me flowers. Since when does a kind man with caring eyes and gentle hands trigger me to tears?

Thank God his brother burst in like a storm cloud, making me want to run for shelter. Now these two powerful and built men, dressed impeccably in suits, growl at each other over my bed as if they're fighting over who will have me first.

I'm under no illusion here. These men are from the same stock as Franco Fiore: Mafia. Just on this side of the pond.

Il Consiglio. There were more brothers in that warehouse yesterday, but for the life of me, I can't place them as a family. And this is for my life. This crime ring has somehow crossed swords with Franco Fiore, and in the bigger scheme of things, with Emilio Randazzo.

The obvious connection is Gigi and Carla Trapani, but I'm not sure how they're connected to these men. I suspect there's history here nobody is aware of. What I won't give for a bit of Interpol intel right now, or just access to a computer. Never mind. Here I'm just as cut off from the world as I've been with Franco.

They're looking for Gabriella Scalera. Beyond actually being her, which is impossible, I have no illusions that I'm nothing but an inconvenience—a big one. If I'm not their little lost sister, I'm as good as dead.

With a deep breath, I try to read the DNA test's instructions, needing to distract myself and get this over and done with so they can leave. Something caused a rift between these brothers within seconds, and as much as I try to read the room, I don't know them well enough to get how this happened without either of them speaking a single word.

At first, Dominic has protected me from Matteo's onslaught of questions, but now he's slumped in the chair, looking murderous. Matteo is just standing there, hovering over me, indecisive, as if he needs someone to hold his hand as he does this test. *Men*. That someone can be so bamboozled by a stupid swab.

"It's not complicated," I say, forcing myself to slip back into the type of side character with zero importance, someone who will appease them and buy me time. "You each take a swab, roll it inside your inner cheek for a minute. I do the same with my own swab. We seal them in these different colored tubes to prevent cross-contamination of the sample, and then you send it off." My eyes run down all the way to the last lines. "Results are usually ready within three to five working days. For expedited results, call this number—"

"We're going to expedite the living fuck out of these tests," Dominic grunts as he tears open a foil package and extracts a long, cotton-tipped stick. "If I could have results today, I would."

He hands me mine, and I obediently rub away, knowing that my days are, yet again, numbered. Once these results are back as negative, I'm just a pair of eyes that witnessed crimes no human should. A woman, on top of it all, one who can easily disappear into sex trafficking, especially now I'm an illegal. I bet *Il Consiglio* is as deep into such depravity as Randazzo was. I don't even want to know where Franco Fiore planned to lead the operations.

Franco is dead.

My stomach tightens. I still can't believe it.

When Dominic picks up the other test packets and pulls out the swabs for my side of the DNA sample, I do what I need to do. Five tests equal five swabs. It's all a big excessive but I say nothing.

"I'll get the others to do theirs and then get it to the lab today," he says in explanation. "If we pay them enough, we might even have the results tomorrow."

Matteo closes his test tube holding his swab, pushes it back into the box, and hands it over to Dominic.

The tension between the brothers is as thick as frozen butter, and I drop my gaze to my lap, not wanting them to look at me. They have many questions, but I only have one: how on earth am I going to escape my new prison and get back to Italy?

Dominic stands and reaches for my shoulder to give me soft squeeze. I don't flinch away from his touch, not like when Matteo wanted to stick his hand out to me and I signaled nobody is laying a hand on me, not even in a polite greeting.

It's too soon. I'm not ready. I've had no time to think or order my thoughts about how I'm going to get out of this mess. I need to escape this place and make my way to the nearest police station. And all this without money, a phone, or proper clothes. With those tests going to the lab, there's a ticking time bomb in the room. Once they have the results, I'm done for.

They won't keep me alive once they know my truth. I, after all, know theirs, and in the Mafia, witnesses never get to tell the story. I don't have a minute to lose.

Dominic sighs and nods to his brother. This meeting was swift, but it's over. Matteo gives a nod, sweeps me with a glance, and with a sigh, walks out.

"Try to rest," Dominic says as he makes his way to the door, the tests in his hands. "I'll see you later, Ariana."

No, you won't.

14

DOMINIC

As we walk out of the clinic, I'm rigid with tension. Matteo looks ready to sag under this knowledge he's kept from me for how long? Years. Twenty-two fucking years.

"Where do you want to do this?" I ask as we head to the back service road where our cars are waiting.

"It will have to be your place, Nicky. I can't do this at mine."

"Fine." The Don's house isn't my fucking place, but Matteo used my nickname as if he's already begging for mercy. Or forgiveness. I'm going to have to dig deep for that one.

He could take his own car, but when he clambers into the back seat of mine, I know my brother is struggling. Fuck. This life...

Stan hits the road, and we sit in stoic silence. Matteo's bodyguard and driver follow our car. To kill time and to stop myself from going at him like a maniac and squeeze everything he knows out of him with my bare hands, I check my inbox on my phone. At times like these, I forget I forged a successful security company out of nothing and it deserves some of my time. Matteo has his own things on the side, but mine is clean. I've gone as pristine as I could have without becoming a fucking monk.

When we drive through the house's gate and the security closes it behind us, I slide my phone back into my pocket. This place. If only we could burn it down and walk away. Disappear into another realm where we aren't who we are, weren't born to the Don, or haven't become who we've become under his iron fist.

With a deep sigh, I get out of the car but slam my door, not waiting for Matteo. As soon as I'm inside, I spot Bruno where he is lying in the foyer and sink my hands into his fur. He's been waiting for me to come home. I breathe, trying to find my equilibrium. Of all the things I can do to my brother, it's going to have to be nothing. Absolutely nothing.

The dog doesn't even acknowledge Matteo as he heads to the Don's office, and I take the minutes I need to get a grip.

By the time I close the door, I'm calm but go over to the bar and pour two neat whiskeys. It's only ten in the morning, but shit's gone down already today, and I need a drink.

Matteo is slumped in one of the wingbacks facing the Don's desk, opting not to take his rightful place. He's cupped his face in his hands, looking completely defeated.

"How long have you known?" I ask as I hold out his whiskey to him.

He inhales a sharp breath and looks up to meet my gaze. "Since yesterday? Since Franco Fiore jerked my fucking chain?"

Jesus Christ. It hasn't been years.

He takes his whiskey, and I sink into the other chair, facing him. "And we're going to go on the word of a fucking lunatic?"

He shakes his head as he waves a hand at the Don's desk. "Have you found anything here? Anything at all that could—"

"Fuck it, Matty, no. I haven't exactly been looking for information on a MIA stillborn sister." I didn't know this could even be a reality. "Why the fuck do you think Franco wasn't just lying? And how would he know anything in the first place?"

Matteo drops his head back and stares up at the ceiling as if he is praying for strength, clinging to the whiskey glass as if it's a lifeline. "That day the Don called me in to tell me he had cancer, he mentioned he had three loose ends he wanted me to wrap up before he died."

Three? Matteo had shared only two with us, and we'd helped him with both projects: eliminating Don Emilio Randazzo and taking care of senator Peter Armstrong's debts.

Then Tasha flung Matteo's phone across the expanse of his apartment, and he gave her a fucking hickey. In that moment, I knew things were going to go pear-shaped. When Matteo defied the Don by marrying Tasha Armstrong, I was so relieved. It pleases me fucking endlessly that the exact opposite of what the Don had wanted happened with Tasha and Matteo.

"What did he say about the third loose end?"

As if a baby girl born to our mother is a loose fucking end. Whatever happened to our sister is a sacrilege I will never forgive anybody for. I will torture every capo who was in the Don's service at the time until I know the fucking truth.

"He didn't elaborate. He first wanted Randazzo dead and Armstrong dealt with, both with proof, before he told me his third and final command."

"What happened when you came back from Cannes?"

The Don was sick, but he was still alive when Matteo and Tasha headed back with Stephano in tow, our younger brother as prickly and moody as a teenager who didn't get the girl.

Matteo sighs, takes a deep sip of whiskey, then looks me in the eye. "I came to see him and lost my shit."

I quirk a brow. Of all the things we were allowed to do, losing our shit was never one of them. Even Stephano learned how to deal with his own vice by starting that Fight Club gym of his. "Why?"

"Because I thought he was asking me to kill Tasha—" He breaks off, running his thumb along his forehead as if he could erase his frown lines. "I mean, what else was I to think with the amount of shit he'd already put her family through and then what he'd wanted me—us—to do to her?"

None of us endorsed what the Don wanted to do with Tasha Armstrong. The unwritten *Il Consiglio's* rule for civilians is two for one. If you take out one of ours, we take out two of yours. The Armstrongs paid for Alex's death. We had no business putting Tasha's virginity up for auction, and I'm still not sure what the Don's real reasons were behind those tasks he saddled Matteo with months ago.

"But that wasn't what he'd meant." He groans. "Fuck it, Nicky. His last words to me were about *the girl. Alive.* I couldn't stop myself. I didn't for one second think about Gabriella. I fucking strangled him before he could explain himself because I couldn't listen to one more word."

Jesus fucking Christ. I drop my head into my palm and try to digest this influx of information.

The girl. Alive.

Jesus. Our little sister has been alive for twenty-two years, and none of us knew it? How many more secrets walk the corridors of this house? No wonder I can't shed this weird feeling that's been trailing me for weeks now. It ghosts over me as if this house is haunted, and it is. With secrets. About Gabriella and what happened to her.

Not only do we have a Scalera sister unaccounted for, but Matteo just confessed that he killed the Don. Our fucking dad. The man whose fist I can still feel choking me.

My big brother did all of us all a hell of a favor. He might have left it a bit late, but here's the thing: you can sense a man's grip weaken, you can watch him wither away with age and then cancer, but if you grew up with his type of discipline, guarded yourself and your brothers against his wrath for doing anything against him, it takes immense courage to disobey his instructions, never mind killing him. I was never able to do it. Ever since the time Alex died and the Don put me in my place, I focused on protecting my brothers. Firstly from the Don, and then from people like me in other crime organizations.

I rub a hand down my face, and with a deep sigh reach for my whiskey where I parked it on the desk. I down the whole thing, stand, take Matteo's empty glass, and get us each a refill.

With this new information, the scales have shifted from speculation to certainty. The Don's third request to wrap up unfinished business must have been for Matteo to find our baby sister, dead or alive.

Suddenly, I don't want to know. Not in this world where we hail from—and I'm the one trained to have the stomach for our cruelest depravity.

"How the hell are we going to find her, Nicky?"

Matteo's voice is a guttural plead, and when I meet his gaze as I hand him his drink, he's distraught.

"Mom's gone," he continues. "The Don is fucking dead. So is Franco Fiore—"

"The retired capos will know something," I say as I sit again. "And we have Ariana Morelli. Maybe she's the real deal."

Matteo smirks as he wipes his face and drops back in his seat. "And when last was something so fucking easy?"

Never.

"We don't have time to lose, Matty. She could be anywhere, subjected to—" It's time to be frank with him and tell him what I know. "Ariana has Randazzo's seal tattooed on her stomach. She has scarification on her lower belly—"

"What the fuck?" he growls.

"It was Franco's handiwork, but who are we going to kill for doing that to her? Franco and Randazzo are both dead."

"I should have fucking listened to what he wanted to say."

"No regrets, Matteo. It's done. It needed to be done." My

brother is gutted, but I stand and walk over to meet him halfway. "Any one of us would have done exactly the same. In fact, if I could kill him again for all of us, I would." I squeeze him by the shoulder. "We have resources and the means to figure this out. It's just going to be a matter of time."

"Which we don't have."

"So let's stop fucking around. How do you want to do this?'

"Pull in Luca and Benedict. Stephano is out for the count." He rakes a hand through his hair. "Gigi needs to see Don Trapani and make sure he's safe. Steph will fly out with them to Italy as soon as Carla can travel."

Fair enough. "Okay. I'll have to ask Gigi a few questions before they go, though. She might know something, if unwittingly. Vincenzo is still around for what he's worth, and with his connection with Franco, he might know something if I ask the right questions."

"Sure, but then he's done."

Yep. Matteo doesn't need to remind me Vincenzo's days are numbered.

"I'll need help going through the Don's paperwork. If there is any trail of what happened all those years ago, it will be here. At least we now have something to look for rather than going through endless papers, having to decide if they're keepers or tossers."

"Rosalia can help. Portia might know something, too."

Great. To think Rosalia and her mom could be into some of the family secrets and never squeaked a word. We're going to have to pull everybody who worked for the Don at that time into this investigation. Somewhere, someone must know something.

"I'll get the DNA results and start asking questions."

"Focus on Ariana Morelli," Matteo says. "She isn't a coincidence. Franco didn't drag her all the way here for nothing."

I drop my gaze. "She hasn't been very talkative."

"I'm not surprised. If she's one of Randazzo's girls—" A shudder runs through his body. "Truth be told, it's a miracle we have one of his women in our care. I bet none of them make it out alive. Who knows what she's been through."

But we both know. Sex trafficking. Forced prostitution. Chemical submission until she can't resist anymore and does whatever someone asks just for a hit. Except for the tattoo and those tally marks on her skin which appeared to be new, I haven't noticed any track marks of injection scars to hint she's an addict.

"I'm not wringing information out of her, Matteo." Fuck knows, that's the one line I haven't crossed in my life. I don't care who she is or what she's done. I don't need to torture a woman for information. I'd rather end her and myself before I go there. The next words could cost me, since Matteo is now the Don and I'm his to command, but I don't care. "I refuse."

Matteo draws his chin back as if he's offended. "I never suggested you torture her like one of those Bratva wannabes we've locked in the basement."

"Thanks for that fucking reminder," I huff out. Another issue I still have to deal with.

"There are other ways to make a woman talk," he fills in.

Fucking hell. He's going there?

"Is that so?"

"For one, we can send in the calvary, now that we have one."

"The calvary?" I ask, hitching my brows. What is he on about?

"Tasha and Gigi. Surely, Ariana will open up to them? Let the women talk. They'd like nothing better than a good chit-chat over a cup of tea."

A chit-chat? Over a cup of tea? So it's not... Never mind. I smirk. I've never heard Matteo use those words before, never mind in one sentence. "You think?"

"And if that doesn't work—" he reaches for my shoulder to

squeeze me in the exact way I squeezed him minutes ago, "—you of all people know best how to make a woman submit to you, don't you, Nicky?"

Fuck. He *was* going there. He only took a detour.

A weighty beat of silence bounces off the walls of the office as I stare at him.

"What the actual fuck, Matty? Can you listen to yourself for a second?" I hiss, incredulous. My brothers know what I'm into sexually, but fuck, it's not on the agenda for discussion—ever. I don't prod and poke around their fucking sex lives, and the least they can do is leave mine the fuck alone. And now—"You're calmly suggesting I seduce her—to the point of her begging me to fuck her—for information? A woman who has been prostituted, violated, used? A woman who could be our little sister?"

Matteo is already at the door and opening it to leave when he throws back at me, "We both know Ariana Morelli isn't our little sister."

Right. As if that makes anything better.

15

ARIANA

It's almost eleven in the morning. I've been lying in bed feigning to be asleep ever since Dominic and Matteo left. I've quietly been observing the coming and goings in this private clinic. The nurse came in with some meds, woke me up, watched me swallow them, and then pulled up the blind to let in some daylight.

I blinked in confusion as I took in the outside world. A low wooden fence separates this house from the next one. Our neighbor has a small vegetable garden with tomatoes and beans already trellised for easy picking. There's a whole bed of sunflowers and another one with lettuce and kale.

Beyond this small, narrow yard, the next wooden fence. The back porch has a coffee table and two rocking chairs. Very companionable, but not a soul in sight. I'm in the heart of American suburbia. I should be able to scale the wall without a problem and cross to the other house, then the next one and so on, until I find a bigger, busier road where I could disappear.

"Do you rather want the blind down?" the nurse asks, and I shake my head.

Sleep isn't my friend right now, and after weeks without sunlight, I'm craving it.

"I'll bring your lunch soon. It's only soup, but better than nothing."

True, that, and I should know. I touch my stomach where the bullet wound throbs as soon as the pain meds start to wear off. One thing is for sure, I won't last out there, not without help. Once I've made my escape, I'll have to get to the right people without any detours. I don't know who the right people are here. My job was never meant to extend beyond Italy into Europe. The States isn't even on our map.

Plus, if this is anything like Italy, I could be running the risk of talking to the wrong police. If I talk to someone who is taking a cut from the Mafia, I'll be back to Square One—and delivered right back into the beautiful hands of Dominic Scalera. There is no way to know, and it's a risk I'll simply have to take. Unless I can bypass all of these risks and get my hands on a cellphone.

The nurse walks out, and I glance around the room. There's nothing here to use as a weapon, and I still haven't figured out how to get around the bodyguard sitting outside my door. Whenever he gets up to go the washroom or whatever else he does, the nurse comes and keeps an eye on me in his place by leaning onto the doorjamb and scrolling on her phone.

There aren't many people here. In fact, today, it would seem to be just me and Carla as patients, the nurse, and the bodyguard.

My gaze snags on the small fire extinguisher mounted on the wall. Perfect. You've got to love building codes. I suppress a giggle—to think these mobsters adhere to building codes. Nothing like butting a guy's head with this and have him out of it for a few minutes.

I'm not fooling myself here. I'm only going to have a few seconds, unless I take him out, grab his gun, and shoot everybody in this house. I've never taken anybody out, never mind innocent victims. All I need to do is buy myself time. The nurse is sweet and not a threat at all. Even in my diminished physical state, I can take her out if I need to. As for Carla, she's pregnant and won't risk her baby. Plus she probably still has a pounding headache from her head bouncing on the concrete yesterday.

The only tricky part is going to be to detach the fire extinguisher from its mount without anybody noticing.

Yep, I'm screwed. First, I need to get my weapon, and then I need to sneak up on the bodyguard and get in a proper swing without him noticing.

I lean to the side, as far as the bed would allow me to go without toppling off, and look. From here, I can see his elbow and his leg where it's stretched out. He's sitting on a chair, similar to the one in my room. Then I spot a framed watercolor print on the corridor wall that screams hospital decor. I hadn't noticed it before, but now with the blind up in my room and the sun pouring in, the framed glass reflects the bodyguard's face perfectly.

My heart starts to thump in my chest as my mind does the math. I can see him, but he can't see me. If he turns his head away as he is doing now, engaging with the nurse in some small talk about coffee, I can sneak up, raise the fire extinguisher, and with one step come down on his head. Then I can spray the stuff in the nurse's face and get out of here.

I'll have one chance. *One*.

With a deep but soft sigh, I slump onto my back and stare at the ceiling. Voices sound from the entrance, the one that leads to the garage, and my ears perk up. Women's voices.

Gigi Trapani. I'll recognize her voice anywhere for the rest of my life. How can I not when the way she begged with Franco to let Carla go is imprinted on my mind? It was futile to beg with him for any kind of mercy. Even now, goosebumps rush over my skin at the memory, and I want to sink deeper into the covers until I'm submerged.

Franco is dead, I remind myself for the hundredth time today, still in disbelief.

Then the voices are closer, and a stranger peeks into my room. She's young and American-pretty, if there's such a thing. Blond hair and light eyes, perfect skin, and dressed casually in jeans and an off-the-shoulder white T-shirt that hangs loose over her hips.

"Hey," she says as she steps into the room, flowers in hand, uncertain as she tucks a strand of hair behind her ear.

The massive diamonds on her ring finger catch the light, and I have to do a double take. Oh my God. The mobster's wife. It could be one of their sisters, though. I have no guarantee they only have the one who's missing.

"Hi," I say, wishing she'd reverse out of my space and I didn't need to do this.

"I'm Tasha. Tasha Scalera, Matteo's wife," she says softly as she walks up to me. "I came to check in on you."

She smiles at me, and it's so warm and genuinely caring, I have to warn myself. I don't do friendly, least of all with Mafia wives.

When I say nothing, she glances around the room, spots Dominic's flowers in their vase, and chuckles. "Oops, we didn't think that far. We just got these on the way here and didn't think there...would...be...a vase problem."

Tasha speaks slower and slower when I don't respond. She's being kind, and who knows how she got manipulated into the position she's now holding.

I reach out to take the flowers from her. "Thank you. I'm sure the nurse can find another vase. They're beautiful."

I'm slightly sour that I won't get to appreciate these gorgeous and expensive blooms. It's not as if anybody ever buys me flowers in my real life. With a fake smile, I remind myself who I am—who I was a mere five weeks ago until Franco got hold of me. That I have a team who is probably going mad looking for me, just as I'm worried sick about them.

"I'm so glad you speak English. I know zero Italian...well, that's not entirely true because Matteo's been teaching me some naughty words," she says with her warm smile never leaving. "I'm so sorry this happened to you, but you are safe now, out of that maniac's hands."

I bet she doesn't know how things ended for Franco Fiore or how maniacal he really was. "I'm going to be fine. Thank you. Where is Gigi?"

"She's just with Carla. She's so worried about her and the baby." For a second, Tasha looks chagrined as if she spoke out of line, but then she shrugs. "I bet you know all of this already."

"It all came out yesterday while—" I break off for dramatic effect. I drop my gaze then look back up at her where she's hovering next to the bed. "Who is *Il Consiglio*?" I ask, knowing this woman might give me more information with the right prodding. "I feel in debt with them for saving me."

"*Il Consiglio*?" she repeats, her eyes widening. "I—I... Sorry. I'm not sure myself, actually. I met Matteo only recently, and well...it's been a bit of a whirlwind."

That could mean anything.

Footsteps fall, and we both look to the door where Gigi Trapani is walking in. She doesn't stop. She comes all the way to me and then leans into the bed to wrap me in a hug. I don't resist. I mean, how do you?

When she pulls away, tears are streaming down her face. Heavens, she looks like she's been through the wringer, and watching the emotions pour from her tightens my throat.

"We are sisters now," she murmurs. "You know that, right? Bound by this thing that happened. Franco is dead. He'll never hurt you again."

Or hurt her, by the sound of it. I bite my lip, triggered by her tears. God. When did I become this weak? Tears slip down my cheeks in a warm but quiet rush. Gigi now has my hand in hers, and I wipe at my face, embarrassed she was able to break me so easily. As she squeezes my hand and I stupidly squeeze back, I remind myself of the rules: Don't get involved. Don't start to care. Don't get attached. *Observe, adapt, only act when the time is right.*

I'm not here to make friends. These women are married to the type I want to put behind bars. For life.

In this quiet moment, the nurse chooses to walk in with my lunch.

"Oh," Gigi says as she gets up from where she perched with her hip and half a bum on the bed. "Is it ever a good time to visit?" she asks deprecatingly. "I have so many questions—"

"Ariana still needs a couple of days, Gigi," Tasha says softly.

"I don't have days...We're going to Italy, and then—"

I wish I could beg her to take me with and not leave me here, at the mercy of people who'd have no use for me once the DNA tests comes through. I hate this part, this moment when you meet somebody you know you'd be best friends with if you weren't an undercover agent in deep shit and she a Mafia kingpin's daughter. In any other life circumstances, these two women could have been my best friends.

Instead, I'm going to go back to Italy—by some means or another—and ruin their lives from afar...unless I choose to turn a blind eye to everything I've seen.

"Come back tomorrow," I say softly in Italian. "We have time?"

"Of course," Gigi says and shoots Tasha a small smile. "They're taking Carla for an ultrasound to check in on the baby at a hospital not far from here. We literally came at the worst time to visit because she asked if we could both go with her."

"Now?" Tasha asks.

"Yes. The appointment is in an hour, and there'll be forms to fill in and so on."

"Okay." Tasha reaches for my arm and gives me a warm squeeze. "I'm sorry we have to go, but we'll definitely see you tomorrow. In the meantime, if you need anything...we'll bring some clothes and so on. Make a list?"

"I'm fine for now, thank you." Inwardly, I curse because if only I had something to wear now, my escape plan would be halfway there.

They leave the room, and in the commotion of everybody getting Carla ready for her appointment, I slip out of bed, reach for the fire extinguisher, and quietly unhook it from its wall mount. I pull out the pin so it's ready for action and place it on the floor, out of sight.

When the nurse pushes Carla out of the house in a wheelchair, it dawns on me I'm alone with the bodyguard and my moment has come.

16

ARIANA

It's quiet. Eerily quiet now I'm alone in this clinic. Every now and then, the bodyguard shifts in his seat, and it creaks. It's hardly noticeable, but I'm on high alert, and every sound is amplified. When the man stands, stretches, and peers into my room, I'm feigning sleep again.

His footsteps fall softly on the floor. Eight. Eight footfalls. Hushed clanging sounds come from the kitchen, a packet ripping. I clamber out of bed, rush to reach the fire extinguisher, carefully peek out into the corridor, and take in the layout of the house in one glance. A small foyer, several doors leading to more rooms. The sounds are definitely coming from the door in the middle: the kitchen.

My lucky break.

He'll walk out of there and won't see I'm not in bed, and with the layout as it is, I can hide in the one door and whack him as he exits the kitchen.

In seconds, I have stolen over to my hiding place, so quiet, the only way he'd know I was there would be in the movement of air. I haven't been trained for nothing, and I'm barefoot. Adrenaline rushes through my veins. I'm pumped.

I wait, my heart in my throat, for him to finish making his coffee. Soon the earthy smell reaches me, and I swallow down my thirst.

What an idiot. If this whack over the head doesn't kill him, he might be dead for letting me escape. It's not a done deal yet, but failing isn't an option. This is my first step back towards my team and the job I set out to do and plan to finish. Fuck Franco being dead, and fuck Randazzo being dead. When it comes to slime, the world keeps on producing. Someone else will step into those men's shoes, and my team is waiting. We *will* get it done.

With this pep talk running on repeat in my head, I get in position, raising my hands, clutching the fire extinguisher.

I home in on his footsteps as he walks past, stirring his coffee, a cookie shoved in his mouth.

Sorry, my friend, it's you or me.

With my whole measly weight and all my muscle power, I bring the extinguisher down on his head. But here's the problem. It's more to the back of his skull because this guy is motherfucker tall and moved around like a freaking fairy.

"Good God," I huff as he sinks to one knee in surprise, the mug slipping from his hand and crashing to the floor, splattering creamy coffee far and wide. He isn't out yet.

I up my swing again, knowing I'm not getting a third chance as he is already reaching for his gun. But this time, he is at a better whack-level, and I don't hold back. I bring down the extinguisher full on his head with a satisfying crack that makes him crumble to the floor like the cookie he spluttered from his mouth.

For a split second, I stare at him, horrified at my own brutality but also knowing I had no choice. I can't tell if he's dead, and I'm not going to wait to find out. If I really cracked his skull, the nurse will know what to do with him. He's already at their clinic, so in a way, I've done him a favor.

I curse. He's fallen onto his side, right on top of his gun. There's no chance I can get it out now. I'd rather use what strength I have to get out of here. For a second, I consider his phone. It will come with a tracking device, and the last thing I want is someone finding me. I need to go. Already, my body reprimands me, whispering how this whole maneuver wasn't the best idea. It has stretched the stitches to my wound that hasn't healed yet.

Now I rush, going around the place, frantically looking for something to wear that isn't a hospital gown with my naked butt for all to see. I don't need anybody to conclude with one look that I've just escaped an asylum.

But there's nothing—not even an extra nurse's uniform. I don't have time to waste.

I'll need to steal some clothes. From next door. From the neighbor with the pretty vegetable garden. I head back to the kitchen. Its windows look out over the street and not the way to go if I want to be surreptitious. I hasten to the garage which I open with a remote by the door. Really? These people need to up their in-house security. Naturally, this clinic is only for their own people, who have no motive to run, but this...*this* is too easy.

With a huff and a deep breath, I peer out into the street. The service road is empty. Farther along, there are some cars parked, but no humans, no rodents, and no Mafia in sight.

I walk, demurely, like I do this every day, to the next house's picket fence that has a nice gate for me to go through. I open it and walk into the yard as if I own it, clenching my hospital gown all the way to keep myself decent.

There are only three steps onto the porch and then I'm at the back door, feeling the doorknob. I softly turn it, and the latch slips as the door opens. Then I'm inside, close the door, and for a moment lean against it to catch my breath with my eyes closed.

Two soft bangs and the almost eerie brush of air by my legs arrest me. And then, I'm almost electrocuted in shock as the silencer's tell-tale muffled 'pip' sound registers in my mind. My eyes fly open.

Fuck. Someone just *shot* at me. I blink into the ill-lit foyer, frozen.

"Just warning shots, *cara*. Don't move," a female voice delivers, calm but clear. "And please don't test me. I'd hate to really immobilize you."

I exhale a shattered breath as I look down to where two bullets have pierced holes in the wooden floor, mere inches from my feet.

Holy fucking shit.

I glance up. Two meters from me, in the dark shadows of the corridor, stands an older woman with an apron on, her thick, curly hair streaked with grey. She smiles. I don't know what she sees, but I bet it's disbelief and horror on my face.

"What? If Christian Grey's housekeeper can wash butt plugs, you better believe that a Mafia Don's housekeeper knows how to shoot a gun."

I swallow, no clue what she's referring to, but I've lost. Again. A whiff of gunpowder and hot metal swirls up to me as I take in her stance. This one shoots and asks questions later. She won't hesitate. She won't miss. She'd take out my kneecap without flinching. Now, she has her phone to her ear, her gun never shifting from its target, her eyes never leaving my face as she watches me.

"Nicky," she says as the other person answers. "She's here now. I'm holding her. Be quick. She didn't hold back, and poor Marco looks dead from what I can see on the cameras."

Fuck. Fuck. *Fuck.*

I didn't notice a single camera in that whole clinic, and it wasn't as if I wasn't looking for them.

Hidden cameras, with *her* keeping watch. *Right next door.*

"Come now, *cara*. You can't run around in that. It's a dead giveaway that you're in *Il Consiglio's* clinic, if you were wondering."

I look down at my gown, which has a pretty pattern of light blue flowers printed on the white fabric. It looks custom-made. I thought nothing of it, but this woman—

"Who are you?" I ask, out of breath with shock.

"I'm Portia. Come with me, and we'll see what I have that fits you. Dominic will be here soon. He was heading this way in any case." She doesn't lower the gun but takes two steps back and nods in the direction of a bedroom.

I have no choice but to follow her instructions, my eye warily on the gun with its silencer. It must have at least ten more rounds, and with defeat, I walk through the door. I take in the homey bedroom, which is clearly for guests, and sink onto the neatly made bed as exhaustion floods over me.

Portia is the real deal, and I'd be dead before I know it.

As if any of that is even news.

17

DOMINIC

Nice.

Now we have a fugitive. Or rather, Ariana Morelli just proved she's a flight risk. I get it, but in the same breath, I don't. Why?

I clamber out of the car and make quick work of the stretch between the picket-fence gate and Portia's porch. Already, Gus and Stan are heading into the clinic to assess the damage she's done to Marco as two more cars with our team arrive on the scene.

Ariana's a feisty little one, too, and gutsy to take a man Marco's size out with a fire extinguisher. Noted. Let's see what she does with this welcome party.

At least Portia was on top of things and almost immediately called me to deliver real-time feedback of what she could see happening on her screens feeding from the hidden security cameras next door. This is honestly one of our strengths: keep the circle tight and the rest of them guessing. There's a reason we installed Portia here after her retirement as housekeeper for the Don—she could keep an eye on things when we needed her.

I knock briefly and let myself in.

"Here, Nicky," she calls out, and I follow her voice to one of the bedrooms.

I lean against the doorjamb, watching the scene in front of me. Portia, despite the gun in her hand still pointed at Ariana's head, has clearly shifted into mother-mode. Ariana is sitting on the bed, but she's dressed in something borrowed, her blond hair brushed into a thick ponytail, and she has sandals on her feet. All very simple, but so feminine, it makes my dick twitch. Fuck it.

"Thank you, Portia," I say, shoving my hands into my pockets. This is literally the last thing I need. Everything seems to spin more and more out of control the harder I try to keep this mess contained.

"No problem, Nicky. I thought you wouldn't want her at the clinic anymore, so I got her to dress a minute ago in some of Rosalia's old things I had on hand. I opted for a dress so there's no pressure on her wound."

"Good, that's perfect." Only a minute ago? Portia is solid. Naked women don't flee, and Ariana's skimpy hospital gown was issued on purpose.

"I'll leave you to it." She slides the safety on then tucks the gun into her apron pocket, touching my arm as I twist to make space for her to leave the room. "There's some fresh ravioli if you feel like it."

"Next time, thank you, Portia. This situation—"

She just nods. She already knows exactly what's going on. It's after all only a three-person grapevine between Ariana and what happened here. Burley, Matteo's bodyguard, was at the shootout, and he is married to Rosalia, who is Portia's daughter...and here we are. We might work on a need-to-know basis, but that's why we're a close-knit family.

"Portia," I say to her as she heads towards the kitchen. "We have some questions."

"I know. But honestly, Dominic, I know nothing about that time and what happened after your mom left for the hospital to have the baby. I didn't even know it was a little girl. In retrospect, I should have guessed, because they didn't speak about it. With you boys, Don Scalera couldn't stop talking about how great it was that your mom was giving him son after son after son."

She gave him an army, and yet, he never stopped beating her. I sigh with a nod, effectively dismissing her. Portia won't lie, not to me of all people. That she even went as far as calling me Dominic and not by my nickname just goes to show she doesn't want to step out of line here.

I'm left alone with Ariana staring at me from where she's sitting, hands clenched in her lap.

"Come on." I hold out my hand. "Let's go."

"Where?" she asks, her voice uncertain.

"Somewhere you can't pull the shit you just pulled," I say, not for a minute wanting to give her the impression I'm not pissed. What she's done isn't on, and if she were one of my team—one of us, a Scalera—there would have been serious consequences for knocking her bodyguard into the next realm, woman or not. As it is, I feel her actions shouldn't go unpunished. We're after all here to protect her, and this is how she thanks us?

As she stands, I take her in.

Fuck.

She's wearing a white summer dress, one of those medieval things with the fabric rucked at the bodice and a tiered hem that ends in a ruffle just above her knee. It has two runs of corset laces in the front, aligned with her breasts, which is probably why Portia chose it in the first place. Rosalia is dainty but curvy, and everything of hers would be baggy on Ariana, who is taller but slim.

Matteo's last words to me—about how I'm the perfect

person to seduce a woman to the point where she reveals all her secrets—conjure up all types of unwelcome images. My hands sliding down her sides, over her hips and catching those little corset bows to pull them loose, one by one, and then watching how the dress gives and those little puffed shoulders slip off to reveal her breasts.

I look away with an inward groan and nod towards the back door. "Come on, I still have shit to deal with today."

She says nothing, and as she comes closer, I take her wrist in my hand and squeeze it softly but in warning.

"Don't do that again, Ariana. I don't have time to hunt you down in Boston, but if I have to, I will. And it won't be a pretty sight when I finally find you."

A soft tremor runs through her, and she drops her gaze from where she held mine for the duration of my reprimand. Instead of holding on to her wrist, I slide my hand to hers and gently wrap her fingers with mine. She doesn't protest, and I lead her all the way to the car, where I open the back door and help her in. She settles in the passenger seat, and I take the safety belt, run it over her chest, and buckle her in.

Her face is close, her breathing shallow and warm over my skin where it flows. I meet her gaze, and for a moment, I'm spellbound. Her lashes are long and lighter without mascara but still accentuate the crystal blue of her eyes. My eyes run down the perfect slide of her nose and land on that full mouth with lips made to stretch around a cock.

"Are you going to tie me up?" she whispers, a tremor in her voice. "And lock me up? In a dark room? For weeks?"

I lean away and out of the intimate space of the back seat, forcing myself to keep my cool. "You know, you have a lot of questions for someone who hasn't answered a single one of mine, so..."

She sucks her bottom lip, and I swear she wants to kill me slowly. "So?"

As I reach for my phone to talk to my team who are still inside the clinic, I give her the only answer she deserves. "So you'll have to wait and see."

18

ARIANA

I glance up and down the street from where I'm strapped in. Earlier, it was empty. Now there's an army of vehicles locking this one in. Men are on standby, watchful. Good grief. All of this for me?

"Is he hurt real bad?" I ask as Dominic rings off and pockets his phone. I got the gist of the conversation.

He opens the back door and slides into the seat next to me. "Marco's coming to. Consider yourself very, *very* lucky."

I chew my bottom lip and look out of the window as the garage rattles open. Dominic is pissed, and this doesn't bode well for me. But even so, I'm not scared of him. Ever since he came and took charge and carried me out of that warehouse, his hands so gentle and caring, I haven't been able to slot him in with the others where he belongs: violent and brutal Mafia.

The impulse to run, to fight my way out of every situation always sits shallow, but something broke me. I'm not sure if it was the weeks in that dungeon, or the fact that my vendetta against Franco and Randazzo has broken to pieces, but I'm winded. Portia's precision shooting rattled me. I don't run around naked. And Dominic—

Earlier, when he warned me not to run away again, his clasp around my wrist had been warm and gentle, even if firm in warning. It had been enough to make my pulse skip several beats. I'm not used to being touched by men. I usually avoid it at all costs, and yet Dominic's touch has never made me veer away in disgust or go rigid in fear.

A man walks out of the garage, closes it again, and then gets into the driver's seat.

"He'll be fine, boss," the driver says. "Going to have a motherfucker of a headache, but he'll be fine. Gus will stay with him for now."

"Thanks, Stan. Pick them up once the doctor's been and Marco's good to go home. Keep me posted. As it stands, we've already lost a man this week."

Unease chases down my spine as I recall the dead bodyguard slumped in the van when Franco kidnapped Carla.

"Yes, sir."

I meet the driver's gaze in the rearview mirror, knowing I've sealed my own fate. I blew my one chance to escape, and I'm not getting another. Everybody is going to be on high alert around me now. How was I supposed to know the clinic is as closely monitored as the Papal Palace? There was nothing giving it away.

Maybe I'm not 'all there' at the moment. I've landed in a Mafia-level hornet's nest, and yet I'm slow to catch on. My weeks in that death-zone dungeon have done me in.

"Let's head to the old house," Dominic says to his driver. "I've activated Code Red, so..."

Another sentence left hanging to keep me guessing.

Dominic pulls his phone from his pocket, and I give him a surreptitious side-eye. He has dismissed me and is working on his emails.

As we drive in silence through the suburbs of Boston, the areas become more and more exclusive, the trees taller, the properties bigger, the houses mansions. Eventually, the road winds through patches of forest until we reach a gate. It opens slowly, the guard getting out of his gatehouse to greet the car. I doubt he knows who is in the vehicle because the windows are tinted.

"Where are we?" I ask, taking in the high wall hidden by the thick forest lining the street.

"Whatever it might look like, this isn't my place," Dominic says, answering around my question.

We drive into the compound, and I drag in a slow breath as I take in the extent of the lawns and garden, the road winding until a magnificent mansion comes into view.

"Wow," I whisper. It's a classical red brick house in a colonial style, two stories high, with a couple of steps to a white-columned front entrance. Farther along, there have been additions to the dwelling, but they blend in, and the massive structure ends with a conservatory...or an indoor pool? Heavens. Hydrangeas bring pops of blue and white to the red brick. It's breathtaking, and the type of place I'd only ever see in a movie, not in real life. "It's beautiful."

"For a prison, it has its charms."

Dominic shoots me a glance that says it all. *Don't try and escape here. Code Red has been activated.*

Then I spot them. Armed guards at various points in the garden, patrolling with Alsatians on short leashes. And that's only the surface-level security he's implemented here.

Shit. I'm so screwed. Dominic isn't messing around, and I know better now than to just take things at face value.

"My prison?" I ask, testing the waters.

He reaches across the seat to squeeze my hand where I have it clenched on my thigh. "Our prison, sweetheart."

This man is in a prison? And here, of all places? What does he mean? He can't escape either?

The car pulls up to the front door, and Dominic and the

driver get out. I'm not making assumptions here, but I release the safety belt and open my door. When I look up, Dominic is holding his hand out for me.

I clamber out but pull free as soon as I'm out of the car. Instead of leaving me be, his hand settles on my lower back, and he guides me to the front door.

"Are you scared of dogs?" he asks.

"I am now," I say, with a little nod to the guard dogs farther afield.

"Good," he says with a smirk. "Those ones aren't for you. I mean pets. We have a mutt here who's more coyote slash wolf than dog."

"Wolf?"

"We're not sure. We down-sell him as coyote, but he's a bit big. He's also old, and to be honest, for most of his life, he's been misunderstood."

"Misunderstood?"

"People are petrified of him, and well, it gets him all worked up, which in turns makes people more terrified of him. It's a vicious circle."

"You're telling me I'm about to meet a vicious wolf-dog monster who isn't vicious at all?"

"Exactly." He leans in and whispers close to my ear. "Don't show fear, and you'll be fine."

I steel myself, reading the subtext right there. *Don't show fear here*, not to him either.

Dominic opens the front door, and a massive ball of fur gets up from where he was lying on the thick Persian carpet, wags his tail, and comes up to him with a few keen steps. It's an old dog, and his eyes looks glazed over with cataracts, but the way he homes in on me shows every other faculty is in full working order.

"Play nice, Bruno," Dominic says as he drops to his haunches.

He is literally cuddling the beast, giving the monster dog time to sniff my hand while he holds him in check. The jaws and teeth on that thing are straight out of Little Red Riding Hood. The fangs...I see where he comes from with the notion of this thing having some wolf in him.

"This is Ariana," Dominic croons in Bruno's ear as he rubs his back and sides. "She's going to stay for a while. Be gentle with her, you hear? She's had a rough time."

His words hit me full in the chest.

This man.

Goddammit.

I blink at the sudden swell of tears. Since when have I become so freaking weepy? This morning with Gigi and now with him. Always with him, showing me a side to men I've never seen before. Has my little pond been so small all these years? Filled with nasty big carps nobody wants to get close to? Probably. That's what I got for choosing my own path after that one night with Franco.

Once Bruno had sniffed every finger, Dominic gives a little. The dog by instinct homes in on my wound, and when Dominic tugs him back in warning, I reach out and caress my hand over his head. Bruno blinks up at me, gives a pant that looks like a smile, and my heart melts. Misunderstood, indeed.

"That's it," Dominic says as he stands. "He's given you the seal of approval."

"And what does that mean in this place?"

He quirks his brow. "Clearly, you are a Scalera in one way or another."

"Ha." If only I can fool the world this easily.

"Come along. There's a room ready for you." He indicates with his hand the direction I should take, forcing me to walk in front. After this morning, I won't trust me either.

I might have been dog-approved, but fear sprouts in my stomach. What if he drags me down to the basement? I have no choice, so I start to walk towards a corridor but glance around quickly to take in, orientating myself.

A gorgeous wooden staircase curves elegantly up to the second floor straight from the double-volume foyer, making a bold statement: here be money. Lots and lots of it. Two corridors split off on the ground floor, and then at the back of the foyer are also two doors. Beautiful modern art hang on all the surfaces, but there are no portraits or any photos to give me clues who this house belongs to. It's perfectly anonymous.

I feel Dominic's eyes on me, studying my every move. If I'm not careful, little things would give me away.

"It's a beautiful home," I say to distract him.

He doesn't respond, and we walk in silence, Bruno tagging along. We walk past closed door after closed door, and at the end of the corridor, Dominic stops me with a hand on my shoulder.

"You're in here."

He opens the door, and I stare into a beautiful bright room with big sash windows that look out onto the garden. No dungeon. No darkness. No death.

As he nudges me to walk inside, I cup my hands to my face. I need to do something to stall the emotions wrecking me from the inside out and calm the panic that rises in me every time I think back of the weeks I lost, forgotten and dying. And my team… I can't tell Dominic anything—he'll see right through my words, whether they're truth or lies.

His eyes are on me, reading me like a book.

"Fuck it, Ariana," he says softly as he gently twists me into his arms. "I know you're not ready to talk, sweetheart, but I just wish…fuck it, I just wish I can reverse everything he's done to you."

He feels so safe, his arms a haven, and I press deeper into his chest, letting the fear and pain flow out of me. For that, we'd have to go back so many years… My tears wet his shirt as he softly rubs my back, letting me cry it out. Why does it feel as if I've only started?

"Do you always cry this softly?" he murmurs against my ear, almost reverently as if he doesn't want to disturb the quiet of my pain, his lips soft and warm and sparking goosebumps down my neck.

"Force of habit," I say as I try to push free, ashamed I'm falling apart in front of him.

"Stay put," he says as he holds me close. "It's okay. It's just your body dealing with what it's gone through."

Something in his tone, his voice, or just his comforting warm scent where I'm pressed to his torso, makes me cave in. My head tells me to woman-up, to be stronger than this, but every other part of me only wants to stay put because it's finally safe to let go.

I lean against him, against his chest that's akin to a wall of warm comfort like I've never known before, allowing his hands to roam over my back, caressing me in rhythmic strokes and circles that are more than calming. They seem to be healing in a way. In me, that thing I've suppressed for twelve long years turns in its sleep.

No.

No-no.

Not this man.

I can't.

As if he feels the turmoil in me, he stops, and with a finger on my chin, tilts my face up so I'm forced to look at him.

"We haven't checked with you," he says as he runs a thumb along my tearstained cheek in a gesture so tender, more tears come out of nowhere. "Is there anybody you need to call to let them know where you are? Someone you trust and want to tell you're safe?"

I blink, then peel away from his body to wipe at my face with both hands. *Safe* is so objective and subjective at the same time. Safe for me, or safe for them? Now he offers me the one thing I clung to those weeks in Franco's dungeon. If only I could get hold of my team, they would come for me. Dominic hands me the opportunity on a platter, but if I do, he'd surely track the number, figure out exactly who I am, and kill me just as Franco had planned to.

Only, he'll be kinder and give me a quick, quiet bullet to the head. Dominic doesn't seem like the type who likes someone to suffer.

Bruno twitches his ears where he's been lying close on the floor and lifts his head. Far off in the house, the front door opens and shuts. Bruno gets up, but not in haste. Now a man is calling for *Nicky*, and with that, Bruno slumps back to the floor. It's clear the dog knows the voice and chooses to stay with us.

Dominic continues to stare at me, not distracted at all. I have hesitated too long in my answer, and he is going to read between the lines.

"It's only my brother, Luca," he says when I still say nothing. "We've got some work to wrap up here so you're going to be alone for a bit."

"Okay." I don't want to be alone. Not when he could be here, helping me deal with this tailspin I'm in. With a swallow and a shake of my head, I tell him my truth. "I've been gone so long now, they'll assume I'm dead."

"And you don't want to—"

"No. It will only put other people in danger."

19

DOMINIC

With a sigh, I leave Ariana standing in the middle of the small guest room. Those words implied so many things, but I don't have time to digest them now. I still have shit to deal with today, and the time has come.

I close the door and activate the electronic lock with my phone. It whirrs, and with a clink, secures the room. I'm not a fan of keeping her contained, but after this morning, I'm not taking any chances. I mean...why did she want to run in the first place? Weren't we being nice? And where did she hope to go?

I make my way to the foyer where Luca is rolling on his heels.

"For a minute I thought you weren't here," he says in greeting.

"Just contained our rogue guest," I huff as I walk over to the stack of DNA tests on a console.

"Making you run around, is she? Is she talking yet?"

Fuck this shit. As if Matteo hasn't made his own decrepit suggestions as to how to drag information out of Ariana already, Luca has one hell of a dirty mouth for starters, and a mind born in the gutter.

"Since she might be our little sister," I spell out to stop him from going anywhere with this. "Can you sort this out later? Benedict still needs to do his swab. As for you and Steph, one will do. If you can drop it off at the lab, it will take a load off me today."

Luca takes the box, studies the outside, then peers inside. "Sure thing. I'll drop it off once Benedict has done his part. Steph is out of commission today." He puts the box back with the others. "Where did you put her?"

"She's in the small guest room. It's the only room the guys had time to sweep before we got home."

It's also the room where it's least likely she'll hear anything we're doing in the basement. The last thing I want is for her to be traumatized by noises. I still don't know what she went through, but I can put two and two together. *'Are you going to tie me up? And lock me up? In a dark room? For weeks?'* Torture takes many forms. Isolation drives people mad. I'd take physical pain any day.

"Let's hope she isn't going to be innovative like Tasha."

I smirk. Tasha did keep Matty on his toes all the way to Sicily and back. Ariana's already shown she's gutsy, which I like more than I should. "There's nothing in there she could repurpose as a weapon. The windows are secure, and they've left her with some old-school puzzles and magazines to entertain herself. Plus, it has cameras in place. I'll keep an eye on her."

With Ariana's brave and rather futile attempt at escaping, I had to make plans quickly. I got the security team to lock all the other doors in the house. Can't be too careful nowadays.

"Won't she be better off at Matty's place, with Tasha there? I mean, she's not our usual profile."

"Matteo has had his fill of house guests." And our older brother needs space after everything that's happened. I've been thinking on my feet ever since he revealed it hit him like a ton of bricks that Franco wasn't bluffing. "I'll take one for the team. In any case, I've messaged Portia to come back and help work through the paperwork. She can keep Ariana company."

At this, Luca chuckles. "Fun and games."

So much fun and games.

We're quiet now as we've reached the basement and things have turned to serious business.

"How're we doing this?"

"Ever played good cop, bad cop?"

"Jesus Christ, Nicky. This isn't my thing."

Don't I know it. That's because it's always been my thing and mine only. Assigned the task by our Lord and Master, also known as the Don, our fucker of a father and a complete psychopath.

I coil all the hate I have towards the Don back into my core. He had a plan for each of his sons, and here we are. The question is really: what was the plan he had for his only daughter? "There're two of them, so no need for it to get messy. We play them off against each other."

Luca huffs out a breath. "Fuck. Should have passed on that burrito for lunch."

"Just remember they came to kill Steph, so..."

"We're not letting them loose in the wild again."

"Exactly, but we're going to skin them for every last piece of information." And that's not a figure of speech. The tally cuts on Ariana's lower belly flash in my mind's eye, and I pull back. Fuck it. That woman is going to toy with my mind when I need it least. The fact that she's in the house is already disarming me from my usual ingrained *sang froid*.

"This is what we know. Steph's team at the gym filled us in," I say. "You read the email?"

"Yep. Our boys are Boris and Boryslav."

I smirk. Fuck my life. "We'll make it easy and just go with Boris."

"Yep. These two boys walked into Steph's gym with baseball bats at around ten in the morning looking for him, the time he usually trains. Russian—"

"Ukrainian."

"Whatever." Luca waves it off. "Asking after their guys who went MIA since the night at the gallery where Vincenzo came for Gigi. Bottom line, we have six wannabe Bratva in our hold, and none of them has spilled one useful bean of information."

"Yep. But these two are still fresh." And they haven't experienced even the tip of my repertoire. I stretch my fingers out and curl them again, allowing my left pinkie to be obstinate.

Pain is nothing. It goes away once you're dead. Something everybody begs for once pushed too far. My time will come. Some days, I can't wait.

"They obviously didn't only have baseball bats," I say as we take the maze to where the men are locked up. Stephano's team confiscated guns and knives once they had these boys cornered.

"Sigh. They should have known better."

We walk past the two guards keeping an eye on our prisoners, and I dismiss them. This isn't a spectator sport.

Then we're standing in front of the two cages. Both men are shackled but have been allowed some space to move. Just enough, though—we don't want them to think this is the circus and they're part of the act. There's a faint whiff in the air, of fresh shit contained in the closed buckets in the corners. Our guys look worse for wear what with their beat-up faces and scruff. They both have buzz-cuts, but these boys will never shave or have a haircut again.

They glance at us, shackles clanging and scraping as they get up, that nerve-wrecking sound of metal against metal, in itself a form of torment if you time it right.

"Okay, Boris and Boris. We're here to talk," I say, pulling up a chair. I gauge their ages at mid-thirties at least. The one guy has a bit of a pouch and is probably pushing forty-five. And he wanted to take on Stephano? Fuckwit.

For now, I'll give them a chance to open up and fill us in. Luca does the same, and we sit, facing the men chained to a system the Don designed.

Each one has a metal choker around the neck connected to a pulley system for partial or complete asphyxiation. With their arms and legs chained to the point where they'll strain in all directions like a star, it's the neck that's the weight-carrying joint. It's right out of some medieval Torture for Dummies handbook, but with a modern twist. These ones are remote-controlled.

It's a system we've perfected, the Don and me. Let's just say, I know exactly how far to push someone with it. And it's clean. Mostly.

"So, Boris and Boris. You work for Franco Fiore. Want to tell us how that happened?"

20

DOMINIC

Boris and Boris glance at each other through the bars of their respective cells. There's nothing for them to gain by being silent. This might not have clocked yet, but at some point, it will.

"We came for him," the one Boris says, his English laced with just a smidgen of an accent.

I glance at Luca. "Why him?"

"He took the Trapani woman and four of our men who are still missing since that Friday night. We were supposed to take only the woman and make sure she got on a private jet to Italy with her brother Vincenzo. That was the deal with Franco Fiore."

Good flow. I nod in understanding. "And what's this guy's name?"

We need to establish exactly how much they know about the Scaleras and our operations before they can't talk anymore. I feel somewhat flayed open as if someone is dissecting *Il Consiglio* from behind a screen. There's a bigger force behind all this, and we need to figure out who it is. Good thing we've gone Code Red on security.

"He's Steph Scalera."

"And what else can you tell us about Steph here?" I say as I reach out for Luca's shoulder and give him a squeeze. Boris and Boris have no clue there's an identical twin in the mix. They clearly didn't do their homework and rushed the job. Imagine calling Stephano *Steph* as if they're fucking family. Now that ticks me off. Fuckwits.

"He is part of *Il Consiglio*."

"And? What do you know about his family?"

"He has brothers. We're not sure how many. One got shot years ago."

"I see." They haven't identified me as one of those brothers yet. "And what do you know about *Il Consiglio*?"

"It's the gang that rules the ports this side of the East Coast."

Gang. I don't really care for the word. We're an *organization*. An *operation* or a *family-run business.*

But it's true. The ports of Boston, Providence, and New Haven are all our territories. Uncontested for decades. Fuck it. The Don is dead, and we might have signaled it's business as usual to the capos of *Il Consiglio*, but outsiders who would want our turf have no need to play nice.

Until they land in here. I suppress a sigh. This better not be the rekindling of a turf war the Don won with blood and brutal force decades ago.

One positive, though: Boris and Boris haven't earmarked the Scaleras as the kings of *Il Consiglio.* To these dumbasses, we're just worker bees. Good.

"Maybe. I'm not sure how this is any of Franco Fiore's business as he has his own operations going in Italy."

"Where is Vincenzo? And the woman?" the other Boris asks. He's been quiet, allowing the one with his mouth on the run to keep talking. "We want them. We go. Leave you alone."

His English is more forced, his accent heavier, his vocabulary clearly limited. This one is very fresh.

I bet their heads were bagged when whoever transported them brought them here. These guys have no clue where they are. They weren't in the loop with Franco's arrival and that he came to sort shit out himself. He also noticed they were incompetent and underperforming. This explains why no Ukrainians were at our little shootout at the warehouse. They were still trying to get the original job done. Yep, fuckwits.

"Only we get to ask the questions here, Boris and Boris," Luca tells them, and both men shift uncomfortably on their feet, setting loose a ripple of clanging metal.

Right. If they're clueless about Franco's movements, these two won't know anything about Ariana Morelli's arrival either. Their value just halved.

"Okay, so you're here to take the lady in question, with her brother Vincenzo, and get them shipped back to Italy. How did Franco Fiore pay you for these services?"

"Bitcoin."

I exchange a glance with Luca. Nice. "How much?"

"Fifty thousand dollars."

We both quirk our brows as we glance at each other and then back at our prisoners. Somebody got seriously lowballed. Or—

"Slim pickings for such a high-profile job, don't you think?" I say, knowing what we know of Gigi Trapani and her family's millions. Fifty-thousand dollars is an insult.

"Very slim," Luca says. "Fuck it, I don't get out of bed for less than sixty K a day."

I smirk, leaning back in my chair. "You for real?"

"Lie in bed every morning and track the numbers and only get up once I've clocked sixty."

He's probably joking, but who the fuck cares. "You're a little shit, you know that?"

Luca shrugs. "What can I say, having made money motivates me to make more money. Come on, Nicky. We all need some motivation to get out of bed in the mornings."

Between him and Benedict, they have some contest going on in which I have zero interest. Money is handy, and it makes life easy, but fuck knows, I get out of bed because if I don't, shit will fly and hit bull's eye.

"There must be more to this deal you're not telling us about," I say as I stand. Time for some real talk. I walk over to the unit by the wall and open the lock with my thumbprint. With a deep but suppressed sigh, I switch on the system and take out the two PlayStation-type controllers. I have my back to the men, and they'd have no clue what's coming.

As I stroll back, I toss Luca one of the controllers. He has his poker face on, but I can almost see that burrito squirm in his stomach. Yep, this isn't Luca's territory. I should tell my younger brother to leave, but fuck it, we're only getting to the *real* good-cop, bad-cop part now, and I'm going to need him.

"Gentle with the controls," I say as I sit down again. "They're sensitive."

"Okay. So, what're we playing?"

"Hangman."

"Fuck. So just imagine we're playing *Call of Duty*?"

"If that works for you." I test my controller's buttons, and the Boris in front of me catches on that his arms are being lifted on both sides, reeled away from his body.

"How did you do that?" Luca asks as he leans in to check what I'm doing with my controls.

"Up, down, left, right. This button for arms, this one for legs, and this little fucker for the head," I say as I play around to demonstrate.

"Okay, jeez, the Don was a committed old nutcase, wasn't he just."

"You can say that again."

Protests come from both Borises now as we are tightening their arms and legs to the side.

"Damn, it's effective. An oiled machine," Luca says. "So neat. And clean. Not like yesterday's shitshow of a party."

With both men stretched out as stars, their arms and legs straining, barely balancing on their tippy toes, but with their necks still fine, I lean forward.

"What else did Franco Fiore offer you over and above the measly fifty K to get a shitty job done?"

Splitting that six ways doesn't offer each man much, not for the bloody risk they were taking with their lives. But they weren't aware of this when they stepped onto our turf, were they?

When neither man answers, I sigh. "Who do you lot work for when you're not fucking around with the big boys, hmm?"

"We work for ourselves," the fluent Boris chokes out.

"I don't buy that," Luca says as he stretches the fluent man's arms a tad too much and he screams in pain.

"Do you talk, or do we torture you until you do? This can take the whole fucking day, or we can be quick about it," I add, not really wanting to spend my afternoon listening to their torment. A gag would be nice, but counterproductive.

Silence stretches until Luca's Boris starts to whine.

"Don't you want to help your friend out, here?" I suggest to my Boris, playing the good cop. "Tell me what I need to know, and his suffering stops."

"We work for us," the man grunts.

Very helpful. "And who is your leader?"

The two Borises exchange glances and turn quiet again. For fuck's sakes. I up the ante on my own controls, stretching my Boris to his full capacity. Then I go for the neck. Soon, he is on his toes, barely able to breathe. He wrestles in desperate breaths as his face turns blue. I release the tension a bit, and he sags, dragging in air like a starving man.

"Are you in bed with the Bratva?"

That's the obvious choice here. And since they raised the question about our ports and who rules which territory, I've been drawing lines between the dots to get the picture. I don't like what I see taking shape here. We rule the main ports north on the East Coast—everything south is Bratva. Once you hit the Carolinas, it gets messy and contested, a bloody situation we've avoided by having agreements in place with our neighbor in New York and New Jersey.

"Give a bit there," I tell Luca. His Boris is bleeding in the armpits and is gasping in pain. "The idea is to hang them, not to quarter them."

"Oh, fuck it, sorry."

"The butcher might be pleased, though. Less work for him."

Luca shoots me a glance. "Fuck, you're a cold motherfucker, brother."

I don't bother to respond but watch how Luca alleviates the tension. The man starts crying, literally sobbing, and it makes me rub at my forehead with a thumb knuckle. Shit needs to get done already.

"Franco promised to help us take over the ports. First New Haven, and then Providence. Finally Boston. With money he would've gotten from the woman. Vincenzo's sister."

Fuck. I knew it. As soon as Matteo steered the Don into the afterlife, the hyenas started prowling, coming for the fucking carcass. Well, we're still fighting fit and not letting go for a long while. There isn't a single weak link in *Il Consiglio's* top tier. There's nothing to have here.

My Boris glares at the talkative Boris, and I bet if he could cut his throat right there and then, he would have. The man just overshared.

"Do you have anything to add, Boris?" I ask my man, and he turns to look at me, his one eye twitching in the corner as if he's about to pop a vein.

He spews at me in Ukrainian, but it could be Russian for all I know. Not that it matters, because we're done. With a final pressing of the neck button and the up button in unison, the man gets jerked up so fast, he hangs, swaying. I lower his arms and legs so he's suffocating from his own bodyweight.

I sigh. I don't care to watch this shit.

"Anything else you think we need to know?" I ask the other Boris. My Boris's feet flay and his arms sway as his hands try to reach for the choke at his neck in an attempt to save himself.

Fluent Boris just stares at me as we listen at each ragged breath that becomes more and more strained. Then it grows eerily quiet in the room.

One Boris down. One to go.

"Well done and good luck to you," Boris grunts from where he's grappling for breath. "Boryslav didn't deserve that. To think he only came to America four months ago. And—" He breaks off to breathe. "You just killed Igor Petrov's long-lost nephew."

A beat of silence tears through the room as Luca freezes on the spot, his eyebrows shooting to his hairline.

Fuck.

21

ARIANA

I stand in the middle of the room where Dominic just left me and breathe deeply, trying to get a grip. Telling him other people could get hurt if I contact anybody isn't a lie. I don't know what dominos Franco had put in place before he kidnapped me and then took me to Boston. For all I know, some of his henchmen will start mowing down my team if I even contact one of them. It's a risk I can't take.

My best bet is still to get back to Italy. Once I'm there, I can make contact after I've sussed out the situation.

For now, I stay right where I am and figure this out while holding my cards close. *Observe, adapt, and only act when the time is right.*

Dominic has locked the door, and I'm a prisoner again. From what I've seen yesterday and experienced today, I now know better than to mess with my hosts. When it comes to *Il Consiglio*, I'll have to wait it out until the time and space is right. It won't hurt to work on my physical strength and mental fortitude in the interim.

At least this is peaceful, what with the stunning garden view from my bedroom window and the sense of light and space with the high ceilings. The room smells of lavender-scented wood polish and is spotless. The antique furniture gives it a homey feel, one I didn't expect to find. There's a small adjacent bathroom with a shower, handbasin, and toilet. It must have been added on during a restoration, because this house is old and wouldn't have come with this type of amenity two hundred years ago.

I close the bathroom's door and cross the room to the desk placed by the window, and the old hardwood floor creaks underneath my feet. My mind is too busy to focus on anything but my dilemma while glancing through the stack of magazines and puzzles. I'm in an *Il Consiglio* stronghold. but it isn't Dominic's place. I don't even know who heads this crime ring, but since escaping isn't an option, maybe I can barter my way out of this situation. With information. I just need to figure out what I have they'd want, desperately. Beyond what I can tell them of Franco Fiore, I'm screwed.

My ears prick. Was that—?

I freeze. Listen closer.

There. Again. A strained scream sounds from afar.

No. Impossible.

My head is messing with me.

After weeks in that dungeon without light, I've started hearing things, making up for loss of sight.

But there—

Chills crawl over my skin as I sink down on the bed. Not here, too. I close my eyes, drop back to the pillows and pull one over my head to block the sounds. And still, the screams slice right through my skin like a scalpel. No, it's just me, hearing my inward screams at the memories of what Franco has done to me. I bore every cut in silence, refusing to feed his sadistic needs.

Dominic said they had some work to wrap up here so I'm going to be alone for a bit.

This is the work. What did I expect? For him to take his laptop bag and go punch numbers at some audit firm? Put on his construction hat and go do stuff on a building site? These people aren't normal, and things went down yesterday. It's never a one and done. Every action has a reaction, sets something else in motion that needs to be contained, controlled, subdued.

With Franco Fiore on the hunt for Gigi Trapani and her fleeing here, things didn't pan out for Franco...but they didn't pan out for someone else either. Someone who is being tortured to death. If I don't watch out, I could be next.

I'm going to have to give them something, or else—

For a long while, I lie there, my head squashed between two pillows, my thoughts and heart racing, and then the sounds die down, and the adrenaline seeps out of me.

When a soft knock sounds on the door, I startle. I'm hardly sitting up when the bedroom door swings open, making me cower.

"Shit, sorry. Didn't think you'd be sleeping. I've been knocking a while, so..."

I blink. It's just Dominic. He won't hurt me.

Outside, the bright summer's light has turned to dusk. I was out stone cold for hours.

"I think the jet lag must have gotten to me." And everything else. I'm amazed I managed to fall asleep at all. My pulse skips a beat as I recall the earlier sounds I heard. "What time is it?"

"It's already past seven." Dominic takes two steps into the bedroom. His gaze jumps from my face to my bare legs and to where the flip-flops Portia gave me have slipped from my feet onto the covers. "I would have checked in with you sooner, but things came up."

I hasten to pull my skirts down to be decent as they've rucked up in sleep, exposing more than I'd ever want to a man, never mind a man who thinks he could be my brother.

He's standing with his hands shoved into his trouser pockets, his white dress shirt rolled up at the sleeves. For the first time, I see the hint of a tattoo on his inner arm that disappears underneath his shirtsleeve. His forearms are dusted with dark hair thinning towards his hands. Muscles flex as he seems to pump his fists in his pockets, veins embossed on his skin from where they run their course from his wrists to his elbows.

My gaze glides from his arm to his face, where his jaw ticks.

"You have blood on your shirt," I say softly. "Just a few specks on your collar." But blood all the same.

"Yeah?" He reaches for his shirt's collar as if he should feel the blood on him. "Occupational hazard. Come, I organized dinner for us."

The way he says those words so casually makes my stomach turn. *Occupational hazard.* How can he want dinner after what he's done? He doesn't even try to hide what he is to me, open and almost mundane about killing someone in cold blood. This evidently runs in the family, but what did I expect after yesterday's brutality?

Get real. I'm familiar with the fucked-up world of the Mafia. I was born into it. Grew up in it. I turned my back on this world, but with a vow to one day tear it apart. Now I'm a sheep in wolf's clothing, but here are wolves aplenty, and they protect their own first. One of them is going to see through me.

I drop my flip-flops to the floor, shove my feet in, and straighten my skirt as I stand. He waits for me to walk out of the room, and then with a hand on the small of my back, guides me through the quiet house. I should shudder at the intimate contact and pull away at a minimum, but I don't do either. I don't want to acknowledge it to myself, but I can't reconcile this man, who looked after me with such gentle care, with one who would torture someone else.

"Portia was here earlier, but I was busy—"

"I know," I say softly. "I heard you."

"What was that?" he asks as I've spoken under my breath.

I'm not even sure why I said anything. I'm literally poking at the beast with a stick, provoking him as if I have a death wish. "I heard a man screaming. Through the vent."

"I'd hoped you wouldn't hear a thing."

He stops me with that soft grip on my wrist, gently turning me to him. For a few beats, we just stare at each other, summing one another up.

"So tell me, Ariana, what would you do if they come for your family? If they threaten to torture and kill every single one of your brothers in the vilest way humanly possible?"

Dominic raises his eyebrows in question, waiting for my answer. Seconds tick by, and I don't know what to say.

"Not just black and white now anymore, is it?" he says when I don't answer him. "Think it over, sweetheart, and tell me what you would do."

I don't have family, and the little I had got torn from me by Randazzo and his machinations. I've promised to avenge both my mom and Elena Bianchi, but now, it's too late.

But I have a team—the closest to family I've ever had since my mom died. And then the Mafia in Italy killed Elena, the only other woman I connected with at fifteen—my mentor who got me through life in the aftermath of Franco. I've made it my mission to be independent and detached from the world, but when it comes to my team, I'd do anything to protect them, as they would protect me.

I can't tell him about them, so instead, I admit to another truth. "I have no family."

"No family? You're a loner with no burdens. My brothers' safety gives me sleepless nights. I think about them about ninety-nine percent of the time."

"Lucky them." What else can I say? That it's fun to have no family and no place to belong? Nobody to think about me ninety-nine percent of the time? How lucky I am!

"For now, you think you have no family, Ariana," he says with a soft smile. "I'm getting the DNA tests back soon, and then we'll know."

He nods, and we continue towards the kitchen, his hand still wrapped around my wrist in the stance that says *bullshit will only be tolerated to a point.*

I bet he can feel my pulse where it flutters wildly through my veins.

As we walk inside the spacious kitchen, all white marble and chrome, he lets go of me.

"From experience," he says, "I can tell you what those men went through wasn't half-bad."

"Experience," I scoff, but I sound bitter. I've had ample experience when it comes to torture, and it started the day Franco Fiore decided it was time to 'train me' for my 'job' in his extortion scheme.

On the kitchen island, there's a spread of take-out.

"I got a variety of things," Dominic says, promptly ignoring my remark. "Reckoned you'd be hungry, and I don't know what you like, so..." He tapers off and draws some of the dishes closer and opens the lids. "Green Thai curry with chicken and rice, some spaghetti marinara—it's really good, gets my vote for the best in Boston—and some pizza. We've beef tenderloin, cooked medium-rare, with Greek salad, and some vegetarian options... You know, hummus with pita and some dolmades, olives..."

I bite my lip. It's extra, and everything looks delicious. This isn't some random take-out either; this looks like food from top-tier local restaurants. "Thank you. I'm starving."

"And by the look of you, you've been for weeks."

"Let's not talk about that," I beg, but I bet it's all he wants to talk about.

He has the plates and cutlery ready and is holding them out to me, but I hesitate. "Do you mind changing your shirt?"

I guess it doesn't bother him as much as it bothers me, since he can't see it. It's the only thing I see when I look at him, and it drags my thoughts all over the place.

He gives me a calculating look and then shrugs. "Sure. Come with."

He shows me the way in the opposite direction of where my room is situated, and I lead, passing closed door after closed door.

"In here," he says and opens the one to his room. He switches on the lights but immediately dims them.

The interior is similar to mine, but much bigger. Darker colors, more masculine, yet impersonal. He walks past me to the mirrored closet, his eyes never leaving mine, and opens it to reveal a row of suit jackets, shirts, trousers, and drawers. It's as if we're in a hotel room but he's been here for a while.

I drop my gaze when he turns to keep an eye on me while he unbuttons his shirt.

"Pick a color then, sweetheart."

I can't stop myself. My eyes flicker over his hands, where they're busy with the suddenly very sensual motions of unbuttoning his shirt. And then, my gaze glues to his chest as the fabric falls away, with every button revealing more of his tattooed pecs. The visual sets loose a riptide of tingles down to my core.

No. Not this man.

I felt it when he carried me, when he held me in his arms. Dominic Scalera is strong, virile, and a man in his prime. Every muscle is toned, his abdomen ripped with subtle ridges of a six-pack, and as he plucks the shirt from his trousers, my gaze dips to the V-shape muscles on his hips that draws the way south, to something I've never wanted. Not after my first time.

And yet, I find myself taking in the shape of him and the subtle hint that he isn't small, not in any way or form. Heat flushes my face, and I look away to the bed, and then I blush even more.

"Grey," I say, my voice edgy and maybe a bit louder than needed. There are several black shirts, but seeing him in one would only remind me of Franco and that's the last thing I need. This man and Franco will never fall under the same category in my mind.

He chuckles as he tosses the bloodied shirt to the laundry basket in the corner, completely unaffected. "Grey, like my morals. Good choice, sweetheart."

22

DOMINIC

For someone who has Randazzo's seal tattooed on her lower belly, she blushes like a virgin while watching a man take off his shirt. And it makes my body react in places I'd rather it not given how—

God just fucking help me here already. Ariana Morelli is the last woman on this planet I should think of sexually. Reminder: *she could be my sister*. And even if she isn't, I have no business with a woman from Italy who has been trafficked to the States.

Our crime is 'clean,' and she is a stain that won't come out.

Il Consiglio has steered clear from anything that level of illegal for years. The Don was never really into this type of shit to start off with. When it came to women, he was a real man-whore, and to say it straight, he was the last fucking guy who should have ever been let loose around women in the first place, but human trafficking? Nope. There are other jobs way less dirty, with easier money, less risk, and a better return on investment. And then came Matteo with bitcoin, Benedict with his hacking, Luca and Stephano with their e-commerce and clubs, all built on the foundation of the real estate empire the Don built. Money-wise, we're untouchable.

We don't traffic people, yet here I have a woman, in my bedroom, and she isn't here of her own free will.

Brushing the thought away for now—because what the fuck are we actually going to do with her once those DNA results come back—I slide a light grey shirt from a hanger and dress again, making sure she only sees my good side. In the dimmed light and with my tattoos, she won't see much to start off with, but I don't want to show her the proof of my experience in the field of torture.

It's quiet as we head back to the kitchen, but I observe her all the way. She's trying to be subtle about it, but this one is on high alert all the time. She's counting the doors, the steps from one place to the next, the light switches as we pass them, mapping the layout of the house as we go.

One thing is for sure, I can't afford to take my eyes off her or let my guard down. Couldn't leave her in the kitchen either. She'd probably wait for me around a corner with a knife and stab it right into a main artery. We caught her escape attempt on camera at the clinic, and Luca and I watched it a few times once we were done in the basement—we'd deal with Boris's revelation soon enough, but first, our other guest. On the footage, she ran around as if she had her escape plan all mapped out. Something about this woman tells me we shouldn't underestimate her.

When we're back in the kitchen, I hand her a plate, and we sit down at the kitchen island. For several minutes, we're busy dishing up from the various containers, and when I take a bite of my marinara, it's already cold.

"Do you want to heat yours up?" I ask, breaking the tense silence which has stretched all the way from my bedroom.

"I'm good, thank you. This is delicious."

She's already two bites down, and my thoughts turn back to Franco and how she watched on as Stephano beat him to death. Then my mind flips over to the business this afternoon.

She watched her tormentor being brutally killed, and I, in turn, became the monster who took photos of Igor Petrov's *long-lost fucking nephew* where he hung strangled, before we let him drop to the floor. More photos. Evidence. Proof. To verify the other fucking Boris's wild claim if we need to.

If I did kill a nephew of Igor Petrov, irrelevant how many times removed, I've fucked up. Badly. And there's a kink in our armor. A weak link. One I'm going to have to fix.

I still haven't spoken to Matteo, and Luca only raised his hands in a *What the?* and *What the fuck now?* and *How fucked are we?* gestures. We decided to defer admitting to the fuckup until tomorrow.

For now, Boris and Boryslav are in the walk-in fridge in the basement, but they can't stay there indefinitely. Especially not once Petrov starts asking about the whereabouts of his two favorite Borises, one being his fucking nephew.

I'm too tired to figure it out tonight, but the question really is how do Fiore, Petrov, and this woman connect? It could all just be coincidence. Luckily, Vincenzo still has a tongue, and he will talk. Tomorrow is going to be a motherfucker.

Whether this woman is connected to this mess or not, she's right in the middle of it, and it's time I start figuring her out. If she really heard anything from what happened in the basement, she'd know better than to test me.

"Want to tell me how you know Franco Fiore?" I ask, taking my food from the microwave.

"We grew up together," she says, without missing a beat. She glances up at me where I've frozen with my plate hovering above the counter. "Well, technically, he was already grown up."

"You grew up together?" I repeat, shocked to my core.

If she grew up with Franco, she's as Mafia as any of us. I don't know why I was thinking she's an innocent woman who got lured into a human trafficking ring run by Randazzo.

"My mom died when I was eight, and I was put into foster care in Franco's uncle's home. He was already twenty-two at that time and only around at random times."

"I see, he's fourteen years older than you. How old are you now?"

"Twenty-seven."

See, no chance in hell this woman is our sister. She looks young, but it's her slight build and delicate frame giving her the gangly look of a girl who hadn't filled out her curves yet. I'm not sure if that's because she's been starved or just her genetics. Either way, Gabriella will be twenty-two years old now, so the ages don't match.

"So Franco was forty-one when he died." Not a bad innings for someone that fucked up.

"Yes." She looks down and stirs the food in her plate. Mentioning his death could kill anybody's appetite.

I wasn't expecting her to open up like this. "Where in Italy?"

"Franco's uncle had a small holding in Calabria. Between Vena di Maida and Cortale, literally in the middle of nowhere."

"And what's his name?"

She hesitates just a millisecond, signaling to me she isn't sure she should share this information. "Antonio Mancuso. He lives on a small holding where he farms pigs."

"Okay." Why does that name sound so familiar? I make a mental note to get information on this guy. It might come in handy. "And who were your parents?" Her dad must have been dead by the time her mom had died for her to go into foster care.

"My mom was an international student from Finland who went to study Italian and Archeology in Italy. She fell in with the wrong crowd...or rather, she fell in love with the wrong man on an extended excavation in Sicily."

I quirk a brow. That's fucked up. And that explains her Nordic looks. "You speak Finnish, then?"

"Not really. My mom never went back to Finland because she fell pregnant with me and then she died—"

"How?"

She puts her fork down and stares at me. "I feel like I'm being interrogated."

You are. I shrug. "Just imagine you're on a bad date with some douchebag you swiped right on when you should have swiped left."

This makes her chuckle, but then her face falls. "She died in a car crash."

Our eyes lock, and so many things hang in the air between us. Terrible. Sad. Heartbreaking. Sudden. *Convenient.*

"I'm sorry for your loss," I say as I put my fork down. "And your dad?"

She sighs. "Can I have some water?"

"Sure." I get up and pull two chilled waters from the fridge, keeping my eyes on her, but she's dropped her gaze to her plate and is thumbing a paper napkin as if she has food on her hand that won't come off.

"Here." I uncap a bottle and hold it out to her.

"Thanks." She takes a deep sip and as she puts the bottle down adds, "Except for money, he wasn't in the picture much. He's dead in any case, so..."

So... Nice. She's pulling one of my own on me by letting that hang. I bet it was deliberate.

Mom dead. Dad dead. Already in Franco's uncle's care. Antonio Mancuso. Now I remember. He's one of Randazzo's henchman if I recall correctly when Benedict scoured the dark net for anything he could find out about Franco. From her birth, this woman was on the slippery slide into prostitution. So why the blush earlier, then? Why did she cower when I stood in the room and came two steps closer, in the most non-threatening way I, with my size, could muster?

And why the fuck is she counting the number of knives on the knife block on the other side of the kitchen?

I know better than to believe anything she says to me, especially when it all comes out without a glitch.

Oh, sweetheart, we been paired up at birth already to dance this little tango. I can't wait to figure out what game you are playing, and what your next move is going to be.

Except I don't have the time or the patience for fun and games.

Time to test this little one.

23

DOMINIC

I drop my interrogation for now, and we finish up eating mostly in silence, except for Ariana complimenting the food. She chose all the high-protein elements of the spread—ate through a man-sized beef tenderloin and then picked out all the chicken in some Thai green curry. This little one is eating for strength.

"I should've opened some wine for us," I say, trying to shrink the quiet while planning my next move.

"I don't drink, not when I'm—" She breaks off and shrugs. "Thank you for the offer all the same."

Not when I'm... pregnant? On the run? On a job?

"An Italian who doesn't drink wine?" I say with a chuckle, ignoring her slip of the tongue.

"Not when I'm held captive," she says, and her gaze locks with mine, her brow cocked in a dare.

"Captive is a strong word." I can show her what captive really means if she wants. The guards did hose down those basement cages, and they're ready for fresh occupants.

"Maybe, but I don't want to get into a situation where I'm not fully there, if you know what I mean."

"Fair enough." I stand and take her empty plate. She stands, too. "No, I'll do it. You stay put."

She sits again and helps instead by closing the various containers. We've made a dent in the food, but there's enough left over for another day. She sits and watches me as I pack everything away and put the dirty dishes in the dishwasher.

"Don't you have help here? This house, the estate, looks like it needs a team of at least ten people full-time to run it."

"Portia's coming tomorrow." *Il Consiglio* works on a need-to-know basis, and as much as Ariana could be family and is Mafia in some way or another, she's still an unknown entity and has already seen too much. I go over to the side counter where Portia left several bags of clothes and other things for her. "She brought this for you earlier."

I put the bags on the counter, and she peeks inside.

"Oh... Thank you. It's everything I need. It's more than I need—" She closes the bags with a sigh. "Thank you for this. It wasn't necessary."

"You were running around in a hospital gown, sweetheart. I think it was necessary." I gave Portia carte blanche to buy as she saw fit; she's after all a mom with a daughter, and knows what a woman like Ariana would need. "And you're welcome. It's nothing really."

The bags are from a big supermarket chain, not where I'd shop for myself, my sister, or a wife, and definitely not where Matteo and Steph shopped for Tasha and Gigi, but it's better than nothing. I'd hate for Ariana to feel uncomfortable here because she's got nothing decent to wear.

The way Matteo plucked Tasha out of the pool at her own home and had her standing there in front of us in only her skimpy bikini still gives me the ick. Then again, my brother doesn't have first-hand knowledge of experiencing something in someone else's shoes. To each their own. Matteo has his own cross to bear. "How're you feeling?"

"Still tired, but I won't be able to sleep now. Not with the nap I had."

Neither would I. Not with the day I had. I haven't had time to digest this afternoon's fuckup yet, and I loathe going to Matteo with a problem for which I don't have a ready solution at hand.

"Let's watch a movie?" I hesitate. Why do I even plan to toy with this woman? "Unless you want to go to your room for the evening."

"No. Not yet. A movie would be great. I've...I've spent too much time alone."

With a nod and a weight to my heart, I guide her to the Don's in-home theatre. She's playing into my hand. Worst is, when we're all normal around each other, it's hard to remember that nothing about this situation is normal and she recently went through a traumatic experience. I've been trained to become numb to it all, sticking to logic and pushing emotions away, solely focusing on what needs to happen next.

I unlock the door with my phone, feeling her gaze on me, taking notes. As soon as the door swooshes open, the dreamy scent of aged leather spills out. I switch on the light, and she giggles as she walks inside.

"Oh my God. I've seen these, but I've never been in one."

"No?" It's silly, but seeing her face light up is like a rubber band snap to my heart. It stings, but in a good way. As if there's life here, after all.

"No...I mean, in Italy? Come on. Everything is so much smaller there." She walks deeper into the room, which isn't in the basement like these home cinemas usually are. This room has no outside windows, so it turned out ideal for this. "Real leather, too! I love the smell. You know, in Italy, we see all these things in America on TV, everything so big and bulky and just—"

She sweeps a hand over the backrest of the closest recliner

and looks up at me. And looks. And then looks some more, with a bit of a swallow. A lick of her lip as she registers the words that just tumbled out of her mouth.

My eyes are up here, sweetheart.

Fuck. I bite down on my jaw to keep a straight face, because there it is: that sugar-sweet blush again. I drop my gaze to my feet because right now, a hundred deliciously dirty things I want to do to her are fighting for a place in line. The fantasy is like a fucking to-do list, one I don't mind adding to as we get to know each other.

I want to start by taking those stray strands and tucking them behind her ear, so slowly, she'll hear the individual hairs slip into place.

Big and bulky. Her words, not mine. I'm way taller than your average Italian. The muscle is what you get when you pump weights like a man obsessed for decades. Ever since Alex dragged me to the side, demanding '*When are you going to stop being a fucking walkover and stand up to him? You have the height, Nicky, build the fucking muscle to take him out. Become the man that fucking stands up to him.*'

So I did. Except I never stood up to him.

I clear my throat. "Grab a seat, and we'll see what's new. We can watch something in Italian if you like?"

"No, it's fine," she says with a weak smile as she slides into one of the front-row seats. "How do you think I got this fluent in English?"

"By watching TV?"

"And listening to radio, songs, and so on, constantly."

"This is how I kept my Italian going. When my mom passed away, we spoke it less and less at home, especially between my brothers as we all had school in English."

I switch on the TV and open Netflix. At a glance, it gives my taste away.

"Anime?" she says, and there's that smile again. "I didn't take you for a cartoon guy."

"Come on, it's anime, not cartoons. What did you take me for?"

"I don't know… I've never seen a man's streaming profile like this before."

Netflix and chill is clearly not high on her dating-do list.

"What's yours like?" I ask, wondering if it is all romcoms and home reno stuff.

"Thrillers and suspense. True crime. Nat Geo channel, that type of stuff."

"No romance," I tease.

"I don't believe in that shit."

"No?" I don't have the luxury to believe in *that shit*, as she so aptly phrases it.

"My mom's life cured me."

So did mine. But I don't say that. Instead, I press play on a new release that seems innocent enough. An action movie about making action movies. "This is good?"

"It's perfect."

I close the door and switch off the lights. Now we're huddled in a dark room with the only light coming from the massive TV screen on the far wall. It's as close to a real cinema you're going to get without leaving home. I'd kill for a glass of wine now—I suppose I shouldn't say this lightly—but Ariana isn't the only one who wants to be 'all there.'

As I sit down, I up the volume a notch and settle in my seat, pushing the control so the footrest is up and I can lean back. She's already done the same with her chair, and observing her trying to figure it out was like watching a kid in a candy store. Everything is new to her. This girl clearly grew up poor, what with her dad dead and her ending up in some Randazzo henchman's house. And also with Franco. I bet that didn't end well for her, either.

With a sigh, I kick off my shoes, and in the most innocent way possible, ruck up my pants a few inches. Just enough for her to see the ankle holster with my concealed carry pistol.

And then I get busy with the hard work of feigning sleep.

Let the fun and games begin.

24

ARIANA

Dominic is asleep. He actually dozed off twenty minutes into this mess of a movie, and I don't blame him. It isn't really going anywhere, and the man by my side has me drawn like a magnet.

I've curled up in my seat, my knees facing in his direction so I don't give him my back. There's lots of space between us, and for a man, he's only been kind and gracious. I'd go so far as to call him a perfect gentleman, which is so far removed from my frame of reference, it's laughable. In the world I grew up in, women were only good for one thing, and the men didn't go about getting it in a gentlemanly way. After experiencing Franco, nothing is going to shake that foundational belief in me, or my plans to vindicate my mom's death, honor her life, and rip Randazzo's trafficking rings to shreds.

I'm delusional, but I haven't given up yet. If my team can't find me, I need to find them. I can't sit here, doing nothing, not with an opportunity staring me in the face. In fact, my pulse is racing with new vigor. I've spotted a weapon and a man disengaged. I'm an idiot, but I can't let this opportunity slip through my hands.

If I slip quietly off the leather seat and to my haunches, then lean in just a bit, gently peel away his pant leg an inch, I'd be able to pull the pistol out and have it aimed at him before he's fully awake.

And then... And then...I'll sneak out of here and make my escape. Or force him to drive me to the airport so I can fly to Italy, and we'll make as if none of this ever happened. I'll turn a blind eye to everything I've learned here and deal with the situation on the other side of the pond. What do they say? Clean up your own house first.

I suck in a deep, slow breath. In the light of the TV and the movie which has hit a night scene, I have more cover. I try to slide from the seat, but the back of my legs are glued to the leather, and I bite down a curse. I peel myself free, and Dominic doesn't stir at the ripping sounds, what with the movie going on in the background. My toes push into the plush rug underneath, and I lower to my knees. If he wakes up now and looks at the screen, he'd see my head etched out, so I shift a bit to be perfectly between our seats.

For a moment, I pause. His feet are massive. I take in his long legs in his dark trousers and higher to his chest. The man is a hulk, and the perfect fit of his grey shirt only accentuates it. To think I saw that sculpted chest naked and had the idiocy to blush in the moment.

God. There I go again. I've been around men all my life, but never around one who is so unaware of his potent sexuality, or more like...he doesn't use it to his advantage. He doesn't play to it all the time. It's just who he is, and he isn't the whole freaking *I'm macho so watch me fuck your pussy to smithereens* personality. All talk and no substance.

With a sigh, I remind myself all men are monsters, and this one is no exception. I'm not privy to details of what happened this afternoon in the basement, but I can fill in the blanks.

I inch my fingers closer to his ankle and peer over the

armrest to pinch his trouser leg and shift it up a bit. He'll feel this, depending on how deep asleep he is. I'm slow, intentionally taking my time to move the fabric and get my hand in position, trying my best to not let my fingertips brush against his skin. I graze a coarse leg hair or two in the process, and my breathing stalls as he stirs. My gaze flicks to his face. His eyes are closed, and his chest hasn't changed the rhythm of his deep and steady breathing.

I don't change my position but now have my fingers on the pistol's grip. I know the gun type. Small and not very heavy, but lethal all the same. The ankle holster is molded to the gun's shape so it will slide out easily as there's no strap holding the weapon in place. The whole get-up is made for a quick retrieval and even quicker shot.

I keep my eyes on Dominic's face. He's relaxed in sleep, and something stirs in me. Not in my core, where I felt wet heat seep from me earlier in his room, but higher. In my heart. I'd hate to hurt him, to be forced to pull the trigger. To be honest, no man has ever touched me so gently as he has, and it's been working on my subconscious where I've packed all desire away. I might be sexually cold and have written that part of life off—but clearly, I'm not immune to Dominic.

It's a first.

It's weird and unwanted.

I can't get my head around it. Before that night with Franco, I'd been pretty normal, all things considered. After that night with Franco, I boxed up every feminine part of me and buried it so deep, I planned to never find it again. I already knew where I was going career-wise, and in my field, men are just complications and problems I didn't need or have time for. Imagine all the questions I'll get from a partner about *where have I been* and *what have I been doing*.

This weird attraction to Dominic is definitely unwanted, and I bet it's because I've been on death row for weeks and then walked out with my life in a fragile hold, Dominic catching me just as I caved. My body is whispering to me that I got a second chance I was never entitled to in the first place...it's time to live a little.

As if things aren't dire enough, the man thinks I'm his sister. Truth be told, it's a bit of a mindfuck. It's a joke.

With a slow inhale, I prepare myself. On a shallow exhale, I slide the pistol from its holster. Dominic drags in a shaky breath, and I freeze, but his eyes are still closed. I lean back and feel the pistol for weight and then in a smooth, slick move, rise to my feet. I cock the gun and aim it at his chest.

I take two steps back, and in this moment, the scene on the movie changes to daylight and floods the room in white light.

Dominic's gaze flicks open, and he stares right at me, as if he knew exactly where I'd be. "Good job, sweetheart."

Goosebumps rush over my skin like an invasion of ants as blood roars through my veins in shock and horror. His voice is crisp and clear. Not that of a man who'd dozed off and was still half-asleep.

He wasn't asleep at all.

He let me take his gun. He *allowed* me to take his gun. My hand is steady, my grip firm, my feet planted firmly apart, ready to take the shot, but all I can do is stare at him, the images of the movie casting a light show around us.

"What now, sweetheart?"

He hasn't moved, but his eyes are taking everything in. From my dress's shoulder which has slipped down my arm, exposing way more skin than I'd like, to my free hand clutching my stupid dress as if it's going to save me.

"You have to admit this isn't very sisterly of you," he drawls.

"I'm not your sister," I breathe. Claiming to be just that could stop a man from raping me—it would stop *this* man—but it's such a blatant stupidity, I can't buy into it.

"We'll see. But you are a thief, stealing my gun like that. What are you planning to do now?"

His words rip through me and zap me back to the night Franco kidnapped me from that sex-slave auction. Back to the day I fled after his assault.

Franco. That night. *Thief.*

My hands start to tremble, and I take the pistol in both hands to steady my grip.

He's dead. *Dead. Dead. Dead.*

Dominic reaches for the remote control where he'd left it right by his hand. With the smallest of movements, he kills the sound. Now it's so quiet, my heartbeats seem to fill the space with heavy, anxious thuds.

He doesn't move, just waits for me to take the next step. To say something.

I lick my lips, all my training withering to dust as a I watch him register how I'm failing. How my head has gotten to me. God. The body is nothing. The mind is everything.

I've never felt weaker than in this moment, with a gun in my hand, aimed at a man I would have given a life sentence with no parole weeks ago if I'd met him in my day job. Cuffed him and dragged to prison to rot like I was left to rot in that dungeon.

But now all my weak mind can do is fill up with Franco, with what he'd done, and this man's gentle voice as he keeps on asking questions I can't answer without giving everything away.

"Let me teach you something, Ariana," he says then, his voice soothing and calm. "Next time you want to know if a man is asleep or just faking it, look at his crotch."

My gaze drops there by instinct, and I snatch at a breath that won't fill my lungs. He is aroused, shamelessly so. And it's...it's...*it's a lot.*

"It's the gentle, almost imperceptible touches that get to me the most."

He lets that sink in, and it does.

Did he just admit that I turned him on? My mouth fills with gravel, my lips parched, and still, I can't say anything. The gun, all for being lightweight, is a brick in my hands, dragging my arms down.

"Go for it, sweetheart. Prove to yourself you can do it," he says. "I bet a bullet from you would make a very pretty hole in my heart."

25

DOMINIC

Something triggered her to lose all focus. And it wasn't my giant fucking cock begging for attention. It was something I said. She was so into getting my gun, I couldn't bring myself to interfere. Firstly, it was kinda cute. Secondly, the whispers of her fingers as they ghosted over my skin, brushing against my leg's hairs, sending sensation to rush under my skin and into my veins...*fuck*.

Now my arousal is abating at speed because a haunted look has invaded her eyes, and I need to be careful. Just looking at the way she stands, how she cocked the pistol, this one is a professional in one way or another.

She knows her way around guns but has never pulled the trigger to kill somebody.

Until you've been forced to shoot, until you've felt the body grapple with a last breath as you keep on tightening your grip on that throat, until you've stabbed and let blood fountain over you, you actually have no clue how you're going to react when the time comes.

Sweetheart. Sweetest of sweethearts...

I sigh as I tilt the sofa's footrest down. It locks in place, and I stand. Ariana has lowered the gun, and it points to the floor now, ready to shoot off a toe if I let her. One step, and I have her by the shoulder, and she doesn't resist. I slowly slide my fingers down her arm and take hold of the weapon. I secure the gun, empty out the magazine and the bullet in the barrel, and toss it all on a recliner.

She's standing there, rooted to the spot, petrified. I'm at least a foot taller than her, and I bet I weigh double what she does. Her mind is spiraling; I can see it in her eyes.

"What triggered you, sweetheart?"

She blinks. This time as I reach for her, she visibly flinches.

"I'm never going to hurt you, Ariana," I say softly, keeping my voice calm, but not retracting my hand where it's folded around hers. Instead, I rub my thumb over her pulse point, trying to calm her.

"Please—" She strangles a sob as she breathes haggardly, forcing herself to be quiet, trying to contain her emotions. I bet she's been bottling them up for years.

"Is this about Franco? And being kidnapped to Boston and whatever happened in the weeks before?" Those tally marks cut on her skin. Her begging me not to tie her up or to lock her away in the dark. "Or is this about something else?"

My jaw ticks as I wait for her to answer, but she's clammed up, and it could be borne out of so many things. Fear for herself, fear for others. There's a reason why she tried to escape the clinic. There's a reason why she wanted my gun. I'm not sure what her endgame would have been, and it's laughable, but also so freaking desperate.

I get that she won't trust me, but fuck, what more must I do to prove to her I'm not going to take her by force? Maybe that's the only thing the Mafia does in Italy, but not here. Not in *Il Consiglio*. Never mind waiting on those DNA tests—if I'd wanted to do so, I've had plenty of time. If I wanted her dead, I would have seen to it already.

Instead, *she's* literally killing *me* here with those quiet tears.

"Tell me, Ariana. If he's threatened people you love on the other side and you are protecting them by not talking, I need to know. Franco's dead, and you're the only one who knows what would happen in Italy once people realize he isn't coming back."

Vincenzo. He could know. Fuck, I'm glad Steph hasn't killed him yet, even though it's been touch and go for days now.

She's closed her eyes, tears streaming, her fingers gone cold and trembling in shock. She's definitely in some PTSD loop, and I can try help her out of it, but I don't even know what dredged up these memories for her in the first place.

"He called me a thief once," she whispers. "And it's true." She looks up at me, eyes like crystal pools. "I stole from him. I don't mind admitting to it. Over a thousand euros. It took me months, skimming."

"From whom?" I ask, and when she doesn't answer immediately, I push again. "Who called you a thief, sweetheart?"

"Franco Fiore. I was so stupid. I thought he wouldn't notice. There was so much drug money in the house—" She shakes her head, seeming in disbelief. "I wanted to run away. I knew what was coming my way... I—I—"

She chokes up and tries to catch her breath, but she's almost hyperventilating now, her chest heaving with sobs and quiet tears. It hits me this woman has never released her pain, and I feel it echo in every scar on my body. I know what's coming next. There's torture, and then there's sexual assault. Men get the brunt of the first one, women always the second, irrespective of age, circumstances, relations.

I keep going with my thumb's hypnotic movement, caressing her wrist and giving her time to gather herself.

Eventually, she shudders on a gulp. "One day, he came and took the value of what I'd stolen. A thousand euros worth of—"

She leans into me, and I inch closer, allowing her to rest her forehead on my arm, right there where a kitten would curl up in the corner of warmth between your chest and arm if you let it. Her breathing is strained, and we stand there for such a long while, it seems she's lost her thoughts. But she's lost her courage. I bet she's never opened up to anybody about this.

"A thousand euros worth of *you*," I say eventually, and she sags against me.

"Yes."

I pull her to my chest and hold her close. From what I've seen of Franco, the assault would have been brutal, filled with violence. Something she's never recovered from. He didn't only take his measly thousand euros from her, he took her *everything*.

I'm tense with her revelation, but force myself to stay calm, my body relaxed to let her take whatever she needs in this moment. This is what gets to me the most about this woman. She's my experience, my photo negative, colors inverted, but mine all the same. Taken by force and done things to that bodies heal from, minds never.

"He'd said if I wanted money," she croaks against me, "I needed to earn it, and that he had the perfect plans for us. That I needed to get practice, because he was going to use me for extortion. He planned to catch men on camera having underaged sex with me, then blackmail them afterwards."

I'm already tense, but now, I freeze. "How old were you, sweetheart?"

She quivers, the memory probably too much. "I'd just turned fifteen."

Fuck. Rage, simple and pure, shoots through me like lightning, and I stretch my hands where I have them on her back, straightening all my fingers, except the one that would no longer obey a simple instruction. Now I'm shaking, too, and it's as every memory of my own riots to escape the cages I have them locked up in.

"Dominic?" she whispers, fear in her voice, a reaction to what she felt in my body.

"Shhh, it's okay," I say, dropping my arms away from her. The last thing she needs is to feel threatened by my oversized, male body, every muscle flexing with the fury raging within me.

She sways and for a second looks like she'll faint without the support, so I take her by the shoulders, steadying her.

"You know if I could kill him for you again and again, I'd do so," I say, leaning in to stare into her eyes, to make sure she understands I'm serious. "I promise you nobody will ever touch you like that again. Do you understand, Ariana?"

It's a sinner's vow, but it's a vow I make with everything in me and one I'll stick to, whatever it takes.

She blushes, and it drives my pulse wild. Has nobody ever stood up for this woman?

"Okay."

And now, I'm fucking pissed Stephano did such a good job. Hacking off that maniac's hands. I could have done so much more, could have gone for days and let Franco suffer in a way even his wildest imagination could never have conjured up. He is dead, but I will do the same to any man who even so much as glances at Ariana in a way that makes me wonder what his intentions are. Yes, these are brotherly feelings. Good. They're the best type of brotherly feelings.

I hesitate to ask the question, but I need to know. "What did you do next, sweetheart?"

She wipes at her face and then hitches a shoulder. "What every woman in my position would do? The next day, I stole ten thousand euros from him and ran away."

It's her go-to, like she's proven twice in a row now, ingrained in her earliest experiences. Everything she does makes sense now.

I shoot her a woeful smile. "Of course you did."

26

ARIANA

I'm drained now with everything that just spilled out. And it isn't only the things I told him—it's the fear that had me in a chokehold once I realized he wasn't asleep at all...and what he would do to me next.

Calling me a thief. Nothing could stop my tailspin then, not with what happened the last time someone called me that.

Even now, chills chase over my back with the memories of that night with Franco bubbling up to the surface, from where they'd been simmering for years. I've been a fool to think I'd dealt with that night. I hadn't. I'd merely cut it out like gangrene, forcing myself to never think about it, and then expecting the flesh wound to just heal by itself without proper care.

For years, I've been functioning on autopilot, until Franco strolled back into my life. Somehow, I managed to get through everything he had in store for me these past weeks, but now that he's dead...it's as if I'm finally free and allowed to deal with what he's done to me. Have I really been watching my back for twelve long years, waiting for him to walk back into my room, just as he had that night?

I have. I don't know how to deal with what has happened now. I can't do it alone. The mere idea of finding myself amongst the rubble of that night makes my knees want to cave in.

I'm cold with the memories, but Dominic's hands are warm and firm where he's keeping me upright.

Dominic.

What is it with this man? This time, I didn't talk because I needed to give him something to latch on to like I did over dinner, giving him random safe facts of my childhood. First it was the fear of what he'd do to me now that I'd stolen his gun. But then… I couldn't hold back, and for the first time since that night Franco came to take as it pleased him, I've told someone the truth.

Not just anybody, but *him*.

Dominic has me. He knows my biggest shame, my darkest secret. I bet he can smell my deepest fear: to go through something like that again.

But he vowed to never hurt me. He'll kill Franco again and again if he could. My knees buckle, and he pulls me to him, into the circle of his arms where I felt safe from the first time he held me. I press my whole face into his chest and inhale his scent through my quiet tears. Freshly laundered shirt, warm male underneath, a hint of cologne mixed with him. It's intoxicating.

"Come, sweetheart," he says softly as he supports me to the door. "You're exhausted."

As soon as he's opened the door, he sweeps me up in his arms and cradles me close as if I'm a treasure, not a woman broken forever by one brute's actions. Instead of resisting him as I should, I close my eyes and sink into his embrace, my hand lying limply against his chest where I can feel his heartbeats, solid, firm, and without the least bit of exertion at carrying me down the corridor.

As we walk through the kitchen, he passes the counter with the bags of clothes.

"The things Portia dropped off—" I whisper, wanting to reach for it.

"The clothes aren't washed, and coming from the store, you can't wear it without washing it first. I'll have something for you to sleep in."

His tone tells me not to even think about giving him grief, and I let it go.

It's only when he lowers me to my feet that I realize we're in his room, and not in mine. "I—"

"It's okay. This bathroom has a bath." He leads me into the adjacent bathroom which looks palatial in comparison to the small add-on in my room. He leans into the tub, closes the plug, opens the faucet, and tests the temperature to make sure it's just right.

As he straightens, the room seems to shrink to him and me. His gaze inches down to my chest, to where the little puff shoulders have slipped off what with the corset laces loosening with time, and then to my bare feet. I've long lost the flip-flops Portia gave me.

For the briefest seconds, his gaze captures mine, and my breathing stalls at the raw look in his eyes. It's like he's clawing back his anger, only being a protector for now. That moment earlier, when he told me where to look to see my effect on him, flashes in my mind's eye, and I force myself not to drop my gaze to his cock but to keep staring back in his eyes, hating the slow blush heating my cheeks.

With a groan, he opens the double vanity's cupboard and puts a packaged toothbrush out for me next to his toothpaste. He takes stock of everything else in there. I bet he's assessing what I could use as a weapon, but I'm done. I'm completely defeated.

"Do you need help?" he asks as he turns back to me, his gaze landing on those two little corset bows that slipped loose.

"No." It's barely a whisper, but it sounds more like a question than a dismissal.

"Take your time," he says.

And with that, he scoots past me, making sure we don't touch, and leaves me standing alone in the middle of the bathroom, water rushing to fill the tub. He doesn't close the door, and I wouldn't dare do so either. It won't help, and I can't afford to mess with Dominic Scalera again.

I strip, quietly giving my thanks to the gods for allowing me the luxury of a bath—another thing I thought I'd never have again. I lower into the tub, and the warm water whirls around my tired body. I touch my bullet wound's dressing, recalling the nurse saying it's waterproof. Still, it won't be a good idea to be in here for hours.

It's quiet as I relax in the water, and I try to screw my emotions back in place and take control of my mind. Next door, Dominic is busy doing things, making noises of drawers opening and closing.

I don't know what to do with this man. He doesn't fit the usual profile of the Mafiosos I've dealt with all my life.

Any Mafioso whose gun got pick-pocketed would have beat me into submission, if not into the afterlife, and then some more. Physically proving who is in control all the way. Instead, he dared me to shoot him as if he has a death wish. Dared me to make *a very pretty hole in his heart.*

He is an outlier, and I'm out of my depth.

I soap up everywhere and rinse off the water, then stand. As I do, I look towards the bedroom door where Dominic is still busy. It's quiet now—he's listening to me, as I listen to him. I tug a bath towel off the heated railing, dry off with swift swipes over my body, and wrap it around my breasts. I reach for the toothbrush and brush my teeth. He isn't watching me, but I can feel his attention on me, dissecting every move to predict what I'm going to do next.

I've left the dress on the vanity, and as I'm done brushing my teeth, I reach for it. His voice comes from next door. Deep, masculine, but gentle.

"I have something here you can sleep in, Ariana."

It isn't a summons, but it isn't as if he brought it over to me. I was naked in the bath, so...

It's an invitation to come fetch it.

I pad out of the bathroom, and he is standing by the foot of the bed, looking at something on his phone, with clothes in his other hand.

When I come closer, overly conscious of his size and the fact I'm literally wrapped in a bath towel he can pluck off my body with one little tug, I blush. The stupid blush that speaks a thousand words. Hopefully, he'll think it's the heat of the bathwater.

"Here," he says as he looks up. "At least it's clean."

"Thank you." Now I don't want to raise an arm to take the clothes, because what if this towel actually drops? I've twisted it tight, but I don't trust anything right now. I chew my lip as I'm stalling, and in these few seconds, his gaze slides down my body, and I freeze up even more.

"Sweetheart," he says with a sigh as he tosses his phone to the bed. "What's it going to take for you to trust me? You're like a deer in the headlights here. And that after—" He breaks off.

After I told him I got raped and have never recovered from it. Yes. I've been a deer in the headlights for twelve years when it comes to being physical with anybody.

"Will it help if I tell you I only have sex with women who have given me their written consent?" he says, staring into my eyes. "Like on paper, word for word what they want and don't want, what they need from me, how I can best serve them, then signed in real ink, while they are completely mentally there?

Not under duress? Not intoxicated? Not drugged? Not on a date? Heck, I don't even do those."

His words are slow to sink in. Written consent. Wants and needs. Ink. He must be into BDSM, and the mere idea sends a warm rush down my spine to my sex. I've always found everything around sex repulsive. But when *he* says things like that, it does *this* to me?

I'm still in a stupor when he shakes out the clothes he was holding and drops the one piece to the bed.

"Come on, you're going to swim in it, but it'll be comfortable." He scrunches up a plain black T-shirt and has the neck over my head in one gentle swoop, then he guides my arms into the sleeves so tenderly, it's as if he is dressing a sleeping child.

He tugs the T-shirt down, and it's clean, smelling of laundry soap, but under that layer, there's more. His scent has been trapped in the fabric or maybe it's just me, homing in on everything about him with my new, sharpened sense of smell.

"I'm going to take off the towel, okay?" he says, and I nod, in a haze. The T-shirt is big enough to cover to my mid-thigh.

He has the towel by its edge, and with a gentle pull, it comes loose and puddles at my feet.

"Now this is going to be interesting," he says with a wink as he picks up the men's sleeping shorts from the bed. "They are wash-worn and soft, so..."

So...

I swallow as he goes on his haunches and then nudges me to step into the wide legs. *His* sleeping shorts. If he looks up, he'd see my sex. The place where Franco ruined me for life, but Dominic doesn't look up. Of course he doesn't.

It's only when both my legs are in and he pulls the shorts up, making sure the T-shirt covers me all the way as he straightens in the process, that our gazes meet. His eyes tell me he doesn't miss a thing, and yet, the look in them doesn't make me want to shrink away in fear. In fact, I can't look away. I want to be dragged in deeper, down into the heart of him.

All those gentle, almost imperceptible touches. *That get to him the most.*

I've never been treated like this before. With such reverence and care.

He lets go of the waistband, and the boxer shorts sag and barely keep up. He chuckles, and I reach for them to keep them in place. If I move in the night, they'll slide right off. He is that big, and I'm that small in comparison. This man is all muscle with the build of a weightlifter—not one who started yesterday; he's been at it for years.

"Let me," he says as I fumble with the T-shirt to get to the short's waistband. His hands slip underneath the T-shirt's fabric, and his fingers kiss my skin as he takes the waistband and rolls it up several times. His knuckles brush against my bandage, and he stills, his touch a warm glow to my skin. "You're still okay here?"

I shrug. "I haven't looked."

"Need pain meds?"

"It's okay."

"I'll give you something in case."

He traces the edge of the bandage with a fingertip, below my belly button. He's checking the bandage's seal, but the delicate touch sends a shiver of goosebumps down, lower, seeming to steal between my legs and right to where a slow steady bass has been pulsing for hours now. I bite down on my bottom lip not to gasp. *All those gentle, almost imperceptible touches.*

"Lie down, sweetheart. Let me have a proper look."

We're right at the bed, and it's only a matter of caving in. My legs don't want to hold me up anymore, so I do.

27

DOMINIC

It's important that her wound heals. If nothing else, I know about aftercare when it comes to this type of thing. I bet this bandage isn't as good as it needs to be, what with her shenanigans escaping our clinic, running around giving me hell, and then taking a bath.

She's giving me hell, all right. But I'm playing her, too, so all's fair in love and war.

"Scoot all the way up," I say, wanting to have her lying flat, so she can't kick me in the nuts without me seeing it coming. This one...she's not to be trusted.

When she's rested her head on a pillow, eyes wide, hands nervously twitching by her sides as if things are about to get really inappropriate, I take a deep breath.

I'm really only interested in making sure her wound is properly sealed.

I don't want to peel the clothes I just put on her right off again.

I don't want to touch her with such gentle care, she'll forget everything Franco's ever done to her. Wipe this slate clean with my own hands, and replace those memories with quiet caresses that would ripple through her, arousing her like she's never been aroused before.

I don't want to mix my antidote into the poison she still carries within her.

With trained stoicism, I ignore the woman in front of me and quietly lift the T-shirt away and lower the pajama shorts two inches, baring her beautiful, creamy skin. I drag the shorts another inch lower because what I really want is another look at everything else going on her skin below her belly button.

First comes Randazzo's tattoo which can still pass for body art if you don't know what it means. And then, the real ugly scars that knot me up with such anger, my fingers start to tremble.

"What do these mean, sweetheart?" I ask, testing the scars by running a finger beside them.

They aren't very long, and they were done in different batches, all at various stages of healing. And then, there're the cigarette burns. Four in a line. I'd guess they're maybe two weeks to three weeks old. Someone killed these cigarettes on her, giving her second degree burns that weren't treated properly. I close my eyes, trying to contain the anger that's got nowhere to go.

"Franco was counting the days he was holding me. Those are the tally marks. The last time I saw him before we flew here, he came with a friend. He didn't have time so they just used their cigarettes to number the days until his return...he was planning to kill me, but he never came, and then things turned around, and I ended up here."

I drag in a haggard breath. I'm a monster for letting her relive all of this. I don't need to ask why he wanted to kill her. People are killed for way less than ten thousand euros.

"Who was the friend?"

I doubt she would know or even tell me, but to give her time to open up, I inspect the bandage, and it's still sealed and watertight. Good for another night. I'll get Dr. Wong to come check in on her in the morning.

She reaches for my hand where I'm still touching her, my fingertips grazing the sensual feminine hollow made by her hip and stomach, my hand burning with the need to slide over the hillock of her hip, down to the beautiful curve of her side, to her breast. Her nipples have hardened in tempting little peaks against the T-shirt, and there are so many things I want to do with them right now. Inappropriate things. Things she isn't ready for.

As she takes my hand and lifts it away from her, it's a clear non-verbal no. But she doesn't let go of my hand as I expect her to. My stubborn pinkie pierces into her palm, stiff, and she adjusts her hold, then squeezes my hand as if for courage.

"It was Vincenzo Trapani, Gigi's brother."

She knows about Vincenzo. This woman is no coincidence.

"What did Vincenzo Trapani want?" It's only our tight family circle who knows where Vincenzo is at the moment, and it's going to stay this way.

"Franco...offered me to him, but—" She breaks off and lets go of my hand, then struggles to sit up and crosses her legs.

Fuck. I almost hiss in a breath. Those sleeping shorts' legs are so wide, she almost flashed me. I look away as she adjusts her seat and drag my teeth over my bottom lip so hard, it diverts my mind from her pussy.

"Vincenzo didn't want me. So Franco planned to eliminate me once he had Gigi locked in."

"And then, that went pear-shaped."

She shrugs with a small smile. "Never underestimate a Mafia princess."

I smirk. And something tells me this one is royalty in disguise. I bet she'll get on with Gigi like a house on fire given half the chance. "By saving Gigi, we indirectly saved you once from a certain fate. We'll do so again."

I'll do so forever, and it hits me that I've adopted her into this family already as if she's belonged to us all these years.

Sister. Family. Relation. Whatever. Bottom line: off-limits.

"Come along, let's get you to your room."

I step away from the bed so she can make her way, but she doesn't move.

"Ariana."

She closes her eyes, and as a lone tear slips down her cheek, it shreds me like one fast hack of an axe.

"I really don't want to be alone. Can I stay here? With you?"

Fuckfuckfuck. NO?

Didn't she see my fucking erection earlier? Doesn't she know what it takes to touch her and still keep the beast in check? It's been the perfect torment, sweet and addictive. I need my fix. My antidote. After a day like today, and she's right here and I can help her, show her my way—

"The bed is really big."

"Yeah...but you're not a good girl. I can't sleep next to you," I say, grabbing for the obvious straw. "You'll sit on my face—with a pillow in between—" *Obviously* "—and suffocate me. Sweetheart, you were ready to shoot me an hour ago."

I should have her under twenty-four-hour watch like I had, mind you, but after she whacked Marco over the head with a fire extinguisher, I'd rather spare my staff. And now, with what she told me about Franco, I don't want to leave her with another man...someone who could make her feel unsafe. She's asking me if she could stay, because despite everything, she feels safe with me. It makes me glow, just a bit. If she knew the real me, she wouldn't feel safe with me at all.

Ah. She does know me. She knows exactly what I did this afternoon. But does she trust me? I'm just a fucking man, like the rest of them.

"I don't have the energy," she says and slumps back against the headboard, drawing up her knees. "Please."

She asked not to be tied up, but there is no way this woman sleeps in my bed without being tied to something.

"Can I trust you to stay put for a minute?"

A weighted silence drags the moment down.

"Yes."

"Then get under the covers." I watch as she does so, then turn my back on her and head to the bathroom where I grab my toothbrush and get busy at speed. While brushing, I look out of the bathroom door, only to see her lying in bed, on her side, exactly as I left her.

I finish up my night-time routine, dim the lights, then head to the closet. Her eyes are on me, watching my every move. I give her my back as I strip. Let her watch. Let her plot. Let her pounce on me from behind and try to strangle me. I'd love to wrestle her to the bed and pin her down with a few little threats and some discipline that comes with this type of behavior. Physically, she's no match for me, but with what she's gone through—

Overly conscious of my experiences displayed on my skin, I turn my good side to her as I drop my shirt. I hasten to put on a T-shirt and strip to my boxers. It's ample coverage. I dip into the drawer with my silk ties I wear to business meetings. I have six here as I have only made a half-assed move of my closet at home. That's plenty.

Ariana Morelli doesn't want to be tied up to something—I bet Franco tied her up while he had her prisoner, maybe even while he violated her twelve years ago to keep her immobile—but I have other plans.

The headboard isn't made for constraints, but we don't need those. There're plenty of knots for a situation like this, and I know them all. I switch off the lights but turn on the one on my nightstand. As I kneel onto the bed with my bundle of ties, her eyes widen, and she licks her lips.

"Nothing to hurt you, sweetheart," I murmur. "Just something to keep you contained. You sleep on that side?"

She nods, and when I reach for her arm, she doesn't resist. I caress her inner wrist's delicate skin out of habit. I love every part of a woman, but there are a few places I always give special care to. The most vulnerable places. Those little nooks and dips that whisper back to me when I lick or nip at them, when I slide my tongue along the length of her pulse points, or drag my open lips and close them in tender kisses in her most erotic and hidden places.

Her breathing is strained as I slip one silk tie around her wrist, the movement measured and slow, and it's killing me how I can't do more for her. She's opened up to me, and she isn't the first woman to do so. I've served women with the sole purpose of reconnecting them with their own sensuality, to overcome their trauma and take charge of their sexuality again. What I'm doing here is nothing new for me, but from her subtle reactions, it is all new for her.

I know the patterns. Women either slide into complete promiscuity, trying to paint so many layers over the original abuse until they can't find it amongst the rest, or they never let a man touch them again. Every signal her body sends me is like a dot on a line plotting to the latter.

Fuck, sweetheart. Twelve years.

And here I am, wanting to make up for all of them.

28

ARIANA

Dominic is on his knees next to me, his face cast in shadows, the bedside lamp's light glowing behind him like a halo.

My guardian angel.

Touching me with what feels like the tips of his angel wings. Featherlight teases dance over my wrist as he wraps a dark blue silk tie around my arm, gliding it over my skin, slow and erotic as he knots it, circles it around itself, and again. I have no idea what he's doing, but I'm mesmerized by his big hands' rhythmic movement, how he binds one tie together with another and then another, making a length looping around my lower arm.

The little finger on his one hand isn't playing along, like an errant child always in the way, but he doesn't seem to notice it. I want to reach for that finger, feel why it's so wayward. I breathe through the need, knowing this could never be. Unsure why I even want to touch him.

But I know why. He's twisted me up like no man ever has, like one of those knots, and the urge to rub my thighs together, to still the secret pulse between my legs, washes over me in waves.

Not him.

When he starts to loop the ties around his own arm, I still even more. I had no idea where this was going, no choice but to wait and see, but now... This is so unexpected. He is tethering me to *him*.

My heart beats slow down, with no anxious little pauses from one thud to the next. My pulse seems to hush where it's been spiked with adrenaline for days. A river's rush finally culminating in a calm lake that only doubles the world in size with its mirror-like reflection. From here, I can take my time. Be still. Just breathe.

This man can take all of me, and more. Like a final destination for everything I've bottled up, and now that I've opened the sluices, taking course in his direction, I don't know if I can stop.

I close my eyes, trying to block every sensation his touch unleashes in me. Every uncharted desire and want, every emotion I've suppressed for years push up to his light. Uninvited and dangerous. Deadly.

I can't. I can never tell him everything. As it is, my life is hanging on a thin thread of some stupid DNA test. *You know what they'll do to you when they've figured you out.* Franco's words when he found me at that sex-slave auction sound like a fire alarm in my head, and it's a bucket of ice water over my body.

Dominic is Mafia. He will be no different from Franco or any of Randazzo's ring. Not once he's figured me out.

The ten thousand euros I stole from Franco got me all the way to Milan and in hiding, but it's what happened next that I can never talk about. Least of all to Dominic, who seems to have me like a faucet in hand. Just turn, and I spill all my secrets.

I try to regulate my breathing so this war of emotions doesn't show, unable to stop staring at what he's doing. Now he's busy with his own arm and no longer touching mine, I flex my hand to distract myself. He's left space between the silk and my skin, barely two millimeters but a snug fit that won't keep me from sleeping. It's expertly done. The knots are complicated, and there's no way I can untie them with my dumber left hand without waking him up.

He's already proven to be a pro at feigning sleep. I bet he's a light sleeper. If he sleeps at all.

Eventually, he's done with his side, and with a last firm tug, he closes the gap between us and weaves the end of the tie into a slip knot. Our hands are so close, I just need to stretch my fingers to touch the tips of his. I don't dare look down to see if this affected him as much as it's affected me. Whatever I tell my mind to do, my body disobeys. I'm aroused, and his sleep shorts are going to bear the evidence in the morning.

God. I hope he isn't here when I wake up.

"There," he says as he finally looks at me again. "Do I tie up something else, or do you only want to play Houdini with this little set-up of mine?"

"Houdini?" I laugh. It cracks the tension in the room, but not the tension trapped in my body. "Next thing, you're going to tell me you're a light sleeper."

"I am. When I don't take something to help me sleep."

I blink. "You've trouble sleeping?"

I'm not sure why I'm even surprised. After what I've heard this after afternoon—

"Don't you?" he asks, his eyes searching mine.

When I don't immediately answer, he leans back to switch off the bedside lamp. I wish he wouldn't. Ever since the dungeon, I've nightmares of being stuck in a dark place, metal clanging, footsteps sounding, and Franco bearing down on me. But *he* is here, and I'm not alone. I push my face into my pillow and breathe out a deep sigh that only wants to be a scream or a sob. I don't know which.

With a few slight tugs at my arm, he gets under the duvet and uses his free hand to plump his pillow under his head. I shift, getting comfortable, but my arm is more stretched out than what I'd like. I inch a bit closer to him, knowing this isn't a good idea.

"What do you need to sleep, Ariana?" he asks softly. "I have a whole drugstore of stuff for you—"

"No, I... Thank you. After everything Franco fed me—" I break off. I don't even know what he gave me to numb me enough to get me into the States.

And then, Dominic's fingers brush against mine, gently sliding between the digits, in the most soothing hold as he strokes a line with his thumb over my index finger. "You're going to be okay, sweetheart. You're strong, but I know you're even stronger than you think."

For a long while, it's quiet as I digest his words and succumb to his caress, the quiet unbroken flow of his thumb, up and down, the slight movement of his other fingers as they follow in his thumb's wake. It's nothing really, just hands, just fingers, but it touches my soul.

As if I have to answer back, I thread my fingers with his, not getting far as the digits are so much bigger and thicker than mine, the skin harder and callused, and yet, he knows just how to skim over my skin to make goosebumps sparkle and pop right to my core.

As my pinkie traces the line of his own, I feel it. The bump of scar tissue in the middle knuckle. It runs like a ring, with the dark tattoo basically hiding it.

"What happened with this one?" I ask, already knowing I'm not ready for the truth.

"Let's not talk about that," he says, an echo to my own words earlier, but he doesn't retract his hand.

"I shared with you." Somehow, it wasn't hard at all. It was like a dam wall bursting, but he doesn't know this. And he doesn't need to know more. I'm going to have to regain control over my head and mouth around this man.

“Hmm, you’ve told me some, but not everything.” There’s a smile in his voice, and it’s warm with kindness, as if he’s opening the space for me to just be and let go.

I drop my hand away from his, but we’re tethered so close to each other, his hand still rests against mine. He’ll lulled me into a false sense of security, and I can’t believe I’ve fallen for it.

I’m a fool. A trapped idiot, ruled by hormones that have never given me a day like today.

“I haven’t talked about it to anybody, sweetheart.” He sighs. “So if you want to know what happened to my hand, you’re going to have to earn it.”

29

DOMINIC

It's still dark out. Ariana is curled up with her back against my chest, and I've shed the duvet down to our hips. I didn't want her to roll away because I'm too hot.

Our hands are still tied, and when she tried to turn around the first time in her sleep, I was still awake, reassessing the shit show that's my life. I didn't block her with our bound arms. Instead, I shifted into her so she could turn with ease and drew closer to her.

Good thing, too, as I could soothe her in the night when she got anxious in her dreams, more likely nightmares. Weirdest thing was how she was so quiet about it, subdued and not even whimpering, but her breathing and the tremors running through her body spoke for themselves. This woman learned from an early age that giving in to emotion is dangerous—showing it, even more so.

I doubt she'd remember anything when she wakes up.

Hopefully not.

And thank fuck for the extra pillow I managed to wedge between my cock and her sweet little ass.

Yep. Rough night.

Shut eye: zero. Blue balls: two. The forecast of sex that's going to be halfway satisfying: cloudy, with a bit of jizz from the jerk-off I plan to have in the shower.

Yup. That's as good as it's going to get.

I slowly sit up and lean in, then reach over her so I can untie the slipknot with a few tugs and then let the whole wrapped business droop off my hand, leaving a pile of ties next to her. Once I've edged away, I tuck the duvet over her so she can sleep in.

I go find my phone where I left it in the bathroom on purpose. Four fucking thirty in the morning. I drag my hand down my face. And all this with the shit I need to deal with today. I have a to-do list neatly written up in my mind.

First, I need to get someone to guard Ariana. It's too early for Portia. There's a small army of men on site, but I won't let any one of them stay with her without a chaperone. I trust our men—nothing is going to get you culled quicker than fucking with a woman in the new *Il Consiglio*—but I want Ariana to feel safe.

Fuck it. Portia's going to have to come now. I find her number on my phone and ring her. When she answers, I kill the call and send her a quick message. *Sending a driver to pick you up. Need you here now.*

Her answer comes seconds later. *Yes, boss.*

I smirk. Sounding just like Burley there for a minute. I make the arrangements, knowing Portia will be here within half an hour because at this time in the morning, there's no traffic. I pad back into the bedroom, where Ariana is still exactly as I've left her.

The second order of the day is to talk to Matteo, and he isn't going to like anything I have to say. I have time to burn so I sink into a wingback in the corner of the room and send him a message.

Me: *Figured out Ariana can't be Gabriella. She's 27 and Mom couldn't have been pregnant with both her and Benedict at the same time.*

There. The math finally did the math. And after I came to this conclusion, I didn't feel half as much like an incestuous freak show when I snuggled closer to her.

I don't expect him to answer, it being this early, but a reply pops into my inbox a minute later.

Matteo: *Unless she's a secret twin. Shit runs in the family after all.*

I suppress a laugh.

Me: *This isn't The Young and the Restless, Matty. Plus no chance in hell Mom would have let go of one of her babies. We would have known. Five years between Benedict and Gabriella. It would have shown.*

In so many ways. The only way Mom could ever give up a child was over her dead body. And that's exactly what happened.

Matteo: *Glad that makes you feel better, Nicky. It only makes me feel shittier about the whole situation. Why you're up?*

I can understand why he isn't sleeping. And it's about to get worse.

Me: *Need to talk to you about the two guys in the basement.*

Matteo: *Yeah, did they talk?*

Me: *Yep. Hired hands. No connection with Franco beyond this job they cocked up. They won't know anything about Ariana.*

Matteo: *You're done with them?*

I suppress a groan. He's indirectly asking if I need the butcher to transport the bodies to his promession site.

I've opened the can of worms now. I didn't expect him to respond, and Luca and I agreed to do this together. But Luca didn't kill Igor Petrov's nephew. I did. We have no proof of the relation, but that won't be hard to get once I set Benedict on a scent to find out who's who in the zoo.

I take a deep breath, bracing myself to face the music.

Me: *I've fucked the pooch.*

Matteo: *Bruno? Poor boy. Desperate times, bro?*

I bite down on my jaw not to chuckle. Jesus Fucking Christ. Now's not the time for jokes. Desperate fucking times? He has no clue. The dickhead. Matteo can probably just roll over and make love to his wife. I bet she's right there in bed with him, all warm and soft and beautiful.

Just like Ariana. My gaze flicks to the bed where her body is outlined in the dark. All warm and soft and so fucking beautiful...with that female scent that basically drove me nuts the whole night.

A stab of jealously pierces through me. Matteo got the one thing we've all known for years is off the cards. The one thing I've consistently denied myself, choosing to protect my brothers instead. And now, Steph's gone and joined the club, too.

Women, love, and *Il Consiglio* isn't a good fit. It's too fucking dangerous. Not only for them, but for us, too. Women from the outside can be bought; they can turn on us. Sell us out. So far, we've been lucky—Tasha's realized her dad is a decrepit loser, and the fact he's still alive serves as security for us. Gigi is from our world and came to us for protection. We're in a stronger position with her marriage to Stephano. There'll be no such luck for the rest of us Scalera boys.

With a huff, I reply to his stupid message, not beating around the bush this time.

Me: *No, Matty, for real. I fucked up.*

Time ticks by, and I bet where Matteo was at first lying in bed reading these messages, he's now sitting up straight.

Matteo: *How*?

Me: *One Boris said the other Boris was Igor Petrov's nephew.*

A long stretch of silence follows as Matteo digests this information. Yep, I just gave my oldest brother more sleepless nights. He'll read between the lines. Our Ukrainians are connected to the Bratva in New Jersey and New York. The Bratva who basically rules the ports on that side and everything in between. To Igor Petrov's organization and one we used to have a watertight agreement with. Well, until yesterday, we did.

Matteo: *Come see me. First thing.*

That's a summons.

Me: *Yep.*

I still have time to find a solution to this problem, but fuck it, I've spent the whole night trying to find one and couldn't come up with shit. I was going to Matteo's in any case. I have some questions to ask Vincenzo while he's still around.

A soft knock on the door makes me close my phone and walk over. When I open up, a bleary-eyed Portia is standing there, dressed and ready to keep an eye on Ariana. I step out of the room and close the door softly.

"Thanks for coming," I whisper. It helps that I've always been her favorite. She'll do anything for me.

"She's sleeping?"

I nod. Her gaze travels to my own pajamas, and I cringe. She'll see the bed. The crumpled ties. She'll know we've spent the night together, but like a good Mafia housekeeper, she won't blink an eye or say a thing. Instead, she'll read the bedsheets and come to her own conclusions: nothing's happened.

And yet, a lot of things happened. No wonder I couldn't figure out what to do with this Igor Petrov situation. I've held a woman in my arms during the night for the first time in years. I can't even recall how long it's been.

"I'm going to grab my things and go for a run. Do some weights. Swim." Anything really to stop my mind for churning and from the distraction named Ariana Morelli.

"You look so tired, Nicky. Don't overdo it," she whispers back. "And don't worry about Ariana. She won't try anything with me."

I nod. "Let her sleep in. She needs it."

I glance down the corridor where a backup security detail

has been stationed throughout the night. He's wide awake, and Bruno is at his feet, still dozing in his old age, not so excited to see me at this hour. At six, there'll be a partial security guard rotation on the premises. Only certain positions. Keep them guessing.

I might have fucked up, but *Il Consiglio* is an oiled machine.

Whatever Igor Petrov is going to do or want in retribution for his nephew's death, we'll be able to deal with it.

30

ARIANA

I roll onto my stomach and push my face into the pillow as I slowly wake up. I've slept so well. This bed is just perfect. After a languid stretch and a happy sigh, I let my limbs relax again.

Something's missing. Warmth and safety and a certain intoxicating scent I want to nuzzle my nose in.

I blink in confusion, not sure where I even am anymore.

A slice of early morning light cuts through the curtains, and then there's movement. Someone is getting up from a chair in the corner. I freeze and by instinct want to curl into myself. Safety amongst these people is just an illusion.

"Ariana, it's just me. Relax."

As my eyes adjust to the light, I take in the short, curvy woman with the crop of wild grey-streaked curls. *Portia.* She's holding a stack of...laundry? I exhale in relief. She hasn't fired warning shots at me yet. *Phew.*

"Dominic won't be happy," she says as she walks over to where I'm struggling up. "He said you need to sleep in."

"What time is it?"

"Seven. Way too early for someone who needs to sleep in." She purses her lips in a reprimanding line, but there's a smile there, too. "Ah, that boy. When Dominic looks after a woman, he looks after a woman. Is that his T-shirt? I bet it's his favorite. Wouldn't let you sleep in my supermarket clothes without having washed them, hmm? Knew it. I would have stayed to do the laundry yesterday, but he was busy, and I didn't want to be out of line, you know—" She breaks off. "Anyways. Slept well?"

"Hmm-hmm." I'm a bit dazed. The ties Dominic had expertly fastened around my arm have loosened to such an extent that they've bundled at my wrist. I quietly tug at them, not wanting Portia to notice, but by the glint in her eye, I'm not hiding anything from her soon.

"Not to worry. I got a guard to do the laundry and dry it, too, so now it's all folded and ready for you." She puts the stack of clothes on the bed.

"Thank you." Right on top is a blush pink satin robe. What was she thinking when she got me *that*?

"You want to try fall asleep again?"

"No." I won't, not now she's chatted me awake. There's no sign of Dominic, which is totally for the better.

"Come then, you look like you need some coffee. A proper one. Not the stuff they sell at shops here. I make the best cappuccino this side of the Atlantic."

This makes me smile. Of course she does. I push the ties to the side and get up, and as I do, Dominic's pajama shorts slip, and I have to catch them. "Oops."

"Why not put on your own? It's right on top."

"Maybe a shower first?"

"No, you're not going anywhere this early."

With a shrug, I go through the first few layers and find the matching pink summer sleep set. "May I?"

I'm under no illusions here. Portia didn't come all this way to make small talk with me and take care of laundry. I bet she's got a gun shoved into the back of her jeans or something.

"Sure, go ahead."

I go to the bathroom where I change, feel whether the bandage over my bullet wound still holds, wash my face and brush my teeth, and manage my bedhead into a messy bun. *Not dressing up. Not dressing up at all.*

"Is Dominic around?" I ask, walking back into the bedroom.

Portia has opened the curtains, and through the windows, there's the beautiful view over the manicured gardens. She's busy collecting the ties on the bed, muttering, "Ruined, all ruined."

"He's probably in the gym," she says as she puts the silky pile on the chair.

I step in and help her make the bed. He's *in* the gym, not *at* the gym, which means he's still here, in the home gym. So much money on display. I'm not used to it at all.

When we're done, she opens the bedroom door and leads the way to the kitchen.

I don't miss the guard who sits two doors down. He stands as we walk past. Portia only nods at him in acknowledgement. All the doors are still closed, but it doesn't feel so strange anymore. I'm building a map in my head of the house for future reference. For now, I'll let this tide sweep me into whichever direction it chooses to take, observing, adapting.

It's quiet as Portia makes the cappuccino. She's relaxed; I'm slowly tensing up again. There seems to be more eyes around than last night. Maybe I was so out of it I didn't notice, but this Code Red calls for a lot of security. I'm out of my depth, but to be honest, I've been from the start.

"Here." She pushes the coffee in my direction. "Drink up, and we'll go find Dominic. I need instructions from him. By the sounds of it, we're going to still tear the house down today."

"Okay." I cautiously take a first sip, but it's the perfect temperature and delicious, like a sip of home. Emotion overwhelms me, because here I am, having another thing I thought I'd never have again.

It's a quick coffee, and when I'm done, we make our way through the house to the other side and the additions I saw when we drove into the property. We walk through the home gym which is so well-equipped, it looks like something from a luxury private sports club, but Dominic isn't there.

"He must be swimming," Portia says as she pushes open a sliding door between the gym and what looks like a twenty-five-meter-long pool, enclosed in a conservatory-style glass house. It's magnificent, with a high ceiling with exposed rafters and glass doors designed to open up to the outside world in summer and keep in the heat in winter. The pool is at least four lanes wide, and in one of them, Dominic is swimming in the opposite direction.

"And Bruno is here, too," she says. "You've met the brute?"

"Yes," I say with a small smile. "We're good."

"Since he's still busy, I'm going to prepare breakfast." She lets the statement hang.

I can either wait here for Dominic or go crack some eggs and help in the kitchen.

"I want to dip my feet in the water," I say, feeling a bit like a girl again. It's not often—no, it's actually *never* that I get to experience life at this level of luxury.

"That's fine." Her gaze jumps to a guard who is standing just outside with an automatic rifle, and when she squeezes my hand in warning, there's no need to verbalize the message.

Don't try pull off any shit, sweetheart.

I watch for a second as she walks away, Bruno now following in her wake, clearly knowing who is going to feed him. I spot another guard who has positioned himself right at the sliding door between the gym and the swimming pool. Code Red. Dominic said this isn't all for me, but goodness, it's a lot.

With a shrug, I pad over to the pool where I sit down on the edge and lower my feet into the water. It's fresh but not cold, and now I want to strip and get into the pool with Dominic. I don't have a swimsuit, and I'm in my new pajamas with no underwear. There isn't a chance in hell I'm getting naked with him.

On the far side, he does that underwater turning thing and freestyles it back in my direction, totally oblivious I'm even here. I'm sitting by the corner of the pool, on the side of his lane, giving him space. He's wearing swimming goggles, and with graceful strokes, glides through the water at speed.

He's clearly an excellent swimmer, and I can see why, what with those shoulder and back muscles. He is so efficient with the movements, it's almost soundless. Each time an arm comes up and pierces back into the water, muscles strained and bulging, his skin shimmers as water sluices off, making magic with the tattoos on his arms. I'd love to have a closer look at them, but so far, he's hardly given me a chance.

As he comes closer to where my legs are hanging in the water, my pulse skips several beats, and the urge to tuck my feet away bubbles up. Soon, he's going to be right here, and I bet by now he's seen me. He slows down as he nears the edge, and before I can pull out, he's brushed my foot with a warm hand, giving me a squeeze as he rises out of the water.

I suck my lip as he stands, the water running off to his waist, where he's still covered in the shallow end of the pool.

"Hey," he says as he pulls off his goggles, chest heaving. "You're supposed to be sleeping in."

When Dominic looks after a woman, he looks after a woman. God, he is sweet. And he did take care of me last night, in a way I never thought possible for a man. There's a reason I slept so well. He was there.

As he rakes his hair from his brow and wipes the water off his face, I take in every inch I can. He's right here, so close and naked from the waist up. His body is majestic, toned, strong, years of weightlifting defining every muscle individually. The morning sun beams down through the glass ceiling, and the water droplets on his skin almost magnify his body. With his arms raised in motion and his side facing me, I get to see his smoother inner arms, tattooed lats, his side, the shape of his obliques as they trail down into that V no woman can resist.

I double-take. And double-take again, sure the water is messing with my head. But then, my mind flashes back to how he dimmed the lights, how he turned just so when he changed his shirt yesterday. How he was overly conscious of his body, even though he has nothing to hide.

Except he does. It hits me, and blood seems to seep from me in shock, cold fingers of horror scratching down my spine. *Experience.*

He's been too focused on his exercise, maybe too taken off-guard to find me here, he didn't think of hiding his scars from me.

I bite back tears, resisting the urge to reach out for him in a soft touch I've only learned about yesterday. A touch he taught me without being aware he did. This man—

"Dominic?" I drag in a ragged breath, but there's no way I have control over my voice now. "Who did this to you?"

31

DOMINIC

Fuck.

I close my eyes, as if it could help. Making as if she were never here. Making as if these scars wouldn't be there when I open my eyes.

I didn't think. I didn't have time to think. She isn't supposed to be here. She's supposed to be in my bed, sleeping, and not distracting me at all.

And yet, it's all she's been doing.

But now... This was the last thing I wanted her to see. Not with those cuts and burns on her beautiful, flawless skin.

Ariana is sitting here in a soft pink robe, staring at me as if I'm straight from some Halloween make-up freak show.

"How?" Her voice breaks, and my heart goes out to her. "How are they all on one side?" she manages to whisper, her eyes brimming with tears when I finally have the guts to look into them.

"He was right-handed." With a sigh, I heave out of the water and perch on the edge just like her, sitting with that side towards her. There's no point in trying to hide it from her now.

Her gaze drops to my scars and shoots back to my gaze. "Who?"

I smirk, but it's sour, and the hate I keep coiled up inside me pushes to unfurl. It's too late. Matteo did us all that favor.

"The Don."

"The Don...like in *your dad*?"

"Yep. He was—" Fucked up? A fantastic strategist. Genius. Focused. Maniacal. "A psychopath. A monster, really."

Those quiet tears of hers are idling down her cheeks, and she blinks at me in confusion. "Parents are supposed to love their children... To protect their children...not do this."

"Did yours? Love and protect you?" I ask quietly, knowing the answer.

Her dad is dead; her mom died in a car accident without plans for her care in case something went wrong. By slotting her in with Franco, in some weird Mafia foster home, they didn't look out for her at all. The reason she got raped in the first place can be tied right back to some parental neglect.

"It's not the same," she whispers, her fingers working her robe's fabric anxiously, almost to tearing point.

I reach for her hand to quiet her.

"In a way, it's exactly the same." I rub my thumb over her knuckles, signaling to her I'm okay. "It's done. It's in the past. It shaped me, but it doesn't have a chokehold on me. It's not...my master," I say, picking my words carefully. "Not like it used to be."

Hasn't been for a long time and will never be again. Not since I discovered the antidote to things done to me and I'm forced to do to others.

"But why?" Her fingers grip mine. "Surely, he didn't do this to your brothers, too?"

"No. It was part of my specific training." And have no fear, the Don had his curriculum for each one of his sons. His plans for his army.

Her eyes widen. "Training?"

"For my role in the organization."

"As?"

"The man who gets all questions answered." The interrogator.

"I don't get it."

I shrug, not relishing the idea of explaining this to her. But we've come this far, and after what she told me, there's no reason not to share with her.

"Understanding pain makes you know just how to hand it out. How to push people to a point where they would tell you anything. I know exactly how every single one of these feels like, and I can read people, know what to do to break them." I speak quietly, but the words are harsh, and she seems to flinch at every single one of them.

We're sitting on two sides of the pool's corner, legs in the water, and like this, she is close to me. Maybe too close. When she pulls her hand from mine, I don't stop her. She reaches for my side, her gaze homing in to where I've disguised some of the scars with tattoos, but not all the scar tissue would take ink. She spotted the cigarette burns, and now, she reaches for the lines cut by a whip, the pattern burned by a clothing iron, higher to where the Don used a scalpel on my skin, cutting the top layer in lines that eerily match hers. As if he were counting.

Her touch is like butterfly wings against my skin, and I let her explore. Feel the uncertain caress of a woman where I've never felt it before. Tears spill ever faster over her cheeks, her breathing becoming strained as she tries not to sob.

"How old were you?" she whispers, leaning closer as she splays her palm over my obliques and higher, her hand like a starfish wanting to cover my scars, as if she could erase all of them with touch alone.

Her warmth seeps through my skin in patches, only where the nerve endings haven't been killed off.

"Once my mom died, there was no stopping him. I was eleven when he did these." I take her hand and guide her forefinger to rest on the cigarette burns, counting them one by one. Cheap torture.

"How did your teachers—at school—how didn't they—"

"We were homeschooled."

"But didn't your brothers—"

"They didn't know, sweetheart. And when he tells you that he'll cut your tongue in half if I told anybody...well, at that age, I was impressionable enough to believe him. He took care of my wounds, so..." Dad and son bonding time. The Don and Dominic version.

By the time Alex had caught on, a lot had happened. The Don did pace himself, but six years is a long time for abuse. And my brothers weren't spared, so I wasn't exactly standing in line to complain. By the time Alex cornered me, telling me I had the height and I needed to build the muscle, he'd been put through his own paces.

And not taking any of it anymore. Alex didn't toe the line.

Alex was becoming the man who planned to cut the Don down to his knees. Kill him, even. I can see it now, looking back. Alex was the Don's weakest link. His son who wouldn't take his bullshit for much longer. Because of this, Alex was the strongest of all of us.

I bet the Don saw him plotting. Took stock of his influence over us. Matteo was the first in line, the heir apparent to *Il Consiglio*, but Alex was becoming our bedrock foundation, rising up slowly, planning to shipwreck all the Don's plans.

To this day, I don't know if the shootout in that warehouse, on the night when Matteo came back with Alex's body locked in his arms, the night Peter Armstrong ratted *Il Consiglio* out, was a real police shootout or the Don's way of getting rid of his son who was becoming his biggest threat.

Clean, neat, perfectly executed to the point nobody could ever point a finger to the Don, killing his own son.

I force myself not to speculate anymore, to focus instead on Ariana and the effect opening up like this would have on her. She's been through all of this so recently, and I bet those cuts on her lower belly pulse in time with mine. Her hand still heats up my skin, her fingertips resting, with the most quiet and subtle movements tracing parts of me no woman has ever explored. Not at this pace. Usually, if a woman got this far, it came to a swift end. I don't talk to anybody, not like I talk to Ariana now.

I close my eyes, my breathing stalling as her caress lingers over thicker scars of a whip lashing that almost cut to the bone.

"Does is still hurt?" she whispers.

"Like an echo."

When I open my eyes, she's right there, cheeks wet, lips plump and red with having been shredded with her teeth as she tried to keep quiet. Lips I'd love to kiss. Lips I'd love to open slowly, languidly with mine, so I can sweep my tongue over hers, and prove to her she's still alive. That she can still feel. That we aren't dead inside.

Lips I want to have on my skin, as much as I want to have mine on hers.

I shift so I can reach for her robe and tug at the whimsical belt keeping it closed. It opens easily, revealing the matching pajama set underneath. A thin-strapped camisole and a pair of satin shorts, riding high up to her sex. I ghost my hand over her thighs, needing to touch her where she's touching me. Her fingertip is tracing the pattern made by the Don's scarification, and she doesn't stop me when I sneak my finger between the waistband and her skin and inch lower to where I can feel the tips of the first set of tally marks.

For a long moment, it's quiet between us as we succumb to each other's touch, to this moment of intimacy I've never had with someone before. When she cracks a sob, I lean in and press my forehead to hers.

"Sweetheart." Fuck, it's one thing to have suffered this, but knowing she's been through it in her own way, it kills me.

"How broken are we, Dominic?" she whimpers, pressing into me with her whole body.

I pull her close, wrapping my arm around her.

"Pretty broken, sweetheart," I whisper. "But if you let me, I can try... I can try to help you and show you how to live as if you're whole again."

As whole as we'll ever be.

32

ARIANA

This man.

This broken man.

He has me in such a gentle hold, his fingertips resting right where I feel the subtle pressure deep between my thighs. His hand needs to slide just a few inches lower, and he'd be able to feel how wet I am. Press his finger to my clit, circle it with that slow and gentle touch of his.

My thighs tense with the need to open wider, and it hits me hard that I want him to. Need him to. That I'm starving for him to do more.

After Franco, I've never wanted a man to touch me there. Now I'm sitting on a hungry yearning I've hardly allowed myself to feed in the past. I've tuned my body out to these feelings, these needs, but it's as if Dominic walked into my personal space and tossed a can of glitter over me, sparking every nerve ending back to life. I'm glowing, despite having all my broken pieces scattered in front of him like shards of glass. He's just offered to put me together again. To show me how to live as if I'm whole once more.

It isn't a magic fix. He's only suggesting there's a way to live life to the fullest around what happened to me. To him... To us.

His breathing is calm, his nose nuzzling mine as he pulls away slightly from where I'm clinging to him. He's indirectly asked me a question: if I'd let him in. I'm not ready to answer. All of this has been too much, his truth a punch to the gut and heart that has me reeling.

But my body already whispers its own answer, separate from my mind's desperate workings.

I want this. I need this. I need *him*.

It's been twelve years of being a nomad in my own body, wandering and not finding a resting place that fits. And now, here's this man. The only one in the world who seems to get me, and he comes with a raging red flag.

He's from the wrong side. The enemy. The hunted.

"Why did he—" I break off, not even knowing how to ask this and if he'd even know whether there was a reasoning behind all this madness. What Franco did to me makes more sense in a way, because that type of violence is the go-to for men when it comes to women. But this—*a father and his sons.*

I lean back slightly so I can look into his eyes, and when I do, he has the softest, the most caring look in them I've ever seen on a man.

"Why did the Don single you out for this...this training... this duty?" My voice wants to break on the words, because the level of evil to plot a role like this for each of your children is unfathomable.

Dominic eases away from me, his hand slipping out of my sleep shorts. He squeezes my hip and settles back. Immediately, I regret making him pull away because in my gut, I know this part is probably going to be the worst if he has a ready answer for it.

"I pissed him off when I was five." He shoots me a wry little smile. "Told him that one day, I wanted to become a cop and take out bad guys."

A shudder traipses down my spine. We've so many things in common. *You'll know what they'll do to you once they've figured you out.*

"I was just a boy with dreams like any other boy to do something big and important, like be a fireman or a pilot or something. At that age, I didn't quite get it that *we* were the bad guys."

"You were five?" I repeat, stunned.

"Yep. From that day on, he was on a mission to play good cop, bad cop with me whenever he could. He made it his personal quest to show me how fucked-up the police force is, how corrupt and full of weak men that make them fail. He made me watch, and later, he made me assist, forcing me to cross lines no kid should cross."

I close my eyes, the visual too much to stomach.

When I look at him again, he's shaking his head.

"Look at me now. In my early thirties, with the Don dead, but I'm still dancing the steps he taught me as if I can't do anything else." He sighs, and it's as if he spills his soul into it. "I thought once he's dead, I'd have a choice, but I don't. And it's fine. I don't want my brothers to do what I do, and someone has to."

He cups my cheek, his hand warm with the subtle scent of chlorine from the pool, making me look up at him.

"You know what we are, sweetheart. You've seen it firsthand in that warehouse. You're from this world and know how it works. It's us or them. And by them, I don't mean the police and their corrupt backstabbing, two steps back for every one forward. It's us or other Mafia, or the Bratva, the cartels infiltrating from the south. I need to keep my brothers safe from all of these factions, and well, I do what I need to do."

"You were only five," I whisper, knowing I'm helpless in so

many ways. I've seen this play out in my own life, until I ran away from Franco and my foster home.

"The Don played a long game, and somehow, I got what I wanted. I take out the bad guys that threaten my family and our organization."

"Have you ever taken out a cop?" My question hangs heavy in a weighted silence that stretches and stretches as he thinks.

"Not to my knowledge, but I will if I have to. And I won't leave a trace."

I'm suddenly chilled to my bones. I'm already missing without a trace. I bet my team presumes I'm dead.

He lets go of me with a sigh, stands, and holds out a hand to help me up. I take it, finding comfort in his touch but also noting the strength of his hand, his veined forearm muscles and biceps, how his stomach contracts and highlights his six-pack as he helps me up, all movements which underscore the ease with which he'll be able to eliminate me if he wanted to. He's tall, too, and overpowering me would be the easiest thing on this planet...except he doesn't want to.

Fear doesn't swamp my body as it should because nothing Dominic has done has warranted this reaction from me yet. I've never felt safer around a man, but it's as if I'm under a spell. My mind yells at me to tread carefully, to watch my step. And get out of here as soon as I can.

Dominic is one of five brothers in a much bigger machine I'm still trying to figure out. An outlier in a lot of ways, but he'll do exactly what Franco wanted to do once he's figured me out.

He lets go of my hand and walks over to a lounger where he's stripped off his training clothes. He swam in black swimming trunks, which are still wet and dripping water. He roughly dries with a towel, puts on his sweat-stained T-shirt to hide everything his dad did to him from the world, and picks up his sneakers.

As I watch him, I close my robe again. My fingers are white

with cold and stupid, slow to perform a simple task. It's shock and dread of what would become of me if I don't make it back to Italy, my secrets intact.

"Come on." He has me by the elbow and steers me to the sliding door. "I need to get to Matteo's place. I'd take you with, but I need you to work with Portia on something for me."

He lets go of me as soon as he's closed the sliding door and leads the way to the kitchen. We walk abreast, Dominic acknowledging the security detail stationed in strategic corners. The heavenly smell of coffee and something frying fills the corridor.

"Portia is Italian like nobody else, but she loves an American fry-up for breakfast. You're hungry?"

"Starving." I don't use this word lightly anymore, but it's a lie. After that conversation, I have no appetite, but I'll eat. I need to regain my strength.

Portia is busy at the stove as we enter the kitchen, and with Bruno lying in wait for a handout, it's the picture of homeliness. She's the grandma cooking, and the island counter is set with a spread from fruit to pastries and more fresh coffee.

Toast pops, and she turns to us. "Excellent! Good timing. Let me fry the eggs."

Dominic winks at me as soon as Portia is back at the stove and pulls out a barstool for me.

"She loves cooking," he whispers, as if I haven't picked up on this already.

We settle, and he pours us each some orange juice.

"Dr. Wong will come check in on Ariana this morning."

"Good thinking, Nicky," Portia says. "What else?"

"I've been going through the files in the Don's office, but I've hardly made a dent. What I really need is for you to find Mom's things. We didn't keep track. Do you know what the Don did with all her personal effects when she passed away?"

Portia stills, and in the quiet, the frying eggs pop and crackle in the pan. “Anything specific you’re looking for?”

“Her journals. The ones she kept during her last pregnancy.”

“Oh, Nicky,” she groans. “You know she’d never allow anybody to read them. She kept them so well-hidden.”

“And therefore the reason why we need them. Those journals could hold the key to finding Gabriella. You’re going to have to look in every nook and cranny in this house. If someone can figure out where they all are, it’s you, Portia.” He leans closer and squeezes my arm. “And Ariana’s going to help.”

33

DOMINIC

When I walk into Matteo's place an hour later, the apartment is quiet. Rosalia is busy in the kitchen prepping a continental breakfast with coffee and pastries. I wave at her in greeting but head straight to Matteo's office from where I hear my brothers' voices.

I walk inside, and as I close the door, sweep my gaze over the vast room. Matteo, behind his desk. Luca and Benedict in the seating area, coffee cups still steaming with fresh brew. Benedict is on his laptop, Luca on his phone. Matteo is playing with a pen as if he needs to hide a nervous tic. I'm not sure what he's told the others, but this thing with Gabriella needs to get out sooner rather than later.

"They know," Matteo says, as if he read my mind.

"Good." This type of secret isn't one we should keep.

Benedict glances up from where he's typing away at speed. "Whatever info I can scrape, we'll have, and we'll put this puzzle together."

I nod as Matteo stands and comes around his desk. We both sit down with the others, Benedict puts his laptop to the side, and Luca shoves his phone into his pocket.

"I feel like we're under an attack of sorts, and I can't fucking pinpoint the source." As soon as I know the origins, I'll know how to protect my brothers—and their wives. We need to get this situation under control *pronto*. "Steph?" I ask, just making sure we're keeping our brother in the loop.

"He's with Gigi and not coming in," Luca replies. "I've already asked him to probe her about anything she could possibly know. It would seem the Trapanis had no idea about Gabriella. There's no reason why Gigi would lie, and as she's the eldest, we'll leave it at that for now. She's offered to ask Don Trapani once they're back in Italy, but it will only be later this week."

"Good. And fair enough. She's Team Scalera now." Matteo turns to me. "The question is, really, what do we do with Ariana Morelli."

"If that's even her real name," Luca says.

"Yeah," I say, knowing I'll have to share the basics of what she's told me in private with my brothers. She'll never need to know, and keeping everything I've learned from them only opens us up to risks. I want to limit those as far as possible. "I didn't get the feeling she was lying about anything she's told me so far, but we need to double-check every detail."

"And what has she told you?" Matteo asks, inching forward in his seat.

"Franco has some type of hold on her, but she hasn't told me yet what it is, or was. She thinks people in Italy are at risk, and she prefers to stay missing in action for now."

"With what she knows of us, she can't go back to Italy," Matteo says.

"Yeah, she's pretty fucked, isn't she," Luca says. "Landed right in the middle of it."

I sigh. Even if Ariana seemed unconscious during the shootout, she's in too deep now, what with trying to escape.

"What else did she tell you?" Matteo asks, and I wish I

didn't have to expose the secret she's been keeping tight for more than a decade.

"She grew up with Franco, and he...he...brutally—" Fuck it. The mere idea of it makes my stomach clench tight, heat curve around my neck in anger, and my heart rate speed up. The words are stuck in my throat, but they'll have to come out. "Brutally violated her when she was fifteen."

It grows eerily quiet in the room as my brothers digest my words.

Here's the thing: if you grew up like we did, with a mom who let us only know love, despite everything she went through, then you become protective like we are. There are reasons why we all had this rule—the one Matteo and Steph have already broken—that marriage isn't for us. On the one side, there's the gnawing notion we might turn out to be like our dad, a violent abuser, cruel beyond words. On the other side, even if we were better than the old Don, we need to fight for dominance in our world all the time. If I can't protect a woman, it would be my ultimate failure. I don't even want to go there.

"Well, fuck," Luca says eventually. "If Franco weren't dead already—"

Matteo and Benedict grunt in agreement, and I slump back in my chair. Whatever Ariana is to us, she's just been adopted by the Scalera brothers. Except she has this happy knack of wanting to escape and to put a hole in my heart. I'm not telling them about that. Or about what happened after, and how I got to learn about this in the first place. They need to know the basics. They don't need to know everything.

"She just told you?" Luca asks, getting right to the freaking point I want to avoid. "Opened up like that?"

I grind my jaw. "We talked and...well—"

"Well?" Benedict prompts.

A knock on the door makes me pause, and when Rosalia

peeks in a few seconds later, I huff out a quiet breath in relief. Saved by a fucking platter of pastries. We wait for her in silence as she carries in the food, but Matteo searches my face as he nods with a quiet thank you. By the time Rosalia has left the office, the atmosphere has shifted.

"Doesn't matter how he gets information out of Ariana," Matteo says, now studying me intently with a glint in his eyes I've never seen before. "Let's just call it Nicky's magic...wand."

What. The. Fuck.

A round of smirks circles the room, and I feel even hotter around my fucking collar. "Bro? Really?"

"Come on, Nicky, take it like the big man you are," Luca says, a grin still eating his shitface. "When it's your turn, it's your turn."

I reach for a croissant with a shrug. Let them razz me, I don't care. I'm going to call order to this meeting. As my brothers reach for their own croissants, I have a moment of reprieve to organize my thoughts. We need to discuss Igor Petrov and my little fuckup.

"I'm thinking—" Benedict says between two bites, "—if you can get me her fingerprints, I can dig and get my contacts to see what they find on the Italian databases. If she's lying about anything, it will eventually show."

I've been brewing the same idea. I don't relish going behind her back to get information on her, not with this newfound trust between us, but it's for her own safety—and ours. "Okay, I'll make a plan."

"This idea Nicky has about us being under attack," Matteo starts as he reaches for a napkin and puts his plate on the coffee table. "It all started with Randazzo. It got worse with the Don's death. The question really is whether this is normal with a power change, or is someone fucking with us on purpose?"

"They're fucking with us, Matty," I say, suddenly tired to my bones. "The Borises admitted that Franco had promised to help them take over our ports once he got Gigi's money."

"But why would Igor Petrov send his nephew to contest agreements in such a way? Blood agreements that were made decades ago?" Matteo asks. "Why stir up shit if you don't have to?"

Benedict clears his throat, raises his hand to pause all talking as he takes a leisurely sip of coffee. "Igor Petrov retired earlier this year. Might be that his successor has the need to prove himself."

"What? Retired?" Matteo says. "How?"

"How the fuck do you get to retire out of the Bratva?" Luca echoes, putting the words there for me.

"His son took over. Ivan Petrov," Benedict says. "It all happened while we were focusing on this Randazzo business and not paying attention. And here we are."

"Ivan Petrov?" Luca repeats, a bit stunned.

Matteo shakes his head, holding his hand up. "So what the fuck is Igor Petrov doing in his *retirement*?"

His tone gives it all away: what a joke, and maybe he's a bit jealous.

"Bought a mansion in Maui and plays golf the whole day," Benedict fills us in with a small smile. "It works out for some, you know."

Instead of keeping an eye on whoever now rules the Bratva and making sure old agreements are honored, Igor Petrov gets to catch a tan and lose golf balls in the links.

"Well, fuck me. What do we know of Ivan Petrov?" I ask, homing in on the obvious adversary here. The new player I need to protect my brothers—and their wives—from.

"Hmmm...uh..." Luca starts. "I might have done a job for him a few months ago."

"What?" Matteo barks. "A *job*?"

"Chill, dude, it was just a cyber scrub and Ivan Petrov

wouldn't know it was me...us—" Luca glances at Benedict, but Benedict only cocks his brows at him. "Yes, okay, it was my turn for one of those and only I got involved. Petrov contacted us via the dark web to scrub some videos and images of his mistress off the web, but I didn't link him to Igor Petrov. Fuck, I thought it was all coming from Russia as everything I swiped originated from there. How many Ivan Petrovs are there on the planet anyway? Both names are the most common ones in use in a motherfucking giant land like Russia."

"Fuck if I know, but this one's looking to become a fucking huge pain in my ass. So he can't trace that back to us?" Matteo asks, still rigid. "Because this type of shit comes home to roost."

"No. Fuck, Benny, back me here," Luca says.

"Our security is top tier, Matty," Benedict says, slightly offended. "We routinely do a fucking deep cleanse, so—"

"And I bet you the reason Petrov got a third party on the dark web to do the dirty work for him is because he doesn't have the know-how in house." Luca reaches for his coffee again, argument closed.

"That sums it up," Benedict says with a nod. "Relax, Matty, this isn't about whatever job Luca did. In any case, it's not the first time one of us have been asked to do this type of shit, so just because it's Petrov doesn't mean he's after *Il Consiglio*."

It's tense for a moment as we all digest this news.

"What else do you know," Matteo sighs. "I bet you have all the info already?"

"Yep. Not just a pretty face here," Benedict jokes as he puts his coffee cup back on the table. "Late thirties, wife's dead, and he's blessed with two young daughters."

Blessed, indeed. With a fucking migraine from hell. If Ivan Petrov took over from his dad, he is now the king of the Petrov Bratva in New York and New Jersey and however far their operations stretch. But with two young daughters...blessed isn't how I'd describe it. I'm already freaked out with wives in the mix...but kids? *Girls*? It's this whole situation with Ariana and Gabriella that's eating at me and how girls become women, and from Day One, they're basically at risk of being hurt or being used as pawns.

"How did his wife die?" I ask.

Benedict shrugs. "Apparently, it was suicide."

Fuck. I quirk a brow as we all shoot each other glances. When last was a death in the Bratva really suicide?

Matteo drags in a deep breath, shifting our thoughts. "Is he looking for a new wife? A mother for his girls?"

"Don't even fucking go there, Matty," I say, my blood heating up. "Ariana isn't going to be your pawn in this mess I made."

Matteo stands, and I have to crane my neck to look up at him as he's standing next to me. "Don't be fucking delusional that Ivan or Igor, whichever Petrov we get to fucking deal with, isn't going to want retribution for his dead nephew, cousin, whatever. We have a woman on our hands who knows too much. You know what that means, Dominic."

I stand, too, eye to eye with him. I know what it means. She's either contained, or she's dead.

"I won't let her get married to some Russian fucker who we don't know from a fucking bar of soap who will use her—" I break off, my voice strained as I inch back a bit, somewhat taken by surprise at my own intense feelings.

Ariana.

What the actual fuck? I need to pull back here, but Ariana... *Fuck.*

She's gotten under my skin. In the time we've spent together, she's actually managed to get to me, to my core. To the part I've been protecting like a dragon its treasure. I drag in a slow breath, battling for control in front of my brothers.

"I will not let her go to any man who is going to abuse her

like Franco did." Time to say it like it is—like it was. How we witnessed it. Lived it. "To be abused like Mom was."

A strained silence swamps the room. Matteo's gaze doesn't break away from mine as everyone digests my words. Comparing Ariana's situation with Mom's isn't a low blow, it's a reality. And my trump card.

With the smallest of shrugs, Matteo concedes my point and makes his way back to the chair behind his desk. This is no longer my brother, but the Don of *Il Consiglio* who is going to overrule me when he wants. And what the fuck do I do then?

"Before we get ahead of ourselves here," he says as he sits down, "let's make sure this Boris you killed is really Petrov's cousin, nephew, whatever. Once we know for sure, we'll know what to do." Matteo sits, and his chair creaks with his weight as he leans back and looks me right in the eye. "Until then, nothing is off the cards."

34

ARIANA

I had a hard time eating breakfast with a cheerful face. Portia is a ray of sunshine, but nothing can cast lightness over everything I've learned this morning about Dominic. I'm just following the motions, whatever Portia tells me to do.

We clean the kitchen after breakfast. I take a shower and get dressed, all while she potters around in the room, righting things needing no righting. A security guard is always on standby, and she ignores him as if he is part of the furniture. Portia is clearly much more in tune with this life than I'll ever be.

I can't stop thinking of Dominic. He left over an hour ago, leaving me with a hollow ache in my chest, one I can't shed. The urge to cry tightens my throat out of nowhere, and I need to swallow every emotion down to keep myself in check. The last thing I want is for Portia to read my face or my feelings. The one I can school; the other I seem to have no control over anymore.

When her phone rings and she answers with a quick conversation, she has me by the hand. "Dr. Wong is here."

When a short and thin Chinese woman stalks into the room

minutes later with a medical case, I almost wither under her cold glare.

"I'm here to check up on a bullet wound," Dr. Wong says as she points to the bed. "Show me."

Portia closes the door to give me some privacy from the security guard. Without wasting time, I strip the jeans I dressed in earlier as Dr. Wong puts on sterile gloves.

As I lie down and lift my T-shirt, she just shakes her head.

"Too busy, too busy here," she grumbles under her breath as she carefully peels off the bandage but making sure not to shift my underwear if it isn't necessary. "Pain?" she asks as she takes a minute to inspect the wound, but her gaze wanders, and she sees everything else down there, too.

"It's fine." And it really is. In comparison to the other healed wounds on my lower belly, I can bear this easily.

"Good. Leave this uncovered now. No soaking in the bath, only careful cleaning. Don't let anything rub against it. Any changes, fever, puss, anything, let me know." She straightens and glances to Portia. "Makes sure she eats. Lots of carbs, proteins, fats. She's too skinny."

The women exchange a look, and I can't help but feel like an outsider. Clearly, these two have come some way.

"Yes, Doctor." Portia has a new sparkle in her eye, and I bet it's because someone gave her the green light to fatten me up to the BMI of a cheap pork sausage.

Dr. Wong is even more efficient in leaving the room than in arriving, like a gust of wind just passing through the house.

"Excellent," Portia says once I've pulled my jeans back on. "Now we can get down to the real work for the day."

"Hunting down journals?"

"Making a nice, hearty carbonara with extra fatty pancetta and Pecorino Romano," she says, listing the ingredients as she ticks them off with enthusiasm on her fingers. "Home-made fettuccine. Organic eggs. Pepper. Lots of freshly ground pepper."

Yes, I'm drooling, but I'm still stuffed after breakfast, as Portia made me finish the packet of American-style bacon she air-fried.

She reaches for my arm with a soft squeeze. "I'll get a driver to fetch us all the right ingredients. As is, Dominic's been living on the bare minimum here. If you're staying a while, we need to stock up."

"But this isn't his place?" I ask, wanting to drill into the layers of mystery that's Dominic Scalera. Plus we need to define *staying a while*, because this isn't my plan. I might have paused any ridiculous escape attempts, but it doesn't mean my brain isn't working overtime to find the nearest exit. *Act only when the time is right.*

Portia just shrugs and looks at her wristwatch. "Doesn't matter. He will be where you are, and that for a while. Come on. Time for us to go do some manual labor."

She leads the way out of Dominic's bedroom, which seems to have become mine now, as she never took me back to my original corner guest room where Dominic parked me yesterday.

The guard follows behind us as we head to the foyer and the magnificent staircase. When Portia scales the stairs and I follow, I glance around the elegant space. It really is something out of a fairytale in a way, one Disney hasn't gotten hold of. No, this place is the real Brothers Grimm, with every gory secret still intact.

"How long have you known the family?" I ask.

"Oh, a long time. I worked for the Don for over forty years. First as just a cleaner when he was still building his business, and then when they moved here, I proved myself enough to become the head housekeeper. He looked after me and my own." She pauses and holds on to the railing, seeming to catch her breath as she reflects back. Then she turns to me and looks me in the eye. "I'd be the first to admit he wasn't a good man, but he rewarded loyalty, and when I came to America when I was only sixteen—"

She takes the stairs again, seeming to need to organize her thoughts, and when we reach the landing, she huffs out a breath. "These stairs didn't get to me like this when I still worked here. Good grief, I need to walk more and stop thinking the garden is enough." She brushes away a rogue curl. "Let's just say, Don Scalera gave me my first job. I was out on the street, and well, it was about to go very wrong for me."

"How did you come to America?" I ask, curious how she came over at sixteen.

"With my parents. As tourists," she says, making quotation marks with her fingers. She nods in the direction of a corridor, and I follow. "Totally illegal. They came with the plan to stay. They wanted to leave the Mafioso crap behind in Italy. But that isn't how it works. My dad got into the wrong side of the turf war, Randazzo's side, and things went very wrong, very fast."

An electric shock would have surprised me less in that moment.

"Who?" I ask, pushing down my surprise, and feigning only mild interest.

"Emilio Randazzo. He and Guiliano Scalera were in this turf war they dragged all the way here from Sicily. And then my dad got killed, and my mom died months later, and I was so to say on the streets."

"Oh. That's...that's terrible." My pulse speeds up several knots, and I make as if to catch my breath, too. What I'm really catching is the thin thread between Franco Fiore, Randazzo, and this family. I suspected there was a connection of sorts.

"Don Scalera won. Randazzo went back to Italy and gave up his American dream." She sighs as she comes to stand in front of a closed double wooden door, signaling to the guard to open it for us. "I got mine, though, and you'll never see me complain. One more day on the streets, and I would have been a prostitute, dead of AIDS ten years later."

The guard unlocks the door with a key and swings both doors open. Portia waves for me to walk in first and as I enter the room, I snatch in a breath.

"Instead, I got to turn a blind eye and work here," she says softly. "Not a day of abuse at any man's hand. Tell me, *cara*, if you only had yourself to think about, what would you have chosen?"

35

ARIANA

This. Obviously this. Any woman offered the choice of a life between prostitution and working in a house like this turns a blind eye and takes the latter.

I breathe in the splendid space. It's a vast room with high ceilings. Big old-fashion sash windows completely line the one side, with a fireplace on one wall and floor-to-ceiling bookshelves flanking it. A comfortable seating area faces the fireplace, and an easel stands in the corner with a half-painted landscape on it. It looks like the beginning of a garden, maybe even the view from one of the windows.

To the other side of the room, a massive four-poster bed takes center stage, made up with crisp white linen. A door leading to a dressing room and adjacent bathroom is cleverly hidden by the wallpaper, which is dated by modern standards. Chintz in pink and blues. The wallpaper, the cream-colored carpet, the pink drapes, everything gives away this is—*was*—a woman's sanctuary, frozen in time.

Portia steps up to a dainty antique desk that stands facing a window and runs a finger along its surface. She inspects her fingertip with a huff and mumbles something involving *standards.*

"Right. Whoever leads the show here now needs a talking to. The Don died, and two weeks later, the head housekeeper left on holiday. If I have any say in it, I'm thinking she's holidayed herself into getting fired." With a dismissive shrug, she turns to the guard who still hovers in the door. "You can leave us now. Close the door and wait outside."

"Portia—" the man starts, but she only pulls up to her full, unimpressive height, gives him a scowl, and shoos him with her hands as she walks up to him, ready to close the door in his face.

"We're fine. This is women's business, and Ariana won't try anything here. She'll have to jump from the window to escape, and there are hounds and guards enough to catch her when she tries to limp off with a broken leg."

The man raises his eyebrows and then his hands in defeat. "Okay-okay. Just watch your back. As I've been told to watch yours."

Portia shuts the door in his face as soon as he gives an inch and rolls her eyes at me. "As if I don't know how to watch my back."

I shoot her a half-smile. She's already stepped in as a mother figure to me, and for someone who lost her mom at such a young age, it's slowly becoming harder to even think of hurting Portia, never mind getting her into trouble by trying to escape. Plus, she's a helluva shot.

She walks past me and murmurs, "Just like this house, Dominic's mom had her secrets. We're here to keep them safe for her as far as possible. I won't have any random guard look on while we do this."

But she'd trust *me*? A total stranger coming in, to help heave a massive skeleton out of the closet? The only people who get to keep secrets are the dead...

"This was Bianca Scalera's safe space," Portia says as her gaze travels the room, interrupting my thoughts. "The only times she got to use the bed was until six weeks postpartum. Then it was back to work."

The way Portia says those words pops goosebumps on my arms. *Work*. By what I've seen of Dominic's skin, I don't want to imagine what work Don Scalera had for his wife. This is a mirror to the life I would have lived if I'd married Franco Fiore. My throat tightens again with helpless fear swarming in me. Bianca Scalera didn't have the same luxury of a choice between housekeeping and prostitution. It's clear she was here to do only one thing: bear sons.

"What was she like? Dominic's mom?"

A full minute passes as Portia mulls over my question, her feelings openly displayed on her face as she goes through them.

"A caged tigress," she murmurs eventually. "Keeping her cubs close for as long as she could. But caged all the same." She sniffs as tears roll down her cheeks. "She did everything to keep those boys safe. Fought for them like a tigress as long as she was able to. God...the things—"

She breaks off in a suppressed sob, crosses herself, and under her breath, she mutters a prayer in Italian. One I don't recognize. My Finnish mom wasn't religious, and once in foster care, church wasn't high on the to-do list for anybody. I reach for her in sympathy, and she grabs my hand, urgently squeezing now.

"If you ever wonder why these men are the way they are, it's because despite everything, their mother showed them enough love to carry them through it all. To this day and beyond. The love she had for her sons will carry them for the rest of their lives, and subconsciously, it sways the direction of every decision they make." She gulps in a breath, her hand still squeezing mine as the other comes to rest on her heart. "I've seen it over the years. Don Scalera might have had a cruel fist and a mental hold on his sons they would bow to all the way, but when it comes to women, these men will never be their father."

Portia's words echo everything I've experienced with Dominic so far. With me, he's been the most caring and compassionate man I've ever met, and I bet he is like that with every woman that crosses his path.

Portia lets go of me to wipe roughly at her face. She shakes her head as if she can shake off memories. "Come, we need to work. To think this whole situation with Gabriella only came to light now. When Bianca knew her time was close, she made me pack everything away, promising me to never look at it, and I honored her wishes. Now I can kick myself for being so naive."

So loyal.

"You didn't know about Gabriella?" I ask, getting the feeling if someone knew something, it would be Portia.

"No." She leads the way into the bathroom which has an adjacent dressing room and walk-in closet. It's stacked with clear plastic crates filled with clothes and shoes. "The Don took Bianca to a different hospital to give birth than the usual. Due to the new doctor, see? None of us were there to see what happened, and with her so weak...we didn't even think to question it. We just took his word. Now I wish I saw the bodies, but even that never happened."

No bodies? How did this happen? Everybody took the Don's word, but without ever seeing Bianca's body, there is no certainty of her death.

Portia picks up the top crate and holds it out for me, and soon, we've stacked those that were against the one wall away to the opposite side. "To think I stored all her things away years ago, and never caved in to the temptation to even look..."

I'm in awe. Loyalty gets rewarded, indeed.

"You cared for her very much, and you still do," I say, reaching to squeeze her shoulder where it's shaking with sobs.

"You didn't know, and you had no reason to suspect—" *Treason. This is a form of treason.*

"I know, right? And after she died, there were the boys...all of them so lost, and poor Benedict hardly five years old. I was busy, trying my best to fill a hole nobody ever could or would again."

She drops to her knees, and I'm readying myself to see her whip out her rosary and go through a string of prayers, but instead she tugs at the baseboard, wriggles and shimmies it until it shifts.

Eventually, it slides out without protest, and Portia glances up at me.

"When the closet is full of clothes, you don't notice, and I was careful to stack the crates just so."

She pulls on the other corner's baseboard, but this one has been hammered in with a lone nail, and she puts in a bit of force. Once it's out, it exposes the cream carpet covering the floor, cut flush to the wall, now only with the baseboards' footprint on it. Portia reaches for the carpet's corner and peels it away, revealing the old hardwood floor underneath. One board has a hole in it, just big enough to fit a female finger. As she lifts it away, the wood creaks, and dust clouds up.

"Have no fear," she whispers. "Everything in here is wrapped in plastic, covered for posterity."

My heart hammers in my chest as this new reality finally sinks in.

"You told Dominic you didn't know where her journals were," I whisper, stunned.

"I lied," Portia says without a blink or a blush. "I'll go to confession on Sunday."

"What? You *lied*? To Dominic? Of all people?" Does she know he tortures people to death? For the truth? He's admitted it to me...not in so many words, but I heard the evidence—there's no misunderstanding the role he plays in this family.

"I did." She glances at her watch again, clearly keeping an eye on the time, then leans back on her heels and gives me a stern look. "Listen, we Mafia women need to stick together. You and I have maybe two hours to scan through everything here and decide if we tell those boys where these are, or if we let sleeping dogs lie."

36

DOMINIC

I prefer to do shit like this on an empty stomach, but it is what it is. We're filing out of Matteo's office and heading to the adjacent secret room where Vincenzo and the rest of Franco's team of hired Ukrainian hands have been kept going. Matteo opens the door with his thumbprint, and once we go through more security checks, we reach the guard who is watching the men on TV monitors.

Yep, all my work and basically an impenetrable prison. There's only one way you get out of here—in a body bag directly to the promession site in the building's basement with Matteo's private elevator.

The men listened to our arrival, and already they're alert, whatever that means. I'm not a fan of this type of situation. I've seen enough of this shit to prefer it to be quick and done with, but they've been slow to talk.

Vincenzo blinks at us through his swollen eyes, and just seeing his face makes me want to choke him to death. He allowed Franco to get to Gigi. He saw what that maniac did to Ariana. Most probably helped—

"Fuck," I growl, but Matteo's grip on my arm holds me back.

"I get it, Nicky, but first, the information."

I purse my lips, clenching my teeth, my nostrils flaring with the need to control my anger. It's weird—it's a type of anger I've never felt before. Somehow, it cuts deeper, but maybe it's because someone else cut into me first. *Ariana.*

Suddenly, I'm getting where Matteo and Stephano come from with their women. Not that I'm so dumb to fall for one, but the need to avenge what Ariana has gone through is real. Franco might be dead, but I'm here to avenge her with whoever else participated in her hurt, in whichever way. Vincenzo is going to be that man. For starters.

Matteo printed out the images we have of Boris and Boryslav, and now he's holding them out to me. "Make them talk."

His tone says everything. I'm never getting out of my role here. As we walked over, I've reconsidered our position. Maybe all of this isn't an attack, but a test of our strength as *Il Consiglio.* I can't afford to be the weakest link here. I'll do what I must do for as long as it takes. I have time to figure out how to protect Ariana. For now, my focus needs to be here.

With the photos in hand, I approach the closest Ukrainian. He drops his head back to meet my gaze. Yup, this guy already wishes it's over.

"Tell us who this is?" I say, starting nice. No need to go anywhere with this if it isn't necessary. The before and after shots will probably be enough to make these men talk.

The guy focuses on the photos, his gaze slow to jostle between the images. "Boris Kovalenko," he grinds out.

"And the other guy?" I push the paper close to his face.

"Boryslav Petrenko." Blood starts to seep from the guy's mouth, and he coughs. Probably from a lost tooth or five.

"And? What makes these boys significant?" Next to me, Matteo, Luca, and Benedict are rolling on their heels, and the guy's gaze jumps to them, then back to mine.

"Petrenko is Igor Petrov's nephew. He got him out of Ukraine. I hope you didn't kill the poor fucker. He doesn't look very alive on that second picture."

I sag in my soul but keep my posture upright. Nothing in my body language can give away what I feel. To make sure nobody is fucking with us, I ask the same questions to the rest of our prisoners, and when each of them agrees on the names, even though I'm holding the images up in random order, we need to take it as the truth.

"Why was Petrov's cousin, fucking nephew, whatever, coming over to our side to fuck around in our territory?" Matteo asks in general.

"It was just a job," one man groans.

"Which you fucked up," Luca chimes in.

We share looks amongst ourselves. If Franco were just a job, and these men were acting on their own without Igor or Ivan Petrov's approval, they might have stirred up shit unintentionally. There's no way of knowing, not until this whole situation comes to a head.

"Can we get rid of them already?" Benedict says. "It isn't as if they're going back to where they came from."

"Hmm," Matteo hums, hands in his pants pockets, looking over the scene. "We keep this contained for as long as we can. For now, nobody else is breathing down our necks to find these fuckers, and we need to sort this situation with Ariana out first." He glances at me. "I suspect when the time comes, Petrov is going to require our full attention."

"We're done here, then?" I ask. "Six of them if Petrov is going to keep count?"

My throat constricts, and I have a hard time swallowing. Six men might be overlooked in the bigger scheme of things, depending on their worth in Petrov's Bratva, but a cousin...a nephew? *Fuck.*

Bottom line, this is a family fuckup. It started with the Don and dominoed to this. Matteo and Steph both have a hand in it, and let's remind ourselves: teamwork makes the fucking dream work.

"There's no going back now," Matteo says as he pulls his gun from his shoulder holster. "Four of us, four of them. We're done here. Party's over."

Fuck. In my head, it's only started. We're all pulling out our guns and pick a Ukrainian at random. The men are whimpering now, begging in whatever language, but I block out the sounds.

Vincenzo hasn't peeped a word during this entire interrogation, but I watch the fuckwit. He is literally pissing in his seat, the liquid spraying into the bucket from his little wilted dick. His time will come. In the interim, let him shit himself.

On Matteo's cue, we raise our guns, and in unison, finish the four Ukrainians in one go. Their bodies slump as blood starts to seep from the holes in their foreheads. Just a dribble. It's the back of the head where the party's at with brains and bits of skull bursting out and splattering onto the floor. It's nothing in comparison to what this room can take, what with the drain hole in the middle and the neat hosing-down options we have in place.

Quiet descends once again, and we all home in on Vincenzo. He's rattling his chains where he's fastened to his metal chair. Boy, oh boy. It's all fun and games, until it isn't.

I go stand in front of him and take in the goosebumps spreading on his marbled skin. He seems to be almost blue with cold, but it's only fear. "Vincenzo Trapani, it would seem Franco Fiore's plans didn't work out, and you're pretty fucked."

He shudders, and I shoot a glance to Matteo where he's standing to the side with Luca and Benedict in tow.

"Tell me what you know about Ariana Morelli," I ask, stepping up to him and putting my foot down on his bare toes. No pressure, but the hint is there. At least he pissed himself already—there's no chance he'll do so now and splatter some on my legs.

"I don't know, man. Franco didn't let me in on all his business dealings."

I put some weight on his foot, and he groans. I'm a big man. I can break the bones in his feet if I want to. "So what *did* he tell you?"

"She's some mafioso's daughter, but he never told me who. Some big shot."

"Any names you care to share?"

"Fuck man, I dunno? It's the fucking Mafia. In Italy. Every area has its capos; there are many big shots. Being Don Trapani's son, I was above the fucking fray."

I glance at Matteo, and he gives me a cocked brow. This guy is a fucking arrogant idiot, going around the world as if he's royalty.

"There're capos aplenty, but was this guy a Don?" Matteo asks. "From Italy?"

Vincenzo grunts as I put more pressure on his foot.

"I dunno. Franco planned to marry her at some point, when they were much younger."

This makes me reel back on the pressure a bit. Imagine the life Ariana would have led as that maniac's wife. "What happened?"

"She ran away." Vincenzo breaks out into a grim chuckling fit, one that shoots the hairs on my arms up in chills. "But he found her." Now he laughs out right. "Funny thing, he said he always knew exactly where she was, but he waited for the right moment to strike. Like a snake."

He looks up at me, and the admiration in his eyes for Franco Fiore is too much. How could this man be Gigi and Carla's brother? Just imagine if Franco got what he wanted. And he so almost had.

I can see it now, how Franco was literally living in an

underworld until his time had come. And then he messed with the wrong people. I reach for Vincenzo's throat and circle my hand around it. With a little squeeze, I choke the laughter right out of him, and he starts to wheeze in desperate breaths.

"And when was this?" I ask, letting go just enough for him to answer my question.

"Fuck, man. Weeks ago," Vincenzo croaks. With a shrug, he drops his head back, preparing to spit on me, but I close his throat again, and it's a battle for air. Human nature dictates you'll always breathe first.

"And then?" I ask, less kind in my prompting now as I step with both feet on his, not sparing him any of my weight.

"We made the deal that made Ariana Morelli obsolete," he croaks. "Gigi." He laughs again, sinister and cruel. "Franco brought me to see her, to offer her to me...but he was just fucking with her. She was his prize. He was going to kill her as soon as his ring was on Gigi's finger."

His prize...

"Good thing that never happened," I hiss. "Tell me, you piece of shit, now that Franco is dead—" I break off, because this would be news to him. Vincenzo has been locked up for some time in here. I feel the change in his pulse where my thumb is pressing against it, speeding up. "Yes, you fucking prick, Franco is dead by our hand. What are the consequences for Ariana Morelli?"

He stares at me, the life seeming to drain out of him. "Franco? Dead?"

I don't bother to answer, just firming my hold. "Answer the fucking question. What hold does he have on her? What would happen on that side when he dies?"

Vincenzo closes his eyes, and I know this move. Resignation. Nobody is coming for you. This is really the end.

"I don't know."

Which is the standard answer when you're dumb enough to be *above the fucking fray* in this world we rule.

"In my opinion, we're done here," I say as I look toward Matteo for authorization to end Vincenzo once and for all.

"What about a Gabriella Scalera?" Matteo asks now as he steps up.

It takes a full minute for Vincenzo to come back to life. He takes in Matteo and then shakes his head. "Never heard of her before."

"We'll let you think about it for a day or two," I say, letting go of his throat where days of beard must be itching like a motherfucker. My finger's imprints have discolored the skin already. He will die with those bruises. All I want is to wash his filth off my hands now. "Do yourself a favor and think over those two last questions carefully."

37

ARIANA

Portia reaches into the hole between the exposed floorboards and pulls out two packets of sealed moleskin notebooks. At a quick glance, I'd say there must be at least twenty of them.

"To think she still did this, wrapped them carefully just like they are now and sealed them herself."

With reverence, she wipes the dust off the plastic Ziplock bags, but there's more. Ribbon with a wax seal that has never been tampered with. Portia kept her word.

She hands me a packet, and I'm suddenly weak with the weight of secrets carried between these pages.

"These are the older ones," I say, noticing a small square of discolored paper with the years written in pencil on it. "You must have the more recent ones. Where do we start?"

"Ideally, we need to read all of them to get the full picture. Right from the beginning," Portia says as she forces a nail between the ribbon and the wax to rip it apart. "But let's just figure out what was going on in her mind during that last trimester."

She rips open the Ziplock and pulls out a stack of moleskins. They seem to be ordered by date, because she hands me one and keeps the one right at the bottom of the stack with her. Even from here, I can see the journal she's holding was never fully used. Where all the others show signs of complete wear with all the pages flipped and written in at one point, the one she's holding looks almost new.

As I open my journal, a photo slides out and to the floor.

Portia reaches for it. "Heavens, there's so few photos of them. Here, put a face to the name," she says, pointing to the old photo. "This is Bianca Randazzo on her wedding day to Don Scalera. See, there's Randazzo."

Bianca *Randazzo*? Heavens help me. Was she his cousin, his sister? My stomach seems to drop to the floor. Here it is—the whole connection captured in a fleeting moment.

"Were you there?" I ask, somewhat breathless, trying to hide my shock.

"No, but she showed me this photo once."

I take it from her, my fingers quivering. *Randazzo.* I haven't seen an image of him in decades. This one is taken from his side, and that tell-tale notch in his ear is clearly visible. Just looking at him like this tenses me up with fury, and I exhale with strain, trying to keep a hold on my emotions. Now isn't the time.

Instead, I focus on Bianca. She was beautiful with lush chestnut hair, tanned olive skin, dark eyes, deep and somehow mournful in this casual wedding photo. But it's Don Scalera's face that pulls me in the deepest. Dominic is the spitting image of his father, if a much taller hulk of a man.

Something shifts in me. *Relief.* Deep, foundation-shaking relief. There's no chance we're related. Neither the same mother, nor the same father.

I slot the photo back into my journal as Portia opens hers with a sniff.

"This is dated six weeks before she went into labor." Her eyes skim the lines.

I lean in to look closer, but she's already flipped the page. She trembles with a few suppressed gasps, then goes over into big heaving sobs. Tears run and splatter down on the page as she grips the notebook.

"Portia—" I murmur, reaching for her hand. This woman is reliving trauma, and I so wish I could spare her.

"I can't...I just can't—" she cries out between sobs. "I can't do this. I've never been able to do it. It's like taking a blunt knife and carving into my heart. I knew she suffered, oh, God, how I knew it, but to see it like this—" She brings her hands together in prayer, closing the journal in the process as she brings it up to her face, already trapping her tears on some of the pages. "You know, after the twins, the doctor told her to never have more babies as it would kill her. And then, she was blessed with Benedict. I don't know what Don Scalera was thinking, getting her pregnant again." With a wild sniff, she looks at me, tears glazing her eyes. "I can't read this."

"So let me," I say, feeling shredded by the power of her emotions. Already, I sense there's a stronger connection between me and this family than I ever thought possible, but Portia lived this time with Bianca and her sons, now grown men. She witnessed Bianca's abuse, her pregnancies, and her last days... God, I totally understand why she can't do this. "Just let me. I don't have the same connection to Bianca as you had."

She nods, tears not stopping. "This is why you're here. This is why God send you to us. To right this wrong that was made decades ago." Her grip loosens on the moleskin, and I gently take it from her. "God works in mysterious ways."

And sometimes, he doesn't work at all. But I keep this thought to myself. As I open the book, Portia slumps back against the wall, looking completely exhausted. Who knows what battles she's been fighting since learning of Gabriella's existence.

I open the first page. It is just a blank journal, and Bianca wrote the date on the top of each page on which she made an entry. I take a quick glance over a few pages. Some days, the entries are a line or two; some days, there are pages. If this was six weeks before she went into labor, then she didn't write much. She must have been exhausted and anxious, clearly not supposed to be pregnant at all, and waiting in dread to see if this birth would finally be one too much.

"Read aloud, will you?" Portia whispers at me from her side of the walk-in closet, where we've cut ourselves off from the rest of the world.

"Okay," I whisper and turn back to the first page:

I can't. I can't anymore. My anxiety for my little girl, for my Gabi, is too much. I know they'll save her because I'm done. I know I'm not surviving this one and I've signed the papers. I don't even have the strength to push her into this world. Already this is so much worse than with Benedict, and I can't bear looking at my sons, knowing I'm leaving them to fend for themselves.

I swallow. "Papers? What papers did she sign?"

"Like a living will," Portia says. "I witnessed it. A legal document forcing the doctor to save the baby if it becomes a decision between saving her or the baby. She had the same in place with Benedict."

A shudder passes through me, having never heard of such a thing before, but in this world, anything is possible. What was this poor woman going through? I jump to the next entry.

The last thing I ever wanted was to bring a girl into this world, to fulfill the final term and condition of the sick pact they made. If only

I could have died with Benedict as was the plan, this would never have come to pass.

I glance up at Portia, and she's stilled, taking in the words, putting them in a context I don't have.

"Benedict. Do you actually think she fell pregnant with Benedict in the hope to—" I break off, unable to say the words.

"No, that was just wishful thinking. The Don didn't stop with her. Ever. It was just a matter of time."

I wipe at my cheek, the cruelty of Dominic's dad being hammered into me from all sides today. "What do you think she means with final term and condition of the pact they made?"

"I don't know. We'll have to read the rest. I told you, to get the big picture here is going to take time." She glances at her watch. "Can you scan through it? Find the salient parts."

"Okay." I skim over several pages during which Bianca only makes short entries, mostly about her sons. She skips many days and doesn't write anything.

When I come to the last entry, I give it a quick glance before I read it for Portia. "This is the last one in this journal." In a way, her final words to the world.

Giuliano came to me tonight. We haven't spoken in days. I'm bedridden and he hates that. I'm too weak to fight him, and when he came in peace, I had to listen. We spoke about all the things that happened. Quietly. For the first time in years. It's as if he knows this is the end.

I refuse for Gabi to go to Italy, but she will. She must. Giuliano will honor that pact but promised me that he will reward my loyalty to him. He'll make sure she'll only go when she is older, and that when she goes, she'll be as safe as possible. For as long as he can keep her safe, forcing Emilio's hand, he will do so.

It's the least he could do, given that both his and Emilio's sons are in this house, born from my womb. They've had each other in this chokehold for years, stags who fought each other, antlers caught in a deadlock from which they can't escape. The least they can do is to care for the little girl they forced me to have. A son for a son. A daughter for a daughter. One for one.

Until death us all part. And then she'll have six brothers to find her.

Finally I can rest in peace.

"Oh my God," I whisper, reading the last paragraphs again and again.

Portia is crossing herself, eyes closed, lips murmuring in prayer.

"What does this mean?" I ask, not sure I even want to know. Do the Scalera brothers even know?

"The fucking Mafioso," Portia grits through her teeth. "Always putting revenge first. No wonder people can't move on. Retaliations, blood, and murder! Vendettas that spread over several generations. I'm so sick of it."

"Portia," I say, reaching for her arm to calm her, but inwardly wanting to shake her in urgency. She's working the gold cross hanging from a thin chain by her neck to smithereens, stalling. "What does this mean?"

"Oh, I'll tell you want it means! Emilio Randazzo killed Giuliano Scalera's first family. His first wife and his first-born son. The woman he apparently loved. In revenge, Giuliano killed Emilio's wife. When they made that pact for peace, Emilio must have promised to give him back a son, but in turn, Giuliano will give him a girl. One to replace Bianca, his little girl Emilio offered in marriage as truce. The original *piccola ragazza,* whom Giuliano agreed to marry and guarantee peace between the families."

At those words, the final piece falls into place and my stomach twists. Bianca was Emilio Randazzo's *daughter*? The wedding photo—

God help me, I'm going to be sick. This means he—

"Emilio forced Bianca to marry Giuliano, so there would be a blood relation to keep the peace. As if we live in medieval times," Portia says, wiping at her eyes. "But she was never anything to him. Least of all blood. He kidnapped her off the streets in Napoli as if nobody would notice. She was never his own child. Nothing but a street urchin, ready for the picking. Just like I was at sixteen. Only...she was so much younger."

I sag into myself, fist to my stomach. Bianca was just another trafficked girl. *The original.* The prototype. And the last man who called me his little girl in that tone was Franco. All these men with their little girls and this sick ring that I was trying to crack and failed at.

Portia's tears are flowing again now, and I close my eyes, trying to appear calm and not succumb to my own inner turmoil. I need to digest everything I've learned. And then I feel them, dripping down to my hand where I'm still clutching the journal tight, my tears now threatening to run the ink of this truth none of us are ready for.

'Both his and Emilio's sons are in this house, born from my womb.'

I have half-brothers here amongst the Scaleras.

Franco wasn't lying.

38

DOMINIC

When I walk into the Don's house in the late afternoon, Bruno isn't lying in wait for me as usual. With a pang of disappointment, I follow the security guard's hint that the women are in the kitchen with my dog.

My dog.

What the actual fuck. When did I make this mind shift?

With a shrug, I make my way to the kitchen where Ariana immediately looks up as I come through the door. She's pale, and although she musters a smile, it's clear she's drained.

Portia is at the kitchen island, grating cheese. Bruno is pert and alert at her feet, gazing blindly up at her to where his nose leads him. Pancetta. A whole pile of it cubed. I bet she gave him some...and not just a taste.

"Nicky," Portia says in greeting as she drops a thick slice of Pecorino Romano cheese to the floor for Bruno.

The dog is on it like a starved beast.

"Portia..." I groan. "Bruno is only supposed to have raw bison. I've stacks of it in the freezer, and the guys know to feed him nothing else."

"Raw *bison*?" Portia says, offended. "This dog?"

"Yes! He's been farting for over a decade, and I can't take it anymore. All the other shit people feed him messes with his gut microbiome. So I decided to go back to his origins and first foods to see if it helps. Bison. Or deer. Rabbit. Nothing else. All raw."

Portia cusses under her breath. "Have you lost your mind? Bruno is Italian! Why would he eat anything raw? Least of all American wild meat! Full of worms and parasites!"

"It's farmed organic bison," I retaliate, equally offended. "And he hasn't fart-bombed me out of a room for weeks. But now—" I cut myself short. It's going to be a proverbial shit show what with the raw bison deep cleanse he's had. That cheese smells like trouble already. Bruno is going to have to sleep outside tonight.

Portia looks like she's been through the wringer, too, and it strikes me this homey scene in front of me has been staged. Portia as always in the kitchen, Ariana measuring out flour on a scale, but something is off.

"What did you find?" I ask, going straight for the target. "Tell me you found something?"

"Nothing," Portia says with a sigh that sounds a bit forced as she keeps grating. "Dominic, this house is humongous. The housekeeper hasn't been here for weeks to do a proper job, and without oversight, the staff is lazy."

"So you cleaned instead?"

"Just a bit—" She shoots me a glance before she looks down at the cheese grater again.

"You know we have a missing sister out in the world—"

"Yes, Nicky, we're all fully aware." Portia gives me her back as she turns to the stove, and my heart sinks.

It's been twenty-two years. For all we know she's dead, and a few more hours won't matter. And I'm still waiting for the DNA results. Apparently, I'm getting them in the morning.

I'm annoyed that a whole day has passed without a shift in

anything or any new information. Except for this fucked-up situation with Ivan Petrov, or his dad, Igor. I don't know either of these men, and the whole fucking day, it's been eating at me that there will be a retribution, that *Il Consiglio* doesn't have anything we're willing to give up, and that Matteo is going to see Ariana as an easy solution. If she isn't a blood relation, he'd give her up if Ivan would have her without a blink if it means we don't take a slice off our territories.

Over my dead body.

With a quiet sigh, I shut the door on my workday and close the gap between us. "What are you making?"

Ariana looks up at me. "Fresh pasta. Fettucine. Portia got all the ingredients delivered for a carbonara, so..."

"So she can technically go home? As I rather like making pasta," I ask *sotto voce* as I take hold of the backrest of her stool.

"Thank God," Portia huffs, already at the strings of her apron. "It's been hot today, and I need to water my garden, otherwise those beans will be good for nothing but compost. I'll leave you to Bruno and his farts."

She's over-exaggerating her movements as if her words weren't enough. I soften immediately. She is, after all, the woman who stepped onto the battlefield when Mom died. Portia tried her best. Not that she was allowed much, but she never gave up on us.

"Thanks for coming in," I say, padding over to give her a side hug. "And for being here at the crack of dawn, and for dusting, and for vacuuming, and for looking after Ariana."

She harrumphs as she glares up at me in mock anger. "You're welcome, Nicky. Dr. Wong was here. All is good with Ariana's wound. But you need to feed her, therefore the carbonara."

I smile at Ariana, and she blushes right on cue. If it weren't for the drained look on her face, I'd say she already looks better since Portia's been feeding her.

"Of course I'll make sure she eats." I drop a peck of a kiss on her grey curls. She's so much shorter than me, I have her completely under my arm. "I owe you one."

"Yes, you do," she teases with a quirked brow.

As I let her go, a silent exchange passes between the two women which I don't miss at all. Portia hands me the apron, grabs her purse where she parked it this morning, and waves herself off.

"I'll see you in the morning."

"Thank you, Portia," Ariana calls to her back as she rushes out of the kitchen.

Someone is way too eager to leave. Portia's running from something, and it isn't Bruno's flatulence.

Right on cue, Bruno slumps to the floor, rips his first pancetta-and-cheese-induced fart, and I drop my head back with a groan. "Fuck me. I need a drink."

"Oof." Ariana hops off her chair and goes to the stove where she puts on the extraction fan. "This will help."

"The only thing that helps is having him out of the house." I call for a guard down the corridor, and the man comes to lead away the reluctant dog. I give Bruno a hard stare as he gives me *those* eyes. Yep, it's been more than a month of raw bison, and clearly, Bruno was enjoying having Portia and her tidbits too much, but— "I'm not cooking with you in the kitchen."

I strip my suit jacket as I watch the dog slink off. I've long ago lost the tie and now take off my shoulder holster and safeguard the gun before I put it all on a side counter then walk over to the wine fridge. "Red or white? I always feel carbonara can swing either way."

Ariana shrugs. "White? You know I don't drink—"

"When in captivity. I know." I reach for a bottle of chardonnay and get two glasses. It's been a long day, and from what I've seen, she needs to loosen her tongue. "So you two got along?"

"Portia and me? Yes, totally. Especially since she didn't wield a gun at me."

"Ha. She takes no prisoners, that's for sure."

I place the wineglasses in front of her and search for a corkscrew in a drawer. I get busy uncorking the wine, overly conscious of her gaze studying my hands, homing in on my pinkie, which for once, molds to the object I'm holding. I can still feel her touch as she traced the ring around it in the dark, asking what happened. My response of how she'll need to earn that answer.

She could have guessed it already, with everything that happened this morning at the swimming pool. I still feel her hand on my side, my fingers resting on the scars on her lower belly. It was a level of intimacy I've never experienced with a woman before. Nobody who has crossed my path over the years had been through this exact thing.

I can't afford to get close to her. Intimacy on that level isn't my thing. It's too dangerous. I'm too needy. It will weaken me and make me lose focus on what I'm here to do: protect my family.

With a sigh, I pop the cork, and to reel myself back to reality, I tally the things that have been off with this woman from the start.

One: Randazzo's seal for his prostitutes on her body but shy as a virgin.

Two: knows how to use a gun and as alert as gazelle getting a whiff of lion.

Three: has a need to run away, even though she knows it's futile and that she's stuck, which she knows because...

Four: clearly, she's from a Mafia background, but not keen to talk about it. This one is protecting someone or something.

After this morning's work, I'm not in the mood for another interrogation, but here we are.

"You're back early," she says as I pour her a glass. "Portia hoped to have everything ready by the time you got home."

I top up my wine and hold the glass up to her for a toast.

"After Matteo's, I went to the office." I needed a reminder that I've got some control over something after getting rid of the last of the Ukrainians in our care. "Everything's going smoothly so I came back early to see if you two were productive."

I watch how she picks up the smooth crystal, leaving perfect fingerprints right where I want them.

"Office?" she asks as she tips her glass to mine with a soft *salute*.

"*Salute*." I take a sip. "I own a security company which I run outside of *Il Consiglio*."

Her eyes widen. "A real one?"

"Yes, sweetheart, a real legit company with a physical street address and an office folks can walk into. Not just an obscure postal address. It even has thousands of reviews on Google. The whole nine yards."

"Oh, wow. How did you manage that?"

It's the easiest thing to answer in the world. Maybe not the easiest answer to stomach, but it's the truth. "When you've done what I have, your biggest fear is that someone you care for, someone you love, falls into the hands of someone like me. To protect my brothers became a bit of an obsession after Alex—our brother who came just after Matteo—got killed in a shootout. The Don knew where to channel my fears, and I have a knack for tech, so..."

"So..."

I smile at the way she teases me. "So I started a security company to protect them, over and above the usual protection we have, but I'm not client-facing. I have a back office at our premises and have a team in place who runs the show." I reach for the bowl of flour she had measured out on the scale and the eggs. "When things are going well, I spend a lot of time there."

"And when things are not going well?"

"You already know what I do when things aren't going well." Which brings me to the real reason why I'm early. "Are you going to tell me what you and Portia discovered, or am I going to have to tease it out of you?"

39

ARIANA

Oh, God, Portia. What have you made me promise?

I'm clinging to my wineglass as if it's the only thing preventing this ship from sinking. Dominic's teasing, in that gentle tone, is the last thing I need.

He must have picked up on something, despite us being so careful to act normal, to just be ourselves, but he is an expert at reading people.

'Just one night. Please, Ariana, just give me one night before we tell them everything we've found.'

After reading through the last journal, Portia and I went back and skimmed through the earlier ones, racing against the clock. We couldn't spend too much time in the walk-in closet, in case the guard got suspicious.

"You understand what this means?" she whispered to me. "There are people who know where this little girl went. Capos in *Il Consiglio*. There's no way Gabriella went missing without somebody knowing."

As we swiped through the pages in a hushed rush, trying to find any information we could, the tension and anxiety in that room became so suffocating, as if we were being vacuum-sealed.

There is a massive gap: Bianca didn't journal from the start. She only picked it up once the twins were born. As to the pact, this sick truce between Giuliano Scalera and Emilio Randazzo, there were no more details and zero information as to what happened to baby Gabriella once she was born.

We sat defeated, journals scattered all around us, when Portia gasped in such shock and horror, I reeled back.

"Oh my...oh my God," she whispered under her breath, fresh tears brimming from her eyes as she clutched at her golden cross again. "The dates... her birth...this...*this* is why he left me."

I froze, holding a breath. "Left you? Who?"

Now the sluices of the dam opened properly. The last thing I expected today was this. Portia's heart breaking in front of me.

"Rosalia's dad, my husband...this...*this godawful secret* is why he left me and told me he couldn't see us anymore. That things were getting too tough at work, and he had to move and—"

I pulled her into my arms, and for a long while, we just sat as she sobbed and clung to me, sputtering out a fractured love story through haggard, painful breaths. A story about a man she loved once, the father of her own little girl, a man who was forced to leave them. And now it dawned on her that he left to protect *them*. From Don Scalera's dirty secret he was the sole custodian of. And her working in the Don's household all these years, pouring all her love into those boys, not knowing their dad was the reason for her own heartbreak.

Eventually, she pulled away on a hiccup. "*Cara*, we must tell Dominic, but you understand that I need to...that I need to protect him, we're not even divorced—" She broke off, gasping between breaths. "This was his way to protect me. God. If I only understood—"

Clearly, Portia had never recovered from this loss as her voice cracked with emotion.

"Yes, yes, I get it. Completely," I managed as I tried to soothe her. "It's okay, we don't need to say anything yet."

"Ariana," she whispered then, leaning close to my ear, as if the walls were listening in...which they might be doing from my experience with this crowd. "The Scaleras will never hurt you. They will never hurt me. But they will pull the limbs off men who know something about Gabriella. I need to go see him to warn him. Maybe he'll talk now? It's been twenty-two years. And with Don Scalera dead...maybe, just maybe..." She pushed me at arm's length, and I rested back on my heels as she stared into my eyes as if the whole world hinged on me. "We cannot talk about this, not until I've warned him. Just one night, promise me, one night."

"Why don't you phone him?" I whispered back. "Right now."

Portia's gaze volleyed between my eyes as she shook her head, frantic. "From here, on my company phone? While I'm in Bianca's closet?" She was quivering all over now and scrambled to gather the journals and seal them in those plastic bags again. "Are you mad? What if they trace the call and—and—"

"It's okay, I get it," I said.

But now with Dominic here, I get it even more.

Dominic owns a security company, and this is why I couldn't whack a security guard on the head and walk out of a private clinic in Boston. In the clinic, the cameras are so well-hidden, I never saw one. In Bianca's walk-in closet, there aren't any cameras, because if there were, Dominic would have been here hours ago, because he has a *knack for tech* and someone might be watching our every move.

I'm trapped under so many secrets, I can hardly breathe... and Dominic is threatening to tease them out of me? I shouldn't drink. I should keep my head clear, but he's here, his tall, masculine frame towering next to me, his elbow brushing against my arm as he unbuttons his cuffs and rolls up his sleeves.

With every fold of the fabric, he reveals more of his muscled forearms, my gaze taking in those strong but elegant hands that touched me with such delicate reverence at the swimming pool this morning. I completely forgot this man can be brutally cruel.

In fact, I can't weave his gentle side and cruel side together at all. I suck my lip, knowing I'm in too deep. I'm treading water, battling a tide I only want to be swept away with, straight into his arms...the last place I should be.

Portia's parting words to me as we put back the baseboards repeats in my head, and I swallow another desperate sip of wine to pull myself together.

"You need to divert his attention, cara. *I've seen how he looks at you, Ariana... Please. I've also seen how you look at him. Just one night. He already has you in his bed, and even though I know nothing happened last night, and I'll never push you to do something you don't want to... but Dominic never has women stay over, or in his bed for that matter, and you...you have Randazzo's seal on your body. Please—"*

I had to stop her from talking before I lost my mind. How do I look at Dominic? How does he look at me?

As he walks over to the sink to wash his hands, I scan his body, his posture, his profile, the way his hair falls forward over his forehead. I've been desperately studying him, looking for anything that might spark my memory of Randazzo, but the photo we found with the journals showed me Dominic isn't Randazzo's son. I'd hazard a guess he's ninety-nine percent Guiliano Scalera's offspring. But is that enough? Not with the fresh knowledge of my half-brothers in the mix.

Never mind our family dynamics, the seal of Randazzo is a temporary tattoo, made to last only a few months.

Then there's the sad fact that beyond being assaulted by Franco, I've never had sex with anybody.

That Portia suggested I seduce Dominic to keep his mind and body occupied is such a joke, now that I'm alone with him, I break out in a nervous giggle. I wouldn't know where to start. In fact, my inexperience petrifies me.

Dominic looks up from where he's doing a surgeon's job washing his hands. "What are you laughing about?"

I drag in a strained breath, forcing my gaze to stay locked with his. "There's nothing to tease out of me," I lie. "We really did spend the day ferociously cleaning. Once Portia got started, she got a bit obsessed."

Because Portia had to do something to kill time, to digest and organize her scramble of thoughts after her epiphany in that closet.

And so did I.

I might be sitting on the biggest pile of secrets here as it is—adding Portia's hardly makes a difference—but my own discovery makes me want to curl back inside a shell I don't have. And with Dominic here, I'm even more open and exposed because he knows things about me that I've never told anybody before. Things that hurt so much, sometimes, I still feel bruised, deep inside my core.

A hurt I really want to shed. With him. Those hands...his voice...the way he touched me. His suggestion that he could help me overcome what Franco had done to me—

The last thing I want is for him to be my brother, because I want him to guide me to the space where I can live with being broken.

40

ARIANA

"So we just make dinner, then," Dominic says as he reaches for a dishcloth to dry his hands. "Portia has prepped all the sauce ingredients, and that takes just a minute. So…it's just the pasta."

"She's very efficient," I say, trying not to look too relieved we're now on safer ground.

I'm fooling nobody here. Until the last secret is out, there is no such thing as safer ground. Only once I'm back in Italy and can disappear, away from this whole mess, would I really consider myself safe.

Dominic comes to stand by my side again and pours the flour onto the marble countertop. I watch as he makes a bowl in the flour and crack the eggs into it. He takes a fork and whisks them in slowly.

"You're a real pasta pro, here, aren't you," I say, feeling exactly as redundant as I did earlier with Portia. She walked into the kitchen and started prepping as if she's a master chef on the clock, which I suppose she'd become out of necessity, feeding a house full of boys.

"I like the ritual of it, the tradition, using my hands," he says without looking up.

Those hands...they're mesmerizing. And he's so good with them. "Who taught you?"

"Portia. I bet she wanted a big family of her own, but instead, she got stuck with ours. She only has one daughter. Rosalia. She works for Matteo."

"Keeping it in the family, aren't you," I tease, biting my lip to hide that I probably heard the real story behind all of that today.

"It's the Mafia way," he says, turning to me with a crooked smile, and then booping my nose with a forefinger smudged with flour.

"Dominic!" I say in mock horror as I wipe my nose, glaring up at him as the flour dusts to my T-shirt.

"Dang. You looked cute with that," he says as his gaze drops to my lips, and lower, then slowly returns from my breasts all the way up to my lips and eventually my eyes.

This man. I feel the invasive heat of a blush as my nipples harden right on cue. He's flirting with me. Easily, light, playful flirting. Everything our lives are not. His whole being is an incongruous mess. About as much as that raw egg and flour blob he is mixing into shape.

I need to get space between us—lots of space—because I swear the next thing he is going to want to do is kiss me, and I —I—

I swallow down the need to feel those warm lips on mine, the scruff of his five-o'clock shadow brushing against my delicate skin.

"What do I do?" I ask as I get off the stool so at least that is between us.

"Set up the pasta roller," he says, unfazed, cool and calm, nodding to where Portia placed it on the counter earlier. "And start boiling the water. It always takes a while to get ready."

I tap hot water into the big pasta pot and put it on the stove to a high heat. Once I've set up the pasta roller, I watch him from afar as he kneads the dough. He is strong and makes quick business of the process, his muscles flexing in his forearms and the veins on his hands etching out hard with each move.

Once he's done, he gives the round ball of dough a loving pat as if it's a woman's ass, and now I want it to be mine. I'm so out of whack when it comes to this man, my body slowly spinning out of control toward something I never understood. Not after Franco. I reach for my wine and take two gulps.

Oh, God. This is the last thing I want even if it is the first thing I need. And not because he's getting to my body, but because he understands mine...he understands *me*.

Dominic raises a brow as he picks up his own glass and leisurely takes a sip as he stares at me over the rim, enjoying the golden liquid as it hits his tongue. From the wine's taste, it isn't some cheap five-euro chardonnay, either. Not that I've checked the label, but it tastes like pouring liquid money down my throat.

"Looks like you're drinking for Dutch courage, sweetheart." He puts his glass down to pick up the rolling pin and goes over the dough a few times. "Want to talk about it?"

God help us all. He's still onto me. He isn't going to let it go, is he? *One night, Portia? What about one hour?*

I drop my gaze and wipe my hands down my jeans. It's a nervous gesture, and I can kick myself for giving anything away. My training has left the building, walked out as soon as he walked in with his soft gaze and masculine body I touched earlier today, his gentle gestures, his slow, sweet teasing. The whole combination only makes need pool into my panties—panties that've never been this wet.

I seep in a slow breath and then go to the only place that will be safe for Portia's secret. For one night, at least. Only me and him.

"You said earlier—" I pause to blow out some tension that

seems to battle for space in every muscle in my body. "You said earlier that you can try and help me...show me how to live as if I'm...whole again?" I chew my lip when he doesn't immediately respond. Instead, he pauses where he'd been peeling the dough off the counter, never breaking our locked gazes. "How?"

"Ariana—" he starts.

"I know. It's weird. We could definitely be brother and sister, and I—I—"

"Yeah. There's that—"

"We don't need to do anything," I say, flushed all over my body now. "Can you just tell me? What you've done for other women? Because it isn't something I know of or..." I trail off, not sure how to phrase my total lack of experience and only want to puddle to the floor in embarrassment which isn't feigned at all.

We're staring at each other, and his gaze softens so much, I have to look away. No man has ever looked at me like this.

Eventually, he picks up the dough and comes over to where I've stationed the pasta roller. He reaches for some flour and dusts it over the adjacent surface.

"I'm a service dominant, sweetheart," he says simply, as if there isn't a whole box to unpack there.

"And what does that mean? You're into BDSM and stuff like that?"

He smiles but doesn't look at me as he sets the machine to its thickest setting.

"Stuff like that, hmm?" he jokes gently. "BDSM is a very broad spectrum, sweetheart, and no, I'm not into most of what that spectrum covers." He feeds the sheet of pasta through the machine, and I wait as he does it a few times, shaping it into a long fat slab that would go through the thinner settings with ease. "Hardcore BDSM is too much like the baseline stuff I have to do, but without the sexual edge. It's me dying slowly. Service dominant stuff is what I do to bring me back to life, for living."

My breathing stalls as those words sink into my soul.

Things for dying, things for living... I've only been doing things for dying, so focused on my vendetta with Franco, with Randazzo, with my job of burning down his empire to the ground, that I've never done anything for living. Too scared even to find out what it would be like to be more than a victim of his choices for me.

Dominic spreads the wide ribbon of pasta onto the surface and takes a knife to cut it in half. With a sigh, he leans into the counter to take a deep breath. "The funny thing is, I need it to somehow find my own inner equilibrium again after doing shit like I had to do today and with the guys in the basement—" He breaks off, his jaw working as he seems to fight for a grip over something.

I trap his hand with mine where he is clenching it tight.

"It's okay," I murmur, my heart in my throat.

He looks at me then, shifting his hand to cover my fingers with his instead. Warm and strong but gentle, too. "It reminds me that I wasn't always programmed to be...to be this fucking monster, you know?"

That rogue pinkie of his quivers, where the rest of his hand is steady. We look down at it at the same time, and then he rolls his hand to the side, still holding on to me, but pressing that little finger against the cold marble, forcing it to be still.

"How did you even start? How did you discover this thing you do?" I ask, hesitant now because he seems to be on edge, going through memories.

"Luca," he says as he pulls away to massage his pinkie instead. "My younger brother. He's one of the twins. He's a little shit most of the time, but he knows how to match people. He introduced me to an older woman who knew what she wanted and needed, and he figured I could use the guidance...to do the opposite of everything—"

He closes his eyes, and I feel like crap making him talk

about something he clearly doesn't want to share. "I'm sorry. You don't need to—"

"No," he interrupts softly. "I actually do. You're not the only person out there who never tells anybody anything, sweetheart."

He rolls his shoulders as he drops his head back with a huffed exhale. He has about as much tension in his body as me, and I inch away slightly. Not out of fear, but he seems to need space.

"I was in a really bad space after this," he says as he lifts his hands, his fingers still massaging his pinkie. "And even though everybody picked up on it, Luca was the only one looking to do something that would actually help me."

"How old were you?" I ask, weary to ask questions about things I haven't *earned*.

"I'd just turned twenty."

"What? So young?"

"What do you mean? Luca was eighteen and knew more about sex than a whole brothel at that point." He looks at me and start to chuckle at something he must read in my face. "Don't make saints of any of us, sweetheart, least of all of my younger brothers. Steph, I'll admit, is a solid one-girl guy. Matteo lost his cool just a few months ago...and fuck knows, that man needed to find Tasha. Benedict... Benedict keeps his cards close. But Luca? Luca is a loose fucking cannon." He shakes his head as he fiddles with the pasta maker again. "We all had a very early introduction into that world, complimentary of the Don, and let's just say, some folks live twenty years in eighty. We Scalera boys all lived eighty years by the time we turned twenty."

It's quiet as I digest his words. Dominic is busy with the pasta, rolling the one sheet through a thinner setting and then the next one. He repeats the process while I watch, his hands guiding the pasta with care, until the machine cuts it into thin strips. He piles them onto the counter in small hillocks of fettuccine.

"But what do you actually do?" I ask, because he hasn't answered my question.

"Touch," he says softly as he shoots me a glance. "It's just touch."

"Okay." I still don't understand, except that he shouldn't be allowed to touch me, even if I want him to. Not if he's my brother. There're some sins I'm not coming back from. "Touching isn't on the cards." Not until that DNA test comes through. And then Dominic's whole agenda is going to change. Do a whole one-eighty on me.

He smirks. "Except that you've been touching me, sweetheart. With your eyes." His gaze brushes down my body in the slowest torment of tingles I've ever felt, and then he lifts a finger to my chin and runs it along my jaw. "Everywhere where you want to go...with your hands."

I blink up at him, stunned.

He rolls his finger over, only to gather a few strands of hair from my temple to my ear, spreading goosebumps down my chest and right to my core. "That's how it starts, didn't you know?"

41

DOMINIC

Her skin is so soft, so delicate, I don't want to stop touching her, but I must. I drop my hand and cut away from her gaze. She's staring at me with sparks of lust in her eyes, chewing her plump bottom lip and basically driving me fucking crazy.

I reach for the wine to top off her glass and distract us both. I'm not even sure she's aware of what she's doing to me. First, she asks that poignant question, and then—

Fuck.

What I really want to do is show her. Lift her onto this counter and ghost over every inch of skin she's got exposed with my lips. Warm breath flowing on cooler flesh, spreading goosebumps like wildfire over her body. Strip her slowly until she's only in a pair of panties that's probably already so wet there'll be no resistance sliding a finger into her tight pussy.

I want to feel where she's at. Smell her need. Taste her. I want to wrap her legs around my hips, carry her to the bedroom, tie her up, and slowly explore her body, tearing down her every last defense so gently, she'll offer herself to me. And then I'll make her come. Again and again. But softly, with care, and on her terms. Terms she hasn't even discovered yet.

Bar her experience with Franco Fiore, this woman is all innocence, stymied due to what happened one night long ago. She's never been a prostitute, otherwise she wouldn't have any of these questions. I'm starting to suspect the tattoo on her lower belly is a fake, and I don't like the segue this thought leads me to, so I brush it off.

The question is really when did she step into character, and when did she slip out of it, subconsciously? And what role is she playing?

"I'll start the sauce," she murmurs as she turns away to the stove, leaving her wine untouched.

"Yes. The pasta is ready."

It's quiet between us as she pan-fries the pancetta. I wrap up the pasta and do a preliminary job of wiping down the counter. The space fills with pancetta's smokey flavor, and I pad over to watch what she's doing.

I place the mountain of finely grated Pecorino next to her. As the water is boiling, I lower the pasta bundles into it and shake the pot. "This is going to be quick."

"I'm ready for you," she says as she stirs the pancetta.

Are you, sweetheart? I want to taste the slope where her neck glides into her shoulder, squeeze her ass, but I need to distance myself from this woman. From this tug-of-war tension between us. This maddening desire I already have building for her, which she's only blazed into fire with her questions.

I force my focus on the food. I feel weirdly at home and awkward at the same time. I've never cooked like this with or for a woman before. As if it's a date. As if she's my girlfriend. Or my wife. If she were any of these things, my hands would've been all over her by now.

My life is so compartmentalized that everything is in a box, stacked in such a way I know exactly where what is, contained, ordered, untouchable—safe—until I decide to pull it closer.

Women have their own container, and they are never allowed to come out like this.

The pasta hardly takes two minutes to cook *al dente*, and knowing it will soften more in the sauce, I turn off the heat and drain the water. Ariana steps to the side as I reach over with the dripping colander and slide the pasta into the pancetta mix. She's prepped the egg yolks and now stirs them in with the cheese.

I'm on standby with the pepper mill, and a minute later, the dish is done.

She smiles up at me. "It's as if all Italians are born with this recipe programmed into our minds."

"Probably," I say, handing her two bowls.

She ladles the pasta into the bowls, and we sit down at the kitchen counter to eat.

I twirl up a first bite on my fork. "Here, taste if it's good." I'm playing with her, taking things maybe a bit too far, but I can't stop myself.

It's a neat bite, and she opens for me, trusting, her eyes locked with mine, those sparks of lust still trapped in her gaze.

"Hmm," she moans as she shifts in her seat. "It's delicious."

"Good." I dig in, knowing I should stop. But the whole night stretches out in front of us, and I don't know what I'm going to do with her. Someone needs to keep an eye on her, and I don't trust the guards. Even worse: I don't trust myself.

After a few minutes of quiet eating, she takes a cautious sip of wine. This one likes her Dutch courage, but she still has to spill the real beans behind her day spent with Portia.

"Do you..." she starts and trails off again, staring down at her food, fork still parked in the fettuccine.

"Do I?" I prompt, watching as she slowly turns the fork, wrapping the ribbons around the prongs like I wrapped my ties around her last night.

"Do you tie women up when you..." She glances up at me, pink blooming on her cheeks. "When you do what you do?"

Fuck. Neither of us is letting go tonight, are we? With a soft groan, I give up.

Submissives usually have a lot of questions when they start out, but training subs isn't my thing. I'm not in a regular Dom/sub relationship and have never wanted one, whatever the outside world might think. My approach is almost sterile, but it works for me and keeps things clear and simple. All I need are reference lines, guiding me where to go and where to stop.

Everybody is unique, and I'm the outlier with a lot of things, but it's better for all parties not to get involved in something long-term.

As for Ariana, being restrained is the one thing she's been objecting to from the start.

"Yes," I tell her. "They're tied up, but it isn't about control for me."

"No?"

"It's a different dynamic, Ariana." I've never had to explain this to someone before, but she's asked, so. "It helps people relax because they don't need to do anything. They don't need to perform. They only get to focus on sensation, on desire...and it helps some people learn to trust and let go of fear."

She's quiet for a long time as my answer just hangs in the space. Something I said hit a nerve, because she reaches for her cheek where she surreptitiously wipes at a tear she hopes I don't notice.

"Sweetheart—" Fuck. If she's going to start crying, I'm going to pull her into my arms, and then every part of her is going to test my already frayed resolve.

"But what about you?" she asks, her voice on edge. "They don't get to touch you, and that seems to be key to this whole thing you do. You got hurt, too, you know."

Her question is a punch to the gut, so profound, it almost winds me. Nobody has ever asked me this or even considered me in this equation.

"Yes... But that's because *nobody* gets to touch me." There are rules on both sides.

Except this woman has been bending my rules one by one, scraping through my layers, hitting me hard. I can add that, in fact, they don't get to see me either, but she hasn't asked, so I'm not sharing until she does.

"Don't you like being touched?" she asks, glancing at me.

I can still feel her fingertips exploring every inch of scarred tissue between patches of healthy skin. I've longed for more of it the whole day, of this thing I crave to give others but deny myself.

"Of course I like being touched, sweetheart," I say softly. In fact, I love it, but— "Women's hands roam, and the first place they go are my sides, my back, and then they feel my scars and —" They get put off, revolted, or worse, they get curious. "They have questions. Questions I can't answer without dragging them into my world."

And once they're in, they want out, and there's only one out for most of us.

"I get it," she says, and her tone is defeatist. "Questions are the worst."

No, they're not. Not getting answers is ten times worse. But the worst is getting the answer you don't want. The answer that breaks the world. The answer that's going to break us. I can sense it hovering around us, waiting to shatter our bubble. I don't want to know what comes next.

"I'm so scared that it will hurt...like the first time," she whispers then, shrinking in her chair, curling into herself as if the memory of that night has strings attached to every part of her body, her heart, her soul, and it pulls tight towards where Franco hurt her the most.

How broken are we? I recall her question, and it shreds me afresh.

"I know, sweetheart. And that's what we work on." I brush a knuckle along her arm. She isn't the first woman who has shared these fears with me. And fuck knows what I'm thinking, but it's as if we're negotiating already. "I know pain. I know pleasure. I only go where you let me in, sweetheart, and we test those limits slowly."

"And you'll never hurt me?"

I push my plate to the side. "There's no pleasure for me in pain. Least of all yours. You know I'll never hurt you."

42

DOMINIC

It's been quiet for a long time as she just sits and pokes at her pasta. Maybe she's lost her appetite. Maybe she's had enough. Maybe she's digesting our conversation and has more questions but doesn't know how to ask them.

"What do I do with you now, sweetheart?" I murmur, knowing I need to separate myself from her, even if I now have this engulfing need to hold her close, stroke her hair, kiss her languidly as if time is standing still, and have her fall asleep in my arms.

Aftercare. That's what I want. That's what she needs.

Fuck. That's what *I* need.

And it's the other thing I don't indulge in because it forms a strong emotional bond that doesn't match my rationale. We haven't done anything, but it's as if she's opened all her little doll house windows and allowed me a peek into her inner world, right inside those secret rooms which hold her fears and desires.

When my phone rings in my jacket pocket where I left it on a side counter, I heave a sigh in equal measures of relief and annoyance. It's for the better, though, to have the outside world come in. Right now, both of us have to get our minds off everything that happened in this kitchen—and everything that didn't happen...and what we both still want. There's no misunderstanding this part.

"I'll clean the kitchen," Ariana says as she waves towards the mess we made cooking, and I nod as I stride over to my discarded jacket and answer the call.

"Matteo?"

"What are you up to?" he asks without preamble.

"Just had dinner. Give me a sec." I lean into the corridor and call a guard over to come watch over Ariana while I take his call.

On purpose, I take her half-filled glass of wine by the stem in passing. I make as if it's mine, as if I plan to finish it off while talking to Matteo, and hope she won't notice. She doesn't notice, but gets the drift as the guard walks in and rolls her eyes at me.

Yes, there's trust between us, and promises, but the knife block is right there, and she hasn't alleviated any of my suspicions yet. In fact, she's only made the pile bigger.

"What's up, Matty?" I ask, walking to a lounge where there'll be some privacy. Portia must have thrown caution to the wind, because all the doors that were closed when Ariana arrived now stand open.

"Tasha's been begging me to bring her and Gigi to see Ariana. Add Carla into the mix, and I'm outnumbered and cornered."

He sounds a bit harassed.

"Your calvary has you with your back against the wall?" I joke with a chuckle, but the last thing I need is these women warming up to Ariana while everything is still in the balance.

"I don't want any of them to come to the Don's house," Matteo says. "That isn't happening."

"And I'm not letting Ariana off these premises, either," I

retaliate. "Not until we have some answers. It's the safest place we have bar your apartment—"

"Fair enough," he cuts me off. "It isn't going to happen then, because the Trapanis are leaving for Italy. If Ariana comes here, Tasha will only convince me to let her stay—"

"And you only want to fuck your wife on every surface you have in that apartment without an audience. I get it." I really do. Fuck. I rake a hand through my hair, cussing inwardly.

"Good. We understand each other. How are things going there?" he asks as I start pacing the room as if I have a nervous fucking tic. Which I have. It's called Ariana Morelli. "Did Portia unearth anything?"

"I don't know. Something's off, and I can't put my finger on it."

"What do you mean?"

"It's just a gut feeling, but Portia couldn't get out of here fast enough earlier. Ariana is definitely sitting on some information she hasn't shared, but she's going to crack. The signs are all there."

"You're speaking in circles, bro?"

I drop my head back to stare at the ceiling, suppressing a groan. "It's just a gut feel, Matty, so just trust me with this, okay?"

"Okay-okay. You know I do."

With a huff, I empty the wine into a potted palm that looks like it needs a drink and place the glass on a side table. "Tomorrow, I'll have the DNA results, and then at least we'll have some answers. I have her fingerprints, and Stan will deliver them to Benedict tonight. Those should be quick, depending on his contacts and how deep they need to dig."

"Good." Matteo sighs into the phone. "What a fucking day."

"You're telling me, bro. I hardly slept last night." And I'm not done yet. "Nothing new from the Petrovs?"

"No, and we're going to ride this wave for as long as possible. When the shit hits the fan, it's going to be fucking spectacular."

True, that. "We're in this together."

"Yep. Teamwork makes the fucking dream work. Let me have those results when you get them."

"Will do."

We ring off, and for a moment, I stare at my phone's screen. We're all on edge with this situation, and going around Ariana's back to get info on her doesn't exactly sit well with me, but in my world, closed books get pried open. I'm going about it as if she's a treasured ancient manuscript.

The one side of the lounge is covered with bookcases and cupboards at the bottom, and I open them at random to look for a container to put Ariana's wineglass in. I find an old shoebox with instruction booklets for dated electronics. I tear the booklets into separate pages and scrunch them up to form some padding for the box. Once I've nestled the glass between the paper, I close the lid. I phone Stan with instructions, and by the time I've walked to the front door, he's waiting for me.

"Get this to Benedict right now. Move it as little as possible. It's fragile."

"Yes, boss."

I wait for Stan to drive off and take in the garden in the last of the late summer's light. There's no sign of Bruno, but the security detail with their Alsatians is patrolling the grounds. It seems excessive right now, but I know how things spin out of control in our world. Better safe than sorry.

When I stroll back into the cleaned kitchen minutes later, Ariana is sitting at the counter, twiddling her thumbs. The security guard stares at her from where he is leaning with his butt against the far-side counter, not taking his eyes off her, his hand resting on the weapon by his waist.

Yep, the word about this woman and how she whacked one

of our men almost into the afterlife with a fire extinguisher has done the rounds.

"It's all good, thank you." I nod to the guard so he can make his exit.

As soon as the man is gone, Ariana looks up at me. My earlier question hangs in the space between us. *What do I do with you now, sweetheart?*

"I'm really tired. Portia worked me to the bone," she says. "Can we just go to bed?"

The way she says this makes me want to smile, but fuck. I'd love nothing more. She should sleep alone, but I bet she doesn't want to be alone, locked up.

"Where are you sleeping, sweetheart? Alone in that small room with a guard outside the door, or in my bed, like last night?"

"You have a really big bed," she says softly, blinking at me as that sweet blush spreads over her cheeks.

Until you're in it, sweetheart. Then it shrinks to all just you. "Yeah."

"I slept properly for the first time in months last night... I know it's weird, but you...you—"

She buries her face in her hands, and my heart pangs as her shoulders shudder with those quiet sobs of hers.

She's been through too much.

"It's fine, Ariana." I'm not sure if I can do two nights of sleep deprivation and still keep shit together, but I'll figure that out tomorrow.

"You make me feel safe, Dominic," she whispers as she wipes at her tears. "I haven't felt safe since my mom died. Least of all with a man." She makes a pathetic little wave between us and shoots me a woebegone smile. "I've never had this before."

That's how simple it is to shatter my resolve, because all I want to do now is to pull her into my arms and prove again and again to her that I am her safe space. That I'm worthy of her, even if deep down, I'm none of these things.

The only thing I've proven to myself is that I'm as weak as any man when it comes to that one woman.

"Come then, sweetheart." I hold out my hand to her, and as she places her warm, slender fingers in mine, it hits me that this woman is going to break me before I can break her.

This one. She's my downfall.

She's going to make me the weakest link.

And I'm not sure there's any way of surviving that.

43

ARIANA

Everything hits different tonight. The way he guides me to his room and leads me inside. Nothing is strange and new like last night, and there's comfort in everything he does.

He steers me to the bathroom where he gives me the privacy I don't crave anymore. I want him to watch me undress. I want him to step with me into the shower. I want to feel his hands on me, soaping me up, massaging, slowly, tenderly until he drops to his knees and kisses me down there where this flight of fancy has taken my mind and where a nagging need has been filling up to bursting point.

Usually, I ignore this feeling, fighting it all the way as I force myself to be consumed by work, but now, I'm wrung tight, every sensual nerve I have poised to receive his touch, with nothing else to distract me. And this is a man in the fucking Mafia.

And not just any Mafia. By the status belonging to this mansion, the most powerful *Borgata* this side of the States.

And not just any man, either. One who wears scars similar to my own, whose story is an echo of mine.

I'm not sure how it happened, but he's corrupted me. I've fallen into trust with Dominic. With the last type of man I ever thought I could trust. With him, I'll let go of my fear, because he understands my pain. He'll take his time. He'll only go where I allow him in.

It's his words. His vows. They make me burn to feel his hands on me, to submit my body to his expert touch, to offer myself to him in some primal and carnal lust I never knew existed, because I'll be safe all the way.

As I soap up in the shower, I let my fingers stray, slip between my thighs, and find the nagging little nub that's the bane of my whole existence right now. I lean away from the spray, my back against the marbled wall, sinking into this need he's provoked in me, basking in it as the steam builds and envelopes me. My breathing becomes strained as I find the exact rhythm that should get me to release, but it's as if I need more.

Dominic pulled the door closed as he left me standing in the middle of this bathroom, but it didn't latch. The idea of him being on the other side of that thin stripe of light, listening to me, his heart pulsing in his cock as it pulses in my clit, drives my movements. As the water sluices down my skin, I close my eyes, arching my back into the wall, needing more. Needing him.

I'm slow to register the change in the room as the door swings wider slowly, dissipating the steam as it shifts and opens like gaps in the clouds. I feel his gaze on me before I open my eyes, in a gridlock of shame and need and lust I have no control over. He's stripping his shirt as he watches me, slow to slide his gaze down to where my hand is working between my legs, the other one on a breast, teasing a hardened nipple.

I pause, wanting to shy away from everything, but my heart seems to be pulsing in every part of my body as my orgasm pulls away. I've been waiting, wanting...needing to sin with this man, and nothing is going to make me stop him from stepping into the shower. I don't care how this all started anymore—all I need is a diversion for tonight.

Truth be told... I need *him*.

His eyes are glazed with desire as I rake him down with my own, from the strained tendons in his neck as he keeps himself in check, biting down on his jaw, lower to his muscled shoulders and pecs, tattooed with images I haven't deciphered yet, then to his six-pack that etches out with the force of his control, to his cock he's fisting...his giant cock that has no place in my body. Not this size, not such force of masculine power that can rip through me and make me bleed for days.

But it's only a glimpse of a thought, a cold draft sweeping through me on which I close the door decisively, making it only a vague memory of something wrong this man said he'll erase until there's only a shadow left of that night. And instead of going where I always go in my head when it comes to this, my thoughts succumb to the control he has over himself as he places one hand against the wall by my head, not touching me, but protecting me from the shower's spray as it comes down on his broad back.

"Fuck, sweetheart," he murmurs as he leans into my ear, his chest heaving with the deep breaths he drags in. "I couldn't stay away. *Fuck*. You're consuming me."

His movements have slowed down, languid pulls to his cock that seem to match my haggard breathing. I'm weak in the knees at having him here, watching me, *consuming* me. At the same time, that pulse is hammering in my clit, demanding attention. His eyes dip to my lips, and I lick them nervously, biting down as I battle the urge to push my body into his.

Sin. This is pure, unforgivable sin. And in this moment, I don't care. Ask me to coast to Hell on the broken wings of a fallen angel, and I'll plunge willingly.

He is so close, I can see each individual eyelash framing his eyes, but we're not touching, his body only radiating heat that seems to cover me in a blanket of love and acceptance.

"Are you going to watch me as I watch you, sweetheart?" he whispers, his breath ghosting over my skin, making my nipples harden even more.

I blink at him as desire flushes through me, the need to look down at where he is fisting his cock, knowing I'm helpless at resisting this. It's only the one percent chance he could be related to me that holds me back from pushing my body to his.

"Are you going to come for me as I'm going to come for you, sweetheart?" he murmurs then, leaning an inch closer and letting the tip of his nose nuzzle my ear.

"God, Dominic, please..." I moan, his words bringing me right back to the edge I've stepped away from.

"Look down, sweetheart. See what you do to me," he says then as he leans back, and I look at our wet bodies, my gaze following the line between his pecs, lower to his abs and then to his cock where it reaches beyond his navel.

The tip glistens with pre-cum, and the veins on his hand bulge as he jerks up and down, so rough with his own flesh, so open in his own need. He is all hard tattooed muscles, his skin this Mediterranean hue I've skipped completely, almost deathly pale against his complexion with a body that hadn't seen proper sun for weeks. I drop my hand to my hip, exposing both my breasts to him, my pert nipples hard and begging.

"Fuck, sweetheart, you're so fucking beautiful," he says as he widens the gap between our bodies to see all of me, the tension between us climbing to the point of no return as his movements become so fast and fluid, they blur with my own frantic circling of my clit. "Let go, sweetheart," he demands then. "Just let go and come for me."

At his words, my orgasm crashes through me with such force, I cry out, fisting my free hand to my mouth to stop myself from calling out his name in desperation.

"Fuck, Ariana," he groans, then hisses as he comes, angling himself at the last second to shoot his release onto the wall beside me.

His body trembles as it comes down its high, his shoulder muscles and biceps straining as he keeps the arm's length between us, his gaze hooked into mine. I'm dazed by his erotic pull, by the intensity of what we've done, with the sweet unknotting of my own release. I want to slide to the floor, feeling weak as I pull my hand away from my sex, slick with my spent desire.

"I want to fucking lick that off you so bad," Dominic says as he pushes off the wall, opening the space between us.

The warm water sprays onto my body again, bringing me back to reality and what we've done.

"I want you to, but this...this already crossed a line." The words tumble out of me on a ragged breath.

"For all we know, there's no line in the first place. And if you think this is a sin... I'm not even sure where sin starts and where it ends anymore."

He reaches for the soap and washes himself as I just stand there, at leisure to take in every inch of his body. And it is magnificent. Strong and virile, with his cock still jutting out. He's perfection.

I want to touch him so badly, but everything I discovered in his mom's journal today is holding me back.

"Keep on looking at me like that, sweetheart—" he murmurs as he rinses off the suds, "—and we'll do all of that again."

"We'll go straight to Hell," I say, as if I haven't been there already.

"All I know is that sin has never felt this good." He smiles at me as he opens the shower door. "And it would be fun burning together."

44

DOMINIC

I get out of the shower and reach for a towel. As I wrap it around my waist, Ariana steps underneath the water to rinse off.

Fuck, she's gorgeous. I can't stop staring. Pale skin, small pert breasts with rosy nipples that are hard, jutting out in perfect peaks. My thumbs burn to massage them, my hands itch to caress her body, flowing with the route the water takes, slowly, testing every inch of her for a reaction so I can get to know her intimately.

Something in my gut feel about today has to do with the fact that she declared we could definitely be brother and sister, something she's denied from the moment we met. Fuck me. If I ever feel about a sister like I do about her—never mind sexually, but with a heart that beats heavy with an emotion I'm unfamiliar with and which I'm not ready to categorize—the devil can have my skin to wear as a trophy.

Tomorrow is the day we cross that bridge, and I'll keep my hands off her until then. As for what I'll do to her when those results come through...fuck knows how I'm going to contain myself if they're positive. Fuck knows how I'm going to contain myself if they're negative.

I'm fucked either way.

And irrespective of what happens tomorrow, I already feel as if I won't be able to let her go if I need to. If she's our sister, her value will go up a million fold. If she's nothing to us, Matteo might have no scruples to throw her to the wolves.

The only way I'm letting that happen is over my dead body.

As she turns off the faucet, I pull a towel from the railing with a suppressed sigh and hold it out for her. She steps into it, and I wrap it around her shoulders, wanting to pull her into a hug, but forcing myself to stay at arm's length. That blush is full on her face, her gaze downcast as she grips the towel tight to cover up. Shy. Ashamed. Embarrassed.

"Hey," I say, lifting her chin with a fingertip, forcing her to meet my gaze. "None of that with me, okay?"

Her blush deepens as she blinks at me, a quiver running through her body. "Okay."

She softens her hold on the towel, and when I reach for it, she lets go.

I take my time to gently wipe her down, starting at the top with her shoulders and arms, lower to her sides and her breasts, making sure to keep the thick, fluffy terrycloth between my skin and hers, but fuck if it isn't even more erotic than what we did in the shower. Her trust in me, and the consequent need to only prove again that I'm worthy, fuels every delicate swipe, every gentle caress.

By the time I get to her hips, I drop to my knees to look at her wound and dab it dry. It's healing well, and even the red tally scars seem to have faded a bit. Only the cigarette burns still stare at me in anger, and for a moment, I fist the towel, bunching it up. A sudden rage pulses through me, and I drop my head to her belly, fighting it, but it has nowhere to go but deep in me where I've been keeping it buried for years.

For a minute, I just have to breathe, battling for control, and then her warm fingers weave into my hair, stroking lower to my ears, and with a soft brush, settle on my shoulders.

"It's okay, Dominic," she murmurs as she holds on to me. "When you're with me, I don't think about it at all."

I could weep at her words. Maybe I should. Finally force that plug out where it's stuffed so deep down in me, everything can finally come out. Mom. Gabriella. Alex. The Don. The fucked-up shit he did to me because I let him.

Because I fucking let him.

I fucking let him bully me, abuse me, too fucking scared to tell him no, to make him stop.

Too fucking weak.

The weakest fucking link. Until he took out Alex, and I finally understood the lay of the land. This pinkie wasn't for nothing. '*Know your place. Play your part. And shut the fuck up. Or I do the same to your brothers.*'

Just like me, a monster did this to her, held her down, tied her up, not giving her a fighting chance to stop him from brutalizing her.

'But when you're with me, I don't think about it at all.' And when she's with me, all I want is to be the man who makes her forget, the man she deserves and needs. I want to be everything the Don wasn't.

A shudder vibrates through me, a quake that seems to ripple from my core. I'm weeping, my tears gathering between us, slipping down her belly as I let go, tired of battling with myself. I'm not sure how long we're standing like this, but Ariana's hands are warm, safe, caring. Touch I always denied myself, never understanding how much I needed it.

"You need to forgive yourself, Dominic, for allowing him to do what he did to you. You were just a kid."

When I eventually rise to my feet, her eyes search mine, her gaze dropping to my lips. Sinking into her would be the ultimate cure for both of us, even just with a kiss, but I can't. Whatever my conscience can get away with—which is a fucking lot given the stuff I've done and been through—this woman is almost virginal in comparison to me. I don't want to fuck her up, too.

The brusque thought reminds me who is taking care of whom here, and with it, I gently wrap the towel around her body again. "Where's your pjs? Let me guess, under the pillow, Portia-style?"

Ariana shoots me a smile. "Yes."

I have her by the hand, and we pad over to the head of the bed. I rummage under the pillows for those light pink satin pjs Portia sourced for her, and when she drops the towel, I almost tumble us to the bed, the need to pull her on top of me, allowing her to explore her own limits on my body, almost gate-crashing all my plans.

Instead, like a fucking monk, I guide her arms into the top's sleeves and help her step into the shorts. I don't glance down at her breasts again, or at her sweet little pussy that deserves a thorough lashing from my tongue, but my cock goes on as if everything in front of me is for the taking.

"Get in bed, sweetheart," I say gruffly, needing to cool the fuck off. I pad over to the closet, finding fresh boxers to contain the beast, and all the way, I can feel her gaze on me. But I've let my guard slip with her so completely, there's no turning back. I don't care anymore that she's seen *me*.

Now would be a good time to put a bullet in my back, if she cared for that shit anymore. Dying was always the way out, the only way out.

I drop the towel and pull on some sleep shorts, giving my cock a unsatisfying fisting en route to tell it to calm the fuck down. When I turn towards my side of the bed, she's sitting on top of the covers, on her knees, just like a submissive, waiting, the ties I used last night unknotted, neatly rolled up and ready.

"I'm not tying you up, Ariana." I'd think what with everything that happened today, everything we learned from each other—

"I want you to tie me up," she says softly, her eyes fixed on mine. "Like you did last night."

"Why? You're not going to try anything." Even if today hadn't happened, surely, she would've caught on by now how this mansion is a prison, a pretty one, but a prison all the same, and I'm the fucking dungeon master.

"I don't know where you went earlier, Dominic," she says softly. "I might have my suspicions, but if you go there again, I want to be with you. I want you to take me with you, so you're not alone."

Breaking.

This is what it feels like to be breaking at the hands of a woman. It's like nothing I've known before. It's nothing like what I learned to do. It's soft and generous, and understanding, and beautiful and warm, an embrace into the gentlest folds I've ever been held in my adult life.

I swallow down my emotions and say the first logistical thing that comes to mind as I kneel onto the bed, matching her pose. "Better I teach you some knots then, sweetheart."

45

ARIANA

Dominic's fingers quiver as he knots the ties into a string, wraps them around us like he did last night, tethering us together as one. Somehow, his movements have become almost like a religious ritual, but every single brush of his fingers against my skin sends sparks of desire to my core.

What happened in the shower was tilting too much in the direction of black in this grey zone we're existing in, but for my body's expanding needs, it wasn't enough. His presence is always calm, but the way he broke down on seeing my scars, it felt as if he was feeling each one individually on his own flesh. All I could do was hold him, be there for him as his shoulders shook in equal anger and agony.

I'm finding the way of this man, his contours, the planes and valleys of his body I've had free visual access to in the shower, but it's his inner world he's been showing me in glimpses. Images that flit past only when the light hits right, covered in the barbed wire of his no-man's land. Things he has gone through, things he's been forced to do, the loathing he has for himself, for the man he was molded into.

He is ruthless, brutal, cruel when he's in his role in *Il Consiglio*, a side I never want to see face to face, but with me—

I bite my lip as he makes the last slip knot, and when he tests the distance between our hands, it's even less than last night. I lean back to the pillows, and he mirrors me as we manage to get under the covers and settle, facing each other.

"You know what my first thought was when I saw you in that warehouse?" I say, almost reverently as his fingers weave with mine in a soft hold. "When I got shot and had no clue how bad it was? I was so sure I was going to die. I mean, it had been coming for weeks, so at that point, the idea that it was finally happening was such a relief, and then—" I break off, too wrought by everything that's happened.

"And then?" he prompts, giving my fingers a squeeze.

"And then you were there, and I thought you were my guardian angel."

He hums a little chuckle. "That's new. I can tell you now nobody has ever seen me in that light."

With a sigh, I close my eyes. "First impressions stick. You'll always be my guardian angel, Dominic Scalera."

We're quiet then, truly exhausted. My thoughts drift, grateful I managed to keep Portia's secret for the one night I promised her, as my brain tries to work through everything I've learned today, the hopes it crushed, the reality it's going to bring with those DNA tests. And then, the biggest question: what are they going to do with me once they've placed me as a pawn on this chess board in the game they play?

Somewhere in the back of my mind, the notion of returning to Italy still hammers away, but it's become white noise with everything else. The fact I've failed in the one mission I've set out to complete when I was fifteen comes with a wave of discomfort. This is why women are still trafficked. People give up too easily. The monsters are too many. The good guys too few and far between.

My team... who knows what has happened to them, if they've given up the search. And then, there's Gabriella. Who knows what she's been going through.

At some point, I shift, and arms pull me close, strong and protective, and I dream of a little girl lost. Me. I'm that little girl. Mom dead in a car wreck that could have been orchestrated as much as it could have been a real accident. A little girl who arrives at Franco's uncle's dilapidated farmhouse. The vast neglect of the place, with all its farm clutter, only distracting from what was really happening on that small holding.

A feeling seems to come to rest on my chest, suffocating in its weight, prompting visuals of another little girl in my mind.

"Oh my god," I whisper, the image becoming sharper, the dream turning from black and white to color, one by one as if it's working through the light prism from one side to the other. "Oh my god," I call out as I bolt upright, clutching the arm draped over my belly, instantly wide awake.

"Ariana, sweetheart, you're having a bad dream."

A shudder runs through me.

"No, no...Dominic...you don't understand," I say, desperate, gripping his hand so hard, my nails bite into his skin.

He sits up, another arm around me, hushing me. "It's okay, sweetheart. It comes to me like this, too. Calm down, I've got you. I had you last night, too."

"No-no-no," I say, urgently. "It was a vision. It wasn't a dream. A memory, I don't know. Triggered...oh, God. She was there, at that house. I saw it, clear as daylight."

Dominic cups my cheek, turning me to face him. It's dark, and all I feel is the warmth of his breath as it ghosts over my shoulder.

"Who, sweetheart?"

"They called her Gabi. Her Italian wasn't great. She had an American accent. It must have been short for Gabriella."

"When?" His tone is already sharper, the hold on my cheek firmer.

"I—I—" I need to think. "Give me a minute." My breathing is jagged, my pulse all over, the conviction that this is real and not a product of my imagination still sinking in.

Dominic works the ties around our arms, and they loosen swiftly as I rub at my forehead, trying to go back, to dig into a time I buried so deep away, never wanting to go there.

"I was around twelve? She must have been around seven? She was only there for a short while. Maybe a week? It could have been longer? I had to go to school, it was the last days before the summer vacation, so I didn't really register her being there."

Dominic switches on the bedside light and gets out of bed, looking for his phone where he left it in the closet.

"What time is it?"

"Two in the morning."

"God. It must have been building in my head, ever since—" Oh, God. I'm going to spill it out now.

"Ever since?"

Dominic stands closer, his hands on his hips, and with the way the light falls, I see exactly what every other person must see when he is in his *Il Consiglio* headspace. His tall frame, his muscles carved ruthlessly in the shadows, and his tattoos menacing in all black ink, the veins on his arms only hinting at the strength he wields with his mere hands.

But it's his face that makes me want to cower back. Eyes dark and hollow, blinking in the little light, the shadows falling under his cheekbones, his lips pursed in a thin line, and the tick of his jaw spelling out that I shouldn't fuck with him.

"Your mom's journals. I know where they are." I swallow as he reaches for a T-shirt and gruffly pulls it on. "Promise me you won't be angry, please."

"Portia knew exactly where they were, didn't she?" he says, his tone laced with budding fury. "Fucking knew it."

"Promise me you won't punish her. Please—"

"Don't fucking insult me, sweetheart," he hisses. "Don't you know me at all? Or is everything between us fake? You're just playing a character in this little skit you're doing in Boston?"

Cold dread wraps me in its icy fingers, but I swallow down my emotions.

"Nothing's been fake, Dominic," I whisper. Nothing between us has been fake at all. "It's only that she begged me not to tell you. Just for one night."

"Why?"

"Because she knows the man who probably took care of your sister after she was born. Until she went to live in Italy. She went to see him last night—" I struggle to my knees and scramble over to where he is standing by the edge of the bed. "Please, Dominic," I beg, reaching for his arms. "She's only protecting her own. It's Rosalia's father."

"Jesus fucking Christ."

He steps away from my touch and paces the room. Eventually, he drags his hands through his hair, and with a grunt, comes to stand right in front of me. For a few painful seconds, he eats into my gaze with eyes that have been stripped from everything they held last night.

"What else haven't you been telling me?"

Heat swarms to my face, and I pray he won't notice in the little light. "Nothing. That's everything I know. There's *nothing* more. As for Gabi being in Italy...I don't know more than what I've just told you. I was just a kid, and the memories are so vague—"

"Is that fucker of an uncle still alive?" he cuts in. "Franco's uncle? Antonio Mancuso? In the place where you grew up after your mom died?"

"Yes."

"If Gabriella was there, he'll talk. Have no fear, sweetheart, I'll make him. I make anybody talk."

And I just lied to him. I haven't told him everything. Nothing about what I was doing in my real life back in Italy before Franco took me to that dungeon. How I could ruin them if ever I get away and back to my team with all the information I've gathered. How I literally—if unexpectedly and totally unintentionally—turned into a Trojan horse, entering their most sacred Mafia inner circle.

Dominic makes anybody talk. I bet once he knows my truth, he'll do anything to make me shut up. Permanently.

"I'll have to take you there," I say, grabbing at this last straw. Once I'm back on home ground, it would be easy for me to disappear. "His house is hard to find, and it doesn't exactly have an address."

"Oh, sweetheart. We'll go to Italy. You'll get what you've wanted from the start. And en route, we'll figure out how this fucking ends. Because end it will as it must."

His words chill me to the bone as goosebumps ride over my skin. He's known all along that I want to go back to Italy at all costs.

Dominic gives me a slow, all-seeing rake down with his gaze, then reaches into his closet for a T-shirt.

"Put this on," he instructs as he hands it to me. "You're too much of a freaking distraction in those scraps of pink satin and lace and shit."

I do as he asks, my heart heavy at his harsh words.

"Now go show me where these journals are, and then, sweetheart, we'll call for Portia."

46

DOMINIC

I march Ariana up the stairs and down the dark corridors of the Don's mansion, to what she called *your mom's sanctuary.*

Once she's led the way to Mom's walk-in closet and tells me to help stack all the crates with her things to one side, my heart sinks. I've been through here. Yes, I did a rushed and shitty job, but it was just old clothes. Some of them sparked memories that had me break down, alone in this room.

Ariana is working the baseboard, and now that she's at it, I can see exactly how I missed it. I'm on my knees next to her to help, and then she peels the carpet away, revealing the loose floorboards and the secret hiding place.

When I finally have a stack of ten journals in my hands, I'm so overwhelmed, my whole body starts to shake. Holding these seems sacred, a saint's relic. A last connection to Mom, and it's as if her graceful fingers are reaching up to me through the pages as I flip through them to brush my cheek. Her beautiful handwriting, her calm acceptance flowing out of pen onto paper.

"The Don never knew about these. It's the one thing she managed to keep hidden from all of us."

Ariana nods. "She made Portia promise to never show these to anybody. They were sealed with ribbon and wax, too. Your mom probably only meant your dad, because why else would she mention the six brothers who would look for Gabriella once she's older?"

"Where? Show me."

"Here." She takes the stack from me, extracts one journal, and opens it to the salient pages. "Read here."

She points to the last lines in the journal.

'*Until death us all part. And then she'll have six brothers to find her. Finally I can rest in peace.*'

My hands are trembling, my eyes wet as I scan the page, but mine won't be the first tears to fall to these pages. It's all here. It's all been here for years, and us boys were totally fucking ignorant of the whole sick business.

I read and read and go back and forth, my gaze jumping over her words, finding them hard to stomach. '*The last thing I ever wanted was to bring a girl into this world, to fulfill the final term and condition of the sick pact they made.*'

"She knew it was a girl." Everybody knew, except us. The plan had always been for Gabriella to go to Italy, the ultimate blood exchange—a life for a life. This has to do with the origins of the war between Randazzo and Scalera. Matteo will know more, but *a son for a son, a daughter for a daughter, one for one* says it all.

I stall as these words finally sink in: '*given that both his and Emilio's sons are in this house, born from my womb.*'

What the fuck? What the actual—

Who?

Feeling totally drained, I lean back against the wall. Those DNA tests are suddenly taking on a whole new level of significance. What if this was the real reason why Don Scalera got rid of Alex, and not Alex's quietly planned mutiny? Alex was

Randazzo's *son*? Fuck it all. Who else knows we're not the descendants of only Giuliano Scalera, but some of us are Emilio Randazzo's sons?

Even worse—did the Don approve of this? Another man fucking his wife with the intention of getting her pregnant with his child? Don Randazzo fucking his own daughter?

Revulsion shivers through me as I recall Bianca Randazzo wasn't his real daughter. Just a little girl he bought, or stole, or kidnapped.

I'm going to be sick. Ariana was once such a little girl. So was Gabriella. All for the taking.

As I meet her gaze, she's weeping, quietly, as she does.

"Come here, sweetheart," I say, holding out a hand for her. If it weren't for her arrival here, none of this would have come to light. "I shouldn't have snapped at you."

Her hand is in mine, small, warm, dainty, and everything that should be wrong in my world. But I clutch it tight, as tight as I can without breaking her delicate bones, and I pull her to my lap so she can straddle my legs.

"It seems we don't have a skeleton in the closet," I say, her hands quivering where she settles them on my chest. "We have catacombs full of them."

"That's a Mafia thing," she says with a weak smile. "I just realized this is how Franco knew about your sister. He was there when Gabi stayed."

Fuck. To think that madman could have had his hands on our little Gabriella. "Tell me she didn't get hurt."

"I wouldn't know." Tears rush down her cheeks, and I want to kiss them away. "Only she will."

I hug her close, her body molding against mine. The perfect fit. All feminine warmth against my muscled male form, soft where I'm rough and calloused, fragile where I'm unbreakable, her smooth cheek supple against my coarse stubble.

Heat pulses to where I've gone hard against her sex, her body's pressure just a tease. This T-shirt does nothing to disguise her allure or quench my need for her. It's because I'm falling for her, for the way she sees me, for how she soothes me. For how she touches me.

Fuck. I need distance between myself and this woman. Permanent distance. Whatever is happening here can never be. I'm fucked up, and I know better than to bring a woman into my world. And this one...this one is poised to plummet into an inner crevice I can never extract her from.

I ease her away and cup her cheek, taking control of this situation. "We need to phone Portia. Franco is dead, but Portia's connection will know enough. And once in Italy..."

She chews her lip, her eyes fixed on mine, and it's more than I can take. Once in Italy, things are going to come to a head.

I brush my thumb along her chin, tugging at it so slightly, the skin dents under the pressure as my thumb pulls her mouth open, giving me a peek of that sweet tongue. Fuck. I want to kiss her so badly, my cock pulses with the need.

She shifts in her seat, almost subconsciously rolling her hips, and I close my eyes. It's the perfect friction that would get us both off within minutes if she does it again and again.

"Sweetheart," I groan, every part of my brain and body going against the logic I try to preach to myself. "We can't. Never mind everything else, if I ever get to be with you, I want to take my time. I need to take my time with you. This is not the place, and we don't have the time you need—the time you deserve—for me to take proper care of you."

From afar, a sound penetrates, strange at this early hour. The house's doorbell. Ariana holds her breath, and I frown. It's perfectly quiet in this small room. I must have heard wrong. Then the distinct ring sounds through the house again.

When my phone vibrates at the same time, Ariana clambers off my lap, and a second later, someone knocks on the closed bedroom door.

"Sir? Mr. Scalera?"

"It's one of the guards," I say to her as I get up and hold a hand for her. "And it's the gatehouse calling." I kill the call, cursing how I don't have a gun on me. And that we're basically cornered in this small room if for some reason shit is already going down with the Petrovs.

Fuck. Nobody breaches this fortress's walls. It must be something else. I notice two missed calls from Portia. Maybe she knew better than to make me wait.

I open the door, and the guard is standing there, looking apologetic.

"Sir, Portia is here at the gate with an unknown man. She's requesting entrance and to speak to you."

Good. If she's bringing this man to talk to me, it means she's wanting to save him from an interrogation. "It's fine, let them in, but do your usual."

"Yes, sir."

They'll strip them naked if needed to see if they have any weapons on them.

"Come," I say to Ariana, my hand on the small of her back. "The party is starting. Best we get dressed for it."

Back in our bedroom, I walk straight to the shower, knowing Ariana won't try anything now. Not with Portia bringing Rosalia's dad here. I rush my shower and walk out in just a towel, water still dripping from my hair.

Her gaze follows me all the way to the closet, and I'm so tempted to drop this towel and let her see what she's missing out on, but I turn my back on her. "Your turn, sweetheart. Who knows what this day's going to bring."

As I get dressed, the faucet turns on, and by the time she

comes out in her robe and a towel around her wet hair, I'm dressed in my usual suit, but without the tie, and scanning through emails on my phone. I'll first listen to Portia's side of the story before I phone Matteo.

Ariana rummages through the small stack of clothes Portia bought her, and a thought zaps through my mind and quietly brews as I watch her surreptitiously. I'd love to dress this woman. Dress her for me. Dress her for her, in things that speak of her worth. Dress her in expensive clothes I'd strip off her body with my teeth, my lips... Not that she doesn't look perfect in those plain white cotton panties, but fuck...the way she looks in cheap satin makes me want to unwrap her out of the most expensive silks.

She skips the bra, probably because it's still early and she's planning to spend the day again at home. I watch with mounting frustration how she pulls on a T-shirt and jeans. When she turns to me, those sweet nipples are hard, as if she felt every caress of my gaze.

A sudden hot flush of possessiveness spreads underneath my skin, fueled by her ignorance about how fucking stunning and sexy she is. I stand, and button my jacket's lapels to cover-up my erection.

"That's not going to cut it, sweetheart," I say, my voice gruff.

"What?"

"If you think you're going to walk out of here with your breasts on display like that for every fucking security guard in this house and beyond, you're mistaken."

Her eyes widen as she looks down, that blush already chasing to the surface. I'm by her side in two strides and pick out the padded beige bra between the other pieces of clothing. "Here."

She turns her back to me as she takes it, flustered, and slips the T-shirt's sleeves off so she can put on the bra. I'm so close to her, if I just lift my arm, I can run a knuckle down the valley of her spine.

My hand is burning with the need to touch her, and her movements have slowed to such a snail's pace, I bet she's waiting for me to act first.

We're fucked, aren't we?

47

ARIANA

He didn't have to do this to me. Turn me on with those simple words, showing me a possessive side I'm begging to see more of. I'm already a knot of nerves as we exit the bedroom into the corridor. Portia is here, and who knows what news she's bringing. The scent of freshly brewed coffee is somehow calming as it lures us all the way to the kitchen.

As we walk inside, she's already whipping up something in a mixing bowl. A man is sitting at the island, and as they both glance up at us, it's clear neither of them has slept the night before.

Her eyes hold mine with a pleading stare, and I whisper to her in passing, desperate for her not to get in deeper trouble. "He knows. About the journals."

"Nicky." She pauses her nervous whipping as soon as my words sink in. "You must be angry about yesterday, but please—"

"It's okay, Portia, I'm not the fucking Don."

Those words hang in the space, and it's as if a ghost sweeps between us.

Portia is on the verge of tears. The man, who seems to be in his late sixties with silver hair and dressed impeccably in a suit, looks as if he's ready to skip his last rites just to get things over with. Clearly, both of them were expecting bullets in the forehead.

"Yes, you're not," she says on a swallow. "This is Arturo Romano. I'm not sure if you remember him? He was one of the Don's capos way back when. He got...early retirement."

Dominic studies the man, and their gazes lock, and then recollection clock on Dominic's side.

"Sir," Arturo says as he stands and holds out his hand, seeming to recall Dominic perfectly. "You've grown into a much-feared man."

"Hmm, I hope that goes for all the Scalera boys." Dominic shakes his hand, his gaze pinning the shorter man in place. "Rosalia has your eyes."

"Yes, my little girl. I haven't seen her in years. Maybe now..." Arturo sits again, looking bone tired. "Rumors go around that you left *Il Consiglio*, what with your security company, but now, I'm not so sure."

At this, Dominic just cocks his brow as he pulls a stool away from the counter and holds it out for me.

"Have a seat, sweetheart," he says as he shoots me a glance. "I believe you have information we're looking for, Arturo. We can all talk over coffee like normal people."

With normal people, I assume Dominic isn't planning to torture information out of anybody yet.

"I'm Ariana," I say as I get comfortable next to Arturo.

"I know. Portia has told me—" Arturo cuts himself off right there.

Enough to have him hanged if he speaks about this to anybody? I bet everybody have these words ringing in their heads, even if it's dead silent in the kitchen.

"Are you making pancakes, Portia?" Dominic asks, a slice of amusement in his voice.

"Had to do something with my hands, Nicky. You must know when I realized yesterday that the timeframe spoke to the exact time Arturo left us, with reasons I never really bought into, I made the connection...and...and—" She breaks off, hands flitting over her cheeks as she gathers herself. "I had some right to the truth, didn't I? To hear it first? So when I asked Ariana not to say a word, it wasn't so much as to warn Arturo, but to get an understanding of what really happened twenty-two years ago and to tell him it's safe to come forward with what he knows, as Don Scalera is dead. We haven't seen each other in years. I had to drive to Providence, and—"

"Take a breath, Portia. Calm down." Dominic closes the gap between them and squeezes her shoulder. "You lost as much as we did, if not more. I'm going to make this right, okay?"

At this, Portia really lets go, and Dominic hugs her close, allowing her a good cry. Then she has him at arm's length and shoots me a woebegone smile.

"Told you he's the best," she whispers at me, her eyes glistening with tears. She urges Dominic in the direction of a chair. "Sit, and have coffee, you poor boy. We all suffered in our own way." She sniffs hard, and with a final swipe of her nose and a pat over her messy curls, indicates that she's in control of herself again. "The batter needs to stand for a bit, so we have time to talk."

Dominic sits as Portia gets busy pouring coffee from a stovetop espresso maker into cups.

"Here. Now, Arturo, tell them everything you know, exactly as you told me last night."

There's no mistaking Portia's tone: don't mess around, and don't mess this up.

"Well, things were like this," Arturo starts. "Mrs. Scalera, Bianca, was going to have a girl, and as one of your dad's most trusted capos at the time, he charged me with arranging an adoption for Gabriella into a mutually approved family. Don

Randazzo also added his two pennies every two minutes, that fucker. In any case, it was an Italian family, part of Randazzo's underground team, who didn't have any children. They were living down the street from me for the first seven years, down in Providence, and then they took Gabi to Italy, as was agreed upon. All the adoption papers, everything was legally done. Correctly, per local laws, so nobody could raise a red flag."

"Did my mom know about this?" Dominic asks.

"Yes. She never met the couple, but they were good people, for what it's worth, in our circles. She gave your dad power of attorney, so everything was wrapped up pretty neatly."

Until now, where they're unravelling at speed.

"Were you there at the birth?" Dominic asks.

"Yes. I was there every step of the way."

"Did she suffer? My mom?"

Arturo shifts in his seat, clutching his coffee cup. "She was sedated. There were complications as the doctors predicted. Even a rushed C-section wouldn't save her. She just...slipped away, minutes after Gabriella was born. Her body was broken. She wouldn't have survived any type of birth."

I glance at Dominic where he's settled next to me around the corner of the kitchen island, his face stoic as he keeps himself together. When I slip my hand to his thigh and give him a soft squeeze, he reaches for my hand and wraps it in his. He's trembling, and his leg jolts up and down with tension. I wish I had the right to put an arm around him, but I bet he wouldn't like that in front of Arturo.

"Did he ever hold his daughter?" Dominic bites out, his knuckles white as he clutches the small white espresso cup with his other hand. A little bit more pressure, and he's going to crush it to smithereens in his fist.

"No." Arturo sighs as he pushes his own cup away. "Don Scalera didn't hold women in much esteem. He was happy to let Gabriella go and being rid of the burden of protecting a woman in the Mafia. But he was even happier that the last terms of his agreement with Randazzo was met. Peace was finally guaranteed and given how Randazzo had become a powerful man in Italy and in Europe, it was for the best."

"Fucker," Dominic grunts as he leans back. "Building his army of boys to fight Randazzo if either of them ever broke the fucking truce." He takes a deep breath and sighs. "Did he even care what happened to her afterwards? Ever visit her in Providence?"

I catch Dominic's gaze. His eyes seem bloodshot with simmering rage.

"No." Arturo leans into the counter, making sure to get his point across. "I was there and kept an eye on her. And then, she went to Italy."

"And what do you know about that time?" Dominic asks.

"Nothing. Don Scalera got seven years and Don Randazzo's word that he won't put her to work until the time is right."

"And what the fuck do you think that means?" Dominic growls as he shoots up, his height immediately menacing. "Put to *work*? In that fucking psycho's world? Randazzo was running the biggest fucking sex trafficking ring in Europe! Where everything fucking goes!" He leans over me, into Arturo's space, and grips the man's shoulder. "Why the fuck didn't you talk?"

It takes me a second to register that Arturo has tears running down his cheeks. Quiet tears, exactly like mine, trained to keep emotion in check until he couldn't anymore.

"Don Scalera had my wife and my own darling daughter in his hold, right here in this very house," he says as he stands, shrugging Dominic off. "If you ever become a man to be in that exact position, you'd understand you'd rather let him slice you into pieces, bit by bit, than speak a word of what was going on in Don Scalera's inner circle. I kept quiet to keep Portia and Rosalia safe, because just like you, Dominic, sir, I know exactly what Don Scalera was capable of."

Arturo's gaze drops to Dominic's hand, where it's now pressing on the countertop, his fingertips white with restraint, but his pinkie, his rogue little pinkie, obstinate and out of place with the rest of his perfect manicured fingers as it points, quivering, to the side.

Oh. My. God. *Holy Mother of Jesus.* Don Scalera. He cut Dominic's finger off. And had it stitched back. Oh my *God.* Why? I'm not even sure why I'm wondering, given what I've seen of what he's done to his son. But this—

"Fucking long game." Dominic sinks back into his chair, driving his hands into his hair. "He always played such a fucking long game."

For a long while, it's quiet around the kitchen island as I get to grapple with what I'd just deduced and everybody else just digesting what had happened decades ago. When I finally come to my senses, I lean closer to Dominic.

"He might have played a long game, but it doesn't mean he gets to win," I murmur, still struggling to keep my own anguish and anger in check. "There's still a chance she's safe, Dominic."

I was safe with Franco's uncle until Franco acted on his own agenda. What Franco did to me was outside of Randazzo's plans. I'm not sure what Randazzo's plans for me were, but I was never trafficked as a girl, not from Randazzo's side. And then, I cut myself off from his world and made my own destiny the day I stole ten thousand euros and fled to Milan.

"Randazzo is dead. This means everybody is in danger, especially those connected to him," Dominic says. "People are going to kill for that network of his, for his money, and wherever Gabriella is, she isn't safe. We don't know who knows what in the bigger scheme of things." He leans back in his seat. "There's only one thing to do. Go to Italy and figure it out from there."

My stomach turns as my pulse beats in my temple. "How soon?"

Dominic stands and takes his phone from his jacket's inner pocket.

"Today still." He gives my arm a squeeze. "Our men cleaned out Franco's truck, and Matteo has the passport Franco used to get you into the country. You'll get out with it, too."

So easy. Everything I wanted most since landing in this mess on this side of the world is right on my doorstep.

"But what about the DNA tests?" I'm not sure why I want to stall us, even if for just a few more days.

"I'll get those via email. We have WiFi on the jet."

"Jet?"

"We have a private jet," he says, already busy on his phone.

"Of course you do," I mumble, more to myself than to anybody else.

My heart sinks as I watch Dominic swipe away, searching for a contact on his phone.

"Get those pancakes started, Portia," he says. "We're going to need energy for this day."

I watch him, his profile as he turns, his firm stride as he walks out into the corridor and away from us to make his call in private.

It hits me then, a sharp punch to the gut that winds me: once in Italy, I have to separate myself from this man. The easiest way would be to alert the police on arrival at the airport. The long-winded way would be to take Dominic to Franco's uncle's farmhouse, help him interrogate everybody in that house, find Gabriella, and then somehow try to escape.

Either way, we're over. Any way you cut it, we're done, and I'll never see him again. And suddenly, I don't know if I can do it. Or if I even want to.

Somehow, it feels as if we haven't even started yet.

48

DOMINIC

I know it's fucking early, but who cares. In our world, shit doesn't wait for you to get ready before it hits the fan.

I'm courteous enough to knock, but by now, Matteo's security team should have alerted him that I'm about to walk into his apartment. Perks of installing all your brother's high-tech security? You know how to breach all of it.

I give him a minute, then walk through the front door and the foyer. As I enter the big double-volume open space, my brother is coming down the stairs in sleep shorts, rubbing at his face.

"What the fuck, Nicky? Jesus. It's like five in the morning."

"Yeah, well. The party's started, and I'd hate for you to miss the good parts." I'm on my way to the kitchen, aiming to make him a coffee strong enough to kick him right in the balls.

"Don't fuck with me," he grunts as he slouches on a stool by the kitchen island.

"Busy night, hmm?"

That makes two of us. I sweep him down with a quick inspection. Hickeys on his chest. Is that a nail scratch on his side? Uh-huh. I called it. Tasha is a little kitten with claws.

Serves my brother right. I bet he fucked her just as she likes it last night, and from the dark circles under his eyes and satisfied smirk smeared over his face, I bet he's now waking up to the memories of it.

"Not exactly getting enough sleep," he says.

"And it isn't just Gabriella and Petrov giving you sleepless nights."

"Now you're fucking with me, Nicky," he says, but there's a small smile.

The thought of the nights he gets to spend with Tasha only makes my own frustrations pop to the surface, and with a suppressed groan, I give him my back to work on the coffee.

Behind me, he stretches and yawns, then drags in a deep breath. "Fill me in?"

I give him a detailed run down of everything that's happened since we spoke last.

"Fuck me," he says as I slide a double espresso in his direction. "He had Arturo in a chokehold what with Portia and Rosalia in his house all these years. Right underneath our noses."

I've been selective with the details I share. I left out the part about Randazzo's sons being among us, as I'm still digesting that fucking tidbit. Deep inside me, I know it's because I want to protect the memory of Alex. Once he's no longer one of us... no longer our blood brother, but that fucking maniac's son—

But there's another conspiracy theory battling for space in my head—one that helps me make sense of everything happening lately. What if that night Alex died, things had gone wrong? Matteo was the real target, the Don's evil plan to get rid of this son that was never his, but Alex got killed instead. That would explain why the Don could never let go of that one vendetta involving Peter Armstrong and demanded Matteo put Tasha up for auction.

Fuck. This is going to torment me for the rest of my days and the only person knowing the real answers is dead.

"Yep," I say, just to say something, then forcing myself to take a sip of my third espresso for the day, swallowing my rogue thoughts in the process. At this rate, I'm going to rattle all the way to Italy.

"What's the plan?"

"First, I'm going to end the fucker in the room next door."

"Good. Vincenzo Trapani has outstayed his welcome," Matteo says with an approving nod. "And then? You're off to Italy?"

"As soon as the jet is ready, we're leaving."

"You know Steph is taking Gigi and Carla tomorrow."

"I'm not waiting. The jet can fly back for them. Let's put some miles on that money drain."

Matteo chuckles, but it's dry. "I don't like you going alone. Take Luca with you."

I knew he'd say something like this. But here's the thing: I don't want any of my brothers with me on this mission. I want to be alone with Ariana because who knows what's going to happen in Italy, and I need time to let go, not a fucking audience.

The thought twists my gut, but I keep my poker face in check. "Not a good idea. Let's not have our identical twins prance around the Cosa Nostra's hideouts in Italy."

"Benedict, then," he counters.

"He's working on the back end." In fact, I know it's still early, but he hasn't come back to me with results on Ariana's fingerprints yet.

"Holy fuck." Matteo leans back in his seat, and from the glint in his eyes, it's clear the espresso has kicked in. "You want to be alone with her."

Jesus. Am I so fucking easy to read? I bite down on my jaw

as his expression turns from realization to something I can't place. Is that *smugness*?

"You're fucking smitten," he murmurs, and raises his cup in a mock toast.

Am I? *Smitten*?

"Who wants to be alone with whom?"

We both look up at where Tasha, in a silky white robe, pads closer. She's barefoot and sneaked up on us. Bet she learned a thing or two from Matteo when it comes to that.

"Sorry," she says, sleep still thick in her voice. "I didn't mean to eavesdrop."

"It's okay, kitten." Matteo hugs his wife to him. "Nicky just came over to let me know he's taking Ariana back to Italy today."

"What?" She eases back from his embrace to look him in the eye, and then back at me. "So soon? How's her bullet wound doing? I haven't had time to check in on her. We haven't even had time to talk...to get to know each other."

And that's probably for the better.

"We're trying to figure out where Gabriella is," Matteo says. "She knows someone who might know, and we don't want to waste time."

"Yes, I get that, but really, I'd hoped—with Gigi and Carla—"

Matteo's hand slides down from her side to just below her hip, where he gives her a forgive-me squeeze on the butt. "She'll be back."

He doesn't look anybody in the eye when he says that, and prickles of premonition spread underneath my skin. He still has plans for Ariana with this Petrov fuck-up. Over my dead body will I hand her over to the fucking Bratva.

When Matteo stands, Tasha shifts to make space for him, and when he tilts her head up to kiss her, I have to look away, jealousy biting around in my insides. A burden? Neither Tasha nor Gigi are burdens. The change in Matteo and Steph attest to that. Fuck, talk about a mind shift that snuck up on me. I'd do anything to be the exact opposite of what the Don was. In fact, I'll welcome the burden of keeping these women safe with open arms just to give him one final *fuck you.*

"Go back to bed, kitten, I'll bring you a coffee. We have some business to wrap up."

Tasha shoots me a reprimanding glance, then rolls her eyes at Matteo. I almost choke on my last sip of espresso at the audacity she has to do just that and how he's taking it so meekly. Hook, line, and sinker. Matteo is a fucking goner for this woman.

It's quiet between us as we wait for their bedroom door to close on the second floor, and in this time, Matteo studies me.

"You have security lined up on that side?"

"Yep. I already set everything in motion this morning. I'm using the same team we used for your trip." And I know some of the men personally, so I'm not worried at all.

"Good." There's a beat of silence. "You know we can't let that woman loose into the world, Nicky."

That woman. It isn't only his word choice that riles me up, but also his tone. I know he's right, but *fuck—*

"She isn't just *that woman.*" He's talking about her as if she's a massive problem the cat dragged in and we need to eliminate. "And she isn't going to become your pawn to play with, Matteo. To use as you see fit."

He just stares at me from across the counter in a silent battle of wills. Of strength. Brother against brother. Matteo is a mean fucker, but I'm meaner. For that, I've the Don to thank.

"We'll see. You go figure out in Italy what she knows about Gabriella. Go find our sister alone, without another Scalera by your side, as you're clearly on a mission here. But understand this, Dominic: you bring Ariana Morelli back here. She knows and has seen too much."

With that, he stalks off, giving me that tattooed back of his, the dragon's body rippling as he walks away, rolling his shoulders.

Here be a line in the sand...sand that could soak up some blood if things between us go wrong, if I cross my brother. For a second, the possibility that Matteo is only my half-brother floods my mind. He could be Randazzo's offspring.

The idea doesn't get a foothold, because even if Matteo was Randazzo's son, that won't change anything between us. We've been through too much to be anything but blood brothers for life, but I won't let him cross me on this. And we have the most important bond, anyway—Mom.

"Fuck," I grunt softly, knowing we're heading for an impasse.

I make my way out of the apartment, this whole fuckup roaring in my mind. I want to protect Ariana, but I want to protect my brothers, too. My duty and loyalty lie with my family first. That's the only way to survive in our world.

I go through the layers of security to enter the chamber where Vincenzo has been rotting away. He's the last man left in here and sways in his seat as he becomes aware of me.

I pull the gun from my holster, and for a fleeting second, other men's faces flash in my mind's eye as I stare into his glazed gaze. The Don. Emilio Randazzo.

Matteo.

I pull the trigger.

49

ARIANA

It's mid-afternoon by the time I head out to the airport with two bodyguards and another car tailing us. I haven't seen Dominic the whole morning. Once Portia and Arturo were done with sharing everything they knew about Gabriella's adoption and subsequent disappearance to Italy, Dominic left, telling me to get my things ready and he'd come back as soon as he'd organized everything for our trip.

He never came back. I was left with Portia to clean the clothes I had, and then she had the bright spark to send Arturo shopping for something 'decent' so I'm *not walking around in Italy looking like a sweatshop.*

"I don't care, Portia," I'd protested, but clearly, she did.

Now I'm heading with a security detail to the same airport I landed at with Franco, still no sign of Dominic, but with a suitcase of seriously gorgeous clothes that's only going to be a waste.

I'm nervous. Not having Dominic around works on my mind, and it's as if I miss him, like going barefoot for the first time in years. I still don't understand how he slipped past my defenses so quickly, but the fact is he has.

The driver pulls up at the terminal building, parks to make a few calls, then navigates his way directly onto the tarmac.

My heart stills. There he is, waiting by the stairs of what looks like a very expensive jet.

Dominic walks up to the car as it comes to a stop and opens the door.

"Ariana." He holds his hand out for me. "I'd thought I'd have time to fetch you, but it didn't work out that way."

"It's okay," I say, putting my hand in his.

There's trust here, and when he doesn't let go of my hand but lets us walk side by side to the stairs, a warm thrill runs through me. This. This is what I've been missing all these years. Someone like this taking care of me. It goes against every rule I'd laid out for myself when I set out to take Franco and Randazzo down, but I never knew or guessed I missed having someone like Dominic in my life. Someone who cares and needs me as much as I need him. Someone who understands me as I understand him.

His hand is on the small of my back as he guides me up the stairs. Once we're inside the jet, past the hostess and pilots who greet us, I swallow down a small gasp. I've never experienced this height of luxury before.

"Let me show you around." Dominic is in front, his fingers intertwined with mine as he leads me deeper into the cabin. "It's a long enough flight that you get a proper night's rest."

He opens a door, and I peek inside. This time, I can't help myself. I gasp. "It's more luxurious than a five-star hotel room."

"Yep. Bathroom to the side with a full shower and toilet, everything you need." He tugs me back into the corridor. "Here, you have a mini-cinema and a refreshment station..." He trails off, looking down at my hand where I'm clenching his tight. "What's up, sweetheart?"

I shrug, trying to shed the memories of coming here. "I

didn't get the tour the last time I flew in a private jet. I can't even remember getting on the plane. I was so drugged."

He gathers some strands of my hair and hooks them behind my ear. "Look forward, Ariana. Not back."

With a small nod, I let him lead me to our seats for take-off. The hostess comes along and offers me earphones for the in-flight entertainment, and I take them from her as I have nothing else to do. I really don't need to be in my own head right now, tail-spinning every scenario to its worst possible outcome.

Dominic is busy on his phone until the last second, by the sound of it making security arrangements. Once we're in the air, he pulls his laptop from its bag, indirectly dismissing me.

Minutes later, he gets up to go sit at a desk farther down the cabin and gets so engrossed in whatever he's doing, I can stare at him openly while feigning to watch a movie.

This man. His hands. That little pinkie which is the smallest part of him that reflects and summarizes his whole existence. Inside, I'm weeping for him, but something else has been blooming for Dominic Scalera over the past few days. A stubborn admiration for a man who had every reason to turn out a total psychopath, a maniac, like his father—like my father—but instead has chosen to turn his back on what had happened to him. '*Look forward, Ariana, not back.*'

He leans closer, clicking furiously at his mouse, and then freezes, eyes slowly blinking, reading again and again. Disbelief floods his face. Something is wrong. When his gaze flies up to meet mine and finds me staring, a hot blush swamps my cheeks.

For a moment, he leans back, cups his hands to his face, and breathes into them, never breaking eye contact with me. I don't know how long we stare at each other, but when his gaze drops back to his laptop screen, I know what he's reading. The DNA results.

"Come here, Ariana," he says, his voice stern.

I already know what's coming my way and had time to prepare my mind, but seeing him like this feels like fresh cracks over places I've already been broken before and only recently healed. I unbuckle my safety belt and walk over to him, trying to keep my cool.

"Who was your father?" he asks me without preamble, his fingers now steepled in front of his mouth as he leans onto the desk with his elbows.

"Why?" I ask, not even trying to hide the tremor in my voice.

"Who was your biological father?" he repeats, his sharp tone telling me to stop stalling.

There's no out. We're miles high in the sky, enclosed in a space I can't escape, and this man will get information out of anybody. He prides himself in this skill.

I no longer have any reason to hide my origins. I have brothers in *Il Consiglio*. How does the saying go? *Blood runs thicker than water.* And in the world we hail from, the blood runs so thick in our veins, it could choke you.

"I wasn't lying when I told you he's dead."

Now, he stands to his full height, towering over me with those eyes that search my face for clues. "Who the fuck was your father, Ariana?"

I bite down my last bit of hesitation. The last time I admitted this to someone, I had changed my name. Before that, I hadn't admitted this to anyone since I was seven years old. It got beaten out of me, *for my own safety*. "Emilio Randazzo."

For a long few seconds, Dominic just stares at me, somewhat frantic as his gaze volleys between my eyes. Then he drops his forehead to mine and murmurs as he clasps my quivering fingers in his. "I knew you were a Mafia princess."

This should make me laugh, but being Randazzo's daughter is the last thing I ever wanted to be.

"Who are my brothers?" I ask, knowing if I don't ask now, the opportunity might never present itself again.

"Matteo."

"Only Matteo?"

He squeezes my hand and turns to the desk to show me his laptop screen. "See for yourself."

I lean in to study the data on the screen, taking a minute to make sense of it. It's only percentages with our names, but there is no mistaking it. Matteo is my half-brother, and I have no relation to the rest of the Scalera boys.

"We won't know about Alex," he says softly then, squeezing my hand where he's still holding on to me. "But that hardly matters now."

But as for Dominic, he's nothing to me. *Nothing*. Except, in a way, he's become everything.

At the realization, every desire I've been trying to suppress, to lock away over the past few days, flies up like a flock of birds in my body, and I lick my lips as need unfurls in my core.

"Show me," I murmur, shy to look him in the eyes, but forcing myself to be open with him.

"Show you what, sweetheart?" he murmurs back, his gaze on my lips, a finger brushing a light circle in my palm.

"Show me what you do? We have time." Alone. In that bedroom with a long-haul flight that's still going to take hours. "Please."

Dominic doesn't say anything. Instead, he closes his laptop screen, signals something to the air hostess which probably means *do not disturb*, and leads me down the short corridor to the bedroom.

50

ARIANA

As soon as the door shuts behind us, nerves rake down my body. They're following his gaze's exact route as it sweeps over me where I've come to a standstill a meter from the bed. I've been so bold just a minute ago, but now my heart beats with more than anticipation. Every beat is laced with fear that has so many layers, I can't count them. They range from the fear of rejection to the fear of physical pain and everything in between.

When he doesn't close in on me, I turn away so I don't need to face him, panic rising.

"Easy, sweetheart. Just breathe."

I hear him step up to me, my stomach clenching with nerves. Then he's right here, his body flush with mine as he gathers my hair away from my neck.

"I know what you need," he murmurs as he presses his lips to my ear and his hands settle on my hips. I lean into him, into this pillar of a man and his body's strength. "Just take a deep breath, Ariana."

I drag in a deep inhale, and on a slow exhale, unclench my fists. "Dominic..."

He gently turns me around, and I look up at him. "Do you trust me?"

I don't even have to think about it. "Yes."

"And are you sure you want to do this? With me?" he asks softly.

"Don't you want to?"

He gives me a half-smile as he caresses my cheek with his thumb. "That's not the answer I'm looking for, sweetheart."

Heat pools in my core at his soft touch. "Okay. Do we...do we need paperwork?"

"We're way beyond paperwork, sweetheart."

He brushes a slow, gentle caress over my lips with his thumb, his fingertips points of heat resting on my cheek, but burning a path right to my sex. The very promise of each fingertip, the magic of his touch, fires up such a deep-seated yearning in me, I have to shift on my feet.

"But I need you to understand this isn't about me. Not in the traditional sense people have of sex. My needs are being met by me meeting yours, and I don't—" He sighs. "I just need you to trust me and relax, okay?"

"Okay." I take another deep breath, not sure how relaxing comes into the picture because I'm wound up so tight, my whole body strains with the pressure, begging for release.

Ever since this morning...ever since... Ever since he first touched me in that warehouse, it's as if he's been untying the myriad of knots I've tied in my body since that night with Franco, wrapping myself in a hopeless tangle nobody wants to deal with, myself included.

Now I've been sitting on this need that just seems to build and build. What happened in the shower was only a prologue to tease me. Now I need the whole book, chase to this chapter where I can drown myself in the words he'll write on my skin with his fingertips, erasing that night, that one encounter, while rewriting over every tear and scratch that monster made on my blank, virginal pages. He'll make me whole again as I lose and find myself over and over in him.

He drops his hand away, and I immediately miss the warmth of his touch. He shrugs off his jacket and tosses it to the side, never looking away, our gazes locked.

"I have a laundry list of things I want to do with you, sweetheart, and none of them involves penetrative sex. We can work towards that. See where you're at and take it slowly."

I blink away from his intense stare that seems to reach into my soul. Once in Italy, this is going to be over. I'm still not sure how I'm going to do it as I have no idea about the level of security he has arranged, but I need to get away from *Il Consiglio,* from Dominic, and this flight might be the only chance I'll ever get to be with him. And I want to *be* with him.

When I say nothing, too overwhelmed to respond coherently, he touches me again, this time tugging at my bottom lip. His touch is so sensual, so tender, that tingles rush from this one connection point down to my sex where the tension is only building. I want more…I want it all with him, tonight.

"It's yes, sweetheart. The word I'm looking for is yes. But no is an option, too. Let me ask you again, are you sure you want to do this with me?"

"Yes," I whisper without hesitation.

"Good girl. I have a few other words you might want to use. Repeat after me: more."

I bite my lip as his thumb slides to my jawline and lower, to trace down the column of my neck. "More."

I already sound like I'm begging, my voice betraying my body's needs.

"Good girl. Now say stop."

"Stop. But please don't."

He smiles, and by now his hand has reached my shoulder, and he gives it a warm squeeze. "Repeat after me: not yet."

"Not yet."

"We're going to keep it simple today, okay?" he murmurs as he slides his hand down to my hip and tugs me into him. "There's only one more: again."

"Again."

I'm flush against his body, his erection pressing into my belly as his other hand comes up and tilts my head so I'm forced to look up at him.

"Now, sweetheart," he murmurs as he takes in my face, my lips which are practically begging for him to kiss me. "I want you to close off all those open doors in your mind, Ariana. All I want is for you to be in this room, and not wander off to all those other rooms in your mind, okay?" He dips his head to brush his nose along my temple. "All I want you to think about is that you are a beautiful woman, with a body worthy of worship, who deserves to be loved."

At these words, I choke up as emotion floods me. So many things. Gratitude for this man who came into my life, who gets me, who cares on a level I've never experienced before. I'm already leaning into him, but now, my knees are weak.

"Okay," I say, but so softly, it's hardly a whisper as I try to hide my tears.

Then he's there, kissing my temples, my eyes, my cheeks, catching my tears before they run out of control. The reverence in those fleeting brushes of his lips uncoil something in me. With him, yes, I'm a beautiful woman, worthy of love. I'll never be broken in this man's eyes, and he'll always treat me right. It's more than I knew I wanted or needed, but his words are everything.

His hands are on my hips, on my sides, stroking rhythmically for me to calm down. It does calm my nerves, but it also stokes this fire in me, as the embers of lust have long since burst back into flame. I need him, in any and every way he'll give himself to me.

I inch my hands up his chest, clinging to him, to his strength, and when he teases his lips over mine in question, asking permission, I shudder at the pleasure of it.

"This is the first thing I wanted to do with you, almost from the moment I laid eyes on you," he whispers as his lips caress the corner of my mouth, and then they are on mine, open, soft, in a kiss that's slow and seductive, yet so profoundly deep, it's like a drug seeping into my veins.

He cradles my head as he kisses me ever deeper, and now there's nothing sweet or innocent about this kiss anymore. As his tongue sweeps into my mouth, so slow and languid, it becomes the most tender invasion, turning the kiss erotic and somehow so deliciously dirty, opening up a whole new world, the floor bottoming out from under me. I moan into him, only wanting to go with him, down into the beckoning abyss. If this is how he kisses, I'm not going to be able to hold back. Already, my panties are damp, my body begging for friction.

Dominic hums as he closes off the kiss and smiles down at me. "So fucking sweet," he murmurs. "So fucking addictive."

His hands are at the hem of my T-shirt, the one I put on this morning, tugging it off. Next, he's eased off my bra. He's just as gentle as the first night he dressed me in his wash-worn T-shirt, but this feels like I'm shedding all these layers that have always held me back.

When I reach for his shirt's buttons, he stalls me. "Not yet, sweetheart."

He drops to his haunches, hands at my jean's button as I kick my ballerina flats off. Knuckles skim my lower belly, over the scars I never think of when he's around. He drags my jeans down, and I hold on to him to step out of them and keep my balance which suddenly seems very unstable. Everything is tilting—my world, my sanity, my very being is ready to fall into him.

There's so much reverence on his face, I still. I'm only in

these simple white cotton panties that came in a bulk pack, my nipples hard, jutting out, begging for him to kiss them as his gaze skates up my body. I'd love to dress for him, let him unwrap me from silk and lace, gift myself to him again and again.

As he straightens, he runs featherlight fingertips along my legs, over my hips, up the sides of my breasts but never touching me where I'm a hot mess already and pulsating with need for him.

He guides me to the bed. "Lie down, sweetheart, in the middle."

God... he did tell me he was going to take his time.

I do as he says and wait for him to tell me what to do next as he glances around the room. My gaze drops to his groin, where that erection I got a full view of in the shower bulges up and to the side in the constraints of his trousers. My mouth wets with a need I don't understand yet, and I lick my lips.

Not yet. How apt.

"Seems I'm a bit challenged in the prop department," he says as he takes his time to remove his watch and put it on the bedside table. He leans onto the bed with one knee and bends over me. "Stay right here in this room, sweetheart. I'm going to raid the bathroom."

He caresses my cheek with a fingertip, so softly it's hardly a touch, and then lower, down the side of my neck, and it doesn't tickle—it only sparks desire down my chest, ever lower where it adds to the build-up in my sex.

I bet he likes a challenge like this, and the memories of his silk ties slipping over my wrists flare up in my mind. Every sensation of those silk ties on my arms is imprinted on my mind, my body, and what it felt like to be so safe with him. Whatever he comes up with, he'll look after me.

"So soft," he murmurs, drawing a circle around my breast,

slowly making ever smaller concentric circles as he draws on me with that fingertip.

Goosebumps flood my skin, my nipples hard, and I arch into him as the current races straight down to my sex, arousal flooding my panties again. Even I can smell my desire in these closed confines.

"Dominic," I moan, reaching for his hand to push it between my legs already.

He clasps my fingers in his. "No, sweetheart. When I told you I take my time, I meant what I said." He raises my hand to his lips and plants kisses on each fingertip. "I thought we might get away without tying you up, but clearly that isn't going to work."

Tied up, by him, with him, for him. No, for *my* pleasure. That's what he said.

I stare up at him, breathless as he lowers my hand, reaches for the other, and traps both wrists in his bigger palm against the mattress. "Keep them there, sweetheart. Push into the headboard if you have to."

I nod, and he lets go as he shifts lower to where he can trace my panty line. Shivers erupt all along the trail of his touch. My chest is heaving as he dips his fingers underneath the waistband and pulls them down slowly, breath stilted and ragged in my throat.

I close my eyes, sinking in the sensation of his touch as he shifts down my legs and slowly peels my panties off in the process. When I lift my hips to accommodate him, I get rewarded with a kiss to a hipbone and a soft murmured *good girl* that basically squeezes wet heat from my pussy onto the bed covers. God, what is he doing to me?

When I open my eyes, he's getting off the bed, my panties pressed to his nose where he stands at the end of the bed.

"So fucking addictive," he murmurs. "I'm not going to get enough of the taste of you, am I?"

Only one way to find out... and I'm squirming already with anticipation, wanting to reach out for him.

"No, sweetheart. Keep your hands where they are."

I comply, but it's a battle of wills. He waits for me to calm down, and I see the pattern here. He is going to take his time, give me space to adjust and find my own equilibrium each step of the way as we walk this tightrope over the canyon of my past experience together. And he's going to hold my hand all the way.

"Spread your legs, sweetheart."

The command sends a bolt of pleasure down my body, but I hesitate. If I do, he'll see everything from where he stands. I inch them a bit apart, wanting to please him, but heat flushes my face.

"Wider, sweetheart."

I comply, with each inch revealing more, his gaze drinking me in as desire pools in my core.

"Such a good girl," he murmurs from where he hasn't shifted, gaze hazy as he watches me. "Almost there, Ariana, just a bit more."

He is undoing me, with ease leading me to do things I never thought I'd be able do with a man, for a man...for *him*.

Dominic.

Now he's ghosting his hands over my inner thighs, not touching me, but promising and withholding everything I crave at the same time. Instead of going to my sex, he glides his hands up, and I open as wide as I can go as he guides me to bend my knees. "There."

I'm flayed opened and have never felt this exposed before, except it's liberating in a way I hadn't expected, because Dominic looks so turned on. It's obvious in the way he stares at me, licking his bottom lip. There's no fear here, just eager anticipation to satisfy him, to follow his command.

"Stay exactly like that, sweetheart. I'll be back in a minute."

As he walks off, a rogue thought rushes through my mind. He's controlling me even though he isn't even touching me. With his words, his soft voice, his gentle commands.

Dominic Scalera doesn't steer away from what he's been trained to do in *Il Consiglio.* This is going to be torture, but of the sweetest kind.

51

DOMINIC

Alone in the adjacent bathroom, I lean into the vanity for a moment, trying to get a grip. Somewhere in my head, there's the nagging thought that I should let Matteo know he's just gained a sister, but I override it. It doesn't matter. It can wait.

The beautiful woman splayed out on the bed next door isn't *my* sister. Thank fuck I'm not that fucked up. To think I've been fighting these feelings for her with every weapon in my arsenal. Now I can convince myself it's pure lust and fuck it out of my system as we have the green light, but something tells me it isn't only lust. There's more. So much more.

Maybe it's because this situation doesn't follow my status quo. I haven't had more than my status quo, my *antidote*, for years. But here's the problem: Ariana Morelli dropped out of nowhere into my life, broke through all my walls and all the way to my heart, and now she wants me to *show her*. I'm not a fucking silver bullet. I'm not the cure, but for once, I really want to be. The one person who makes her forget *him*.

My cock is so fucking eager, what with the image of her and her spread legs flashing behind my closed eyes, I fist it through the layers of my pants and underwear to give it some reprieve.

My mind is on board, because like every other dickhead on the planet, I can argue for sex until all logic has left the room. But my heart...my fucking useless heart keeps on whispering this is madness.

You aren't the one she needs. You have no business bringing her into your world. You have no right to endanger her by making her yours. Even worse: by becoming hers.

My heart tells me to walk out, find a fucking parachute, and jump out of this plane. Except that isn't an option. We're trapped for a ten-hour flight, with nothing to do but think about everything we could do to each other if we give ourselves free rein.

I'm not a complete dumbass. Ariana is on a route of re-discovery, she's finding herself, and neither of us needs her in love with me—or rather with my process—at the end of it.

Because I'm already in love with her.

The thought comes down like a ton of bricks on my heart. I exhale a haggard breath, clutching the vanity tighter. *Fuck.* When did that happen?

I blink at my reflection in the mirror. I look at least five years older than my mere thirty-one. Hard lines cup my mouth, the signs of shit I've gone through carved out in the deep grooves on my forehead and between my eyes. And here comes the bitter line of my lips as I face reality. *I'm in fucking love with her.*

The status quo has been fucked from the start with her. If she falls for me, too, I won't be able to push her away as I will have to when the time comes. No woman falls for me. I don't let anybody get close enough for feelings to develop.

Now, once I go all the way with her, show her the world as I function in it, I don't know if I can go back to life before Ariana Morelli. Or if I'd even want to.

I have my antidote...but what if she's my cure? My silver bullet.

After a few deep breaths, fighting my indecision, the body and brain win. The heart will break either way—it's the sunk cost in this whole mess.

I pluck open the bathroom cupboards. Towels. Robes. Pajamas. There's a big medical aid kit with all kinds of rolled up bandages and gauze that could work. It's also stocked with everything you need from razors to scissors to shampoo and condoms. Well, well, there's even some lube. I'll make sure to add a list of sex toys for next time to please whichever brother gets to fly with the love of his life.

What the hell? Love of my life? Did I just think that? *Fuck.* Matteo called it earlier. Smitten. That fucker.

I smirk as I walk back into the bedroom where Ariana is exactly as I left her, wet, wanton, and so fucking beautiful, I stop in my tracks to stare at her. She's closed her eyes, but her chest heaves as she becomes aware of my presence.

As I step up to the edge of the bed to drop my loot to the mattress, her instincts take over, and she collapses her legs together, closing up.

"No, sweetheart," I say, kneeling onto the bed to rest a hand on her knee. The command is there to open up again, to let me in. I was just about to get up close and personal with that sweet pussy.

"Dominic," she protests as she struggles up, eyes begging, hands reaching for me. "You made me wait."

I tip her chin up, trace lines with my fingers down her neck, and splay my hand over her chest. "Part of the process, sweetheart."

I guide her back down as I straddle her, effectively trapping her with my body but not putting my weight on her yet. I wait for her to react to this position, to the power I have over her like this, to leave this room we're in and go back to that night in her head, whichever room it exists in, but her hands are on my thighs and sliding up to my cock.

A quiver of need ripples down my spine, tightening my balls as my cock hardens even more.

Fuck.

Here's the thing. I'm planning to spend hours here, edging her, kissing her, caressing and teasing her until she comes with a single lick to her clit, but if she starts touching me, I'm not going to last.

At least she's still completely with me, and she doesn't react to some trauma memory. *'I don't think of any of that when I'm with you.'* What man doesn't fall in love with that?

When she's on her back, I take her hands and gather them above her head again.

"Here, sweetheart. Keep them here for me," I murmur close to her lips, and then I kiss her. Deeply and ardently, my revelation in the bathroom in every sweep of my tongue, in every kiss I close off, needing to pull away but finding I can't stop. I need more.

When I eventually come up for breath, I reach for the gauze and unwrap it. She's staring at me in a haze, arms limp above her head, and she doesn't protest when I tie her wrists together.

"This is good?" I ask as I do a simple bow.

"Yes. More, please."

She bites her lip to hide a smile, and my heart swells.

My sweetheart is a fast learner.

52

ARIANA

Cold shaving gel drops to my skin, and I shiver, but it's more with the idea of what he is doing than the actual feel of the gel as he gently spreads it over my skin. His touch is featherlight yet sure, each slide of the blade down my sex a promise of what's to come.

When Dominic takes care of a woman—

I can think of nothing else as he prepares me for whatever comes next. He's fast, his fingers deft as he makes quick work of shaving me. I'm embarrassed, but I'm too turned on to really care. This is as much for his pleasure as mine, and the pleasure is intense as he traces each slide of the blade with his thumb, making sure never to touch me where I want his touch the most.

I look down. The picture of him leaning into my pussy, concentration etched on his brow as he wipes away the gel, makes my clit pulse. He hasn't touched me there yet. It's as if he is teasing me—torturing me—despite the fact I'm dripping wet with desire.

"Dominic...I need more," I whisper as he puts everything he's used in a towel and drops it to the floor.

"Soon, sweetheart."

He dips his head to press a soft kiss to my mound, his hands now on my knees, holding me open. As he opens his mouth and with a slow, intense lick, slides down to the tip of my sex, electricity shoots through the short stretch between his lips and my clit. I jolt against him, suddenly getting why the shaving was as much for my pleasure as for his own. This is going to be intense.

He smiles against my skin as I tug at my bonds, quivering with the aftershocks. Nobody has ever done this to me before, and it's...it's a lot.

And I want more.

Instead of going down on me as I'm praying he would, he runs his bottom lip up and kisses my tally scars, my bullet wound, my tattoo, higher to my navel as he spreads open-mouth kisses to what seems like every inch of flesh between my sex and my breasts. It's fire trailing a path on my skin, and ice whispering wherever his lips leave, the incongruous sensation making me squirm.

His lips reach that sweet spot behind my ear. "Anything specific you want, sweetheart?" he whispers. "Or do you want me to just do everything I want to do to you?"

"Make me come already," I beg, shameless. "With your fingers. I want to have your fingers in me." To see if I can take it. If it would hurt. I have no doubt he'd know exactly what to do to get me there. At this rate, it's not going to take much.

"Not yet, sweetheart. When you're ready," he murmurs in my ear, his warm breath sparking goosebumps down my chest.

"I *am* ready," I beg, needing friction.

"Maybe, but I'm not."

He kisses me then, a slow and erotic turn of his tongue with mine while he lowers his body, his erection belying his words as he rides it into my thigh.

All I want is to touch him, to make him feel what he makes

me feel, but Dominic is on a mission of his own, wandering the panes of my body with his lips, his fingers, strong but almost weightless as he twists each nerve ending on my skin into a tight bundle, kindling for the fire he's igniting in my core.

When he presses a palm to my pelvic bone and massages a slow circle, applying the perfect pressure, my hips drive into his hand all by themselves.

"Oh my—Dominic," I whisper, feeling the pleasure right there, a flame to my fuse that suddenly seems very short. "Oh my... More," I beg as I roll my hips into his hand, and then, as if there is a god out there, listening to my mumbled, desire-laced prayers, Dominic finally flicks his tongue over my nipple, and then, as if he knew I'm on the verge, gently sucks it and tugs.

An orgasm starts to ripple though me, from deep inside my core, and for a split second, I think it would stave off, but then it explodes, and I gasp at the pleasure of each pulse through my sex as I strain against the bonds.

"Dominic," I whimper, breathless as he keeps suckling at me, every tug of his lips seeming to drain my orgasm into the bed. I had no idea it could be like this.

"Good girl," he murmurs with a smile in his voice.

"How do you... how do you know I've come?"

He looks up at me, his dark brown eyes liquid with lust.

"Let me count the ways," he teases as he trails a fingertip round my sex, still not touching me where I must be drenched. "The way you quivered under my palm. The way your breathing turned a bit frantic. The way you moaned?"

I'm already flushed, but now the heat suffuses my face. I didn't even realize I was moaning.

"And then there's your scent, sweetheart. I can smell the release on you." He kisses my inner arm, working his way up to my shoulder and then to my face where he presses a sugar-sweet kiss on my forehead. "You're still good?"

He is so gentle, so kind, so considerate, so experienced, I

feel like a virgin in the hands of a master seducer. In a way I am, and now, I see right through his process. By being the opposite of everything Franco was, he is slowly erasing every memory I have from that night until the only thing remaining are slight indents on the page, to remind me that someone was there before, a very long time ago.

God...this man. I lean up to press a soft kiss to his lips. "Are you still good?"

"Sweetheart, I've just started. That was the warm-up."

"Let me touch you," I plead, feeling cheated that he has free rein to my body, where my desire to touch him is only building. He isn't going to orgasm that need out of me. "I know you never let someone touch you, Dominic, but please..."

I've seen him. I've seen every scar he has on his body. He has nothing to hide from me.

There's hesitation in his gaze, but behind all of it, the need only I can probably understand. I haven't let anybody touch me for years, out of fear, and he has been broken differently, but it's the same. He needs the same healing that comes with touch.

When he reaches for the gauze to untie my wrists, I've crossed a bridge to a side I didn't know existed. As soon as my hands are free, I cup his face. "Let me in as I let you in, please."

He drops his forehead to mine, and as I brush my fingertips over his tense shoulder muscles and the broad expanse of his back, a shudder runs through his body.

"When it comes to you, the status quo has been fucked from the start," he murmurs, nuzzling my nose with his. "Take what you want, sweetheart, take what you need. Take everything."

53

DOMINIC

All my plans for her are derailing. This is about her, but I am the lost cause. I can't say no to her. Not with her warm, needy body molded against mine, not with that sweet, begging tone in her voice. Not when her need to touch me overrides every other desire. She is so sincere and maybe, just maybe, I should let someone in. Not just someone—*her*.

Ariana is busy with my shirt's buttons as I untuck it from my pants. As soon as I can shrug the shirt off, impatient, I toss it to the side. Her hands are on my chest, soothing over my pecs, my shoulders, then her fingertips slide into my hair as she pulls me in for a kiss.

I sink into her as if she holds captive all the air I need to breathe, and the notion only intensifies what's happening between us. She's caught on, and her touch is almost reverent as she explores my body, her fingertips brushing over the coarser hairs on my pecs, tracing the lines of my collarbones, molding to the shape of every muscle I built into this power tool that is my body. I am not weak in any way or capacity, but with Ariana...she's going to be my biggest weakness.

I roll onto my back, pulling her to me, my hands in her hair and on her breast, massaging her nipple's hardened peak. She half-straddles me, her wet pussy pressing against my thigh as her hand travels south, following the line dividing my six-pack.

When her arm brushes against the tip of my cock, she freezes for a second. I smile into her mouth then kiss her deeper. This one...she's the sweetest thing with so many little tells which reveal her inexperience.

Her touch is addictive, emulating my own: soft, gentle, caring, and when she finally strokes over the silky flesh of my shaft, I arch off the bed with a gasp at the intensity of having someone else's hands on me.

"Is this okay?" she whispers as she plays with me, running her fingertips up and down and finally testing my girth. "You're so...huge."

I bite down on a groan as she tentatively tugs at my cock, knowing both her hands will cover its length neatly.

"Sweetheart," I choke out as I circle my palm over hers, upping the pressure as I ride our hands in unison, adrift in the eroticism of her and me together like this. "At this rate, we're going to have to tie you up again."

She smiles as she kisses me down my neck, and for a few seconds I enjoy her attentions, then remind myself this is about her. I flip us over, and she giggles as I hook her knee with my thumb and pull her wide open. Her other leg latches over my hip, and like this, I can put pressure on her clit as I position my cock just right to ride against her. She is slick with need, and she moans as I find a rhythm, sliding my cock up and down her wet pussy without penetration.

"Dominic," she whispers, sounding rather desperate. "How do you know how to do this?"

I cut off her question with a deep kiss, not wanting to recall all the women I've had when she's only been with one other man, and that against her will. I don't stop kissing her, perching on one arm to make space and have access to her body. I brush knuckles along her breasts, over her nipples, down her belly, and by the time I reach her hip, she's heaving with pent-up need, and I bet if I give it another minute, my girl will orgasm again.

I slow down, allowing her to catch a breath as I slip my fingers ever lower, between her legs, sliding two fingers up and down over her drenched sex. When I finally circle her clit, she bites down on her lip and buries her face in my neck.

"Oh, sweetheart," I murmur as I slowly move on to circle her entrance. "You're ready for this. Just breathe, okay? Easy now."

"Hm-hmm."

She doesn't clench her legs closed—in fact, she's splayed open with trust. When I finally push a fingertip into her, I expect her to clam up, but she breathes and opens her eyes, staring straight into mine.

"Does it hurt?" I ask, cautious as I push deeper into her tight, tight pussy.

"No...it's...*oh*....more."

I take my time to enter and stretch her with one digit, and when she picks up the rhythm of my hand, rolling her hips into each gentle thrust, I kiss her.

"Good girl," I murmur against her lips. "More?"

"More. Harder."

I didn't expect her to be ready for that, but I comply, testing her every inch until two of my fingers are lodged inside of her, my fingertips pushing against her g-spot. When I stop and just hold still, her glazed eyes brighten.

"Don't stop," she begs as she reaches for my hand, prompting me into action again. A beautiful pink glow spreads over her pale skin, a telltale sign of another pending orgasm. I extract my fingers and grab her hand to press a quick kiss to her palm.

"I need to taste you," I say as I get off the bed.

Her eyes are on me, wide and desperate as she takes in my body, my rampant erection that won't need much to go off like a rocket right now. I need to slow things down. When I reach for her ankles and pull her to the edge of the bed, she struggles up in protest.

"Lie back, sweetheart, relax," I instruct, guiding her until her butt is on the edge, her sweet wet pussy right there. As I kneel down, I hook her legs over my shoulders and start to press kisses from her knee to her inner thigh. She gasps as I lick the smooth sides of her sex, arousal already spread over her skin, every inch of her a delectable taste of her need and desire. She jolts and arches her back into the mattress, her hands desperate as they rake into my hair to hold me in check.

She's close, so fucking close, it won't take much.

I gently untangle her fingers from my hair. "Hold on to the bedding, Ariana."

"Dominic—"

"Easy, sweetheart, let me take care of you."

I slide my fingers into her body again, holding still, curving them to put pressure where she'd love it most, and then I get down to business. She's writhing under my tongue, needing to find a rhythm to crash into orgasm, but probably also overwhelmed with each new intense sensation. When I fuck her a few times with my fingers, my tongue in her slit, then shifting so my lips close over her clit to suck, she bursts.

Her inner walls pulsate around my fingers as I feel her release drenching me, and I lap it all up, thirsty for this proof of our passion. She's quivering all over, a fist to her mouth to stop her from screaming. I work my fingers, rubbing at that spot deep inside her, and still she comes, buckling at my hand.

When the intensity subsides, I slowly extract my hand and press a tender kiss to her mound. Her grip on the bedcovers has relaxed but left a twist in the fabric. I rise up and crawl over her, wanting to check in. She seems out of breath, but in a good way, flushed in bloom with her eyes closed and fingers still pressed to her mouth.

"You're so beautiful, sweetheart, like this, I—" I catch myself from going too far. From telling her about this invasive feeling I have that is both foreign and destructive to the inner peace I've clawed together over years.

She opens her eyes slowly, in a daze, and then she smiles at me, and it's as if her joy pierces straight through my heart to light up my whole being.

"That was beautiful," she murmurs as she cups my face. "You're beautiful."

I dip in for a kiss to hide my emotions, and this time she traps me with hands weaving into my hair, her legs settling over my hips and hugging my erection to her body. When she pushes one shoulder, I collapse to my side and pull her close. Her hand trails over my hip, fingertips tenderly brushing over my scars, sending patches of feeling to my core.

This is dangerous. More dangerous than so many things I've been through. Love is not allowed. Not like this. Not with her. Tying her to me would be the worst thing I can possibly do to her. She won't be my burden, but I will be hers, forcing her into a lifestyle few can adapt to.

"I want to try something," she whispers between kisses.

"What do you want to try?" I'm wary she's going to push this too far today and something will trigger her, but I need a distraction from my spiraling thoughts.

"Like this...it won't remind me of—" She breaks off as she peels away from where I've cradled her. She nudges me to sit up, and I comply. "Criss cross your legs."

I study her intently, my erection searching for the bull's eye. She'll have more control in this position. "I get where you're going with this, but I'm not sure this is a good idea, Ariana."

Uncertainty flashes across her face, and that's the last thing I want for her. To doubt herself, to doubt me. "Ariana..."

"Help me, then?" she asks, her voice small.

"Always, but this might be too soon. I don't want you to push yourself to do something you're not ready for."

"I don't feel pushed. I feel liberated. Don't you get it?" She stares into my eyes, tears brimming in hers. "This is so different —" She breaks off and swallows down her emotions, and when she looks at me again, our truth hits me hard as it sits shallow in her eyes. "We might not have another chance."

And that's going to break me. This could be our only chance to... I press kisses to her eyes, not wanting her to feel failed, for me to fail her. I lean over to where I've tossed some condoms to the side. I figured we wouldn't be using them, but what my girl wants, my girl gets.

I rip open the package and roll the condom down my shaft.

"Go slowly, sweetheart," I say as I gather her to my lap, knowing it might hurt. My fingers did prep her to some extent, but I'm not exactly made for semi-virginal pussies that haven't had any action in over a decade. "And promise me you'll stop if it hurts."

"It isn't going to hurt," she says softly. "Because you'll never hurt me. Nothing will ever hurt with you."

Oh, sweetheart, but it will. And it's going to hurt both ways.

I'm already steeling myself for it.

54

ARIANA

Dominic has his hands on my butt, raising me into position. Like this, I'm splayed open, his cock right there, nudging to get in. I press down on his broad, muscled shoulders, hovering in place, my legs hugging his hips. I have enough control to sink down on him slowly, to give myself time to adjust to his size.

When I let go and he breaches into me, I snatch at my breath. "Oh, God—"

"I've got you, sweetheart," Dominic says as he supports me with an arm around my waist, my chest flush to his as he cups my cheek. "Take your time."

We're staring into each other's eyes as I move a bit and then he meets me halfway, pushing his hips up. I have no clue how he does it, holding me this gently, keeping me in check, seeming to enter me a millimeter at a time.

"Easy, sweetheart, breathe," he whispers, pausing to give me time.

I kiss him then, needing the connection as he ends up guiding me onto his cock. I'm so full, so stretched, and it hurts, but just a little bit. It's nothing like that night so long ago now, where that hateful man didn't stop, going at me like a dog for hours.

It's just a glance into one of the many rooms in my mind, and I close the door firmly on it, blocking the memories out. Instead, I focus on Dominic's scent, warm and with undertones of pine and musk, the soft sweetness of his lips in contrast with the five o'clock shadow along his jaw. How my nipples harden against the feel of his pecs where they strain against my softer parts. The feel of him drawing out, pushing back in with a smooth glide that already builds to something again.

I've always thought I was frigid, not made for this, but he's torn every one of those walls down. With him, anything seems possible. And when, after what seems like just a few minutes, I feel the tension build in my core again, I lean back to meet his gaze.

"Can you come like this?" I ask, unsure. I always assumed it needed to be rough and violent, but Dominic is making me reassess everything.

"Yes, I'm almost there, sweetheart. I've been holding back like I'm walking a pack of horses," he says with a chuckle. "I feel you gathering, and it's...it's driving me wild."

"Oh." I bite my lip to hide a smile of pure pleasure. For a man who is almost wild, he's never shown it or lost control in the moment. He really is taking care of me. How do I give this up? How do I let him go? "Let's come together."

"Kiss me," he orders.

I open my lips for his invasion which comes with a rhythm that matches every rise and fall of my body onto his as he takes charge, hitting me deep and meeting a need I've never felt before. I've never been closer to any human, and with my current track record, this will be the last time.

I hug him to me, clinging to him with desperation as if it would keep us like this forever. And then I come, slower this time, but it seems to ripple from inside my heart, down to where I feel him rippling up into me as he comes, too. It's powerful, it's intense, and somehow so sublime, it's as if we've entered a next realm together.

"Fuck, Ariana," he whispers as he keeps me in place, holding still so we can both revel in the moment together.

I'm breathless, and his chest is heaving against mine, a sheen of sweat over our bodies, mixing with our spent passion as we kiss each other again. This is so intimate, I never want to let go, but eventually his grip on me softens, and he fumbles between us as he slips out of my body. He's so gentle when he lays me down, pressing a soft kiss to my cheek.

"I'll be back in a minute."

Trying to catch my breath, I prod at my bullet wound which has closed up in a scabbed scar. It doesn't seem worse for wear, and I still, listening to Dominic opening and closing the faucet. I roll on my side to watch him walk back inside the room. God, he is gorgeous. Tall and manly, and yet he has the tenderness of a poet in him.

"I feel a nap coming on," I say as he kneels on the bed with a wet facecloth.

"A nap is definitely on the to-do list. Here," he says as he nudges my leg, and I let him wipe me clean. "Gorgeous little pussy," he murmurs, the same concentration from earlier back on his face. "What I won't give to eat you out every day."

The words hit my chest where they boomerang around looking for a place to land, but when he shoots me a wicked playful grin I haven't seen before, I realize he's only teasing me.

"Said pussy is at your disposal, but only with a pre-approved schedule," I quip back.

"Is that so?" He tosses the cloth to the floor, helps me get under the covers, then switches off the cabin lights. "Tell me how busy you plan to be over the next few weeks, and I'll slot myself in where I can."

Keep this light, keep this easy. He's only joking about the next few weeks. Ideally, I'd separate from him as soon as I get off this plane. I can't afford to get any closer to this man than I already am. Somehow, he has breached my walls. He's conquered my body and is banging at the door of my innermost sanctum, at my heart, which I've always protected with a steel will and the full force of a resting bitchface that gives most men hives.

When I say nothing, he pulls me to him.

"Welcome to the mile-high club, sweetheart." He sighs, and it's somewhat desolate. "Sometimes it's fun to imagine things would work out just perfectly."

When he presses a kiss to my temple, I curl into him, never wanting to let go.

55

DOMINIC

I never closed the cabin windows, and we've flown into the night. Ariana is curled up against me, and for a last minute, I treasure the feel of her soft body against mine, the sweet scent of sex still clinging to her skin, begging me to lick it off her inch by inch. I could do all of that again, but I best check in on the time as I've lost track completely.

I get up and go dig in my jacket pocket for my cellphone. We've less than two hours of flight time left, and I'm freaking hungry. Several missed calls and messages from both Matteo and Benedict, but I'm not going to read and reply to them now. The knowledge that Matteo is Randazzo's son weighs on me, but it doesn't feel like something I want to throw into the void via an email. It doesn't change anything between us brothers, but it changes everything for Ariana.

I dress in a robe, quietly open the door, and slip out to where I've left my laptop earlier. I indicate to the hostess we're ready to eat, and with my laptop in hand, retreat back to the bedroom. I want to spend as much time with Ariana as possible. I can't shed this ticking time-bomb feeling in my stomach, which is weird since most of the issues I thought we had have been ironed out. It's this situation with Gabriella which is working on me subconsciously.

We're heading for Lamezia Terme, a smaller international airport in the south of Italy, closest to where Ariana told me she grew up in Calabria. Once we land, we'll have vehicles to take us to the small town and from there to the farmhouse where Franco's uncle still hides out. We'll arrive at the crack of dawn, and for Antonio Mancuso's sake, I hope he's a morning person.

It's good we had a nap. This day is still going to be a motherfucker. There's been one too many of those lately, and I'd be happy to have this whole mess sorted out.

I settle back on the bed and flip open my laptop screen, go through the security checks with my thumbprint and codes, and finally, the home screen opens. I give it a minute to connect again to the WiFi, relieved Ariana has her back to me and won't be disturbed by the laptop's screen.

Once I'm connected, I open my email, my eyes by habit skipping over all the weeds in my inbox, homing in on the important ones. Benedict. Fingerprints.

I open the email and read the short message.

By the time I've read the last line, my heart thumps in my chest, and my stomach is twisted into a fist. I fucking knew it. Deep down in me, I fucking sensed it, but I was too blindsided to see what I knew was in front of me.

I read the message again and again, getting to grips with this reality slap in the face.

Nicky,

I had to dig and get others to dig even deeper. And then dig some more. Ariana Morelli is buried deep, but my team likes a challenge, especially when money and bets get involved.

The bad news:

Ariana Morelli is a DIA agent, working for the Direzione Inves-

tigativa Antimafia. It's a police force tasked with combating organized crime in Italy. She's an undercover agent, which explains some of her arrival in the US. If Franco Fiore knew she was working undercover, he'd have no scruples in using and offing her.

Franco had no scruples to begin with. I read the rest of the message again, my fist clenching.

The good news:

The DIA already thinks she's dead. She's been declared missing on their files, presumed dead, and this dates back to the time of Randazzo's death. Not sure how this all connects, but don't cradle that one too close. She's dangerous and has seen too much on our side of the pond. Matteo will have more instructions for you.

Fuck. Benedict has copied Matteo in on this message, but our new Don already made his instructions clear. I bet if he knew this about Ariana, he would never have let her leave the US in the first place, where she'd be less of a liability to us.

If I knew about this, I wouldn't have let her leave the fucking Don's house. I would have kept her locked up, where she's safe.

In the old Don's *Il Consiglio*, Ariana would have been an automatic execution. No questions asked. Not with what she's seen, witnessing Franco's death at our hands, irrespective of whether he deserved it or not. Plus she's ready to identify us all in a fucking line-up. My fingers quiver over the laptop keys as my chest tightens at the mere thought of the Don and Ariana. Together. Face to face.

A tsunami of emotions unleashes in me, and I have to remind myself again and again that the Don is dead and he can't hurt her. Not like he hurt mom while I was too weak to protect her. I swallow down the painful pebble in my throat and groan. We have a new Don, and he might be her brother, but Matteo hasn't been tested. He could use Ariana if things get desperate enough.

Once she's back in Boston, she'll be deemed an *Il Consiglio* asset, and right now, this could mean being fobbed off to an asshole like Ivan Petrov. For all I know, he's the type who'll have no qualms using her, raping her, and then offering her to his men for their fucking pleasure.

I'm trembling so much, I grip the laptop screen and breathe through it as my gaze drags over the lines of Benedict's message again. Eventually, my fear is crushed under anger and desperation.

I'm fucking pissed off that I'd been so slow to catch on with all her tells, but now this idea of her suffering at the old Don's hand—now Matteo's hand and maybe even Petrov's hand—evokes something else in me. A protective demon I didn't even know existed. I'm a fallen angel who only wants to wrap her in my charred wings and keep her close, hide and protect her from this sick world we live in.

A world she's as much part of, even if she's chosen to step out of the herd and become a hunter.

My skin crawls with strands of information I can't tie together, with all the knowledge and secrets we keep to ourselves. I already see the connection Benedict and Matteo can't see because I haven't told them Ariana is Matteo's half-sister. Randazzo's daughter. A Mafia princess. Working for the Italian police. As a fucking undercover agent.

I reach for her and ghost my trembling fingers over her hair. She is so delicate, beautiful, so treasured that I can't find it in me to wake her and shatter this moment and drag her into this new reality, her final secret exposed. She's still asleep, but she stirs as if she could feel my caress.

Fuck. I can't let her walk free ever again. We all know she knows too much about *Il Consiglio*, but now her insider knowledge's value has multiplied thousand-fold. She could hang us all. She could also be immensely useful. She'll have insights into how some things work in Europe and knowledge is power.

I glance down at her, a delicate, fragile woman who doesn't give off the robust, gun-wielding, no-bullshit type usually associated with women in the police force. It works. I bet if it weren't for her beauty, she'd almost go unnoticed. What the fuck was she doing, undercover, to such an extent Franco knew where she was?

And then my stomach turns. '*Franco always knew where she was.*' Vincenzo said so in his own words.

I just breathe for a minute, all the ramifications of Vincenzo's words sinking in, and then she stirs, rolling over onto her back and blinking into the night. I switch on the lights by the side of the bed, and she moans in protest, but this party is fucking over. She needs to talk, *now*.

Our gazes meet, and she sits up straight in a daze. "Dominic, what's wrong?"

"A fucking cop, Ariana?" I hiss. "You're a fucking *sbirro* and fuck knows I should have seen it, but—" I break off, waving at her in general. "Freaking distraction."

"God, I'm not," she says, clawing the bedding to her chest to cover up.

My lips pull into a thin line, and I get that look on my face —the one that hints of the devil in me. "Don't you fucking dare—"

"I'm still waking up, Dom—"

"Wake up faster, sweetheart."

Several beats of silence pass as we just stare at each other. Her mind's racing. She's doing the math and can come to only one conclusion: she's fucked and at my mercy. Who are we kidding here? She's been at my mercy from the moment I saw her crumbling to the floor in that warehouse. At any point, I could've crushed her. Except, I didn't.

She doesn't cower away from my death stare, though, and I've had grown men crumble, so I'll give her this.

When she closes her eyes, I have to restrain myself from reaching out to her because whatever else she is, she is also the woman I made love to earlier. The woman who found the only bridge to my soul and bravely crossed it—to be with *me* and meet me where I'm at, despite everything she went through.

"How do you know?"

"You're not denying it, then?"

"Clearly, there's no point in denying it. How do you know?"

"It doesn't matter how I know."

I push my closed laptop to the side and get off the bed, needing to distance myself from her. I'm a fucking wreck. I pace the room as I find my clothes scattered all over and toss hers to the bed in passing. Fuck. If only I can rewind the clock and be on an infinite flight with her, in this room, just as we were hours ago, but we can never go back there.

"We're landing in two hours. That's the amount of time you have to tell me exactly how the fuck you ended up in the DIA, then with Franco, and then—" And then in my fucking arms. "Go shower and get dressed."

She reaches for her T-shirt where it droops over the edge of the bed, and for a blessed second, I have a last visual of this perfect woman I've crashed into love with. Already, my every resolve when it comes to her has started to oscillate between dragging her back to the US and locking her up where she'll be safe forever, forgoing this hunt for Gabriella, and doing what my trained instincts instruct me to do: kill her. The dead can't identify my brothers in a line-up.

The DIA already thinks she's dead.

There are many reasons we Scalera boys don't get to love. Women make us weak. Ariana is a walking, breathing personification of my weakness, and I'll be damned if a woman drags me—*us*— down.

But then I look at her, and I know I'd never be able to hurt her, never mind kill her. It's the cop in her, the part that's deceived me, that I want to cut out like rot, but I can't do it, not without killing the whole.

Bottom line: Ariana is my Achille's Heel.

56

ARIANA

Dominic's gaze burns holes straight to my heart. How is it I'm always just that one step behind? I have no clue how he figured out I'm with the DIA, but just like Franco, his timing is impeccable.

I was stupid to think he wouldn't keep on digging until he'd figured me out. Dominic is after all the type that leaves no stone unturned and nothing up to chance.

He won't let me out of his sight now. I won't be surprised if he handcuffs me to him just to get off this jet, if I get to leave this jet at all. The obvious end for me, as it's always been, is death. You get to know too many Mafia secrets, and they figure out you're an undercover cop? That I'm still alive is a miracle.

I'm a threat to him, but more importantly, to his brothers. As I step into the shower, I recall in a haze that Matteo Scalera is my brother, too, if only a half-brother. Maybe I'm not so dispensable anymore. Matteo, if I understood correctly from what I've seen, is also the head of *Il Consiglio*. I've always been someone's property, or beholden to someone. I'm a parcel that once again switched hands.

At some point, Matteo will give Dominic orders, and the

thought makes acid turn in my belly. They will decide what happens to me, but until that moment, I have one last thing of value: the connection between Franco, his uncle, and Gabriella. I'm not done for yet.

As I shower, I try not to think about Dominic's hands on my body, his slow seduction, or the tenderness I'm feeling in places where he's been. These are memories I want to keep drifting on, like on a cloud, high above my reality I can't escape, and ordering my thoughts is almost impossible. For minutes, I lean against the shower wall and let tears cleanse me. If only it were this easy to let go of the memories of him.

Once I'm dressed, I pad out of the bathroom and find the bedroom empty, the bed still a mess. I walk out into the short corridor and out into the bigger living space of the cabin. Dominic is sitting at the table with his laptop, furiously typing a way, an empty plate pushed to the side.

When he becomes aware of me, he looks up and rakes me down. I'm nervous, my hands gathered in front of me, waiting for his instructions. He gave them so tenderly earlier, so gentle, but now a dark scowl has settled over his face, his lips pursed with angry lines cupping his mouth.

He slaps his laptop closed, picks up his phone, and stands with both items, keeping them out of reach. I'm not sure why he's worried. It's not as if I'm going to jump on the internet and email the whole DIA that some Mafia crime ring from the States is about to land at Lamezia Terme.

"Eat something," he says. "And when I'm back, we'll talk, so get your story straight."

He doesn't need to add that he'll drag tiny details out of me like nails from a hand. Or what he'd do to me when he catches me in a lie. I just nod, and he doesn't even look at me when he walks past. I suppose part of him feels betrayed, and I understand why. He wanted to be a cop when he was five years old and then got the brunt of his father's abuse for the rest of his childhood for just uttering something so sweetly naive.

With a sigh, I sit down at the table, and when the air hostess comes over with drinks and a meal fit for a king, I dig into it, knowing it might be one of my last.

When Dominic comes back, in a fresh suit he got from who knows where, hair still wet, freshly showered and smelling like Heaven-is-This-Man™, I lean back in my chair and weep inwardly for all I had and lost in mere hours.

"Did Franco know you are with the DIA?" he asks without preamble as he sits down across from me.

God help me here. Dominic has gone over into interrogation mode.

"Yes. But I didn't know that he knew or how he knew. The night he came for me was the first time I saw him since that night when—when—"

"Right," he cuts in, his tone softer. "Let's go back to when you ran away. Stole ten thousand euros and escaped to Milan. Why Milan?"

"In Antonio Mancuso's house, that's Franco's uncle—"

"Yes. Yes, I know all about Antonio Mancuso." He waves at me to carry on.

"In Mancuso's house, there was always a lot of talk about the *guardie*, the *sbirri*, especially the ones fighting organized crime. There was a new *direttrice,* a director, in Milan, Elena Bianchi. Imagine, a woman heading the DIA in one of the biggest cities in Italy. They were constantly making jokes about her, how weak she was, how she was only a woman, and how they would crush her if she ever came south." I swallow down the bile pushing up my throat. "Problem was, she was good. She cleaned up Milan. When I ran away, I knew there was only one person in the world who could help me, and I put all my eggs in that one basket. Elena Bianchi was the best thing that happened to me."

"How did you gain access to her?"

Of course he'd know she had protection.

"I played on my super power. Just being a girl." The look on his face makes me smile. "We're not perceived as a threat. I managed to get to her car and corner her, then told her, in front of her bodyguards, that I have information to share. This got me a thorough pat down and a two-hour ride about town, in which I told her everything. I don't know, we just kept driving around until everything I had to share was out, and I didn't hold back."

It was the first of many long talks I had with Elena, and in a way, just being able to download with her might have been my saving grace.

"What happened then?"

"By the end of the ride, she actually took me to her home. I went from the heart of the Mafia in Calabria right into the core of their biggest enemy. Elena arranged witness protection for me. I legally changed my name, and Emilia Korhonen was 'killed' in the process, and even made the local newspapers to keep the Mafia off my scent. I spent three years in a Swiss boarding school in Geneva on the Italian taxpayers' dime, then went to university in Switzerland."

"What did you study?" he asks, not showing an inch of surprise, not even jumping on the fact I gave him my real, birth name.

"Criminology, law, and languages. English, French, Russian." I was preparing myself for service in the police force, taking my first steps in my vendetta against both Franco and Randazzo.

At this, he quirks a brow. Well, it's not as if he asked. He just assumed from the tattoo I have on my lower belly I was just another Randazzo prostitute, with nothing else to offer.

"So the fluency in English via endless movies and pop songs was a lie?"

"No, it was the start."

He exhales a deep breath and leans back in his chair. "What happened next?"

I close my eyes for a second. I've never spoken to anybody about this and maybe it's time I should. I've told him everything else and it's been liberating. To finally be open about my past with Dominic would break down my last barriers and maybe he'll understand why I became a DIA agent, how my past shaped me and fueled my vendetta.

"You can look it up on the internet. Elena got killed. Gunned down like a criminal in a drive-by assassination outside a restaurant in the suburb where she lived. We're still not sure who did it, but her death was obviously connected to her work."

Dominic stares at me as I try not to lose my composure. Elena was my original guardian angel. She built the bridge for me out of the Mafia, once and for all. Franco was always my stepping-stone vendetta. I planned to get him annihilated en route to killing Randazzo.

Vengeance for my mom and Randazzo's treatment of her was first on my to-do list, but then Elena happened. I always assumed Randazzo was the man behind her death and killing him would have avenged her and my mom in one smooth blow. Then Franco dragged me back into the Mafia over that same bridge before blowing it up. Now that Dominic knows my truth, I'm stuck, and there's no way I ever get back to the other side again.

"Sounds like you had a mentor who cared for you. I'm sorry for your loss."

At his words, so unexpected, I have to blink back the tears pushing behind my eyes. "Yes. We didn't see each other often. In fact, our interactions were limited as far as possible for my safety, but I never forgot what she did for me. I finished my basic studies and got integrated in the DIA via a program for people with my profile. I was already on their radar, thanks to prep work Elena did when I first met her."

"Your profile?"

"Orphans. People who won't be missed. People who have an intense hate for an institution and who would give their lives to take it down."

We glare at each other. Dominic's jaw ticks as we're brutally honest with each other. I am a hunter, and in my world, he is prey. Except I'm weakened, in my heart and in my soul. First by the ordeal Franco put me through, and then by going to Boston, constantly on the run in my mind, and then by him, this man who made love to me earlier as if I'm the woman he's been waiting his entire life for. Letting me touch him. Being human, caring, vulnerable, not the kind of cookie-cutter Mafia brute I grew up with and loathe.

I am a compass that lost its truth north.

Maybe I lost it when I learned Randazzo had died. Killed at someone else's hand.

And then Franco met his fate with this lot.

None of it happened by my hand. In fact, I had no impact at all. I could have been wiped from the picture and it wouldn't have made a day's difference.

I didn't count for squat.

I can *observe, adapt, and only act when the time is right* as much as I want, nothing has prepared me for this.

My whole life's goals, the two things that kept me going through every up and down got ripped away from me, leaving me winded. I haven't been able to catch my breath again since that night, stumbling through everything that led me here.

And now, I'm at the mercy of a man who I know has none.

57

DOMINIC

Jesus Christ. I didn't miss it; I just didn't heed my sixth sense, choosing to be blind to all her red flags.

As she talks, giving me glimpses into her life, little things add up to her truth. The way she gathered information as she walked through the Don's house, how she tried to steal my gun and then wielded it like a pro, but unable to shoot me. Something short-circuited in her head in that moment, and I'd love to think it was me. But it wasn't. It was the past she keeps on running from.

Or maybe she's running towards it, to annihilate it once and for all. People don't join the police force for no reason, especially not special units like the DIA.

Ariana Morelli—Emilia Korhonen, as she admitted—was in witness protection and changed her name, disappeared from her prior life, and yet chose to be integrated back into the Mafia as an undercover agent as if she belongs—because she does. No wonder she fooled me.

"What training did you have in the DIA?" I ask to keep her talking.

So far so good, but at some point, she might stop, choosing

to protect her team over giving me information. Not that I would do anything with it. We have enough shit in Boston to keep us busy, and I don't need to poke around the Italian police force or kick the hornet's nest further down the field, hoping to shoot a fucking goal with it. It's bad enough Matteo established the kick-off with killing Randazzo.

"The usual basic training, firearms, tactical, some combat training," she says with a shrug, as if this is old news. "And then the specialized training in organized crime, surveillance, intelligence, hostage negotiations. Extensive psychological preparation to go undercover. That's just the broad brushstrokes."

Typical training, but nothing about this woman is typical or average, and I'm looking at her with fresh eyes...and admiration. Through everything, she kept her cool.

"What were you involved with when Franco came for you?" This is the inflection point in her story and where our paths start to merge. How did our paths cross? I'd love to know.

She glances to where the air hostess is busy on the other side of the cabin, preparing for landing. Nobody can hear our conversation over the hum of the jet's engines. My bodyguards sit in their usual spots by the front and back of the plane, out of earshot.

"We were working on a long-term infiltration operation of Randazzo's sex trafficking rings in Italy. The plan was to penetrate and take down the ring leaders and make the whole structure crumble." She shakes her head with a frustrated sigh. "It took us years to get people undercover. I prepped as a make-up artist to gain entry and access to the auctions. And then—and then—"

"Wait a minute," I say, holding up a hand. "A makeup artist? At sex slave auctions?"

A feeling I'm starting to associate with her, one of burning fucking rage fueled by everything she's telling me, flares up in me. It's only doused by this intense need to protect her.

"What?"

"They put you, a rape survivor, under-fucking-cover on a sting operation that deals with sex trafficking? What the actual fuck, Ariana?" I growl, wanting to wring the necks of the men—without a doubt—who thought this would be a good idea. I'd think of all the things that would disqualify her from getting involved in a gig like this, it would be a brutal rape which left her stunned for decades.

"They didn't know, okay," she says, her voice thick with anger, on the verge of tears.

Tears she always shed quietly. Not only because she grew up in the Mafia, but because it would make her seem weak in the police force.

"How did they *not know*? You have psychological assessments, endless tests to make sure you're mentally fit for a job like that."

I don't even want to know what she witnessed in some sex trafficking shithole in Italy. What I've seen as we researched to prepare Matteo for his job to kill Randazzo, where I needed to go to ensure he had the proper security, was enough to give me fucking nightmares.

Me. Nightmares. Dominic Fucking Scalera, expert on human torture, had nightmares of the women ensnared in that world. And there she just walked in, a lamb into a lion's den. At any second, they could have flipped on her and thrown her on the stage, subjected her to more of what Franco did to her and worse. So much worse.

"I was fucking mentally fit for the job!" she hisses at me as she slams her hands on the table, leaning into my face. "I was after Randazzo. He killed my mom after he abused her for years, and then he tossed me to the wolves as if I was worthless. I had my own fucking agenda, and I was mentally strong enough to fool all of them. I got in exactly where I wanted to be. And if it wasn't for Franco Fiore walking in on me, I would eventually have gotten to Randazzo and looked him in the eye as I slit his fucking throat."

She stares me down, the anger in her voice reflected in her eyes, and I feel it vibrating through me.

I get it. I completely get every emotion she has.

"And then someone went and killed Randazzo before I—before I could get close enough—" She breaks off, tears flowing, her face flushed as she slumps in frustrated anger, stymied in the one thing that kept her going. "I have no idea who it was or how they managed to get close to him."

I do, but she doesn't need to know this.

I reach for her hand where she's fisted it on the table, and it trembles as I wrap it in mine. She's so delicate, but with this passion in her, I don't doubt she would have killed Randazzo if she'd had the chance. But to kill anybody else? No. Not this woman. And it isn't as if they could give you target practice with real humans, not even in the DIA. I'm relieved someone else avenged for her, someone she can now call family.

Maybe it's time to share that secret. He is, after all, her half-brother. Maybe they even get to know each other, get to care for each other.

"Matteo. It was Matteo," I say softly, squeezing her fingers as it hits me. Things suddenly makes sense. This is why Matteo got access to Randazzo so easily—he was his son. "Matteo killed Randazzo on our Don's command."

Even Matteo questioned it at the time, and the Don assured him Randazzo would see him, which means Matteo doesn't know. Or maybe he does...he's after all been fucking distracted lately.

"He walked straight into Randazzo's compound, because he's Randazzo's long-lost son. Instead of negotiating taking over Randazzo's operations, which I think was Randazzo's end goal, well...Matteo did what he did, and looked him in the eye all the way."

"I can't believe it," she says, her voice quivering. "Matteo?"

"Yes, sweetheart." I reach for a napkin and hand it to her, and she buries her face in it.

I give her a minute, but time is ticking. I'm not at the bottom of this whole fuck-up yet, and my sixth sense tells me I need to dive deeper to find the real nasty business behind everything that led to her sitting across from me.

"Ariana," I say, reaching for her again. "Franco knew exactly where you were. How?"

"I don't know," she says, between two suppressed sobs. "We moved so many times, I lost track of my team, and my team lost track of me. I even got separated from Lorenzo, my partner, and that was never the plan. In the end, I had nothing to notify them of my location. They confiscated everything bit by bit. From my phone to my makeup kit that held my last tracking device. They even took my shoes and gave me new clothes. I had nothing but my training to go on. When I heard Randazzo got killed, I wanted to run, but that was the night Franco came, and it was too late."

Because it was planned.

A chill sweeps down my spine as Don Scalera's voice echoes in my head. '*The police are so fucking weak because they can't trust their own.*' Bought, bribed, rotten to the core, and so dysfunctional in places, people would rather ask for Mafia protection than trust the police.

Planned. Franco Fiore knew where she was because it was all planned.

"Have you had any contact with any of your team members since Franco took you?"

"No," she says with a dry smirk as she wipes at her nose. "I was locked up for more than a month in a dungeon straight from some medieval horror hell. I still don't know what happened to any of them. I haven't had access to anything, as you well know."

True. And with fucking reason. She's a Trojan Horse, and we were all idiots to let her walk in, buying into her disguise. *Just a girl...* Blindsided, all of us.

"Here's the thing, sweetheart. The DIA thinks you're dead. Or at least, they've marked you as missing, presumed dead, on their files. What if this whole undercover operation you were working on was a Mission Impossible, with the only goal to wipe out agents who are actually desperate to get the job done?"

She glares at me, not buying into my reasoning as she shakes her head. "No...there were good people on my team, really—"

"Exactly. All the good people gone in one operation that goes disastrously wrong."

She studies me, the color draining from her face. "Impossible. No. I won't believe it."

I take in a deep breath as memories of Alex's death wash over me. Nobody would believe my conspiracy theory either.

"Get used to the idea, sweetheart. There'll be ways to prove it." I pull my laptop closer. "Tell me your team member's names? Any information to identify them on the DIA's internal records? We have time, but not a lot. Benedict and Luca can help us dig to see where they're at."

"I can try to log in on the DIA internal website—"

"No. You're presumed dead. Whoever is watching, waiting for you to reappear as there's been no body, would be notified if you log on. We're going to keep you dead, sweetheart, because right now, dead is safe." And I'd do anything to keep her safe. I log back into my laptop, knowing we're on borrowed time. "Benedict and Luca can hack their way into the system, or would know who can, not leaving a trace."

My mind is racing, because if she was part of a covert undercover plot to end her, which doesn't seem far-fetched from where I'm sitting, just getting off this plane could endanger her.

"Pietro Garlini. He is our *direttore operativo*, leading the operation. Then I have three men on my team. Lorenzo Ricci, Manolo Diconti, and Alesso Romano, but I can give you their agent numbers, as well."

"Okay, give me a second."

When I'm ready, she gives me the names again, with the numbers of her brothers in arms which they all memorize as part of some strategic plan. I send off an urgent email to Benedict and follow it up with a message on my phone. I wait for it to deliver and watch as it confirms he's read it. Trust Benedict to be up at any goddamn hour, and thank God he is. When he shoots me a reply that he's on it, I sigh in relief.

"This should be quick," I say, placing my phone back on the table. "And good to know because wasn't your goal to join your team again, should you manage to escape Franco, and then escape Boston?"

Ariana is starting to show me what she's made of, and the respect I had for her has multiplied exponentially. She's been brutally hurt, but that didn't stop her for going for Randazzo in her own way to avenge her mom. To avenge Elena. She plays a long game.

"Yes. The only thing that kept me from going insane in that dungeon was the fact there's always work to do. My team waits for me. Just because Randazzo's dead doesn't mean the trafficking stops."

"No, it doesn't. Let's see how many of your team are still standing." I'm not sure how she'll cope with the betrayal if they're all dead.

She rolls her eyes at me, and I want to lean over the table, take hold of that perfect chin, reprimand her for it, because how dare she roll her eyes at me. It makes my fucking dick twitch, and now is not the time, because after reprimanding her, I want to kiss her. Hard.

The air hostess walks over to us, and I curse under my breath. Now is definitely not the time.

"Sir, we are landing in twenty minutes."

"Good, thank you." I stand. "Come, let's go strap in."

It's quiet between us as we prepare for landing, lost in our own thoughts. If her team is wiped out, it will prove I'm right and the police, the DIA, is in bed with organized crime, with Franco. I bet they have no clue where he's at, and they're all in a fucking tizzy.

One thing that eats at me is the passport Franco used to get her out of Italy and into the States. Without a doubt, it's fake, but if it's linked to her personal file in any way, using it now to enter Italy could alert whoever is waiting for Ariana Morelli's body to float up. Shit. We're going to have to disguise ourselves however possible before we walk off this plane.

"Best you give me your home address," I say, using the last minutes before landing to get instructions out to my team on the ground. "It could be that your apartment is under surveillance."

"Really? You think?"

"I'm certain."

She gives me an address in Rome, and I save it on my maps, then send the coordinates to my team lead to park someone in the vicinity and keep an eye on the traffic going to her place.

Ariana Morelli is only presumed dead. Until there's a body, death isn't certain. If her team has been eliminated, and Franco's job was to end her and he failed, she's a rogue unit. A threat to whoever is in bed with Franco. She'll be hunted for the rest of her life.

All she'd have left in the world is us. *Il Consiglio.* Her new family.

And me. I'm one of the few people who has the resources

and skill set to protect her against police corruption. I'm the one man who stands between Matteo and the destiny he'll decide for her as Don.

Fuck if I let Matteo pawn her off to anybody else.

Tasha and Gigi are already part of the clan, and I might have been fighting this with every fiber in my being, but I'm the one man who can really protect her. I don't know when this has happened, or how, but you touch this sweet woman, you're fucking dead.

I might still have to convince her, but she's mine. *Until death do us part.*

58

ARIANA

I'm drained after all the talking and digging into the past. My emotions are raw, and my head spins. Dominic's point of view on our whole operation and it being a Mission Impossible is shaking my foundations. All those weeks in Franco's dungeon, I was haunted with why and how things went as wrong as they did, but I buried these thoughts. I refuse to believe there are crooked cops in the DIA, least of all in my team, but with the way things went south with my mission, it's a possibility.

I'm going through the motions of exiting the plane and through passport control on autopilot, not really paying attention as I should. All I wanted was to come back to Italy, and now, I feel like a stranger on home soil. If I can't go back to the DIA, even if Dominic would release me, who am I? My whole life was built around this one goal, and now, a swift chain of events has robbed me of everything I lived for. My team was the one thing that kept me going.

Dominic has me by the elbow, guiding me through the small terminal building. His hold isn't threatening, but the message is clear: don't even think about it. Earlier, as we taxied to our parking bay, he'd gone into the bedroom and changed.

He's now wearing jeans, sneakers, and a T-shirt he's borrowed from one of the bodyguards. My blond hair is shoved under a dark blue NY cap and with sunglasses—and a pair for me he took with a smile from the air hostess, promising to get her a replacement—we're as 'disguised' as we're going to be. I look down so you'll see as little of me as possible.

It isn't dark outside, as the promise of another day is seeping in on the horizon, but it's early. Once we're outside the terminal building, we get into the back of an SUV with dark tinted side and rear windows. One of the bodyguards gets in the front of the vehicle with us. I've lost track of the other one. As we drive off, I realize we're in a convoy as we're in the middle of two vehicles shielding us. It's all so smooth and I have no clue how Dominic arranged this so quickly, but it's clear he had all the contacts in place.

I don't bother checking if I can open my passenger door. There's no chance for escape.

"The car in the front needs to know Antonio Mancuso's address," Dominic asks as we head out.

"Tell them to go to Vena di Maida, and then towards Cortale. From there, I'll have to direct them." I haven't been down here in twelve years, and hopefully, I'll be able to find the place without problems.

It's quiet in the car as Dominic is busy on his phone, passing on my instructions.

"It's at least a thirty minutes' drive, and by the time we arrive it will be light," Dominic says as he plots the route on his phone's map. "You're okay?"

"Yes." But I'm not. The familiar landscape flitting past pulls at my gut. "I don't know if I want to see him."

"Who? Antonio Mancuso?"

I bite down hard on my bottom lip to get some control over my emotions. "Yes. I spent seven years in his house. He never touched me, but he isn't a good man."

"No need to explain, sweetheart." Dominic rests his hand on my thigh. "I'll deal with him alone."

"Thank you."

Fields of golden wheat glow up in the first sun rays, intercepted with the odd empty field already harvested. Untamed swatches of forest are cordoned off by rows of old olive trees. This is home, but I've never been at peace here. I close my eyes and rest my head back, weirdly exhausted. It's the jet lag, the lack of sleep over the past days, and being emotionally wrung out.

When Dominic's phone pings softly and he follows it up with a curse, I glance at him.

"Benedict's come back to me with info. Let me check my email."

I sink deeper into my seat, bracing myself. If he finds they're dead... No. I won't start doom-thinking. As he swipes open his email, I try to glimpse what he's looking at, but I can't see.

"Put up the conversation screen," he says to the driver, and we have to wait excruciating long seconds for the screen to close. "I knew it. Lorenzo Ricci, Manolo Diconti, and Alesso Romano, all dead."

"What?"

"I'm sorry, Ariana. Your team's been wiped out."

My heart breaks as prickles of cold fear and despair spread on my skin and I start to shiver. "No-no-no. It isn't true."

These were my close colleagues, the men I would have given my life for. What if they gave their lives for me?

"Benedict has added the screenshots of the DIA internal website. See for yourself."

I take his phone from him with trembling fingers. He's already opened the attachments. I swipe through all three of them, finding it hard to breathe as reality stares me in the face. The screenshots are from the real internal DIA portal. There's no way Benedict could have conjured it up in so little time.

"They are all marked as deceased," I whimper. "They're all really dead."

There's even a screenshot from my own agent page. I'm missing, presumed dead, but looking at the dates as I swipe between the screenshots, my team was eliminated within two days, Lorenzo last...on the day Franco came for me.

My hand goes limp as I drop the phone to my lap. It rings, and Dominic takes it from me.

"Benedict," he answers. "Yep. I got your email. Yes. All killed around nine days after Randazzo's death. Yep. Let me put you on speaker for Ariana to listen in."

"I'm sorry, Ariana," Benedict says as Dominic puts him on speaker. "There must be a link with Randazzo's death, but for that, we'll need time and more resources."

Nine days after Randazzo got killed...just days after I went undercover. Oh my God—

"What about Pietro Garlini?" I ask, suppressing a sob. There was no screenshot, and it gives me hope. I can't stomach that, too. Not the only dad amongst a group of singles.

"Last man standing," Benedict says. "Unscathed. For now."

Dominic's gaze meets mine, and he hitches a brow. "I'd ask some hard questions if I were you, sweetheart. My guess is he is your bad apple. I'll bet you a million dollars he's working for the 'Ndrangheta or Cosa Nostra's highest players. And the buck doesn't stop with him in the DIA. There'll be players higher up."

I don't want to believe it. "But how? Why?"

"Money, sweetheart. Everybody has their price."

Seconds tick past as I just sit there, unable to compute this new reality. I've never imagined this would be my life, that the work I've been doing for years can be null and voided within minutes by simple police corruption. And we were getting so close...

"You should lie low," Benedict says. "If Pietro Garlini was in cahoots with Franco Fiore, entering Italy with that passport could flag you on their system."

"Benedict's right, but it's too late now. We had no choice but to land and enter the country," Dominic says. "We're one step ahead, though, and can plan to ambush him."

"What do you mean?" I ask, not keeping up with him and Benedict, still reeling with my new reality.

"Ariana, in this game, you kill them, or they kill you. Until Pietro Garlini has your body, and your status changes on their system, you're a threat to him and his cronies. I bet he is desperately trying to hunt down Franco Fiore, to be reassured that their sick little plan worked out exactly as they envisioned it." Dominic's voice has gone deep, his eyes dark. "We're the only ones who know Franco is dead. Do we still have Franco's phone on hand, Ben?"

"Sure do. Want me to see what's going on in there?"

"See if there are any messages to someone you can pinpoint as Pietro Garlini."

"Sure thing. What else?" Benedict says as he stifles a yawn. "I need some shut eye."

"What are the chances you can arrange for *missing, presumed dead* on Ariana's file to be changed to just *deceased* on the DIA's systems?"

Benedict chuckles, but it's dry. "Everybody has their price, bro. How much money do you have?"

"I don't care. Don't do it yet, but I'll spend what you need to get it done. Get a quote, and line up your resources."

"Right." For a second, Benedict hesitates. "What aren't you telling me, Nicky? Did you get those DNA tests back?"

Dominic sighs as he shoots me a glance. "Yeah, about that... now isn't a good time, but I'll fill you in as soon as I can."

"Killing people with suspense now, are you?" Benedict says with a chuckle. "Have you filled Matteo in?"

Dominic huffs into the phone. "No."

"Uh-huh. I'll read between the lines there...good thinking. Let the poor man fuck his wife for a little longer in oblivious bliss."

"Language, little brother, language." Dominic mouths a sorry in my direction. "You're still on speaker."

"Oh, fuck. Sorry, Ariana," Benedict says, smirk in his voice. "Better get used to it. It's a big party we're throwing here, in true Scalera style. I'll check with my contact and let you know."

"Thanks," Dominic says and kills the call.

"What does he mean with a big party?" I ask, my head spinning, trying to keep up.

Dominic shoots me a sly smile. "Just a bit of a bash to properly welcome you to the family, sweetheart."

59

DOMINIC

The roads are quiet at this time of the morning. Once we're off the highway and drive by the small town of Vena di Maida, we take to country roads that pass through dry summer woodlands and olive groves.

"Can we stop a minute?" Ariana asks. "We aren't far now."

"Sure." I call the front vehicle, and we pull off on the side, cars fairly far apart to not cause suspicion at a first glance. "What are you thinking?"

"I don't know if he has guards or if he is by himself. He never kept much company except for the purposes of a halfway house."

"Okay, it's also the crack of dawn."

"Which means you can approach the house without him noticing until you are there. There's a path through the olive groves and another one hidden through the woods."

"Okay, where's the road to his house?"

"It's about two kilometers on."

I study her face. I'm putting all my trust in this woman, but for some reason, I don't think she'd be lying to me. Not anymore.

"Anything else I need to know?"

She blinks, seeming to rake her brain. "He sleeps with a gun and has a machete hanging by the door. He is very good at knife-throwing."

"Good to know."

I take ten minutes to consult with my bodyguard and the men in the other cars, and we come up with a plan which isn't foolproof. It seems one of the older guys I've hired for this trip knows about Antonio Mancuso as he grew up close by. Everything Ariana said rings true.

I instruct the driver to continue on a crawl until the side path through the olive grove comes into view.

"Be a good girl—" I whisper to Ariana as I lean closer to her, "—and wait in the car."

"What if you don't come back?" she asks, real fear in her voice.

"I'm coming back, sweetheart, because I promised to protect you. Help me by staying put."

"Okay."

I tilt her chin towards me and kiss her full on the mouth. It's soft, and I linger there for a moment, deepening the kiss. "Remember, we have plans for that sweet pussy of yours."

With that, I tap on the conversation screen for the driver to open it again so he can keep an eye on her. I exit the car, leaving her with a soft blush on her cheeks and something to think about.

I'm not worried she'd run. What she doesn't know, as she wouldn't have been able to see them through the tinted windows of our two other cars, is that I have eight men with us, over and above the two we brought on the jet. Three of them are to have eyes on her at all times. Maybe Ariana Morelli has caught on and knows better than to test me.

I don't have a weapon on me, but the men from the other cars are weaponed to the chin with concealed guns, knives, and possibly a grenade or two. I indicate to one of them that we should take the path through the olive grove. Another team will hit the farmhouse from the woodlands' side, and a third team will continue on and block anybody from driving to the old man's house. As soon as the road and cars are out of sight, the man hands me a semi-automatic I push into the back of my jeans.

It's a beautiful morning. Dried grass stands thick and tall between the olive trees, and I inhale the fresh, sweet air, perfumed with hay and sunshine. As we come through the grove, a stone homestead comes into view. It's surrounded by old farming equipment, rusting away between sheets of plastic and old tires. What a fucking decrepit nest. The foul stench of pigs comes from a side structure, and already they are squealing for breakfast. Good thing, too, because when an old dog spots us coming through the trees, he gives a few unsure barks nobody would hear above the pigs' racket.

I stop, hold out my hand for him as I block the other man. "Here, puppy," I croon, and as if the dog can sense I mean him no harm, he stops barking, his eyes only blinking as he makes no attempt to jerk against his chain. Poor dog. In this moment, with his age, he reminds me so much of Bruno, I swallow as I inch closer. He leans in and sniffs at my hand, makes a turn, and slumps down in the dirt to scratch himself behind the ear. Fleas. Flies aplenty buzz around him. Poor fucker.

A few chickens are scratching away in a coop, and once the dog has lost all interest in us, clearly way past his prime and with several itches to scratch, I nod to my bodyguard to move on.

There are no lights on in the house, and I soft-foot to the side where I peer into a window. Dust and grime make for a blurred view into a sitting room, with torn couches and wine bottles on the side table and floor. Fuck. I hope the old man is still alive.

A rush of water comes down a pipe just to the side, and I freeze. Seems someone just took a dump and flushed the toilet. Excellent. I don't need anybody shitting themselves. The rest of my team has arrived, the old dog beyond caring. Slack, so fucking slack.

We take corners, and when I approach the front door, I feel the handle. Locked.

Might as well be polite about it. I knock. No response. I knock again.

"*Chi è?*" comes a gruff voice, still sleepy.

I indicate to my friend who claims he knows Antonio Mancuso.

"*Nino,*" the man calls through the door. "*Nino Mancuso? Sono Paolo C, vengo con notizie di tuo nipote.*"

It's Paulo, I come with news of your nephew. That should tickle the old man, if he still had time for Franco.

Feet shuffle to the door, and when the man swings it open, I have to lean away from the stench emanating from the house.

Fuck. This guy let himself go. And he is hungover. But there's more. His one eye is rudely stitched closed where he must have lost it, a nasty scar running from his brow to his nose where he seemed to have patched up his nostril. Maybe he wasn't such a good knife thrower, after all. He hasn't shaved in days, thick grey beard sprouting in patches on his chin and jaw.

He's dressed in an old-man's vest that was once white, and sleep shorts, thin legs protruding like sticks out of their wide holes. His toenails are long and yellowed, speaking of neglect, and his back is curved in age. This guy looks like he's knocking hard on ninety and regrets making it this far.

There's more, though. He has the same gaunt look the Don had in the last months of his illness. Shit, he's dying.

"Antonio Mancuso," I say as I step into the house, and the man shuffles to the side as if he knows he shouldn't even try to stop me. I switch over to Italian for his sake, although I bet if I wring that throat just right, he'd start speaking English just perfectly. I take the room in with one sweep of my gaze. The machete Ariana warned me about hangs on an opposite wall, right by the front door. A gun lies on a side table, but nothing more.

As I take in the space, I nod to the stairs, and Gus takes them two at a time to make sure we're alone.

"And who are you?" the old man croaks, his rotting breath hitting me in the face. "Which nephew?"

"Dominic Scalera. I don't know your nephews," I lie. "I'm here to enquire about the whereabouts of a girl that came through this house fifteen years ago. Gabriella Scalera. She came from America."

The old man cackles, and it goes over into a coughing fit.

"Now-now," I say as I grip him by the shoulder, firmly in warning, but also to keep him from keeling over. I'm repulsed at the dirt crusting his skin, the oily feel of his foul-smelling vest under my palm. "You can't die on me now, old man."

"Gabriella, Isabella, Anabella, Amar, Petra, so many." He drags in a ragged breath. "How do people expect me to remember all these girls? Too fucking many. Nobody cares. All whores."

I don't like to lose my shit with this guy, not yet, but he mustn't push me. I shift my hand from his boney shoulder to the thin skin of his neck. He doesn't fight me. He might be hungover, but he's been conditioned to know his place.

"I'd think a bit harder if I were you." I put pressure just there, where the blood flow to his face will thin. "Gabriella Scalera. Gabi. Fifteen years ago. A girl named Emilia Korhonen was still living here."

"Emilia? That fucking little thief. She's dead."

I put more pressure on his neck, and now he grapples with my hand with both of his as his eyes go wide. I'm so much taller than him, in the prime of my life—it would be nothing to take him out. I step on his foot, and he stills as the pain registers. Fear flashes through his eyes.

"Indeed. Emilia Korhonen is dead, but she remembers Gabi, though." Nothing like fucking with an old man's head. "Gabi was here for maybe a week, and then disappeared."

Antonio blinks, and I know something triggered him to remember.

"Gabi," he croaks. "From America. Emilio Randazzo's other daughter."

"That's the one. See, I knew you knew something. Now where is she?"

"With Randazzo dead, she could be anywhere."

Prickles chase down my spine. If we're too fucking late, I'm going to have to kill somebody to avenge Gabriella's death.

"Where did she go when she left your shit hole?"

At this, the man croaks some cackles again, but I cut it off with my thumb.

"The convent," he groans, and I release the pressure a bit. "The convent in Potenza."

"Are you sure about that?" I ask with another squeeze. "The convent in Potenza?" Fuck knows where that is and where she went after that.

"Yes, yes, Potenza. Randazzo kept her there, locked up with the religious sisters, to use, you know, when the time was right."

"And when was the time right?" I ask, my blood boiling.

"He ran out of time," the man says with a snarky laugh. "He's dead if you haven't heard. Dead."

Gus comes down the stairs. "There's nobody here. Just the old man."

"Why are you so lonely, Antonio?" I ask, releasing some pressure off his throat.

He stares at me, his brown eyes sunken into the deep holes of his eye sockets. "When you're old enough, when you've made it to my age without pissing anybody off too much, they leave you to die by yourself."

What a fucking loser. Alienated from the world, a pitstop for humans in the sick trafficking business, here on a derelict farm in butt-crack fucking nowhere. How long will it take them to discover his body? Long enough that it would appear as if he died of natural causes.

"Get info on the convent in Potenza," I instruct Gus. We might just be lucky. "Is there anything else you care to share, Antonio? Think over your answer wisely, because it so happened that you pissed me off."

"I've done nothing to you," he says. "Let me be in peace."

Peace? After what he's been part of? So much so, he can't remember their names? All those girls...*Ariana*... I'll hang him up to dry like cured meat. With the alcohol sweating from his pores, he's practically cured himself already.

"Here's the thing, Antonio. You allowed shit to go down in this house, and if you think you could stand by and let it all happen and die in peace, you're fucking wrong. You let Franco Fiore rape Emilia Korhonen under this roof, and I bet it was with your fucking approval."

"She's dead."

"Yes, and yet, she speaks to me. I know exactly what went on here. It's time you pay." I twist his arm into a lock, and his weak body is no match for mine. "This is for Emilia Korhonen and the hell you put her through."

"Make it quick," he begs.

I don't think he deserves quick.

"Tie him up, gag him," I say. "Then toss him with his pigs where he belongs. If we find out that Gabriella is still safe in Potenza, we'll see what to do with him, if he's still alive."

"They haven't had breakfast," the man whines. "Can't you hear them squealing? The boars...they're big. They'll trample me to death, and then—and then—"

"Eat you? Eventually, yes." The fucking pigs haven't shut up since we arrived. "Let's hope you weren't lying about my little sister's whereabouts then." With that, I let him go, and he crumples to the ground.

I walk out, set the dog free, and stalk off, letting the men do as I told them to do.

60

ARIANA

I'm a bunch of twisted nerves as I wait in the car. It feels like hours. I don't know what Dominic would find at Antonio's place. When I escaped twelve years ago, it was already a dump, and to my knowledge, nothing's changed.

When Dominic appears through the olive grove, I have to hold myself back from getting out of the car and running to him and jumping into his arms. He's safe. My heart is a mess where it beats in my chest with a mix of fear and hope, and an ache I've started to associate with him. Not pain—more like bubbles of joy that have nowhere to go, pressing against my ribcage. I thought we were done, that he'd end me once he learned I'm in the DIA, but then I recalled Matteo is my half-brother. I might be a pawn in their hands now, but they won't just kill me to be rid of me.

And then he said, so casually, we still have plans for *that sweet pussy*.

I'd love to hear—to experience—all those plans. Memories of last night flood my mind, and I squirm in my seat. Now I can't think of anything else as he opens the door and slides into the back seat. I blush, the full range of red heat invading my face.

"What happened?" I ask, forcing myself to think about where we are and what we came to do, not sure I want the finer details. "Was he alone? Is he still alive? Did he know anything?"

"Give us a minute, and map out the direction to Potenza already," Dominic says to the driver who waited with me in the car. The man gets out and closes the door, giving us privacy. "For now, sweetheart, he's still alive. Apparently, Gabriella went to a convent. I have the number, but it's too early to phone."

"A convent? What are the chances she's still there after all this time?"

He shrugs. "It's our next lead. We'll go there and figure it out."

His gaze locks with mine, and then it wanders over my flushed cheeks and down my neck. As if he could read my mind, his slow inspection only intensifies the heat.

"Fuck, Ariana," he murmurs as he leans in and cups my neck to pull me closer. "Don't look at me like that. We have work to do."

"How do I look at you?" I protest, having done nothing I'm aware of.

His lips slide along my cheek to my ear. "As if you'd like me to fuck you in the backseat of the car...amongst other things."

Goosebumps spread down my body as his warm breath ghosts over my skin, his lips teasing my ear. That's exactly where my mind had gone, my core just paces behind. To think he read it all on me like I'm an open book. My nipples harden against my bra, a disconcerting wetness seeping into my panties. How is it that he turns me on with a few select words and then just touches me right—

He kisses me then, and all logic leaves my mind. I'm in trouble. So much trouble when it comes to this man. I have fallen for the enemy, for a Mafia man with gentle hands, a kind heart, and a dark side he'd loathe to show me, because he hates it. But needs must. This is how he survives his world.

He groans as he pulls away. "Damn. Matteo's obsession suddenly makes sense, so much sense."

"What obsession?" I murmur as I look up at him, shy, my hand still on his chest where his heart is thumping wildly, too. I affect him, and it's somehow the most beautiful thing I've ever experienced in my life.

"His obsession with Tasha, and particularly with the fact that he doesn't want to do anything but, and I quote, fuck his wife."

"Oh." The implication of his words leaves me breathless, but then other men appear through the olive grove, and Gus gets back into the front passenger seat. The driver clambers in and meets Dominic's gaze in the rearview mirror.

"It's done, boss," Gus says as he straps in his seatbelt.

"Good."

"What happened to Antonio?" I ask, not sure I should or want to know.

"We left him feeding his pigs. There's nothing much else keeping him company here. Let's get going," Dominic instructs the driver. "You've mapped the directions to the convent in Potenza? Where is this place?"

"Yes, sir," the driver says. "It's a drive. Eight hours at least as it's on the other side of Rome."

"Fuck. Should have kept the jet on standby." Dominic reaches for my hand and rests it on his thigh, leaving me buzzing as the driver starts the car, and we head off again.

"Did you kill him? Antonio?" I whisper, scared they went in and let the asshole live.

"He's been taken care of, sweetheart. He won't talk about our little visit."

His phone rings, and he answers, thankfully sparing me the details.

"Benedict. Yep. Fuck it, you're breaking up. Okay. Yes. What? What the fuck? Okay, send it through, and we'll have a look." He kills the call and shoots me a glance as he sweeps open his phone.

"What?"

"Benedict hacked into Franco's phone. He's sent us some things to analyze."

"How does he do it so quickly?" I ask, stunned at how Benedict just seems to walk digitally into any room he wants.

"For starters, he's freaking smart and has been playing around for years. He's got a gift for this type of thing and unlimited money to spend on the latest tech, and a team of weirdos just like himself working for him. Plus he's addicted to the high of breaking and entering where nobody is supposed to go." Dominic groans and drags his hand through his hair in frustration. "The internet is useless here. We need to go somewhere with better reception. Speed up where you can?"

"Yes, sir," the driver says, and for the next ten minutes, we bump along old country roads until we connect with a main road.

"Here," Dominic says as he hands me his phone. "These are transcripts of messages. There are several between different numbers and Franco's phone. Can you figure out if any of them is from Pietro Garlini?"

"How on Earth...?" I ask as I scan the pages and swipe between them. "How did he know to pick these specific ones?"

"Probably used AI. Asked it to analyze the content and narrow it down to the most likely suspects."

I shake my head as I read through the short lines of messages on one file, then jump to the next. Franco was a busy man, and even though the messages are clearly coded, it's obvious he was knee-deep in criminal activity.

"I'm getting car sick," I say, but it is more than that. I'm sick to my stomach by having access to this information, seeing straight into that sick mind's workings. Here I have raw evidence the DIA would do anything to get their hands on... except there's nobody in the DIA I really trust right now.

"Pull off at a gas station and tell the others to stop close by but elsewhere. Ariana needs to work through this before we make any further decisions."

"Yes, sir."

I look out of the window, trying to get a grip on the growing ball of churning bile in my stomach, and when the driver pulls off again, I take my time. There are ten sets of messages, in code, I need to work through. I disregard the first seven after nothing in them gives me any hints as to being related to Pietro Garlini.

A flicker of hope lights in me. Maybe Dominic's theory is wrong. My team wasn't ambushed during a mission we were never set to complete; it was something else that led to our demise.

And then my gaze snags on one little line.

EK in position. LR detained. MD done. AR done.

Pins and needles prickle over my skin. Those are our initials. Lorenzo Ricci, Manolo Diconti, and Alesso Romano. And I...I was known as Emilia Korhonen between Franco and... and it must be Pietro Garlini. I swipe up to the page where the number and a name is included. It's not Pietro's DIA phone number, and nothing else gives it away. But it must be Pietro Garlini because the only way anybody could know my birth name is if they had access to my Top Secret file. Emilia Korhonen was 'killed' twelve years ago, but only someone with access to my records would know I'm alive and have turned into Ariana Morelli.

Oh my God. I check again. The message is dated on the last day I was in contact with Lorenzo Ricci, the team member who was supposed to look after me and protect me. Detained. I'm in position. *MD done, AR done.* Code for killed.

"Ariana?"

Dominic tries to take the phone from me as I'm trembling so much, everything is a blur, but I cling to it as tears fall like stones to my lap. I drag in breath after breath, forcing myself to try to calm down.

"Oh my God, he sold them out. He sold us all out."

I wipe at my eyes, focusing on the rest of the message chain, which details their plan like a to-do list in which they tick off every step.

LR done.

Oh my god. Dead.

EK detained.

Is she done?

No. Detained.

Do her already.

No. Now that I have her, she might be useful.

Not what we agreed upon. Do her.

Soon. Need time.

There are several more call outs from Pietro Garlini to kill me, but Franco had lost interest as he doesn't respond.

And then comes a line from Pietro Carlini that chills me to the bone:

Why the fuck did you leave Italy with her and where the fuck are you going? Not our agenda.

Franco's response is simply, *She'll be back.*

And then the last line from Pietro: *I want to see her body.*

Franco never responded because we were going to the US by then, and he had me in that dungeon with his own plans, which didn't include Pietro Garlini's plans to end me immediately.

"I can't believe it," I sob. "He sold us out. He butchered my team...he—"

Dominic takes the phone from me, and I let go, already in his arms.

He holds me close, trying to calm me with gentle strokes on my back, his lips pressed to my forehead as he murmurs. "It's going to be okay, Ariana. Eventually, it's all going to be okay."

I'm crying ugly tears, sobs tearing from my chest like I never allow them to, but there's no hiding this grief. My whole life, my whole idea of self has been wiped out by the man I trusted the most, trusted with my life—trusted with my team. And they all died except me.

"What if they died because of me?" I cry into his shoulder.

There's no doubt I could have been the sole objective of Franco and Garlini's mission—I am, after all, Randazzo's daughter. An heiress to a sick underground network and a Mafia fortune. A prize in the right man's hands. I was the only thing Franco wanted out of his deal with Pietro Garlini.

"The only way it will ever be okay is if I end him, like he wanted to end me." I don't know where the words come from, but with Garlini alive I'll never be safe. The idea is a one-eighty from everything I've come to trust and believe, but a sense of rightness is spreading into me like the cool reassurance of Dominic's touch on my skin.

"That's the only way, sweetheart, and together, we'll get it done. Give me the list of names, and I'll make it happen."

61

DOMINIC

She's a wreck, and I can't begin to imagine what she's feeling. Disillusioned, her life ripped from her again and now dunked in grief. She lost the people closest to her in her adult life, and worst of all? Their deaths wouldn't have been quick and painless. Not from what I've seen of Franco Fiore's handiwork or from what she's experienced first-hand.

I hold her close and let her cry, knowing that arriving in Italy has set things in motion at a speed we can't keep up with. It's clear from Pietro Garlini and Franco's messages that her fake passport was rigged. Whoever is waiting for Ariana Morelli to come back to Italy just got notified she's entered the country.

We're sitting on a ticking bomb, and something's going to have to give.

When my phone pings a message, I glance down and quirk a brow. That quick, huh? An underlying buzz to avenge her ripples through me again. It's a need slowly ballooning in me. That motherfucker. I'm ready for him.

"Ariana, sweetheart," I murmur where she's pressed against

me, right where she belongs. "Pietro Garlini is already on your case. Your passport was rigged to trigger your movements."

"What?" she asks, pushing away and staring up at me with tear-washed eyes.

"Ah, fuck it, sweetheart." I slide a thumb over her cheek to catch her tears. Seeing her like this fucking hurts.

"I never break down like this," she murmurs as she wipes at her chin.

"I know. It's okay, I know you're strong." I press a kiss to her forehead. "You have to look at this, though. Here." I open the image on my phone and hold it out to her. "Does this man look familiar?"

I can't fathom how I would have done any of this if it weren't for Matteo's trip to Sicily, for which we had months to plan. I made contacts in that time and set things up I can just fall back on now, taking action with ease to put the right people in position.

Ariana wipes at her nose as she takes my phone. "It's my apartment block."

"Yes. Who's at the main entrance?"

She zooms in on the image and inhales in shock. "That's Pietro Garlini."

"Thought so. He got notified you entered the country. He's either coming over to see if you're in Rome already, which is impossible because you don't portal from place to place, or he's there waiting in ambush, or plans to rig your apartment with a bomb or something. Could be anything. For all we know, he is de-rigging stuff he'd put in place. Best I get a team on it."

"A team on it?" She checks the photo's date and time stamp. "This is minutes ago. How?"

I hitch my brows. "I've got you, sweetheart. You're under my protection now, and I don't fuck up."

Ariana blinks at me, and then her shoulders sag. It will take time for her to let go of her past and accept the only future she really has.

"What do we do? He's out to get me." She pushes a fist to her stomach, looking like she's going to be sick.

I tip her chin up, forcing her to look at me. "We're going to take him the fuck down, and we're going to do it in such a way that nobody would ever link it to you, since you'll be dead on the DIA's side of things. I know Garlini's type. He would have swept clean as he went, making it impossible for anybody to pinpoint these crimes on him."

And how the fuck does it seem the universe had this plan for me...for me and this woman, with the Don's iron hand shaping me to his will, but actually preparing me for this moment when I get to avenge the woman I love?

My mind reels with the realization, but now isn't the time to contemplate our future. Now is the time to secure it.

"We'll lure him back to your apartment when we are ready. And then we take him out."

"How?"

"Benedict has Franco's phone. Franco might be dead, but nobody knows this except us. It's time for Franco to have some last communications with Garlini, and we'll stage it for when we are ready, but it needs to be soon. Strike while the iron is hot."

She drops her head into her hands as a sob rakes through her. "I'm still getting my head around everything, I can't—"

"Leave it to me." I've killed before. This woman has never pulled the trigger or cut a throat, irrespective of her plans for Randazzo and her vendetta. I'll be her henchman.

I lean in to tap Gus on the shoulder. "Find a space where we can work and spend the night outside of Rome. Somewhere inconspicuous, touristy, but not flashy."

"On it, boss."

"What about Gabriella? We're going to Potenza?" Ariana says. "You can't drop everything—"

"We must. We're sitting on a ticking bomb here, sweetheart. Potenza is on the other side of Rome. We need to deal with Pietro Garlini first." Because who knows what the fuck else he has planned. I know my position, my strengths. I can guess his, but at this point, surprise is our biggest weapon. "I'll phone the convent and take things from there, but for now—"

"There's several smaller guesthouses in the countryside outside of Rome, boss."

"Pick one with enough rooms available for most of the team, with the rest on standby close by."

We carry on in silence until Gus announces he's found the perfect spot. He passes his phone to Dominic who scans the bed and breakfast and gives it a thumb's up. "Good, we'll take three rooms but with a tiered arrival."

"Yes, boss."

I don't have to give detailed instructions. My team understands my needs. We'll have guards in-house and men stationed in the vicinity as back up.

As soon as we drive up the guesthouse's driveway, I know it's the perfect spot. We're in the country, surrounded by vineyards, hanging heavy with grapes in the late summer sun.

It's early for a check-in, but the elderly owner seems only too happy to have guests filling her empty rooms and offers us breakfast, too. We get the room keys, and I send Gus ahead with the little luggage we have. He knows what to do. Check the room for hidden cameras. He will sweep the general guest areas later, but this isn't the type of establishment that seems high on tech solutions, or on invading your privacy.

We have a coffee while waiting for the all-clear, and as soon as Ariana and I are alone in our room, I suppress the urge to pin her to the wall and kiss her, just to do something with the fucking tension in my body.

"Can you call the convent?" I ask instead, focusing on where to hit hard first. "Speak to the Mother Superior or whoever runs the show and ask about Gabriella?"

"Me?" She looks stunned.

"Yes, you. It would be better for a woman to ask around. Plus, in a way, you are related. It isn't far-fetched to call her your sister."

Ariana sinks down on the bed, and I hold my phone out to her, the number already on the screen. "Please."

"I've... I've never had a sister before," she says as her hands go limp with the slight weight of the phone. "I've never had family before. I—" She taps on her chest to get a grip on her emotions, and I give her the time she needs, then squeeze her shoulder.

I can't even imagine a life without my brothers or how lonely and isolated she must have been. "Just press dial."

I look on as she calls and puts the phone on speaker, my heart in my throat, beating wildly as the ringing cuts through the room. We're bound to be disappointed, and this internal hype is all for nothing.

When a soft-spoken woman answers, she makes some small talk, then Ariana clears her throat. "I'm enquiring after my sister. I believe she might have been staying with you for some time. Her first name is Gabriella, and we were split at her birth. It's a long story, but she'd be twenty-two years old now."

"Gabriella? Just a moment," the woman says. "I'll put you through to the Reverend Mother."

Ariana stares up at me, eyes wide. My knees go weak. It isn't a *no*. What the fuck is this? I was expecting a dead end.

"Tell them you're Ariana Scalera," I whisper to her as we wait.

It takes a minute for us to be connected up the chain of command, and when an even older woman's voice answers, I sit down next to Ariana.

"This is Reverend Mother Lucia speaking. How can I help you?"

Ariana repeats what she'd asked earlier.

"And who may I ask is enquiring?"

"It's Ariana Scalera," she says, and the name glides off her tongue with such ease and has such a beautiful ring to it, I wrap my arm around her back and hug her close.

"And you claim to be related to Gabriella?"

"Is she there, with you?"

"We have several Gabriella here. It's a beloved name amongst the sisters at Potenza."

"I see," Ariana says with half an eye roll. "The one we're looking for came to the convent in Potenza when she was seven years old. She had an American accent as she was born there. We've only recently learned about her...and her being here in Italy. I'm so sorry, but there have been grave misunderstandings, and we've been on a mission to locate her."

For a long spell, it's quiet on the other side.

"What did you say again your name was, dear?" the Reverend Mother asks.

I stare at Ariana, finding it weird she asks Ariana to repeat herself. "Scalera. Ariana Scalera."

"And you are looking for?"

Strain settles in Ariana's shoulders as she says, "Gabriella Scalera? But she had a name change when she got adopted—"

"To Randazzo? You're looking for Gabriella Randazzo?"

My gut twists as Ariana's eyes widen.

"No," she says. "Although...although there is a family relation."

"I see." The Reverend Mother clears her throat on the other side, and it suddenly feels like a dead end.

"Why are you asking?" Ariana asks.

This circle of questions feels like a slow puncture to our plans.

"I'm asking because someone else called and asked after a Gabriella Randazzo yesterday. It can't be a coincidence."

"Fuck," I hiss under my breath.

"What did they ask for?" Ariana asks, urgent now. "To speak to her?"

"No, testing the waters, just like you, to come and fetch her."

I sag as I press a fist to my forehead, my pulse racing, my heart in my throat. "This only means she is there," I mouth to Ariana, and she nods.

"Is she safe?" Ariana asks, and I salute her quick thinking.

"With the name Randazzo linked to her?" the Reverend Mother says. "Have you been following the news?"

Fuck. This woman is messing with us. She doesn't know who she's dealing with...or does she? I take the phone from Ariana. "This is Dominic Scalera, Gabriella's brother. I'll send extra security your way. Please, we just need a day—"

"A brother, you say? And how many brothers does Gabriella have?"

It feels like a test. "We were six, but now we're five. Matteo, Alessandro, Dominic, Stephano, Luca, and Benedict," I rattle our names off, in case it does something for her.

A chair creaks over the phone, and then a soft whimper sounds.

"I've kept that girl safe for more than fifteen years," the Reverend Mother says. "I'd like to think I can manage a few more days, Nicky."

Holy *holy* fuck.

Ariana's hands fly up to her mouth as she stares at me, wide-eyed, in shock.

"How—" I ask, but the question breaks off in my throat. Secrets...so many secrets.

"You're the gentle one," the Reverend Mother says, her voice straining with tears. "Bianca—" She breaks off with a swallow. "Never mind, we don't have time. I'll need proof, my son, of your relationship to Gabriella, before I can release her to you. She is safe, and I've moved her because of everything that's been happening, but you don't have much time."

"We'll bring proof, everything we have," I say, dumbfounded. "There're documents. I'll ask Stephano and Gigi to bring my mom's journals, it explains everything. Please...just keep her safe."

"I know the world you hail from, no need to spell it out for me, Dominic Scalera," the Reverend Mother says, back in control over her own emotions.

How do I get more out of her? Here is something afoot I never expected. "I have questions—"

"Of course you have, but I also understood the assignment from the start. There's to be no answers, *but* I've been waiting for this call for as long as I can remember. Gabriella is here, and she doesn't know it, but she's been waiting for you, too."

"I just need a day," I beg, knowing we don't even have that, not if someone else is looking for *Gabriella Randazzo*. "Two days max, please—"

"Yes. I need time to prepare her mind, too, for God finally answering our prayers."

I close my eyes as I ring off. We just bought ourselves enough time to deal with Pietro Garlini. And more, we've found her. We've found our long-lost little sister. The one we thought had died. She's alive, and she'll be with us as soon as possible. As soon as we're done with this fucker in Rome.

62

ARIANA

I'm stunned. Dominic just handed the phone back to me as he stood. He's raking his hands through his hair and breathes into his palms as he paces the little space we have.

"My mom must have had some connection with her, whether through Randazzo or not, before the birth."

"Yes."

"We don't have time to work through whatever that means now, sweetheart. Fuck, I'll have to deal with my head later." He's already setting up his laptop at the small table in the room. "Bottom line, someone else is hunting Gabriella down, and we have one day to deal with Garlini."

I can't believe it. One Mafia princess, hidden away in a convent for years, protected at all cost—another one thrown to the wolves. I've lost track of who the bad guys and who the good guys are. I always thought I've aligned myself right, with the police force, fighting against everything I've witnessed in my time in Antonio Mancuso's house, with what happened with Franco, and how Randazzo treated my mother, but even that world has been toppled on its head.

I watch Dominic as he gets busy logging in on his laptop,

his phone still unlocked and ready. I can call the emergency number for agents and have people come fetch me within the hour. I can even sit here, quietly, and without a sound send out an SOS message with my location. Someone will come...and his instructions might be to kill me.

Pietro Garlini butchered my team.

By some miracle, I'm the last one standing.

He will pay.

I will break their ring. I had to pass on Franco, I had to pass on Randazzo, never knowing I had an enemy closer to home. There must be a whole line of corrupt police in the DIA. I can't be sure who else is involved or what their ultimate plan is, but if I can make one dent in their numbers, I will.

A shudder runs through me as I weigh my options. This is the moment where I choose one last time. Align myself with the traditional bad guys—the Mafia—and kill a crooked cop, or oust the man who sparked me back to life, and live with the consequences. From what I've seen of *Il Consiglio*, I won't live long.

I can't hurt him. Dominic has his back to me, the ultimate position of trust. I'll never have his physical strength, but as he sits now at the desk, it's the best fighting chance I have. But he is showing me that he trusts me first.

I close my eyes and exhale some tension.

"You're okay there, Ariana?" he asks, not even looking over his shoulder at me.

Trust.

I choose trust. In a man who has shown me nothing but compassion. Who had been through worse at his own father's hand, and who has promised to protect me, whatever it takes. I've never had this before. I've never had what I had with him last night on the plane, either, and if there is one thing I want after years of isolation, it's more of *him*.

I choose family, the other thing I've never had. The thing

Randazzo stole from my mother when she got pregnant, and he refused for her to go back to Finland. My mom knew what she'd gotten into by then and chose to protect her own family, by staying put and disappearing from their lives. But now I have a half-brother, a sister via that connection, women married to men like Dominic and seemingly in love and happy. Gigi even told me we were sisters now at the clinic, after everything we've gone through with Franco.

A real family is something I thought I'd never have. But now—

I'll go and reclaim what Randazzo took from me, even if it is with people who I've vowed for years to hunt down. My blinkers have been torn off, exposing the corrupt underbelly of the DIA which I can't fight alone.

"I'm fine," I say softly, pulling all my strength together, my decision made. "What can I do to help? Give me something to do."

He turns towards me and holds out a hand. I place my hand in his, and his warm, strong fingers wrap mine in a hug that tugs me towards him. I'm not sure where this will ultimately lead, but a foundation of trust and family is a start, and I have feelings for this man that I haven't had time to analyze or even begin to comprehend yet.

"Make a list of things we're going to need to disguise ourselves," he says as he pulls me to his side. "All the make-up products and props, whatever you think best. I'll get one of the guys to go shopping. We can't walk around as ourselves when we go for this hit."

"Okay."

"Do you want to use my phone, or shall I get one of the guys to hand over a laptop?"

"I can do it on your phone. I'll find a location for them to go source what we need. Luckily, it is still early in the day."

He nods, and we work together, side by side, setting things up for the ultimate takedown of Pietro Garlini.

As Dominic calls both Benedict and Stephano, he doesn't shy away from letting me in on their conversations as he sets up a team to go *keep an eye* on the convent in Potenza. Benedict is front and central to arranging many things. Stephano will bring their mom's journals over, and anything else that could be used to pinpoint Gabriella as their sister. Even Arturo and Portia are being called in to find some photos of her as a child and might come along to help Gabriella recognize an aged, if familiar, face.

I get swept up in making arrangements, giving input around my apartment, my neighbors, the area, and seeing how he goes about putting things in place has me in awe. What the DIA won't give for this information. These brothers are a real team. No wonder we are always five steps behind the Mafia. Never mind the bad apples in the DIA, the Scaleras are on top of the latest technology where we're always waiting for tested products, approvals, budgets. We'll never win.

It hits me that the only way to probably stop Randazzo's trafficking ring is from the inside out, and not from the outside in. I'll have time to think that over once we're done here.

At some point, Dominic gets food delivered through one of the bodyguards, and once my list of items arrives, and I've gone through our disguises, exhaustion hits me. It's early to go to bed, but I feel like I can sleep for days.

When I stifle yet another yawn, Dominic puts his hand on my thigh where I'm sitting next to him.

"We should get an early night. We have an hour's drive to Rome in the morning, and it would be best if we get going while it's still dark. Go to bed, sweetheart."

"You're sure?"

"Yes, I'm almost done here. Just need to double-check a few things."

I nod and get up, really taking in the room for the first time. We've been working non-stop for hours, and my shoulders are stiff with sitting. The room isn't big, furnished with wooden antiques and faded printed landscapes on the wall, and a crocheted bedspread right out of the seventies. There's something nostalgic about this place, stuck in time.

I take my suitcase and go to the bathroom, not sure what the arrangement is. I've just been following Dominic's lead, and here we're sharing a bedroom like a couple. I don't want anything else, but my future hangs in the balance, and we haven't spoken about anything.

I'd hate for him to break my heart, especially now I've found I actually have one...and it already belongs to him. I take a long time to shower, letting the water run course with my tears, still trying to come to grips with the reality of what Pietro has done. If all goes as planned, I'll have the chance to ask him some questions, but maybe the moment might be too big for me.

By the time I'm in my pajamas and slip between the covers, Dominic is still at the table, still on his phone, his back towards me. Outside, the sun is setting in warm, golden hues, and now I'm awake again, my mind racing, my body anticipating, longing for him to come, hold me close and take my mind off things.

Last night on the plane, I was bold and asked for what I wanted, because I still had options. Now I'm shy, insecure, because the coin's sides are both the same—whichever way it falls, it falls to this man. I don't know how he feels about me, or the fact I've basically flooded his life with my problems, my mere existence.

"I'll be there in a minute, sweetheart," he says as he closes his laptop, shutting off the last of the artificial light in the room. "I'll just take a quick shower."

As he stands and turns to the bed, his full magnificent

height towers over me, and my heart skips a beat. He knows exactly what I want, what I need.

"Please be quick," I say, heat already gathering between my thighs at the way he looks at me.

He bends over and brushes my lips with his thumb. "In the shower, yes, but with you, I'll take my time."

I lie there, praying for him to hurry up, listening as he brushes his teeth and gets in the shower. I burn with the need to watch him, and one day, I'll walk in on him, just as he walked in on me that night that feels like ages ago. I'm still contemplating doing so now when the faucet turns off. When he steps back into the bedroom, he's drying himself, no towel around his body to hide his budding erection.

I blush as he stares at me, towel-drying his hair as he pads closer, his cock hardening with each step, the room seeming to shrink.

"Having a hard time falling asleep?" he asks as he hooks the towel over the back of the chair and drops some condoms onto the nightstand.

"So much has happened, but now I can't think about anything else...but this. You. Me."

He gets under the light summer covers, and the scent of him, shower-fresh with the guesthouse's lemon-scented soap, makes my heart skip a beat. He is so close, I feel the moisture of his shower still radiating off him as he finds my hip, glides his hand over my stomach to the other hip, and nudges me closer.

"I hope they're only pleasant thoughts."

"Very pleasant..." I murmur as I cup his jaw, my leg hooking over his hip, his cock nestling against my sex. "If a bit uncertain."

"Uncertain?" he murmurs as he nuzzles my ear and nibbles at my lobe, sending shivers down my body that harden my nipples and draw a moan from me.

"What's going to happen, Dominic? After Pietro and after

we pick up Gabriella?" I need to know. My future isn't mapped out anymore as it's always been.

"Well," he says as he finds purchase on his elbow so he can look me in the eye. "I was thinking we'd go lie low in Lake Como for a few weeks. For Gabriella to get accustomed to the idea that she's part of our family now. As long as it takes to get you a new passport and other legal documents that will free you from your past."

I have no doubt he could arrange that. "Lake Como?"

"The Trapanis have a house there. You can get to know Gigi and Carla a bit better, since...you know..."

Since we're all family now.

"And then?"

"And then... I have this burning need to show you my place in Boston."

"Your place?"

"My house. I'd love you to see my house and see if you could live there...with me."

My breathing stalls. "Live with you?"

"Yes. With the aim to eventually get married. I don't want to force you into anything, sweetheart, but you know how it works. Matteo, as our Don, as your brother, will manage your life for you if you don't take yourself off the chess board as a pawn first. If you're mine, nobody touches you. I'll protect you —with my life. I'll care for you—with every means I have. And I'll love you, Ariana, because I already do. Every day, I seem to fall in love with you a bit more. I don't think it will ever stop. I don't want it to stop."

His beautiful words are so unexpected and pure, I press my face into his neck as I choke up. He hugs me even closer, and joy wells up in me. Nobody has ever held me this close, so protective, and spoken these beautiful things to me. They are vows, and each one of them speaks to the things I've been searching for my whole life.

"Hey, my sweetheart," he murmurs as he presses warm and tender kisses along my hairline, to my temple and lower until he finds my lips. "Tell me those are happy tears and that you're not petrified."

"Of course they're happy tears," I say as I push closer to him, needing to be one with him. "I'd love that, to be with you, because I've somehow stumbled into love with you, too."

He chuckles between kisses as he works to open the buttons on my pajama shirt. "Stumble is a good way to put it."

His lips are on my chest, sliding down to my breasts, and when he sucks a puckered nipple into his mouth, I arch into him, my fingers raking into his hair, a desperate pulse picking up between my legs.

One last, desperate thought zaps through me. "What about Bruno?" I whisper.

Dominic pauses where he's working his way down my stomach. "Bruno?"

"That dog needs you," I whisper. "And he loved you first."

"What a time to talk about Bruno." He chuckles as he nudges my bottoms down, his fingertips hot pools of heat sinking into my skin and straight to my sex. "As long as we only feed him raw organic bison, Bruno is welcome. Now...no more talk about Bruno."

I giggle as he nips at my hipbone and ever lower. When his tongue sweeps down to my pussy, I get lost in the love that's Dominic Scalera.

63

DOMINIC

This woman is something else. To think of Bruno in all of this just goes to show who she really is. My heart swells, and I force myself to slow down, even if I want to rip the covers off and devour her. We're still getting to know each other, and the last thing I want is to be too forceful, too much, and in some way trigger her.

Her hands are in my hair as she splays open, and my tongue teases down that secret furrow, dipping into the wet crevice to taste her. She bucks against me, and I grip her butt, keeping her in place as I take my time, licking and sucking and circling that sweet little nub until she fists a hand to her mouth to still her moans. I pierce her with my tongue, sensing she's close.

"More, Dominic," she moans. "I need—"

"I know what you need, sweetheart." I pull away and drive a finger into her pussy, tentatively, but my girl is so wet and ready, her inner muscles already clamp tight against my rhythmic invasion.

She snatches at her breath as I add another finger, and when I lick her clit in passing, a tremor runs through her body. She's on the verge, and this time, I want to kiss her as she comes. I rise up and find purchase on my free hand and bend down to kiss her mouth, my fingers not once losing their pacing.

She opens for me, and as our tongues collide, she moans, fingers digging into my skull as wet heat releases and gushes over my fingers where I'm buried deep inside her.

Fuck...this one comes so beautifully. Her orgasm still pulses around my fingers, my cock trapped against her leg and begging to let me shoot my load already.

"Keep going, sweetheart," I murmur as I roll onto my back, reach for the condom, and in seconds have one rolled on. I pull her on top of me, urging her down on my cock. As much as I would like to plunder into her body, she isn't ready for that yet, and like this, she's always in control.

"Dominic—" She gasps as she inches down on me, that perfect pussy stretching and gripping me so tight, it won't take much. Between everything else we worked on today, images of her, just like this, invaded my mind literally every fucking minute. I'm a man thirsting for this woman, and as I help her roll her hips, we find a rhythm that will make her come again and drive me there, too.

A sheen of sweat sparkles on her skin, and she leans in, gripping my shoulders. "You're so much," she whispers.

"Not too much?"

"No, perfect much." She closes her eyes as she drops her head back, and it arches her back at just that angle to squeeze me even tighter.

"Sweetheart—"

"I'm going to come—"

"Fuck, Ariana—sweetheart—" My heart is pounding, and I'm out of breath as her pussy spasms in orgasm. My balls throb, and then everything in me tightens. There's no stopping me now. I explode into her body, my cum rippling up and riding the wave of her release. Fuck. It's beautiful.

For a moment, we're still, focused on the intense sensations at our core, where we're connected, and with a feral grunt, I feel the last of my load shooting into her.

I go limp as she drops to my chest with a giggle, and I gather her in my arms, smiling as I kiss my way to her lips. We kiss for a long moment, light and easy between bursts of teasing little laughs that only make me want to pull her even closer.

"I don't want to be anywhere else but here," she murmurs as I caress my hands down her back and circle her butt.

"Me neither," I whisper back between kisses. "We wrap up business, sweetheart, and don't look back."

"Yes."

I ease her off and make quick work of the condom, only wanting her back in my arms. She nestles into me, her head on my shoulder, an arm on my chest, and I cover her hand with mine. It's only when she slides a fingertip over my crooked pinkie that I become aware of it again, and I stiffen slightly, before exhaling a deep breath.

"Have I earned this one yet?" she whispers into the dark as her fingers weave with mine, her lips traveling up my neck as she presses sweet, enquiring kisses to my jaw.

"It isn't a good bedtime story, sweetheart." I whisper against her forehead, my lips caressing her hairline.

"Neither are any of the real Grimm brothers' stories...but they have happy endings."

"Mostly," I chuckle. I take a deep breath, bracing myself. Maybe this will give her too much, but with her, I want to give everything. "There once lived a Mafia Don who fathered six sons with a wife he was forced to marry. When the mother died in childbirth, the Don was free to rule his tribe as he saw fit and did so with ever-increasing violence towards his own sons.

"But boys grow into men, and soon, the Don realized he'd underestimated his sons, in brains and brawn. He feared a rebellion in their ranks, amongst his eldest sons, who had grown tired of his brutality which they'd suffered from an early age. The three eldest in particular were protective of the younger ones, and when the Don saw the influence his second-oldest son wielded over the tribe, he conspired to have him eliminated as he rightfully started to fear for his own life.

"He put a scheme in place to put his sons in danger and sent the two eldest out, with the express instructions to wound and maim the one and kill the other. The first son was shot twice, the second died. The third was at home, dreading the news because, in his gut, he sensed something was off...something had gone wrong.

"When they came home, one son dead, another hanging by a thread to life, the father called in the third son. He made him promise loyalty and vengeance for his older brothers, but forced him to swear an oath of allegiance to him, the Don, and him alone.

"When the younger son refused, too traumatized with the loss of a much-loved brother and the older one's life in the balance, he saw through the machinations of the Don, and refused. The Don had him strapped to a chair and chopped his finger off, telling him he'd do so with their younger brothers unless he toed the line. From that day on, the third brother toed the line, keeping all this knowledge to himself, but secretly building his own empire to protect his brothers."

Her hand has curled into a fist on my chest, and I exhale softly as I hug her close. She's crying softly again, only the wet heat of tears on my skin and the slight quiver of her shoulder whispering her distress.

"They saved it, though?" she murmurs in question.

"Yes. To stop the others from asking questions. It was, of course, a simple kitchen accident."

I exhale slowly, the weight of my secret seeping out of me,

into the mattress to the floor and beyond, like a puddle of stale water that's finally found a funnel to escape to and drain away.

"How broken are we?" Ariana whispers in the dark.

"Pretty broken, sweetheart," I murmur. "But somehow, when I hold you like this, to this broken part of me with its sharp edges, I find you're the perfect matching broken piece that makes me whole again."

She tugs my hand closer and presses a warm, gentle kiss to each of my fingers, her lips slow to pull away from the last, little one. "So you see...there's a happy ending, after all."

64

ARIANA

We're on the highway speeding towards Rome. It's no longer dark out, the sun glowing on the horizon. We're driving in convoy, our SUV in the middle, flanked in the front and the back by the hired guns who have been with us since we landed.

Our plans are in place.

I've turned into a brunette student—thick glasses and ponytail, loose-fitting low-flung jeans and a T-shirt so tight, I feel exposed. It sells because with a slouched posture, aided by my heavy backpack and worn-out Converse, an annotated copy of Herodotus's *The Histories* in my hand, I'm almost a carbon copy of my neighbor's granddaughter.

At a first glance, whoever keeps track of the comings and goings in the apartment block would mistake me for her. It helps that my elderly neighbor always blurts out her granddaughter's plans for the summer, and I know she's working the American summer camp circuit to improve her English. They started planning for it already in February.

Dominic is sitting next to me, my hand in his as he stares out at the passing landscape. He doesn't look like himself, either, and I've done such a good job of his make-up, looking at him makes me shudder. The shading and contouring, the extra temporary tattoos on his neck and arms to match Franco's, the nose...everything to make him look like Franco at first glance. He's in plumber's coveralls and has rolled up the sleeves to expose more tattoos. There's one problem universal in Rome—the plumping in those old buildings is a disaster. Something always blocks.

I'm not aware of the whole string of triggers he's put in place with Benedict and Franco's phone—I just know 'Franco' has messaged Pietro Garlini, and Benedict is communicating with my old team lead. He's in charge of luring Pietro to my apartment, under the guise that Emilia Korhonen holds documents there both Franco and Pietro need. Documents related to Randazzo and his assets. A meeting time has been set for ten in the morning, and now we're on a ticking clock.

Pietro Garlini has been keeping an eye on my apartment block since my passport tapped back into the country. We got this confirmation from Dominic's team which has been stationed there overnight. It takes one to know one, but hopefully, Pietro's team won't spot ours. Dominic got the feeling that Pietro's position is weakened, now that he can't tap into Franco's network to help him with his shady dealings. I in turn gave Dominic all our little tells, and it irks me to think I'm being watched for as if I'm the enemy.

Pietro will come early. I know his type, and we'll be waiting in ambush. We timed this right to align with Mass. As it's Sunday, my neighbor will be at church, and her Sunday ritual usually takes her two hours. Things I know that I'd never thought would come in handy.

As we enter Rome and head ever deeper into the heart of the city, traffic tightens, and so do my nerves. We've gone over this plan twenty times. We won't fail. It isn't even an option.

Dominic drops me off at the bus stop where one of the bodyguards is already waiting. It's busy, despite it being what should be a lazy Sunday morning. Tourist season never wraps up, and as some of the cheaper hotels and youth hostels are in this area, people are out and about already.

For a moment, I just stand, taking in the familiar scenes of my city. Pigeons, cobbled streets, constant honking coming from somewhere, and there... the lovely stench of trash nobody's collected in weeks. Yep. I'm home.

I don't make eye contact with my bodyguard as I get onto the bus, and when, four stops down, I get off again, he is behind me, following me to the apartment block. I spot Dominic, now in a marked cheap-and-chirpy plumber's van, as he gets out of the driver seat. He already has his worker's gloves on, hiding the give-away pinkie that had me in tears last night. Two broken people, fitting together perfectly to make a whole.

I ignore everybody as I put the code in the door, walk into the apartment building, and hold the door just a second too long so the bodyguard can get in, then I go straight for my neighbor's postbox where she's got a key stuck to the box's ceiling. I take the stairs to the second floor, with effort not glancing around, looking for anything inconspicuous as I've been trained to do.

I unlock the apartment and walk in, praying Paula won't be home and has stuck to her usual routine. The familiar smell of her morning espresso, wrapped in stale cheap perfume, hits me, and it's like a blanket of comfort wraps around me. I'm in my element. I can do this.

With a deep breath, I pause in the dark apartment, waiting for Dominic's go-ahead. He was following me with his tools in hand. First, he's going to use a signal jammer to block any hidden cameras in my apartment from taking footage. We have about three minutes to get into the place before he'll have to switch the jammer off. It's after all illegal in Italy, and we don't want anybody to get a whiff of what's going on here with a simple outage complaint.

Dominic's message pops onto the screen of the phone I've been commissioned, and now I have to move fast. Paula and I share a balcony, and I open the door, go on my haunches to hide from the outside world, and crawl over the few potted plants that separate our spaces.

Once on my side of the balcony, I peer into my own apartment through a small slit in the drapes. I can't see anything. I fumble for the key, right where I left it underneath one of the pots, and unlock the door. I slide it open, crawl in through the door, and close it again, then listen intently where I'm on the floor.

Nothing.

Nobody.

I exhale, and with speed, rush over to the front door where Dominic knocks twice, pauses, and twice again. I open for him, and as soon as he's slipped in, he pulls me to him for a quick kiss.

"Closet," he says, and I get into the narrow closet by the front door, the only space for winter gear and other random stuff, and wait. In the apartment, Dominic searches for any hidden cameras and shuts them down.

"There were only two," he says through a crack in the closet door. "And they've run out of battery now. Definitely not the tech we have."

"Now we wait," I whisper.

"Garlini's on his way."

Of course, Pietro Garlini has a tail now, but whether he would notice or not is the question. Pietro has always been outwardly calm, but I bet with Franco going off on his own tangent, he might be getting nervous. He would like to see the man eye to eye and figure out what the hell he's done with me.

A body. That's what Pietro Garlini would want to see. *It's him or me.*

Through the thin slit of the closet door, I watch as Dominic waits. He's getting real-time updates from his team and is in on the messages 'Franco' and Pietro are sending each other.

"God help this fucker," he murmurs under his breath. "He's walking into it as if he's fucking blind."

Pietro is so arrogant, he won't imagine Franco would double-cross him. Maybe Franco wouldn't, but Franco is dead.

"One minute, sweetheart," he whispers, and it seems to become eerily silent in the apartment.

I'm blocking out all other sounds, trying to listen to Pietro's familiar gait. When a knock sounds on the apartment's door, I pull in a sharp breath and freeze. Of all the things I've imagined since learning about his duplicity, the reality of facing him was very real…but now that the moment is here, I'm petrified.

Dominic opens the door. He only has a few precious seconds to drag Pietro into the apartment before Pietro realizes he isn't Franco and he's been duped. I can't see anything, but I hear the scuffle, moans, something ripping, then bones cracking as Dominic forces Pietro in an armlock that goes too far.

Holy hell…Dominic isn't messing around. Through the gap, I watch as he drags Pietro deeper into the apartment, kicking the door closed in the process. I'm not sure which move he pulled on him, but Pietro's body has gone limp, and blood is already dripping to the floor.

Dominic is almost superhuman in the way he hauls Garlini around, a gag already stuffed in his mouth, the fight twisted out of him in an arm that hangs useless. His hair—

I push open the door with a trembling fingertip and watch in horror at a rip of hair that's been torn straight off his skull. My stomach turns as vomit pushes to my throat, but I harden myself. This man is responsible for my team's butchering, and now he gets to experience it first-hand. How many other agents have died because of his duplicity? I bet enough to fill a graveyard.

I step into the short space between the living room and the front door and wait, breathless as Dominic has Pietro slumped on a dining chair, restrained with cable ties in seconds.

Inside this man, this beautiful broken man, with hands that touch and love so gently, a dark monster lurks. And he lets him out only to protect those he loves, with precise and efficient brutality like I've never witnessed before.

"Don't look, Ariana." His voice comes quietly, without strain, as if he didn't just manhandle someone into a chair. "It's the stuff of nightmares."

But it's like a car wreck, and I find I can't look away. "This is personal."

"Yes. It is."

He slaps Pietro in the face, but the man seems to be stunned into shock. I'd also be, and yet after the third slap, he bobs his head back and stares up into Dominic's demon eyes because I swear, he's become possessed.

"Have something to say?" Dominic asks softly, his hand on Pietro's throat, squeezing.

Pietro drags in a haggard breath through the gag and a nose that's bleeding, eyes glazed over.

"Want to tell us what happened to Ariana's team? What your plans were for her?"

Pietro's head sways, and I meet his gaze across the short expanse of the room.

"Are they dead?" I whisper.

He nods and attempts a shrug, already knowing his own fate.

"How could you?" I step closer, crossing my arms protectively over my body. "And me, too? At Franco's hand? Do you even know what type of monster he is?"

Pietro closes his eyes, not even looking at me anymore, and fury splits me in two. How dare he?

We don't have time for this. We need to wrap up the job and get the hell out of here.

"Talk," Dominic growls as he plucks the rag from Pietro's mouth. His fingers are gripping Pietro's throat with just the right amount of pressure, he can only croak.

"You're—" Breath. "Not—" Breath. "Franco."

"No. I'm fucking worse, and when you get to Hell, spread the fucking word. I'm not the weakest link. You are. Who else is in on it?" Dominic demands, gripping his throat. "Who the fuck else in the DIA is in on Randazzo's ring?"

Pietro's eyes roll back, and Dominic gives a little.

"Massimo Eposito. And Enzo Caruso."

So fucking weak. So quick to talk. The bile that sat in the shadows of my stomach wants to push to the light. The head of the DIA in Napoli and in Milan respectively. I'm trembling now, my whole body in a lock of shock. For all I know, it wasn't Randazzo who had Elena Bianchi assassinated, but someone in the DIA.

"Anything else we need to know, before you leave us?" Dominic asks.

"My daughters—"

Dominic kills off any further comment by choking him to the point where Pietro's eyes pop.

"You're a fucking psycho," he hisses as he leans into his face and shoves the gag back into his mouth. "Allowing vermin around other people's kids while you have your own safe at home, playing both sides for the money. You're a rat, and you will die like one. Your daughters will be better off never knowing who their father really was...unless—" Dominic shoots me a glance. "Unless Ariana here decides to tell."

At the mention of his own daughters, something snaps in me. Here I am watching Dominic basically being a ruthless, brutal killing machine, draining a man's life from him, but in my mind's eye, a string of girls of various ages that stayed at Mancuso's house in the time I was there walks past.

Now here is this man, supposedly working to protect women, to stop human trafficking, but he played both sides to enslave innocent women for his own financial gain. He killed my team and had instructed Franco Fiore to end me.

I walk over to the small kitchen where I reach for a serrated knife. Pietro Garlini doesn't deserve a clean cut. As I take the few steps to where Dominic has tied Pietro up in the middle of my small sitting room, I have every intension to hand him the knife.

Dominic is holding out his hand, ready to do what needs to be done. A broken man who has killed so many times, I bet he's lost count. A broken man, who fits my broken pieces perfectly, making us whole again.

There is only one way to show my commitment to him, to our future, and to lock my fate with his.

Instead of handing over the knife, I nod at him, indicating with my chin that he should expose Pietro's throat. Dominic doesn't hesitate and holds Pietro's head back, giving me access. Pietro protests as much as his position allows him to, and I might have never killed before, have never been tested like this, but there's a demon in me, too, one I never knew existed until I saw the truth.

With a few decisive saws, I slice him open, blood fountaining from his neck at such speed, his body goes limp in seconds.

I stare at my handiwork, numb.

No. Alive.

Dominic drops Pietro's head and reaches for me.

"Brave, so very brave." He leans in and kisses me deeply, love so incongruous with the scene right in front of us. "Welcome to the family, sweetheart."

There's no turning back. I've crossed sides back to where I've always belonged.

Nothing has ever felt this right before.

I lean into him, seeking his strength to hold me together. Dominic hugs me close, and it's a gift, a promise, and a future all in one.

65

DOMINIC

Three hours later, we're on our way to Potenza. Ariana is sitting next to me, out of her disguise, her hand relaxed in mine as she glances out to the passing landscape. She's the most at peace I've ever seen her, as if she's finally come to terms with everything she's been through, but I know better. It's going to take some time for her to work through this morning's build-up and Pietro Garlini's demise.

What she did to Garlini didn't surprise me. Every human has that dark side in them, but not everybody gets tested to see where their tipping point is. I vow she'll never get to this point again with someone—the point where this beautiful woman has the urge to kill.

I bet she's still digesting, and when she drops her head to my shoulder, I brush a soft kiss over her hair.

"We need to have a call with the family, sweetheart," I murmur softly. Matteo needs to know the results of the DNA tests.

"Yes." She turns her face up to me, and I press a kiss to her lips.

Bar getting the hell out of her apartment, leaving her whole old life intact and taking only the handful of small mementos she wanted to keep, we haven't spoken much. We left the apartment building separately in the way we came, and united again once on the outskirts of the city. I spent most of the drive to the meeting point wiping away the makeup she'd applied and scrubbing off the fake tattoos she'd painted on me, leaving Franco Fiore finally in the past. Still, I itch for a shower.

"Get us a hotel somewhere close to Potenza, Gus, to freshen up and have lunch," I say to my bodyguard. I don't feel like making this call in the car.

"Yes, boss."

So far, the security team keeping an eye on the convent hasn't raised any red flags about another team stalking around, looking to kidnap 'Randazzo's' daughter. I bet the Reverend Mother has an exit strategy in place, what with all the knowledge she seems to have of us, and how she *understood the assignment from the start.*

Jesus Christ. I hope she'll tell us some of everything that happened and how she knew my nickname was Nicky, because that came out of left field.

For now, I only have scanned pages of Mom's journals on hand and a few other salient documents Luca emailed me. If the Reverend Mother is going to want more, she'll have to wait for Stephano with the originals.

Gus directs the driver to a boutique hotel on the outskirts of Potenza, and once we've gone through our security procedures and find ourselves alone in our room, I cup Ariana's face in my hands.

"I know it's been a rough day, sweetheart. You're ready to do this?"

"Yes."

"Okay."

I set up a call with all my brothers in an hour's time and then lead her to the shower where we wash off the morning's business. I take time to wash her with tenderness, take care of her, and when she breaks down in my arms after a shattering orgasm, I hug her to me.

"I'm just so tired," she whispers against my neck, trying to find any excuse for the emotional turmoil she still cares to hide.

"It's okay, sweetheart. We'll be home soon, and then, you can rest." Her ordeal doesn't only include the events this morning. She probably has to go back to the day her mom died, and I will be there for her, every step of the way.

Once we're dressed again, I set up my laptop and start the online call.

Ariana reaches for my hand just before I let in my brothers, who have all already dialed in and are waiting for me to connect them.

"Please, don't tell them about this morning."

"I won't. We work on a need-to-know basis, and this morning stays with us." This is how it starts, all these secrets...

She nods, and I squeeze her hand. When she squeezes back, I finally let the others into the call, and within seconds, my brothers' faces fill the screen. From their background images, Luca and Benedict are in Matteo's office. Steph is sitting on a verandah I don't recognize—he's recently arrived at the Trapanis' house in Lake Como.

Well, this is one way to break it to the others that Matteo is Randazzo's son. At least Matteo isn't alone and it's better for this to come out sooner rather than later.

"So, I got the DNA tests back," I start, then pause.

"And?" Matteo prods.

"Uhm, so, turns out Ariana is part of the family."

At this, eyebrows all quirk up, and my brothers shoot each other glances.

"Fuck, is she one of the Don's by-blows?" Matteo asks, shifting in his seat.

"She's right here, Matteo," I say, my tone suggesting that nobody even thinks of giving her a smidgen of disrespect. I prompt Ariana to get her face on the screen. "And no, turns out she's one of Randazzo's children…and your half-sister."

I can hear a needle drop all the way across the Atlantic Ocean, in that fucking soundproof apartment of Matteo. In the shocked quiet, it's somewhat eerie to see the color drain from his face.

"How long have you known, Matty?" I ask, trying to break the tension.

Maybe this wasn't a good idea. I should have waited to do this in person, all of us together. A hand comes to rest on Matteo's shoulder. It's Benedict's, and on his other shoulder, Luca's.

"Fuck," Matteo grunts as he drops his head back, dragging his fingers through his hair. "I had my first suspicions the day I met with Randazzo, but the Don confirmed it on the day he died."

And this was probably another reason to kill the old man, because who wouldn't be triggered to learn that years of abuse was at the hand of a man who wasn't even your father? Fuck, I'd do it in a twitch.

"That doesn't change anything," Luca says, breaking the tension and confirming what I felt when I learned about Matteo's parentage. "You know what they say, boys, teamwork makes the fucking dream work, and as far as I see, the family just got bigger. Welcome to the party, Ariana."

Thank fuck for Luca. He might be a little shit, but sometimes, he's so on point, it's a relief.

"We'll have to throw a welcome party once you're home, Ariana," Benedict adds. "I look forward to getting to know you."

"Same here," Stephano says. "We'll get to see you soon. Gigi and Carla can't wait to properly suss you out."

Next to me, Ariana breaks into a small chuckle, but her eyes are glued to Matteo's face on the screen, probably scanning his features for any that could match her own, or those of Randazzo, so she can tick off some family traits.

Matteo blows out a deep huff, and it's dense with relief. "Welcome to the family, Ariana. We should do...we should do dinner or breakfast or something together once you're back home."

Oh, boy. Poor Matteo. He's had enough mindfucks for a lifetime, and this in a few short months.

"I'll email you the DNA test results, so you have it on hand." I glance at the time. "It's time to change her profile on the DIA site, Ben. Can you arrange that?" It would take the DIA some time to find Garlini's body, and the sooner Ariana disappears forever, the better.

"Consider it done. I'll send you a screenshot when I've received the confirmation, and I'll double-check, you know, just in case."

"Good, thank you." Benedict will deliver. I've one less thing to worry about. "We need to head out to the convent."

"Yep, keep us posted, will you?" Matteo says.

I nod and ring off.

"That wasn't so bad," I say to Ariana as I close my laptop and take hold of her hand.

"Poor Matteo. He looked a bit shell-shocked. At least, I've had a few more days to get used to the idea."

"You're a Scalera now." Not in name yet, but soon. "By the time we're back in Boston, he would've adjusted."

She nods as I stand.

"Ready for a short drive?"

"Yes."

She stands, and my gaze flows down her perfect body.

"You look lovely, sweetheart." I'm not sure where she got the suitcase full of clothes from, but she's wearing a beautiful summer's dress that fits her like a glove, and in this soft shade of blue, it only illuminates her eyes.

"Portia got busy online and gave Arturo directions as he hit some upscale shopping mall in Boston."

"Those two," I say with a smile as I lead her out of the room to where Gus is waiting in the corridor, printouts of Mom's journals in hand. "I really hope they have time to be together again, at least as a family, if not as more, if that's what they want."

It's been quietly killing me that the Don would have pulled such a fucked-up power move on one of his men, but it was par for the course in the old *Il Consiglio*.

We're quiet as we drive up into the small town, its medieval cobbled streets getting narrower and narrower as we go higher. My pulse beats faster, my stomach twisting tight. To think this moment could somehow be too big for me. I'm relieved to have Ariana by my side, to see me through the next couple of hours.

We're only here for a preliminary meeting with the Reverend Mother, and hopefully, we'll get to meet Gabriella. If all goes according to plan, she'll leave the convent with us tomorrow.

The driver pulls up at the convent's gate, and we clamber out. It takes us a minute to get clearance through the intercom, and then we're inside, Ariana holding my hand, Gus and another bodyguard making up the rear. A nun meets us half a minute later and guides us through the courtyard and up the stairs to the second floor and the Reverend Mother's office.

She's waiting for us, seated at her desk, indicating we should come in and take a seat. She's an older woman, maybe in her mid-fifties—the same age Mom would have been now if she'd lived—and dressed in full nun regalia.

As I sit down, I hold out the printouts with Mom's handwriting, her secrets, out for the world to see and dissect.

"That's all, Sister Maria," the Reverend Mother says as she reaches for the copies and gives them a swift glance.

The door closes behind us seconds later, but now the Reverend Mother takes her time to go through my paperwork. Eventually, she looks up and searches my face, and I read her eyes as she takes me in. She's putting a face to a face she knows from somewhere else. Only the smallest twitch to her lips tells me something has triggered her, and then she slips a photo from a Bible laying to the side on her desk.

"You look just like your father," she says as she holds the photo out to me.

I glance at Ariana, but her eyes are on the copy of the wedding photo that was hidden with Mom's journals.

"How did you know my mother?" I ask, taken aback that the Reverend Mother would have one of these photos.

"We were best friends, grew up together in Napoli. Impoverished to a point where we were basically living on the streets. The day I got placed in a church orphanage was the day Bianca disappeared. I never knew what happened to her, but somehow, years down the line, she found me, and we reconnected. Seems she knew where I went, and then I learned what happened to her—" She breaks off, pursing her lips as tears glaze her eyes. "She was a very brave woman," the Reverend Mother says as she opens a desk drawer and pulls a stack of letters from it. "I think these would be better for you to keep. It's the last connection I had with Bianca and explains how I got to find and look after Gabriella until her brothers came for her."

The stack of letters is like a window to a past life, just like Mom's journals. Here is more of Mom, more than we'd ever think we'd have of her. I'd need to be alone with them to digest the contents once the time is right.

"My sister?" I ask, anxious now to get eyes on Gabriella.

"She's here." The Reverend Mother picks up her old desk phone and dials, and after a short conversation, puts the phone on its hook again.

A knock follows, and now that the moment is here, I cling to Ariana's hand as we stand and turn toward the door.

When it swings open, my heart stalls. A young woman walks into the office, in a plain dark blue pinafore, a white shirt underneath, sensible shoes with stockings, and a gold cross hanging from a thin necklace I recall as vividly as if I've seen it yesterday—Mom's cross.

Our eyes meet across the short expanse of the room, and my throat tightens as she reaches for the golden cross in a gesture so familiar, with a hand that's a carbon copy of Mom's, it chokes me up.

This is Gabriella Scalera, and there's no doubt in my soul she's my sister, for she's a soft echo of our Mom, from her dark brown eyes, the perfectly arched brows, to her regal nose, and the gentle pull of her mouth—the exact one Mom had when she reprimanded us, never scolding, only loving.

"I'm Dominic Scalera, your brother." I hold out my hand, fingers quivering, and she slips hers in mine, soft but tense, hesitantly giving me the short, compulsory shake.

She drops her gaze as she pulls away.

"I'm ready," she says, so softly, I need to lean in to make sure I heard right.

"You're...ready?" I repeat, wanting to make sure that's what she said.

"I'm ready," she says. "To serve in the way God sees fit."

I glance at Ariana, who hasn't moved an inch next to me, and in a split second, all my worst sins seem to fly by in my mind, in front of this young woman—my sister—who seems to be as pure as the day she was born.

Oh, boy. Gabriella Scalera might be ready...but I'm not sure the rest of the Scaleras are ready for what her addition to the family will bring.

Epilogue - Ariana

"It's done," Dominic says as he hands his phone to me.

I take it from him and read the short message as he sits down. It's from the mole. Dominic rests his hand on my leg, softly, gently, and squeezes as my hand starts to tremble at the news.

We've been waiting for this, but now it's real. My breath sits trapped in my throat as my mind spins around the enormity of what I've done. I've gone rogue to the point of no return.

When we flew back from Italy with Gabriella in tow, Dominic offered to orchestrate and fund an operation to take out Massimo Eposito and Enzo Caruso, the two big shots in the DIA who were working with Pietro Garlini and Franco Fiore. The rotten apples in the core of the police force supposedly fighting organized crime in Italy.

I never hesitated to share the DIA's insider secrets with Dominic and his team, and they didn't just go on Pietro Garlini's word that those two were involved but investigated first to make sure. Massimo Eposito got gunned down in Napoli a week ago, and now they've finally found Enzo Caruso's body floating around a lake close to the Swiss border.

For the past weeks, I've been on pins and needles, waiting for the news to break. Worst of all is, we've realized we've only scratched the surface. Those two were in the DIA, but the corruption ripples into every corner in life and includes politicians, city councils, hospitals, charities. It's become ingrained.

"You're okay, sweetheart?" Dominic asks as he leans closer to me where I'm sitting at my favorite place in the whole house —the sunroom sectional where it overlooks the verandah and stretch of lawn that meets up with the sandy beach and the blue ocean glimmering beyond. It's the perfect reading spot, peaceful, and in truth, a slice of heaven.

This is his place—*our place*: a beautiful beach house located in one of the most exclusive seaside neighborhoods south of Boston. The only downside to being here is the longer drive to the city. The Hamptons-style house is crazy big in comparison to what I'm used to, but in this neighborhood, it's one of the smaller ones. We share a private beach with only five other families, and I'm still getting used to the luxury of it, but this is home. This is where Dominic found his peace and where I found everything I've always craved: love, belonging, family.

And it's been heaven. This man...he crawled right into my heart, but nowadays, it feels as if I can almost burst with love for him. The way he cares for me...the longer I'm with him, the more my past becomes history. Not something invading my every thought like it used to, when I was still hellbent on my vendetta with Franco and Randazzo.

"It's a start," I say, my voice quivering. "There's so much more to do."

I've caught on over the past few months working on this project, and we have our work cut out for us. I've got a new team, and it makes all the difference. With Stephano and Gigi in Italy and Don Trapani's support, Benedict's help from here, Luca's involvement, and Matteo's blessing, we've been disrupting Randazzo's network in Italy. It's going to take time, but even a small win is a win, and having these two crooked cops out of the equation is huge.

"Still as ambitious as the day I met her," Dominic says with a smile then presses a kiss to my head.

Bruno nuzzles my leg, then rests his head on my knee, staring at me with those two soulful eyes. It's as if he feels my distressed relief, and I caress him fondly with a gentle rub behind his ear. How is it that this dog had become another anchor in the time I've known him?

Dominic leans in, rests his hand on mine, and together, we stroke Bruno's fur.

"It's going to be okay, sweetheart," he murmurs.

I can only nod. When I look up at him, tears in my eyes, he pulls me to his chest where I burrow into him. Without this man's support, his love, none of this would have been possible. I'm so much stronger because of him, and this family—these brothers, *Il Consiglio*—are next level. They've got such unique skills that drilling into Randazzo's crumbling empire seemed to be a walk in the park from where I'm standing. I know it isn't, and they carry most of the weight of this operation, but at last someone is doing something real to stop the human trafficking.

For a long while, Dominic comforts me, just lets me be in his arms where I've belonged from the start. He doesn't need to say anything, and we can just be like this, a thousand words said in a single embrace. Eventually, I look up and kiss him tenderly, and when I pull away, he cups my head and keeps me close.

He kisses me properly then, and we're quick to engage in that erotic dance we now do so well as I open up to him without hesitating, our tongues colliding and heat already settling between my thighs. My hand strokes up his chest, and I press into him, feeling him hardening. Shit, was it only two hours ago that he made me come last? We have plans for this weekend, what with Stephano and Gigi here from Italy. It doesn't matter. We can't be late—again.

When he breaks off the kiss, he murmurs close to my ear. "This calls for champagne."

I laugh as I slump back into my seat. "This early in the morning? We have so many things to do today."

"Yep, nevertheless." He hitches his eyebrows at me as he gets up and saunters over to the adjacent open-concept kitchen, heading straight for the wine fridge.

Oh, hell. He's serious.

Bruno's eyes follow Dominic's every move, brows twitching up or down as he registers his 'Dad's' intentions, now that he has his eyesight back. After two eye operations, Bruno is like a new dog. Well, it wasn't only the cataract operations; we've been working on his diet, too. It's been touch and go trying to figure out what Bruno can have and should steer clear from, but at least, he's no longer on a diet of only raw bison. Puppuccinos are on the menu with a few other delectable treats.

I suspect it all has to do with the amount of exercise the dog's getting; the fresh ocean air was the last tonic Bruno needed to get a spring back in his step. It seems he was slowly dying of boredom at the old Don's house. He loves it here and seems to have grown younger in the time we've been together, and I get it. I totally do because I feel the same.

Dominic returns, two flutes and a bottle of chilled champagne in his hands. I'm not sure what, but something's been up for a while now. We don't have secrets from each other, but something's brewing, and it's more than just a culmination of months of work to take down the two corrupt DIA directors.

"I've waited long for this moment, sweetheart," Dominic says as he settles next to me again.

"For what moment?"

"For the moment we put the DIA behind us."

"It's been behind me for a while," I murmur.

I've done my best to move on, and Dominic has been a key player in that process, but somehow, it isn't enough for him. He looks after me in every way possible, and if he could serve me by killing my enemies one by one, he would. As he has. I've never felt safer in my life before.

"It couldn't have come soon enough. I promised...I promised myself that only once I've seen this through, once I've made certain those fuckers are dead, would I ask you—" He breaks off.

"Ask me what?" I murmur, my pulse suddenly gathering in a riot.

It's got to do with this coming weekend and the family gathering we're having with everybody getting together for Easter. Steph and Gigi arrived last night from Italy, even though Gigi loathed to leave Carla and her newborn behind. It could be about the puppy he wants to get—a Belgian Malinois, no less—as extra security for me, as if I need extra security with everything else he has in place.

He says nothing, and the love in his eyes as he studies my face is all-consuming.

"Dominic?" He's going to pull a puppy out of a hat, isn't he?

He pops the champagne and pours two glasses, taking his sweet time, seeming to gather his courage. I don't mind another puppy. I'd love to have one...but my heart's desire is to have more than just puppies. Lately, my mind has been drifting to babies, so often, it's become a quiet obsession I haven't had the courage to raise with him yet.

"What is it, Dominic?" I'm getting impatient now he's held out a champagne glass to me. "We've got so much to do today with the drive to town and the day I'm spending with Tasha and Gigi and dinner tonight and—" I glance down to his light blue button down where my make-up has smeared on the collar as he let me cry it out. "And now, I've ruined your shirt..." I've run out of steam.

"Already, she's ruined my shirt," he says, a tender tease in his voice.

He takes a deep breath and tilts my chin up from where I've been staring at his open collar and the delectable smooth skin peeking out. I want to lick it.

"Ariana, you know, when we first came back to Boston after everything that happened here and in Italy, I was smitten." His gaze jumps between my eyes as he takes me in. "Now I'm so much more, sweetheart. I'm this weird and wonderful combination of in love and loved and loving you, and it still feels as if I still fall in love with you every day. I didn't even know all these feelings were possible."

He is so open and sincere, my heart squeezes.

"Do you feel the same?" he asks then, and I bite my lip to contain my emotions.

God, this man. If he carries on like this, I'll be in tears again. Sometimes, he just comes at me with words, and I melt. "Of course I do. You know I do."

"Sweetheart," he murmurs as a thumb brushes along my cheek where a lone tear already slipped free. "I don't think that's ever going to stop."

No. I shake my head. "No, I don't think so either."

"Then let's make this official," he whispers. "Marry me, my love, and be mine forever."

My heart stalls. My blood seems to pause in my veins and then rush through as if all sluices have been opened. This is so...so out of left field, but it's as if he's been peering into my mind, knowing exactly my deepest wish. Months ago, Dominic had said he won't rush me, that he'd give me time. And this man is all about taking time when he cares for a woman...and I am his. I never want to be with anybody else.

"Yes," I whisper on a choke, my heart suddenly stuck in my throat. "Yes and yes again."

He smiles and kisses me tenderly as his hand slides down my back to my butt, where he nudges me to straddle him. I'm on his lap, giggling as he fidgets in his pocket, rolling his eyes as he struggles what with the champagne flute in his hand so I take it from him.

"I've been sitting on this for a few weeks," he says as he manages to pull a small pouch from his pants' pocket.

Here is another moment I thought I'd never have: Dominic pulling a dazzling ring from that little pouch and holding it to me.

"This is part of my mom's engagement ring and wedding band. Matteo offered, and I love that he thought about this—for all of us—to have engagement rings made with Mom's ring. It had so many diamonds, and now it keeps her with us."

Oh my God. Now I'm really going to cry.

"It's so beautiful," I whisper, the moment too big. "It would be an honor to wear it," I say, putting our champagne to the side so he can slip the ring on my finger. The size is just right, and I smile at him through my tears, and from the twitch in his jaw, he is moved, too.

I close in and kiss him softly. "When, my love? Do you have a date in mind? Tell me it's soon."

As I pull away, there's that smile I love so much lightening up his face. "This weekend? We're all together, and it's the perfect time to have a family wedding."

"This weekend? Goodness…where?"

"Right here, on the beach. In fact, we need to go so you can pick a dress with Tasha and Gigi, and Portia can execute the plans she's been working on for the past six months. It involves a marquee tent for outside and a ton of flowers and what not. You know both Portia and Rosalia love this type of thing."

"But…here?" I feel breathless and elated at the same time.

"It's perfect, don't you think?"

He nudges me off his lap, and I clamber off as he pulls me to stand, then hands me back my champagne. We clink glasses, and I take a sip, happiness rises in me just like these little bubbles. He leads me to the French doors, and we step out to the verandah that overlooks the lawn and the sea where it shimmers in the sun this time of the morning. The fresh breeze still has a bite to it, but by afternoon, it is going to be gorgeous.

"It is perfect," I say on a sigh, resting my head on his shoulder. "How come you're so perfect?"

"Just found my perfect matching broken piece, sweetheart. I've never felt more whole in my life."

He presses a kiss to my hair, and I lean my head on his shoulder. Yes, it's going to be perfect. Small and just perfect for the growing Scalera family. "One day soon, we'll have kids running around, dogs in the mix, endless amounts of love, and a big family where children are cherished and loved."

Dominic raises his glass to my words. "To be honest, it's the best up-yours we can give the Don, living the life he never intended for any of us."

"Lead the way," I say as I smile up at him. "I'm right here next to you."

ABOUT THE AUTHOR

Sophia writes sensual, emotional, and evocative contemporary romance. Some snark might sneak in. When she's not writing, she's binge-watching the latest TV series, being walked by her beagles, or planning the family's next trip into the wilds. She's ghosted Facebook, is failing at Tiktok, and has little time left for Instagram, however, she hasn't given up (yet). Check out her efforts at @sophiakarlson or @sophiakarlsonauthor

Sign up for her newsletter to get updates about new book releases and free stuff! Rest assured, you won't be bombarded! https://BookHip.com/RKDPHT

ACKNOWLEDGMENTS

Thank you to my book besties who have been fabulous in helping me write and polish this book! Amanda Holly, my sister Tilla for reading and saying "This one was my favorite" (but you say that each time, lol), and Zee Monodee, my editor. Thank you Zee for making my writing shine! Ladies, you are all rockstars!

ALSO BY SOPHIA KARLSON

The Love Nests Series - four contemporary romances exploring forbidden love.

The Paris Apartment - James and Mila's story

The Shrink - Stacy and Ivo's story

The Neighbor - Ruben and Marlène's story

The Intern - Bryce and Izzy's story (they pop up in HATED VOWS)

The Mafia Vows Series - a crime family saga where each brother meets his match. Open door spice with one book flowing into the next. Please read in the below order!

Hated Vows - Matteo and Tasha's story

Broken Vows - Stephano and Gigi's story

Sinner's Vows - Dominic and Ariana's story

Ashleigh Lake Series - Small Town Romance

One Sweet Summer - Raiden and Georgiana's story

When I Fall in Love - Hunter and Beth's story

Standalones

Just My Type - a Rugby Romance

Perfect Series

Perfect Mistake

Perfect Obsession

Printed in Great Britain
by Amazon

59260308R00249